MW01601438

# Defenders of Becknor

Jack O. Crabtree

All rights reserved. No part of this book may be reproduced or used in any manner without the express written permission of the publisher except for the use of brief quotations in a book review.

This is a work of fiction. Names, characters, places, events and incidents are either the products of the author's imagination or used in a fictitious manner. Any resemblance to actual persons, living or dead, or actual events is purely coincidental.

Copyright © 2017 Jack O. Crabtree

All rights reserved.

ISBN:
9781521988176

FOR MOM

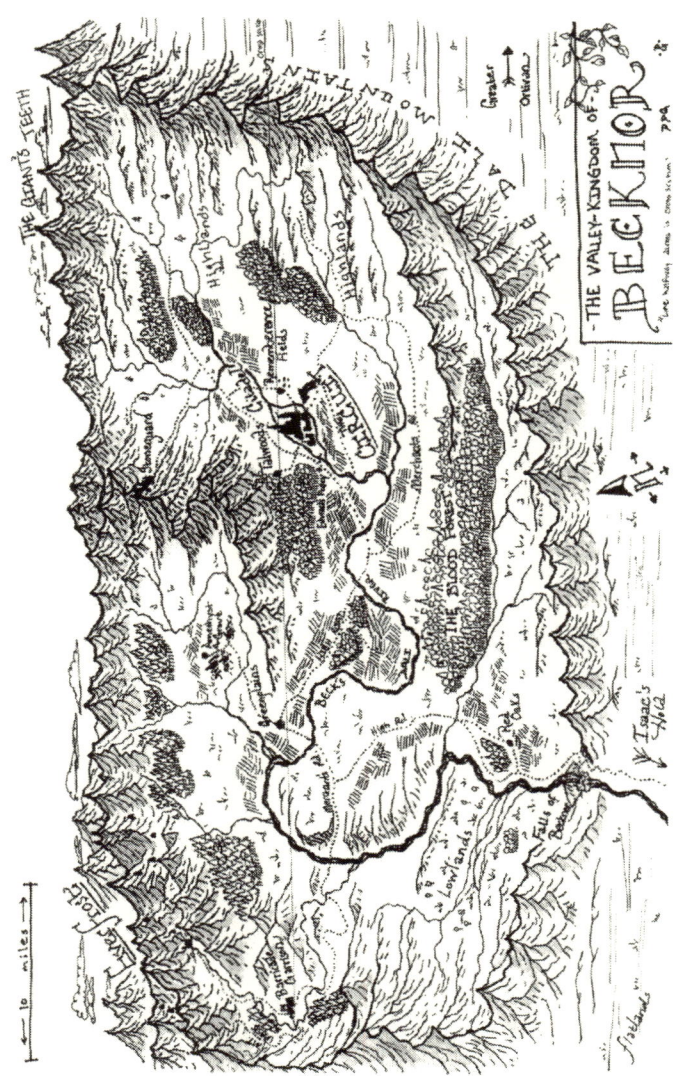

# PART ONE

# THE
# THREE TRIALS

# CHAPTER ONE

The wind blew lazily over the fields of white, filling the air with a sweet aroma. The flowers, and tall grass moved in the rhythm of the wind; like waves upon the sea. Above them, standing tall and mighty, like a lone sentinel, was a weeping willow. The sun setting on the horizon bathed the scene in golden light. Into this windblown "sea," wading hip deep, like one may wade into the water, was Lydia. Her white gown blending in with the field making it appear as if the flowers themselves were spinning her into existence. She walked with her hands out, palms down, skimming the surface. Her back was to him as the wind gently blew her golden locks around her. Suddenly, as if feeling that she was not alone after all, she slowly turned to regard him, smiling warmly and contently. Her blue-green eyes reflecting the day's final rays of sunlight. This was the first time Hector, son of Felix, had laid eyes upon the Lady of Talwoods, and it was this memory he was desperately holding on to as he rode hard for the horizon.

After a fierce ten-day war, Lydia, Regent of the Valley Kindgom of Becknor, had been dreadfully wounded. Hector, Captain of the Knights of the Valley, was tasked with the quest to retrieve the cure and bring it to her. The Wise Men of the kingdom had deemed that only the rare Blue Orchid Elixir would be powerful enough to undo her injuries. But time was against him and so he urged every last ounce of strength from his horse, Lawrence.

To win the Elixir he would face three unknown trials. Time was his only enemy now. He would need to save as much time along his journey as possible to best the trials and return in time to save his Regent, his friend.

Horse and rider emerged at the foot of the mountain. The world before him opened up into a grand and wide-open plain. Having lived all his life surrounded by mountains, none would have blamed him if the openness of the Outer World would have distracted and, perhaps, intimidated him. He payed the openness no mind. Even if there had been a fleet of dragons, a hundred strong, before him, he would have merely taken the reins tighter and charged. Turning Lawrence towards the southeast, he forced his mind from the world and to Lydia. If the war had not intimidated him, then there was nothing that the Outer World could threaten him with.

* * * * *

The Ten-Day War had been as brutal as it had been relentlessly swift. A century of peace had been broken, when the goblin armies of the Everfrost Mountains came marching down the Mountain Pass. For over a thousand years, those that dwelled inside the mountains had gazed out upon the Valley-Kingdom with greed and malice. A countless number of the rulers of the Valley, the Lady Lydia included, had attempted to sue for a lasting peace; to share the resources of the land. Time and again the answer from each and every Dread Overlord had been the same, "Why share what you can conquer."

Indeed, before the peace, the armies of Everfrost had conquered the Valley-Kingdom over and over only to be pushed back into the mountains years later. A thousand year cycle of endless blood and death.

That was until the noble Prince Achelon did what no one else who had called the valley home had ever done before. Something unheard of for this proud and isolationist people. He made a pilgrimage out of the valley to seek help from the Alliance of the Four Greater Kingdoms. The Prince spoke boldly and passionately and won a treaty of protection for his people. The Great City-State of Isaac's Hold dispatched but one legion. That legion was outnumbered three to one, the goblins were outmatched. Everfrost watched helplessly as the well-trained foot soldiers of the City-State slaughtered their army. Achelon's gambit had been successful, but he would not live to see the end of the first full year of the peace he had helped to usher in. He would die by an archer's arrow months later. An apparent victim of one his many rival, isolationist, political foes. With a treaty of protection guaranteed from the Alliance, Everfrost never again attempted an invasion.

But that all changed a mere three months before the war. First, it was Hector himself that noticed all was not well upon the Mountain. One morning, during his private sword drills, he noticed a strange haze clinging to Everfrost and a faint acrid stench wafting through the Valley. The Captain feared then that the goblins were preparing for war. Then, in the dead night came the news. A courier from Isaac's Hold informed Lydia, that with a war breaking out far to the east, the Alliance could no longer spare the forces to guarantee Achelon's treaty. How ironic, that the news would be delivered to her ladyship, as she was the last descendant of Achelon.

It came the same day that news of a new Dread Overlord had taken the icy throne of Everfrost, and that he was rallying his forces. Seeing his opportunity, the goblin leader intended to attack. But this time, the war would not just be for the valley itself, but to wipe out every last man, woman, and child of Becknor.

For the first four days, the armies of the Valley were seemingly pushed back with ease by the goblin hordes. Yet, these were only

3

skirmishes planned by Hector. The Captain was "herding" Everfrost towards Pinnacle Field, the highest natural point inside the valley. With the bulk of his forces lying in wait a day ahead of the coming battle, the Knights of the Valley would be well rested, while the goblins would have to walk up and down a series of steep grassy hills. As Everfrost approached in the late afternoon on that fourth day, Hector expected their commanders to make camp on one of the surrounding hills or, at least, the base of Pinnacle and launch their attack at dawn. He never expected the goblins to march up the hill towards them so late in the afternoon.

Within minutes, Everfrost was lined up in perfect formation. Row upon row of the black and green clad horde. Hector looked over the ranks of goblins apprehensively. They looked neither winded nor fearful, but eager. A vicious bloodlust was in their black, doll-like eyes. Their numbers were an even match to his own. Ten thousand to ten thousand.

Looking over his own forces, Hector found his knights determined, but startled. None, including himself, had ever faced a real battle in a real war. The majority of his army consisted of those between the years of sixteen and eighteen. Centuries ago, Becknor, then and now, was nothing more than a kingdom of farmers. It was the will of Beatrix, the Battle Queen, that instituted the required two Years' Service. Service was the true backbone of Beclnor. All were called upon, boy and maiden, once achieving their sixteenth year; The Age of Responsibility. While not all chose the sword, a good number did choose knighthood. On the other side of the field, however, was an army practically bred for this day.

Having already made one miscalculation, and before fear could take the hearts of his brave men and women, Hector was determined not to lose the last advantage he held. He would test their stamina then and there. Rallying his knights, Hector called for a charge.

While the people of Becknor had enjoyed their century of peace, the goblins had spent that same time preparing for war. The goblin armor was as strong as the fabled dragon-stone, and their blades seemed sharper than steel. Yet it was not their superior armaments, but Hector's second miscalculation, that nearly ended the war in one battle. With his slaughter.

After days of harrying the goblins with his reserves, and with every Knight of the Valley engaged at Pinnacle, no one had been spared to watch the Mountain Pass. Secretly, a second army of goblins had come marching down in the dead of night. With only moonlight to guide them, they made their stealthy descent and had marched unchecked across the valley floor. It was only as the sun began to dip into the west that Hector realize this second force had arrived, and was marching up the slope behind him. Outnumbered, they would soon be trapped on a field tall enough for all of Becknor to witness their slaughter. Fortunately, Hector had one last trick.

Hector had purposely chosen Pinnacle Fields for a specific tactic he had meant to employ. In the spring, Pinnacle was the first region of the valley to see the sun. His plan had been to blind the goblins with the dawn. Now, with the sun about to set behind the western slopes, Hector order his knights to turn and charge the warriors coming up behind them. Before the lines crashed into one another, the setting sun, which had been obscured by the mountains, flashed through a crevasse known as the keyhole. Taken by surprise, the goblins before them howled in pain, covering their sensitive eyes from the setting sun. The commanders of Everfrost seemed to be unaware, that Pinnacle was also the last spot in Becknor to see the sun. Hector's forces slammed through the blinded line and fled to safety.

* * * * *

Watching from a distance via spyglass, Lydia had been witness to the entire battle. Seeing that their armies were no match for Everfrost, she called for a council. Hector turned aside and met with her and the Wise Men of the Valley in a tent not far from the battlefield.

"Are you well," Lydia asked as Hector entered the tent. Acolytes of the Wise Men and Knights were scurrying all around them, packing for departure.

"Nothing but my pride after losing my first engagement in a real war," Hector said frowning. "But I am sure it will grow back. However, we have lost too many brave brothers and sisters."

"As I have witnessed," she said motioning towards the spyglass. "I will be brief as I and the Wise Men are retreating back to the Circuit. I do not mean to further injure your ego my friend, but their numbers are too great. I see very little chance that you can defeat them in an open field."

"Do not doubt yourself, Captain," said Galen, Grand Master of the Wise Men. He wore the blue and silver robes of his office. He was stroking his long, neatly trimmed, white beard thoughtfully. "Never, in our long history of combat with Everfrost, have they come down from the mountain with such great numbers. Undoubtedly, they had been planning this war for some time."

Hector's anger took over just then, staring Galen down he said, "A fact that the Regent and myself have been warning for months now. We would not even be as half prepared if we had not gone against your 'wisdom' and prepared for the inevitable."

"I am not infallible Captain," Galen said heatedly. "Yet, I think the Wise Men, in our combined centuries of experience, are capable of a level of discernment beyond someone who has just lived over a quarter of a century or a Regent that is not even twenty-one."

"Discernment," Hector mocked. "More like groping in the dark."

"Children," Lydia raised her voice sternly. It only took one look at the fire in her eyes for Hector to shrink back. Even Galen had enough wisdom about him to take a step back. "You can have your schoolyard fight later. Your governess is speaking. Let us now continue with the lesson at hand. The hour is dire but this war is far from over. We need to draw them in somewhere we can exploit their numbers as a weakness."

"If we can funnel them into a chokepoint, we could hold them off for a time," Hector said nodding.

Galen added, "If we could lure them to the Gateway Bridge, we could close the gates and allow our archers to thin out their numbers as they attempt to breakthrough."

"I was thinking of letting them move freely over the bridge and luring them into an even tighter trap," said Lydia. "We bring them to the narrow streets of City Citadel."

"How would you go about this," Galen asked.

"We make a show of evacuating the people to Citadel for refuge."

"It will be quite crowded with both our Knights and citizenry trapped inside the walls."

"The people will only be there long enough for Everfrost to follow the trail. Once inside, we lead the people to the catacombs beneath and then into the caverns below the valley floor. From there the people can be taken to safety out of Becknor, by way of Gavin's Labyrinth. They can then be escorted to a village or fort loyal to the Alliance. Leaving only the Knights of the Valley behind to face Everfrost. What say you Captain," Lydia asked.

He began to shake his head and said, "It is a sound enough plan."

"And yet," Lydia asked.

"This would make one battle an all or nothing proposition," he said turning and walking about the tent. "It sounds of desperation."

"I believe that is the sentiment our Regent is attempting to convey," Galen said dryly.

Hector ignored him and continued, "Once Everfrost was inside, they would be trapped by their own ranks pressing in from the back, but we would have no place to retreat. We would have to break their army then and there."

Hector looked out of the tent and back towards the recent battlefield. Night had fallen and most of the goblins were still upon Pinnacle. He could see a swarm of activity, as goblins, by torchlight, seemed to be pacing to and fro.

"Yes, It would trap our foe," he said as Lydia joined him by his right side. The movement had caught her eye as well. "But this could be the opportunity that they wish for. If it were to drag on for days we would be broken. If this strategy fails we will never again have sufficient force to retake the valley," he said his voice trailing off as Galen joined him on his left. "Our people could be refugees for generations…."

Taking a spyglass, Hector looked back upon the field. His insides began to twist at what greeted his eyes. Everfrost was checking the bodies of his fallen knights. The dead were hauled away to a growing pile. Those that were yet alive, but injured, the goblins took their swords and ran them through. Hector's memory flashed back a month ago, as he stood at Lydia's side, as she attempted one last negotiation with the Dread Overlord. His last words to them were that after the war, the Becknor Valley would be renamed in the goblin tongue, Nil' Becknond. Meaning Grave of Becknor. Now as he watched the armies of Everfrost slaughter the wounded, he knew that his words had been no idle threat. It did not matter if the Citadel gambit was an all or nothing battle, the war already was.

Turning to Lydia, Hector said, "I will see to the plan at once. I promise you, we will break them. Even if it is our undoing, it will be another century before they attempt something so foolish again."

With that Hector left the tent and mounted his horse. Already he was forming strategies. His mind's eye beginning to see the advantages those narrow streets held. He rode off, unaware that Lydia had held back part of her plan. A bold but dangerous strategy of her own. As the sound of his horse's hoof beats faded, she turned to Galen and laid out the rest of the plan.

\* \* \* \* \*

The next five days would prove to be a delicate balancing act for Hector and his knights. The safety of the people was of the utmost importance but there had to be a clear enough trail for Everfrost to follow. The margin of error proved to be razor thin. More than once his knights had finished evacuating a village or farm just as Everfrostian warriors began to raze it.

Towards the end, a long line of refugees stretched from the gates of Citadel, all along the cobblestone road that ran across the length of the Circuit, and back across the Gateway Bridge. The latter, a gift from the best engineering minds of Isaac's Hold, was the only safe route onto the Circuit. The Circuit itself was an "island" completely surrounded by the Becks-Dali River. The bridge took its name from the two massive iron and wood gates at its center. It was meant as a stopgap against invasion by keeping the people safe inside the Circuit while invaders spent weeks breaking through the bridge. To ensure that Lydia's plan would fully trap Everfrost, the bridge masters would feign cowardice and abandon their posts.

Hundreds of feet below, the catacombs were filling fast. Refugees sat by torchlight, waiting. If the coming battle gave even the slightest hint of a goblin victory, their escorts were to take them out of the valley.

Sometime on the ninth day, one of the goblin commanders caught on to the destination of the refugees and made haste for the city. Seeing the cadre of warriors moving to cut off the last of the refugees, Hector pulled a group of his knights aside and met them head on. The battle was harried and brutal. Each goblin they faced fought as if they had been personally wronged by their opponents. Hector ordered his men to hold the line at all costs. He knew if but one goblin made it inside they could very well spoil the trap they were setting.

As the last refugee crossed the threshold, the gates began to swing ponderously closed. Hector called for his men to retreat while he and a few at his side continued to fight, while they too slowly backed towards the gate. Seeing their opportunity, the goblins pressed in viciously. Growling and snarling, they clashed with the Knights covering the retreat. With fewer comrades at their side, Hector and his men were facing more and more warriors. Just a few steps away from the gate, Hector found himself crossing blades with no less than three. He parried, turned, and twisted his way out of the path of many a sharp blade.

After what seemed to be an eternity, the last of his knights squeezed their way into the city. Leaving Hector the last one on the wrong side, with at least a dozen of Everfrost's best staring at him. For a moment they could not make up their mind on whether they should rush the gate or pursue personal glory, and dispatch the Captain of Becknor. Hector used their momentary indecision against them. He saluted them and backed through the gate with just a few feet to spare. One hapless goblin, coming to his sense far too late, tried to follow him only to be crushed by the heavy gate.

News spread quickly through the ranks of Everfrost; within an hour the City Citadel was surrounded. A roar began to rise from outside the walls, followed by victory chants. Climbing to the top of the wall, Hector looked out and was shocked by an army of goblins much larger than any in the history of Becknor had ever faced. Regiment upon regiment, it was as if the halls of Everfrost had been emptied.

The sea of goblins parted for one solitary figure. Taking a spyglass Hector focused upon this sight and his blood ran cold. It was the Dread Overlord himself. He was broad shouldered, and heavily muscular, easily filling out the greenish, black armor he wore. Shoulder length black hair that matched his dark eyes. His skin, like most goblins, was so white and pale it looked as if his flesh was covered in frost. He smiled a vicious, predatory smile as he looked upon the city.

"She was right," a voice said to his right. Hector turned to see Galen standing beside him. He wore a worried expression.

"Right about what," Hector asked.

"That he would be here at the end. That the goblin hatred for the line of Achelon was so great, that he would come and personally end her life."

It was the second part of Lydia's plan that Hector had not been privy to. To ensure that Everfrost committed everything to this final battle, she would use herself as bait for the predator.

Prince Achelon's act had never been overly popular with the people of Becknor. The Valley-Dwellers were a proud but solitary people. The ancient motto had always been "A strong Valley is an isolated Valley." Even a century after Achelon's Peace, only members of the Royal Family, a few select Knights, and some merchants had ever set foot in the Outer World. But the act was even more hated within Everfrost. The Dread Overlord of that day, seeing the battlefields drenched in black goblin blood, had vowed that either he, or his descendants would see to the end of Achelon, and all who followed. Lydia would be the goblin's final trophy.

As darkness fell on that ninth day, an eerie silence fell upon the valley. On both sides of the walls, final preparations were underway. The Knights of the Valley shored up the last of the city's defenses while the warriors of Everfrost sharpened their blades for the final kill. After seeing his final orders were being carried out, Hector went out in search for Lydia. He knew it would be a short search. There was only one place in Citadel she could have been.

High above the cobblestone walls and streets, at the center of the city, surrounded by a lush green courtyard, was the Grand Viewing Tower. A tower so tall it could be seen halfway across the valley. Many viewing platforms were built into the sides of the tower but the one from the top was the best, it offered a perfect view of the Becknor Valley. And it was the perfect place to be seen by your adversary if you wanted his attention.

Hector found Lydia sitting on the floor at the room's center, gardening. Dressed in white and wearing light armor, her long golden hair pulled back into a single, tight braid, she sat filling clay pots with soil. The blackest and richest soil his eyes had ever seen. From a burlap sack at her side, she pulled from it what looked to be a flower bulb and planted it halfway down before covering it in the rich soil. Placing it to the side she began to work on the next in a tall stack of clay pots. Never once did she look up or acknowledge him.

Hector wordlessly walked to the center of the room and sat with her. After watching the process for a moment, he took over the task of filling the clay pots for her. They sat and worked silently. After some time had passed, he finally asked his question.

"Why?"

She did not turn to look upon him, only paused long enough to ask, "Would you have agreed to my plan regardless of the danger to me?" When he did not answer she smiled sadly, "We have been friends a long time and I know you all too well. You have an unwavering devotion to this Valley and the people within. This devotion grows stronger for those you call friend."

Lydia finally turned to him and said, "Can you not see? If we can break him here, even if it were to mean my death, it will buy our people some time. Maybe years. Perhaps, even enough time for the armies of the Alliance to return and once again ensure our peace."

Turning to work on the last clay pot she added, "That look in your eye is the very reason I did not tell you. It was difficult enough talking Galen and the others into agreeing. Your voice alone could have turned the tide against me. You may have even persuaded me against this action."

"Is that not the duty of a friend? To dissuade us from folly?"

"It is not folly, it is a sound plan."

"Then I shall stand by your side."

"No," Lydia said sternly. "For what I have planned you will only be in my way. Or worse, you will get yourself killed and I do not want to see your blood spilled in a selfless, but misplaced noble act. Besides, you have your own duties to see to. Your knights will need you, you are their Captain."

"And what of the other, more important rank you bestowed upon me years ago," he asked. Padding the soil down for the last time she did not turn to look upon him. He could see a stiffness in expression and posture. Almost as if she was silently begging him, *Please do not make this any more difficult.*

Aloud, she offered, "If it will sooth your conscience, I hereby release you from your post as Friend to the Regent."

"I am still sworn to protect you," Hector calmly protested despite the tidal wave of emotions running through him.

"Your Knight's Blood Oath is to protect our people as well as its leaders."

"And if you die we are leaderless."

"Only briefly, but not entirely. In half a year, my cousin will reach the Age of Responsibility and will take his throne. Until then, there are the Wise Men, the rest of the Royal Court, and you. I can afford to take this risk because I am only the Regent of Becknor. I am expendable."

"No, My Lady. This is not true."

13

Smiling sadly again, she turned to him once more and said, "That is kind of you to say my most trusted and dearest friend. But we both know it is."

*Not to me,* he began to say, but the words sounded hollow within his head. So he said nothing. Yet, in his heart, he felt he should have said those very words and much more. Even as he took his place among his knights down below, even as he glanced up at the viewing tower, he wished he had said more.

* * * * *

The last day of the war came. Silence fell. No one in the city said a single word. Outside, the goblins stood tall and unmoving, like statues. From morning to late afternoon both sides waited. When would the battle come? When the tension and anticipation had reached its silent crescendo, he appeared. The Dread Overlord stood before his army, flanked by his personal guards, facing the gate.

"Hail Becknor," he said, addressing the city in a mocking tone of the traditional military salute. "Have you finished your prayers? Are your souls prepared for their walk to the Halls of the Divine?"

His men around him laughed and mocked. He raised his arms into the air to encourage their merriment. After a short time, he slowly let his arms fall to call for silence.

"As if the Divine would accept murders and usurpers entrance." Turning to gesture towards his armies, he said, "Behold the day of the reckoning of Becknor has come. It is the goblin right to rule. Would we not have been just taskmasters? Would it not have been better to live under the lash then to die cowering in this miserable refuge? No, you had to have your freedom. And what has your freedom brought forth? You farmers, you toil all day only to see the profits of your labor fill the coffers of the monarchy. You brave knights, how often have your forebears died in needless bloodshed just to continue an obsolete line of kings and queens? Now do you see? Freedom is but the millstone that grounds you down into the very dust you toil in every spring and harvest. My ancestors only wished to free you from the bonds you have placed upon yourself. Your efforts would have been in service of a great and noble race; not the greed of your Royal Court. But now our patience wears thin."

Those upon the wall watched as the Dread Overlord's face contorted into a hateful sneer. "A century ago, one among you brought forth an abominable act. The attempted genocide of this goblin tribe. Despite the actions of Achelon the Cursed, we thrive. And today we will pay back the treachery of Becknor, a hundred fold."

A deafening cheer erupted from the goblin army. All within the city, and below, heard the war chants of Everfrost.

"But fear not Becknor, you will not be forgotten from the pages of history. In fact, we shall build a memorial right here in your glorious city. A monument whose stones will be made from your crushed and ground bones, and your blood shall be mixed with its mortar. Its height shall be seen from the balconies of Everfrost. It will be so prominent, that any trespasser that stumbles upon this valley will take warning that the goblins of Everfrost are not to be crossed lightly. Today, Becknor dies!"

One last cheer erupted, but it was short lived as their master called for silence. For centuries, it was widely known that the Dread Overlords of Everfrost had been studying the magic arts. The goblin rulers had lured an unsuspecting wizard into their ranks, and deceived him into teaching them his magics. Once all had been learned, the wizard had been disposed of, violently. Afterward, each Overlord wielded these powers with varying degrees of success. It was suspected that this Dread Overlord was possibly one of the more powerful adepts to use these arts. What happened next confirmed that suspicion.

All watched as the Dread Overlord stood at the front gate. His arms were folded across his chest and his eyes were closed tight in apparent deep concentration. Both sides watched transfixed as he threw his hands out in front of him, palms outward. For a moment nothing happened.

Then a shout came from the gate master, "The counterweights! The counterweights have broken!"

The Dread Overlord slowly opened his eyes and smiled evilly as the city gates began to swing helplessly open. The Armies of Everfrost unsheathed their weapons all at once. The sound of scraping metal seemed to echo across the entire valley.

Throwing his fist in the air, the Dread Overlord shouted triumphantly, "Unleash a flood of blood and death upon them!"

As their master had commanded, they rushed through the useless gate like a flood. Unchallenged, the goblin horde made their way down the narrow cobblestone streets of the city looking very much like a putrid wall of death, clad in their black-green battle armor. Holding their swords and battleaxes high over their heads, they unleashed a thunderous battle cry as they moved towards the city's center, Hector, and the Knights of the Valley. At Hector's orders, all knights had sheathed their weapons and were standing at a calm repose.

As the goblins rushed towards him screaming, Hector could not help but admire their enthusiasm. Even if they were enthusiastically running past every sign that they were running into a trap. Hector raised his open hand into the air, and began to count backward mentally.

*Three.*

None seemed to be very interested that each side street was barricaded with overturned carts and debris.

*Two.*

Nor did they seem to notice that the entrances to all ground level

16

buildings and towers had been sealed off with brick and mortar.

*One.*

Not a single soldier of Everfrost even bothered to look up. If but one had, he would have seen row upon row of archers, lining up on the rooftops with their bows drawn back.

Hector let his hand fall back to his side. Upon his silent command, he and his men fell to their knees allowing the archers at their backs' a clear view to take aim. Looking up at the charging army, he watched with grim satisfaction as the bloodlust drained from their faces and their eyes went wide with surprise.

"Let fly," he called from his knees. The battle cry of the goblins died on their lips and was replaced by the sound of hundreds of arrows singing through the air. As the arrows found their targets a new sound came from their opponent, one of agony.

Hector and his men were back on their feet in an instant, drawing their weapons. His sword in his right hand, a shield in his left, Hector ordered his men forward. In the madness that followed, Hector glimpsed the Dread Overlord moving through the narrow streets. He locked eyes with Hector and smiled. Then, just as quickly, he was gone. From above, there was a deafening crash of thunder from the Viewing Tower and Hector knew exactly where the Overlord had gone.

While the armies clashed below, Lydia and the Dread Overlord dueled up high in the viewing tower. In between raining blows down upon his opponent and raising his shield in defense, Hector would occasionally steal a glance up at the tower. Each time he was greeted with one frightening show of power after another. Great bolts of lightning were crashing into the tower, followed by even more dreadfully rolls of thunder. Next came balls of fire out through the windows and sometimes followed by sharp shards of ice. As the sun set and night fell, the inside of the uppermost room of the tower was alight with blinding menacing lights of red and pure rays of white.

Down below Hector and his men fought for their very lives. The warriors of Everfrost quickly recovered from the shock, and began to strike back with vengeance in their souls. Hector never left the front line. Even when his shield was broken in two by a large brute of a goblin. He simply took hold of his sword with both hands and leveraged his large opponent down. He fought on even when his helmet went flying from his head after a glancing blow from a battleax. Battered and bloodied as they were, seeing their captain unflinching in the face of death emboldened the Knights of the Valley, and they began to push back as the moon climbed higher. Shortly after, the armies of the Valley had turned the battle one last time and the Goblin Hordes were being routed.

It was in that very last moments of the war, that all began to feel the whole of the city hum with power. The battle below fell silent as all looked up to the viewing tower and watched as the red and the white lights began to merge and pulse. With each pulse, the humming became stronger and more forceful, until the cobblestone began to rattle. The pulses of light began to move quicker and brighter. Both sides became transfixed on this strange sight. Without warning, the top of the tower exploded upward and the scream of the Dread Overlord echoed across the valley.

Fearful, the goblin army dropped their weapons and fled back to their homes in the Everfrost Mountains. While many of his allies gave chase, Hector sheathed his sword and ran for the Viewing Tower. Fearing the worst, he mounted the stairs of the circular staircase two and three at a time.

Once Hector finally reached the top of the tower he found an odd site. Only the floor of the top room remained. The walls and ceiling had been completely blown away in the blast. The wooden benches, what little that remained, were smoldering. The air was heavy with the stench of smoke and brimstone. Before him, standing in the midst of broken pottery with her back to him, was Lydia.

Hector would later learn that those had been no mere flower bulbs he had helped Lydia pot. It was an alchemical weapon known as The Blooming Death. In ancient times there was a fear that the practitioners of magic would one day band together and subjugate the so-called mundane peoples of the world. For the most part, their fears would prove to be fruitless. Yet many of the early practitioners of alchemy began to work on offensive and defensive variants of their work. The Blooming Death was one of the few that had proven useful. The bulbs would absorb a portion of the magical energies. Portions so small the casting magician would have no clue to the danger he was in. Once the bulbs had absorbed their full amount, they would unleash the absorbed magic back upon its user. The one limitation being that one had to stay alive long enough for the bulbs to work. Against a full-fledged wizard, there was little chance it would succeed. But the Dread Lord, as powerful as might have appeared, was no wizard.

Lydia was standing over the seemingly lifeless form of the Dread Lord. Sensing Hector's presence she turned. Her armor was singed and dented. Her golden hair had come undone from its braid and now hung limply around her shoulders. She was breathing heavily in exhaustion. When she saw it was Hector she smiled.

"The day is won Hector," she said quietly. "Victory is ours."

Without warning, the not-quite-dead Dread Overlord sprang to his feet and seized Lydia from behind. He proclaimed with the last of his strength, "No, My Lady. Victory is mine."

Hector's hands moved quicker than thought. With years of battle-hardened reflexes, he drew his dagger and sent it flying for the Overlord. It flew true and found its target deep in the goblin's skull. But it was too late.

The Dread Overlord of Everfrost was already dead. He had used the last of his life energy to whisper something in Lydia's ear. At first, all seemed well. The Dread Overlord fell to the floor, his dark blood pooling around him.

Hector and Lydia exchanged one last nervous glance at one another, and then her eyes rolled up in her head, and she began to fall. Hector ran to her side and caught her just before she hit the floor. It was as if she had merely fallen asleep while standing.

"My Lady," Hector called to her grasping her shoulder and lightly shaking her. "Wake. The war is over. Lydia, wake."

But she would not. Her skin was hot to the touch, and as he held her she began to mutter to herself. His heart seemed to freeze at the sound of the anguish and uncharacteristic fear in her voice. Through all the mutterings, only three words were discernable, "Not the fire."

Behind him, a familiar voice was calling, "Captain, Everfrost is scattered to the four winds. There will to fight has," the voice trailed. Hector turned to see one of his two highest lieutenants, known as Hands, had come up behind him. It was Darius, his customary jolly grin had fallen from his face at the sight before him.

"The Regent has fallen," is all Hector could manage. "Bring Galen, quick."

# CHAPTER TWO

"It is the Fever-Sleep," Galen declared three days later. Hector stood before the Grand Master within the Hall of Study, inside the Palace. The Wise Men were made of the most knowledgeable, senior, and wisest of the Kingdom. They were the Healers, Master Planners, and Historians of the Valley. The Hall of Study itself was, in better times, a place of quiet contemplation and study. The books and manuscripts found within were always filed away in a neat and orderly fashion. After three days of twenty men and their acolytes fervently searching for the cause of the Regent's illness, the Hall looked as if it had been ransacked by a horde of goblins. Many of their records were centuries old, the smell of musky paper clung to the room.

Stroking his beard, Galen continued, "It is an ancient curse. Ironically, we only know of it thanks to Prince Achelon. Only recently has our order began to share knowledge with the scribes of the Alliance. It is within their books we have found the affliction."

"That is truly wonderful Galen, I am greatly pleased for you," Hector said sarcastically and did not care if it offended him. For the past three days, Hector had stationed himself by their door waiting for word. He had only left long enough to wash away the blood of battle and dress in a fresh tunic and trousers. It was a breach of protocol for the Captain of the Valley to be within the Palace outside of ceremonial dress but he cared not for protocol today. "We now know the cause, how do we cure it?"

21

Galen hung his head for a moment as if to gather his strength, and then looking up he answered, "We cannot."

Hector's stomach tightened. Galen attempted to place his hand on his shoulder in an attempt to give comfort but Hector shrugged it off and walked away.

"Are you certain? Perhaps you should study more. It took three days for you to conclude it was the Fever-Sleep, a few days more…."

"We knew it was the curse two days ago captain," he said grimacing in frustration. "The rest of our efforts were spent looking for the solution. We did not want to leave the Kingdom without hope."

"I refuse to accept this High One," Hector said turning towards Galen. "Perhaps there is a potion or some sort of alchemy that can be performed."

"This is the deadliest of curses," Galen said raising his voice. "It is of the Abyssal Magics. Curses such as this cannot be cured, they can only be dispelled by a full wizard or the magician who cast it."

*And the Dread Overlord is in his royal tomb within Everfrost by now,* Hector thought sourly. "No one has survived it on their own," Hector asked aloud.

"Only a brave few," Galen admitted. "Those with the strongest constitutions, and will to survive."

"You see," Hector said latching upon a hope. "There is none stronger in Becknor than her Ladyship. Lydia will come through. You will see."

Galen would not meet his eyes as he said, "They did not live long after the ordeal, and their minds were shattered."

*Their minds shattered,* Hector thought to himself. "Why would that be? What are you not telling me?"

"You are better off not knowing."

"I will not be left ignorant of my friend's ordeal, tell me," Hector said so forcibly that all activity ceased and the room went eerily silent.

Galen shook his head in frustration and said, "It is more than just a fever, though the fever is tormenting enough. Her mind is being assaulted as we speak. The Lady Lydia is trapped within a world of nightmares. The survivors speak of a place where your worst fears are played out in vivid realism. Any pain incurred in the dreams is felt bodily. As her fever climbs, the nightmares will become even more traumatic. Physically the curse will preserve her. She will not waste away, her muscles will not atrophy, and she will be the very model of good health up to the end. It is a torment that no soul has known this side of the abyss. On the very last day, her flesh will blister as her blood boils, and then she will wake so that her mind can embrace the pain fully just moments before death."

Each new detail was maddening for Hector to listen to. He felt a physical pain within every corner of his being. Three days she had already been suffering.

"How long for the process to finish," Hector asked, his voice strained.

"Generally, the length of one lunar cycle."

Hector looked upon Galen incredulously and said, "She will suffer another twenty-five days?"

"It is a hateful curse. I am sorry Hector. I understand that your allegiance goes beyond the chain of command. You both have been friends for many years. I cannot imagine the pain you...."

"You have to keep searching," Hector insisted, cutting Galen off midsentence.

"Captain, we have already exhausted our records here. There is nothing more."

"The records at City Citadel are just as extensive, are they not?"

"Yes, there may be some writings that slipped through, but most would be copies of what we have here. I am sorry Captain, but you must accept the fact that there is no hope."

Hector raised his hand, and said, "Follow me."

"Where? To Citadel? You grasp for the impossible."

"Just, follow me to the window," Hector said motioning again for Galen to follow. Together they left the Hall of Records and into the antechamber beyond. Hector had not expected for the others to follow, but was glad to see that they had. Turning his back to the window, he leaned against the frame and crossed his arms. He did not need to look out, for he knew already what was before them.

"Tell them they grasp for the impossible," Hector said as Galen took it all in. Thousands upon thousands crowding around the Palace in the dead of night. Farmers, knights, laborers, rich, poor, young and old, all gathered around for one purpose. Lydia. They stood, waiting for news and praying. Praying that the woman who had saved their lives would recover.

Hector never took his eyes away from Galen. He watched as the Grand Master of the Wise Men took it all in, stoically. After his years of service, Hector knew that to Galen, nearly unemotional Galen, there might as well have been tears in his eyes.

Without looking away, Galen said, "Send acolytes to Citadel. Fetch any records we do not have here. In the meantime, we shall reopen the books. Perhaps there is a vital clue we missed."

* * * * *

Hector went to Lydia only once.

Two Knights of the Inner Circle, the black-armored palace guard, stood on either side of her chamber door. They recognized him on approach and offered a salute. Hector automatically returned it, barely aware of doing so. His gaze was fixed upon the door. He knocked gently upon its surface. A maiden on the other side bid him enter.

His eyes fell immediately on Lydia, asleep in her bed. Asleep, but not resting. Even by candlelight Hector could see that Lydia's cheeks were flushed and hot. Her eyes were darting about wildly under their lids. Occasionally they would flutter as if she were trying to wake herself. Hector feared what horrible vision was before them now.

"There is no change," the maiden said as if anticipating his question. The girl sat beside Lydia, holding a damp towel to her head. Hector moved quietly to her bedside.

"Cecilia is it," he asked the maiden.

She smiled wanly and said, "Yes, Captain." She sat quietly as she tucked a strand of her long dark hair behind her left ear. Her blue eyes were tinted red from many tears.

"You are Lydia's political acolyte?" She answered with a silent nod. "I would not have expected to find you here."

"The others needed a rest, and this is the least I could do for My Lady," the girl, not quite eighteen herself, said with a shaky voice.

"She speaks highly of you," Hector told her.

This time she did smile genuinely and said, "And of you as well. These past months I have been regaled with the tales of the great Hector. Your many heroic deeds and the finer points of your character. Constantly informing me that a maiden could not ask for a better man in both character and handsomeness. Despite my dedication to study, I believe she was attempting to make a match."

A more pleasant memory drifted to Hector of Lydia attempting to encourage him to look Cecelia's way. If it had not been for the war, he would have begun to hear of the maiden's best qualities as well. But that was Lydia, always concerned someone was not living their life to the fullest.

"I would not be surprised," he told her.

Abruptly, Lydia began to murmur under her breath. An agonized, fearful sound that tore Hector's heart in two.

"Every hour," Cecilia said removing the towel to replace it with a fresh one from a basin on the bedside table. "It is as if whatever she is seeing comes to a crisis about this time each hour."

"Are there any discernable words?"

"Occasionally," she said looking across the bed. "It is always the same three words. 'Not the fire.'"

Now knowing the full extent of what was happening to Lydia, it was much more than Hector could take in. Nodding towards Cecilia, he turned and left the chamber wordlessly. Hector moved quickly through the Palace. His feet moved him aimlessly while his mind was fractured and worried.

For nearly ten years now, Hector had been a man of action. If there was a danger, he would meet it head on. Blade work was dangerous, regardless the foe. But in the end, Hector knew the repercussion of battle. You won and made safe the Valley or you were retired from the field. For him, life and death was not as simple as victory or defeat. Whether you walked away from the battle or were carried away brought varying degrees of victory; you celebrated with your comrades or you awoke in a place that knew no war. But this, what Lydia now faced, brought the specter of a defeat that was irreversible.

Finding himself alone in a secluded hallway, Hector leaned against the wall and closed his eyes. Closing them did not block out the vision of Lydia's slow and agonizing; no, he would not say death, illness. It was an affliction, but one she would recover from. There was a solution out there in the world. Had to be.

That was when, to attempt to block the sight of her suffering in his mind, he began to hold one image in his mind. His very first memory of

26

her. Lydia, standing in that windblown field, turning and smiling.

* * * * *

From that point forward, Hector stationed himself outside the Hall of Records, perpetually. He would be there the moment the Wise Men found Lydia' salvation.

Three more days would pass. Hector would take his meals when he had an appetite, which was not often; perform his morning exercises, and lightly doze in a chair by the door. Each time it opened, he would stand straight and watch for news. He could tell that the Wise Men were becoming sick at the sight of him. So it did not surprise him, shortly after Galen offered him a sour look, that one of his Trusted Hands appeared shortly after.

"Have you been sent to fetch me," he asked her.

Helena, tall and lean, her red hair pulled into a single long braid at the back, smiled and said, "In a manner of speaking. Galen seems rather put off. Apparently, there is a wayward knight perched at his door. I would say the old man has grown tired of him."

"Respect," he lightly reprimanded.

"Apologies, the blind old man that is the Grand Master of the so-called Wise Men Order has grown tired of him. The trouble is, this vagrant knight is someone of high rank and importance. It seems he has not the authority to order him away himself so he turned to his two Trusted Hands to try and persuade him back to his duties. I was the second pick, as Galen is obviously intimidated by my feminine whiles."

"Obviously," Hector said joining the private joke. The only feminine traits Helena exhibited was that she was born and looked female. In practice, she was rougher and more dangerous than any ten muscle-bound men. In fact, if a fight broke out between Helena and said ten men, Hector's coins would have been on Helena.

"He went to Darius first," she continued. "Even though he and his forces are posted on the Mountain Pass to stall any counter attacks and leave goblin stragglers stranded in our domain. Old Galen sent a rider with a request to come back and fetch you."

"What was his response," Hector asked and Helena told him Darius' very rude reply. "I wager that greyed his beard and extra shade. Still, less respectful than he is used to."

"If he had wished for respect then he should have had the wisdom to open his ears to the danger you and the Regent warned of. In any case, I have now been asked to come and speak with you."

"Hmm, so what speech are you to give that will move me back out into the valley," Hector asked.

"I am not here because Galen requested it. I am using it as an excuse to see how you are," she said.

Hector offered a faint smile and said, "I am well." He then added a shrug as to say under the circumstances. "I eat when the need comes and I doze when I grow weary."

Helena nodded and said, "What Galen does not realize is that we do not resent you for your vigil here. If the circumstances were different, and it was you afflicted, this hall would be filled with a hundred knights at all hours. The Knights of the Valley take pride in our Captain. As your comrade in arms, I wanted you to know this."

The words warmed his heart. But not as much as her next.

"And as a friend since childhood, I want you to know I understand why you have to be here. Furthermore, all you need to do is say the word and I will wait by your side."

This was more refreshing than any food or drink would have been for his body. Helena had been by his side through many hardships and dangers. Even as children they faced off against frightening odds once or twice.

"Under better circumstances, I would be proud to have you by my side here and now. The Valley has need of you more this day. Go and make safe the people."

Helena reached out and placed her hand on his shoulder, "My hopes are with you and my prayers are with Lydia."

\* \* \* \* \*

It was a few hours before dawn when Galen nudged him awake. "You found something," Hector asked, looking up at Galen. "A dispel?"

A half smile creased his lips as he contradicted himself, "A cure." The smile faded just as fast, as he added, "A distant and fast fading hope."

A moment later Hector was standing once again within the Hall. If it was possible for the room to look even more disorganized, they had found it. Everyone inside was exhausted. Some were even slumbering with their face planted firmly within a book.

"There is an elixir, a long distance from here. It is believed to have powerful healing abilities. It is made from the petals of a rare flower. A blue orchid."

"I am not familiar with blue orchids," Hector said.

"That is because there is only one left in this world. It is the lone survivor of a great destruction. It was found over a thousand years ago on the edge of the Glass Desert."

Hector's spine chilled and he asked, "Excuse my ignorance High One. The Glass Desert and the Wasting Desolation that surrounds it are well known. The history of how they came about is taught to every child in study. It was one of the last tragedy that precipitated the Great Migration of our ancestors into this valley. But I was left with the understanding that nothing can live within."

"You would be correct," Galen said with a nod. "There are several notations within the books from Isaac's Hold about this Blue Orchid Elixir and its keeper. It is said that a traveling alchemist strayed into the Desolation after his caravan was attacked. This nameless man wandered within for days. As he neared death, a strange sight caught his eye. It was the orchid. Amazed at how it could even survive, he began to experiment on the spot. He concocted the elixir on his first attempt and nursed himself back to health. Some of what is recorded after seem to be part legend and part truth. It is said his first mixture was so potent he achieved immortality, although I am rather dubious about that."

"Is it said where this miracle is stored," Hector asked eagerly.

"Yes," Galen said with a frown. "This alchemist built a vast tower fortress inside the Glass Desert itself. There he keeps watch over the blue orchid and the elixir."

"What price does he ask?"

"Hector, did you hear me? It is in the Glass Desert."

"That matters little. What price?"

Galen sighed and answered, "There is no earthly good, amount of gold, or oath he will trade under. The only way is to win the elixir. He has devised a set of trials, three in all. You must complete them to be deemed worthy. Fail but one and the elixir is lost forever."

"I must prepare myself for the road," Hector said turning. Before he had even taken a step, Galen's hand clamped down hard on his shoulder and turned him back.

"Hector, it is a fool's errand. It is a ten day journey by horse, and that is pushing it to the point of death. Ten days there, ten days to return, a dangerous wasteland to survive, and an unknown length of time to complete three trials you have no guarantee of besting. It has been a week already. I am sorry, but in all likelihood, Lydia will pass before you return. Accept the reality. It is too late."

Hector looked upon Galen defiantly and said, "Lydia's strength is made of fiber that is stronger than steel. She will endure until I return with the elixir in hand." *Or I will not return at all*, he added silently as he turned and left Galen's presence.

As the sun crested the mountains to the east, Hector was already on the Mountain Pass. He had gone to his cottage to prepare himself, he was clean shaven and his brown hair was cut close. His appearance would be in strict adherence to the code. From there he rode quickly for the Barracks and a fresh set of light armor. The armor was the traditional ice-blue color of an officer. The chest piece bore the crest of Becknor and the insignia of his rank. Today he was not just the Captain of the Knights of the Valley, he was the Champion of the Kingdom.

At the top of the Pass, just before leaving the valley, Hector looked back. He had never in all his life stepped foot beyond this point. It was not that he held the same isolationist views of the rest of Becknor. It was because there had never been any need for him to go further. His family, his rank, his friends, everything in his life was inside this valley. If it was not for Lydia's need it was doubtful he would have been leaving this time. Turning his back on it all, he urged his horse forward onto the road and the Glass Desert beyond with but one memory to motivate him. Not Lydia tormented in her sick bed, but Lydia full of life in a vibrant bed of flowers.

JACK O CRABTREE

# CHAPTER THREE

There is a folly to spending your days in a secluded valley, and living in a kingdom that practices deep isolationism. Chances are, your maps of the Outer World are less than ideal. The few dignitaries that had traveled out in the last century found no need in maps. If you wished to visit Isaac's Hold, follow the river. Head due south and you will enter the Great Desert Kingdom of Mar'gev. Traveling to Espertine, the capital of the Alliance, take the King's Road. Never go north unless you wished to be murdered by highwaymen, raiders, feuding warlords, or any number of strange beasts or perils. And to Hector's knowledge, no one from Becknor had ever traveled this far east. As a consequence, the map that Galen had drawn up with the best route to the Glass Desert was less than ideal. Some of the landmarks that were meant to be Hector's guide were still there, but most had been altered or removed altogether. That was the hazard of two-thousand-year-old maps. So between an ancient quarter accurate map and Hector's poor directional judgment; both horse and rider found themselves in a dire condition close to the end of the fourth day.

It had taken two days of hard riding to pass the southern tip of the Dali Mountains. The Glass Desert was on the northeastern edge of the Kingdom of Greater Ortivan. Greater Ortivan, the strange feudal republic, was the easternmost kingdom of the Alliance. This Greater Kingdom was the largest of the four in land. Frustrated with Galen's map, Hector had tried to shave as much time as possible. In hindsight, he could now see the folly of going off the map and relying on compass alone. By taking them off the road, he had ridden into overgrown forests, rocky terrain, and had nearly drowned by attempting to ford a river that was deeper than its appearance. Now back on the road, he and his horse were near exhaustion. Hector knew if he did not stop and allow his horse, Lawrence, an extended rest he would be dead. It was then, as the countryside had turned from forests and rock, to a hilly, grassy plain; in the midst of cursing himself for losing time, he saw them.

Goblins! It was unmistakable. Up ahead, about three hundred yards, he had seen two of them poke their heads over a hill to glance at him. Dark hair, black eyes, and pale frost-like skin. Everfrost must have seen his departure and sent an ambush party. Again Hector cursed himself for those supposed time-saving detours. He had given them all the opportunity they needed to get ahead and set a trap.

Hector pretended to be admiring the countryside as he watched the spot out of the corner of his eye. After a few heartbeats, the two heads popped up again. He could not tell how well armed they were, but at least there seemed to be no archers present. There would be at least two more, well-hidden, he wagered. Anything larger took the risk of being spotted. If he allowed them to spring their trap he could be overwhelmed quickly. As exhausted as he was, Hector had no choice. He would need to ambush the ambush.

Loosening his grip upon the reigns, Hector turned his head back toward the party. The two heads fell out of sight again, and Hector made his move. Kicking his feet away from the stirrups, he slid out of the saddle to the right. Lawrence continued to clip-clop away from him. The moment Hector's feet hit the ground he started running to close the distance. Any moment the two scouts could look up again and call the alarm. His only advantage would be the closer he approached, the less time they would have to react. Ultimately, fortune favored him. Hector crossed the entire distance unseen. Just a few running steps away, Hector unsheathed his sword and leapt over the hill. Landing upon his feet he found five sets of eyes staring up at him in horror, three goblins, and two humans. All of them children, all of them shrieking.

For a moment all Hector could do was stand dumbfounded at the sight. Goblin and human children? Together? Slowly, as Hector came back to himself, he became aware that the children were still wailing as they looked upon his drawn sword. Looking upon them, to the sword in his hand, and back upon the children, Hector loosened his grip on the weapon immediately. It fell to the ground and his hands went up in a pose of surrender.

"I beg your pardon," he said sincerely. "I thought you were an ambush."

"You there," an angry male voice called behind him. Hector turned to see two angry men, one human, the other goblin, approaching him with mattocks. Their eyes fell upon Hector's sword on the ground. "What is the meaning of this?"

Hector took one side step away from his weapon and said, "Many apologies good sirs. I was horribly mistaken. I was alone upon the road and I thought they were," he paused before saying an ambush party from Everfrost and said instead, "highwaymen."

The men eyed Hector suspiciously a moment longer before the human man began to laugh. "Aye, that's our children I wager. Destined to be highwaymen. Third time in the last month this lot have startled a hapless traveler."

"Gryndella, have I not asked you to stop spying upon the travelers," the goblin man said to the oldest of the group, a goblin girl of roughly twelve years. "I have told you that you are bound to scare the wrong one and it will spur violence. Look what you have nearly wrought today."

"Again, my good men, I beg your pardon," Hector said, allowing his hands to fall to his sides. Placing his right hand upon his chest he said, "I have been traveling nearly nonstop for the past four days, and my imagination ran away with me." Hector looked back up the hill to see his tired horse looking down upon them. Hector had a theory that horses were easily amused with their riders, Lawrence included, and was sure his was laughing at him now. Hector turned to see the goblin man staring directly on the emblem upon Hector's chest piece.

"I imagine that being so far from home has your senses on edge as well, Valley-Dweller," the goblin said with an uneasy smile. "One does not normally find a Knight of the Valley in Greater Ortivan."

"Becknor," the goblin's companion said oblivious to the sudden staring contest between his friend and Hector. "There is the tale of that one mischievous fellow, has a reputation for merriment. Every two years he comes riding out to the various villages and cities of the fiefdom. Usually ends with him being chased away by angry husbands."

Hector sighed and said, "That sounds like Darius. I would be his," again Hector changed his word choice from Captain to, "his superior officer."

"Excellent," the man said smiling. "That is a relief. I'll not have to hide my wife."

"If I read your emblem clearly you would be the Captain of the Knights of the Valley," the goblin spoke up again, more worried.

No point in pretending now, Hector answered, "That is correct. I take it you are familiar with Becknor."

"Only from what was passed on to me by my father. He, along

with a group that included my mother, fled Everfrost cruelty to find a new life here. If you do not mind my bluntness. One does not normally find the highest ranking military officer, of any kingdom, riding alone."

The goblin was worried at the sudden appearance of such a high ranking knight, and Hector could guess why. Even if his family had fled from Everfrost, they would have still believed the stories. To maintain control over their subjects, the Dread Overlords had demonized the people of Becknor. The people of the Valley had been cast as villainous butchers who killed goblins on sight, drank their blood, and used their bones for fertilizer. The man standing before him would be fearful for himself and his family.

"An escort would only slow me down," Hector explained. "I am on a quest for our fallen Regent. I am in search for a medicine that will cure her of a dreadful curse."

The two men exchanged knowing looks with one another. The human asked, "Can we be of service General?"

"Our monarchy abolished that rank long ago so that their title may include Supreme General of Becknor. I am but a captain," Hector said. "As I said, my journey has been almost nonstop. I fear for my horse. He needs to be stabled for the night at least."

"You are in luck," the goblin said with a cautious smile. "Our village happens to have one of the best stables, and horse master, in all of Greater Ortivan."

"I would be grateful if you would show me the way," he said, directly to the goblin.

"I would be happy to, Captain?"

"Hector, son of Felix," he answered.

The goblin hesitated for a moment and then said, "I am Elster Mativilies. Welcome to Bear's Sanctuary."

\* \* \* \* \*

Hector's expectation for the appearance of any village was informed by the numerous villages of the Valley. In comparison, minus the surrounding walls and viewing tower, Bear's Sanctuary was a small replica of City Citadel. Although many of the outlying structures were wooden, and the roads leading to the center were simple dirt, the village square was a marvelous exception. Various shops and a small fort were built of stone and mortar. They ran along a recently built paved road. But the sheer size of it all. Hector, leading his horse on foot, could not help but gawk at this wonder. The goblin Mativilies, walking by his side, watched him with a bemused smile.

"Our humble village takes you by surprise," Elster asked.

"Humble? In the valley, this would hardly qualify as a village. This would be the second largest city," Hector said shaking his head.

"And yet we are one of the smallest villages in the fiefdom." When Hector turned to him with an obviously perplexed expression, he added, "Well, probably not the smallest within all of Greater Ortivan. Lord Trask's fiefdom is one of the more prosperous. Yet, this new village square; I will admit, has taken some getting used to for us as well," Elster confided. "This was an empty field almost a decade ago. We have already passed through the old village center."

"What inspired your people to build this new center?"

"It was not our idea or design. Though our mayor takes much pride in organizing and inspiring the local workers," the goblin said with a laugh. "This is the designs of the ruling Duchess of Greater Ortivan. Nine years ago, upon her election, she decreed that every village in every fiefdom would have a new center of commerce and government. She now promises to begin the building of a new aqueduct system. One that will rival even the great City-State of Isaac's Hold. If she is elected to a second decade, that is."

"We have heard of your democracy. Though we do not understand it," Hector admitted.

"That is quite alright. I have been a citizen of the Kingdom all my life, and sometimes I do not understand," he said with a frown. "Greater Ortivan is comprised of twelve democratic fiefdoms. Where a normal fiefdom is ruled by a lord's birthright or appointment, as it is still done in the Realm of Old Ortivan, we have the power to elect the Lord or Lady who will rule over the fiefdom every half decade. Every ten years there is the Grand Electorate. All twelve fiefdoms unite in the election of the One Voice of Ortivan. The elected Duke or Duchess oversees the protection and wellbeing of all the fiefdoms. They also are our One United Voice that speaks for us in the Assembly of the Alliance. Our democratic system is not unlike the one the Alliance uses when it comes time to electing the High King."

"The other refugees from Everfrost, did they stay here or move on," Hector asked.

"We are all here," said Elster. "Those that escaped made sure we knew well the hardships they had to endure. If you are the strongest, healthiest of the Mountain, you are trained for war. Only the rulers and warriors benefit from the work of the rest. Everyone unworthy is sent deep into the mines. You work for days without a break. If you can manage to live through the brutal work ethic, you are allowed sanctuary in the lower levels. My father was part of the work detail that burrowed into one of the caverns below the valley by accident. The foreman demanded it be sealed immediately. My father said the other's saw the opportunity and killed their overseer. They moved swiftly to collect their families and escaped; sealing the entrance behind them. Eventually, they found their way here," he said smiling and gesturing to the village around them. "Bear's Sanctuary is a special place. It is a place of refuge and rest. The people here will gladly take in anyone earnestly searching for a fresh start. Whether they be refugees, wanderers, or just simply broken in spirit. Not unlike the horse master I take you to now."

"How so?"

Elster smiled apologetically and said, "It would be best if he told you. It is his story if he wishes to tell it. But trust me when I tell you, you have never met his like before."

* * * * *

There is one constant in all the world, a stable will always look and smell like a stable. Though Bear's Sanctuary's was much smaller than those found in Becknor, there were horses, hay, the odors, but for the moment something was off. Hector and his goblin companion entered to find the horse master missing.

"Clovis my friend, are you about," Elster called out.

A deep, rumbling voice called out somewhere behind one of the stalls, "Where else would I be this time of day? Come for another game of cards?"

"I am afraid not, but I promise a rematch soon. I have brought you some business."

"Oh?"

"Yes, a high-ranking representative of Becknor."

There was a sound that came from the horse master just then, Hector guessed it was laughter but it was odd and raspy. "It would not happen to be that jolly soldier of fortune we have heard so much about. The one that rid Lord Trask of that small band of raiders by besting their leader in single unarmed combat, before running away with Trask's wife?"

"Afraid not. But he may regale you with his tales, for we have his commanding officer," Elster said. Hector could not believe his ears. Darius

40

had been taking quiet pilgrimages out of the valley for years, but he had never suspected he had made such a name for himself.

"Too bad. Please take no offense, good sir. I am glad for the business, and proud to have the opportunity to meet someone new. Allow me just one moment more friend and I will join you. The name is Clovis, Clovis Ran'Mar."

"Hector, son of Felix," Hector called back.

"Strange, you have no surname," Clovis asked.

Hector smiled and answered, "One of my people's peculiarities. When my ancestors migrated to the Valley two millennia ago, to escape the last Blight War, they left behind everything they felt separated each man and woman from one another. They abandoned the tradition of surnames and took up the old custom of genealogy."

"Fascinating. Over the course of your stay, you will have to initiate me in the ways of the Beck."

Hector tried, but he could not keep his expression from souring. He knew the horse master had meant nothing by it. Yet, it was hard not to take offense. Across from him Elster visibly flinched.

The goblin called out, "I am afraid you have just issued a rather nasty insult by accident, dear Clovis. The people of the Mountain refer to the people of the Valley as Beck. It closely mirrors the word Bek' in the goblin tongue. The most common translation is," he glanced to Hector and said, "Perhaps it is best left untranslated for now."

"I am certainly not putting my best foot forward," said Clovis. "Perhaps it would be best if we meet face to face before I chase you away."

There was movement somewhere just out of sight. Hector craned his neck to see but still found nothing. It was only as the horse master came into view, out from behind a tall stack of hay bales, that he understood Elster's words that Clovis was unlike anything he had ever seen.

He stood just under five feet. He wore tan colored tunic and trousers. The clothes were quite unnecessary as Clovis Ran'Mar's entire body seemed to be covered in a thick mane of mostly dark grey fur. There were splotches of white fur at his throat, hands, and feet. He had strong shoulders and arms. He was barrel-chested and his legs were bulging with muscles. The rest of his features were most assuredly of the feline persuasion. His hands were slightly smaller than his feet but, like his feet, were more like the paws of a great cat than the hands of a man. His head and facial features were even more exaggeratedly cat-like. Clovis' big bright eyes looked Hector up and down studying his armor.

"My compliments to the smithies of Becknor," Clovis said. "I have never seen armor so exquisitely crafted."

"The armor is custom," Hector said, regaining his speech. "The highest ranking officers of the Knights of the Valley go before the master blacksmith. Together they forge the armor and sword they carry to the officer's desires."

"I have never seen this color on armor before."

"Officer's armor has varying shades of color so that knights can find their commanders."

"And enemy archers too, I wager. Still, it is exquisite," Clovis said with approval. "Unique. Just as unique as meeting one such as I, I would wager."

"Even Becknor knows of the far western Islands of Threshold and the warrior race of Loe," Hector said as Clovis looked on in approval. "I have never met one of your people until today. Though, like my people, I was told you rarely leave home."

"You would be surprised how many take to the seas when offered work aboard the great ships of the Alliance. However, I would be the first to have traveled this far onto the continent in decades."

"We are both far from home."

"Indeed," Clovis said as he walked up to Hector's horse and gave him a pat. Talking to the horse in a soft melodic voice he said, "Now my noble friend."

"His name is Lawrence."

"Ah, fine strong name. Let us see what can be done for you."

\* \* \* \* \*

Elster left Clovis and Hector in the stables. It was now well past late afternoon and into early evening. His stomach was growling and he could not wait to relate today's strange encounters with his kin.

"Elster," a man called out to him. He looked to see Rodrick, the man who had been at his side today in the field, walking towards him.

"Our Becknor friend is with Clovis," Elster said to Rodrick upon his approach.

"Are you safe," Rodrick asked in sincere concern.

Elster smiled and said, "Quite safe. My father never did fully believe what the rulers of Everfrost called, the atrocities of Becknor. Though, he passed the story on to us just in case a glimmer of it were true. This Hector seems to be a good man."

"It is a shame then," Rodrick said.

Elster nodded in grim agreement. Hector has said he was on a quest for medicine for his fallen Regent. The Captain's destination was obvious.

"He seeks the madman," Elster said in little more than a whisper.

"May the Divine have mercy upon his soul," Rodrick prayed.

\* \* \* \* \*

Hector stood studying the one handed battleax and shield hanging upon the wall. It appeared that Clovis Ran'Mar was no exception in that he, like many of his people, had at least been a warrior at some point in his

43

past. He pondered what would cause someone to leave their people behind to work stables three thousand miles away?

"I see you have found my wall decorations," Clovis said behind him.

Hector turned and said, "I was admiring your ax. I would have expected the handle to be thicker, not thinner, in the middle."

"If these were man-like, then yes," he said holding up one of his massive hands. "Our grip is surer. Once something is in our clutches you would have to end our life to pry it free."

"Curious decoration for a stable," Hector observed.

"They serve as a reminder."

"You mean to never use them again?"

Clovis tilted his head to the side in thought, then answered, "If ever there came a day that they or I were called upon, in that dark and terrible hour when the need was great, then yes. But I have no intentions of ever touching them for no longer than is needed to clean the dust from them."

"A member of a great a noble warrior race who would happily live the rest of his life as a horse master. Sounds as if there is an interesting story there," Hector said innocently.

"That I am sure of," Clovis said enigmatically. "But it is a long tale and your horse has need of me. I assure you captain, that by morning, Lawrence shall be so well rested it will be as if your horse had never left your Kingdom."

"That is a bold promise."

"One that I have never failed in my ten years here," Clovis said with a touch of pride. "Now, I understand you have a meal and a bed waiting for you in the inn. I am sure you are just as in need of rest yourself."

Hector frowned and said, "No, I am staying here tonight. I will take rest in one of your empty stalls."

"Hay is a poor substitute for a warm bed."

"I am on a quest, not a tour," Hector was adamant. "It would be a selfish notion on my part."

"Surely your quest is better served with a rested mind and body," Clovis said. The Loe warrior, sorry, horse master, would have been correct if the matter was not so dire.

"My Regent lay dying in her bed as we speak. How can I take rest when she has none," Hector said.

Clovis studied him for a moment. Hector could see the gears of his mind at work. Twice he began to ask and stopped himself. On the third attempt, he was successful.

"You seek that which is hidden away in the Glass Desert."

"You know of the Blue Orchid Elixir," Hector asked.

"I am familiar with it," Clovis said gravely and looking away. "You are not the first journeyman to wander this way upon that quest. Doubtful you will be the last. Suffice it to say, I understand your mindset and I will not belabor the point. I will send word to the inn and prepare a stall with fresh hay."

"I thank you," Hector said gratefully. Clovis locked eyes with him in what he supposed later was a Loe smile, but his eyes held a melancholy look.

"It is my honor to serve the champion of Becknor, but if by chance you would allow me one last question," Clovis asked and Hector nodded his consent. "Your Regent, she is, shall I say, important to you?"

"She is important to our Kingdom," Hector said all at once. Clovis' face changed, again later Hector would guess it was a frown. Wordlessly, Clovis turned to leave. Before he was out of sight, Hector asked, "If you would be so kind as to also allow me one last question."

The former warrior of the loe stopped but did not turn. It was almost as if he knew the question before the words were spoken.

"In ten years, you have never thought of returning to the Threshold Isles?"

The answer was without hesitation, "There is nothing there for me to return to." With that, Clovis turned the corner and was gone.

Later Hector sat in a pile of hay, eating his meal. One of maiden's working in the inn had volunteered to bring him his dinner. She stood by while he finished and then took the empty plate and flagon away wordlessly. Upon her arrival, he offered to pay the master of the inn for the food, and her for delivering it to him. She was told to refuse his money just as she refused payment for carrying the meal.

Night fell on Bear's Sanctuary, and Hector sat with his back against the wall looking across at nothing at all. His mind was elsewhere, in a windblown field. In a better time. His mind's eye watched as Lydia turned toward him yet again.

Not far away Hector could hear Clovis with Lawrence. The loe was giving the horse a rub down, speaking in his own native tongue as he did. The loe-speech was soothing and had a kind of melody to it. Hector began to become drowsy at the sound of it. His surroundings, the smell of horse, caused his mind to drift just before sleep. He was reminded of another memory of Lydia. Their second meeting. Ironically it too had been in a stable.

# CHAPTER FOUR

**Five Years Ago....**

Hector dismounted and made his way quickly to the Palace Gate. As one of ten High Lieutenants, it was his privilege, and duty, to escort his Captain from the Palace and back to the Barracks once the Royal Court had adjourned. He was now an hour late, but then this had not been his detail for the day. Thankfully, it seemed the session was running over. A common occurrence for the last three months, the total span of the regency of Lady Lydia so far.

Hector did not wait for the Gatekeeper to finish swinging the gate open. The moment there was a gap large enough for him to slip through, the young High Lieutenant ran past, drawing the ire of the Gatekeeper. As the grey-haired man shouted a reprimand Hector's way for the breach of protocol, to which Hector merely waved and offered an apologetic expression, he made his way quickly to the Great Door. Upon his approach, the other high ranking Knight watched him in amused silence, knowing very well this was not Hector's duty. Hector offered a shrug as if to say *what can you do,* eliciting a laugh from the other.

The outer walls of the Grand Palace of Becknor belied the majesty and grandeur within. It's basic outer construction gave one the impression that it was no more than any other fort in the greater world, giving no hint to the majesty that just lie beyond the door. The simple stone walls that encompassed the perimeter gave little clue to the lush green lawns and colorful flower beds of the many courtyards.

Hector, now standing just outside the entrance to the Great Hall, had to this point never laid eyes upon the former, but took the time to appreciate the latter. Being now one of his Captain's High Lieutenants, one grade in rank below one of the Two Trusted Hands, Hector was free to enter the Palace whenever the mood suited him. Yet, he had never taken one step beyond the threshold. Instead, Hector was content to wait until the day came that official business brought him within the walls. To enter was not a right but a privilege in his sight. One Hector felt he had yet to earn fully.

And so Hector gladly waited for his Captain, Vitus, to conclude his business with the Royal Court. In the meantime, he watched as the Palace gardeners tended the flowerbeds. These men and women worked the beds almost constantly from spring to autumn. Planting, watering, replanting whatever was in season, followed by more watering, and finally preparing the soil for next season. With harvest quickly approaching, the beds would soon be devoid of color. For now, the gardeners were busy weeding and watering the very last flowers to grow this year, mums. The beds were arranged in semi-circle fashion in three tiers, each expanding out wider from a central point. The outer tier was a solid maroon in color. The middle tapered from maroon to yellow to blue towards the center. At the farthest end was one last bed, here the Master Gardner had decided upon purple. From above, Hector imagined, the scene resembled ripples upon the water from a stone falling in from the shore, only in flower form.

"I am not sure I have ever seen any of our knights so taken with the grounds here. Especially the gardens," a voice called to him from the opposite side of the archway he occupied. The words pulled Hector from his observation.

Olivia, Trusted Right Hand of Vitus, stood with her helmet in the crook of her left arm, watching with a curious smile across her lips. She was slightly taller than Hector. A three-decade veteran of the Knights of the Valley, her hair, tied up into a bun, was now becoming an equal mix of sandy and silver. The most distinguished characteristic was the patch covering her left eye. Lost when she was but still a squire, the eye had nearly cost her a chance at Knighthood. All knights in Becknor had to meet strict physical measurements. Any physical handicap was seen as a potential weak link in the chain that was the Knights of the Valley. A weakness that could be exploited to the doom of all.

Working twice as hard, it was said that there was not one squire or knight who could match Olivia's prowess in any fighting style, with any weapon. Still, the Captain of her day initially refused her entry into service. There was but one thing for Olivia to do, challenge her Captain to combat. The duel itself had become a bit legendary and after three decades had fallen into the realm of blatant exaggeration. Oliva herself never spoke openly of it nor did those still within the ranks who had been present. It was said the duel lasted hours. Olivia ultimately lost the battle but won her Captain's respect, and her knighthood. The only fact that had not been distorted by time was the compliment of her captain after the duel.

"Thy sight may have been reduced by half, but thine vision has increased tenfold."

Looking over and smiling towards his superior, Hector offered, "Perhaps it is the farmer in me. One does not come from as many generations of farmers as I do without feeling a call from the Valley's soil. After spending years in the hot sun, laboring over crops with my father, perhaps I find it puzzling that others would work twice as hard over something so trivial."

"Trivial?"

"Well," he said with a shrug, "No crops, no food, no benefits to the Valley."

"Are there truly no benefits," she asked. "Are you certain?"

Hector looked again. This had just become a training exercise. No matter the rank, Olivia was known to occasionally test even the most experienced. Her tests were not always in the realm of combat or physical strength, but of the mind.

He moved his eyes away from the laborers and to those who were currently strolling through the courtyards. He watched as those who exited the Palace, their faces hard and expressionless, walked about the stone paths around the garden. Those that had been there for some time showed signs of a growing serenity, taking deep breaths, relaxing their stance and allowing their hands to fall to their side. Lastly, Hector looked upon the men and women leaving the garden and walking back to their duties within the walls. While a few continued to look stony, others looked relieved after a moment of respite.

"It is a place of refuge," Hector said carefully. "Somewhere to go to when the burdens of the Valley begin to weigh them down. An opportunity to see something of beauty and to breath. To help forget, if only for a moment."

"Very good," she said with a nod. "There is more to being of service than just growing food, building roads and homes, or even protecting our kingdom. Do not misunderstand, all are very important. But somedays, the soul needs nourishment as well. We are not all monks, priests, or scholars. We do not always have the time to devote to meditation, study, and quiet contemplation. But at the very least, if nothing more than a quarter of an hour, we need to escape ourselves. And we need a place to do so," she said motioning towards the gardens.

Despite himself, Hector had to ask, "Why would one want to

escape themselves?"

Her good eye narrowed and she said gently, almost sadly, "To find what was lost. While it can still be found."

The Great Doors of the Palace swung open and a steady stream of high officials and Wise Men began to exit. By the looks on the faces of most, Hector could see a multitude in need of escape.

Near the back, Captain Vitus came into view. His bald head gleamed as the sun invaded through the door. His long, fiery, red goatee easily seen. Facial hair was not strictly forbidden by the Knight's code, but strongly discouraged. It was the one tenant Vitus had ignored altogether. After going completely bald early in life, he would not think of shaving the only hair he had.

Upon his approach, both Hector and Olivia snapped to attention. Dressed in the traditional ice-blue armor of an officer of the Valley, and ceremonial silver cape for his meeting with the Royal Court, Vitus walked swiftly with his head down and lips moving. In his five and a half years of service as a Knight of the Valley, Hector had learned how to read his Captain's mood. Especially now that he was a high lieutenant, and after accompanying his captain to several meetings with the Royal Court. A slow moving Vitus with his head up was a sign of a good day (these were rare). The lower the head and the swifter the pace the worse the meeting. If his lips were moving, cursing under his breath, he was quite irritated. But if Vitus was cursing in the goblin tongue, the Divine help you.

Vitus passed the pair of them without looking up, cursing violently in goblin. Not just the light curses, but the foulest and filthiest words he knew. Hector exchanged a worried look with Olivia as they moved in step with him. Olivia moved to his side and Hector slid to two paces behind as protocol demanded.

"Do I even hazard a guess," she asked Vitus.

"Por'fetti non Galena," he said angrily, coming to a sudden stop and turning towards her. If Hector's ears heard correctly, Vitus had just uttered quite the insult towards Galen and his ancestry. One so violent it would have possibly curled the elder statesman's beard.

"Galen again?"

"No, it is not just Galen," Vitus said waving his hand towards the front of the Palace as if he were shooing it away like a fly. "The entire Royal Court has lost its collective mind over her ladyship. The poor girl. What was the king thinking of upon his deathbed? Appointing her Regent. Imagine, only to just have come to the age of responsibility and be saddled with this lot. You find more common courtesy on the battlefield."

"They question her age then," Olivia asked.

"They question her age, they question her tutelage in Isaac's Hold, they question her loyalty to the Valley after spending five years in said city-state, and worse of all, they have begun to question her lineage." Vitus turned and began to walk for the gate as he added, "Almost a century of peace is not nearly long enough for the isolationists to forgive Achelon."

"Court politics has always been fluid, perhaps once the Lady Lydia finds her footing…," Olivia left the last unsaid.

"I think that is the plan, to deluge her with procedure and study until she washes away like silt in a riverbed. Frustrate her in pseudo-protocol procedures until she steps down and the Court can choose among themselves the next Regent."

"You believe Galen is positioning himself for the role?"

"Actually, no. I believe his second Cassius is pushing for such, but Galen has no desire for that type of power. If I were a wagering man I would say the Moneychangers are behind the bulk of this. Seeing the anger of the isolationists, they are manipulating the Court so a member of their ranks can be stationed to the Right of the Throne. Perhaps even Klytus the

Guild Master himself. Their greed would see the selling of the bulk of our wheat and goods to fill their coffers while our bellies go empty in the winter. My quarrel with Galen is that he sees this and does nothing," he said as the trio reached the front gate and stepped through and to their waiting horses.

"He knows if he stands up to the Isolationists and the Moneychangers, and the girl stumbles and falls, he will fall with her. Unless someone comes to her aid; she will not last. I fear unless Lydia can find her voice soon, her Regency will be a short one," Vitus said shaking his head. "It will be a shame. I knew her father, Lord Marcus, very well. He and his wife, Anastasia ,would be quite proud of the young woman she has become. And their anger would be to the boiling point."

Vitus gave his horse a pat on the side and was about to mount up when something caught his eye. Checking his saddle on both sides he began to curse under his breath again.

"I asked the Palace stable master to give her a good rub down, not lose my possessions! My saddlebags are missing. Darius go back," he stopped short when he saw it was Hector, and not Darrius, who had met him. His eyes narrowed and Hector could feel the heat rising off of his captain even at this distance. Hector had to resist the urge to back away. One never retreated from Vitus unless you wanted a worse verbal thrashing from his whip-like tongue.

"Where is Darius?"

"He was," Hector searched for the right word, "indisposed with, um, personal affairs."

"Out fraternizing with yet another barmaid I imagine," Vitus snapped. Then pointing a finger at Hector, "I will deal with you momentarily."

Turning to Olivia, Vitus said, "When High Lieutenant Darius

graces the Barracks with his presence, be sure to confine him to the grounds for the next two weeks."

"He begins his furlough in a week," Oliva said.

"Then a week of it will be confined to post. Proper punishment for trying to begin early. I would have his hide if he was not so blazingly efficient the majority of the time," Vitus said, clinching his teeth and wringing his hands as if they were around Darius' throat.

"As for you," he said turning toward Hector, "I thought we agreed you would begin *your* furlough yesterday."

"As I said, my Captain," Hector said strongly, but keeping his voice as gentle as possible, "I am in no need of rest."

"Everyone needs rest. I need rest, Olivia needs rest, my horse needs rest, every Knight of the Valley needs rest. It is one of the greatest benefits of being among our ranks. Every two years, we are granted a season of furlough. Upon attaining the rank of High Lieutenant you are granted and an extra season of furlough. Three glorious months away from everything."

"Hector has yet to take a single furlough," Olivia added, and if Hector did not know better, gleefully.

"Five years of service, and you have never taken a furlough," Vitus said incredulously. "Nine months due you and have taken none?"

"I require no rest," Hector repeated. "I believe it is my right to refuse furlough."

"It is your right but it is not right," Vitus said shouting. "You cannot refuse furlough."

"May I ask my Captain why?"

"Because it makes me look bad. What will everyone say next year when I take my furlough and I have knights under my command who refuse theirs," he said rubbing his face with both hands. Dropping his hands back to his side, he said, "We will discuss this another day. For now, go to the stables and retrieve my saddlebags. Once you have delivered them to the front gate of the Barracks, you will take the next seven days as a holiday. No arguments, that is an order," he said stabbing a finger Hector's way as he began to speak. "You will be barred from the Barracks for the seven full days and nights. Perhaps once you have enjoyed a few days of leisure, you will see all that you have been missing and take at least one season of furlough."

Hector opened his mouth again to protest, but Vitus cut him off with, "Do I not speak plainly or have you been struck deaf?" With no other options, Hector saluted his Captain and marched off, grumpily, for the Palace stables.

* * * * *

In contrast to the Barracks' stables, nearly always active, Hector found the Palace equivalent to be empty and quiet. Granted, after the Royal Court had adjourned for the day and the various participants had taken their horses or carriages home, there was very little for the stable masters to do. Yet, that did not explain why Hector could not find even a single stable boy.

Walking to and fro, to every corner of the stable, there was no one on duty. At first, Hector thought he was only just missing whoever was supposed to be tending the horses. He continued to pace back and forth, turning down every corner.

While most of the horses were busy eating their oats or laying down in the hay, one chestnut colored mare simply watched as he passed by. Hector recognized the horse instantly. One does not forget the late King's chosen horse. On the third pass, Luna harrumphed at him. Hector looked back and merely shrugged. On the fourth trip by, finally giving up on his search, he walked over to her and patted her on the side of the neck.

"You would not happen to know where my Captain's saddlebags have gotten themselves to my dear," he asked. "Or where any of the stable workers have run off to?" Her only response was to nuzzle up to his armored chest so he might scratch between her eyes. "I thought not."

"I suppose it gets rather lonely down here for you lately," he said soothingly. Hector looked about Luna's stall, the ornate woodwork that was unique to the entire stables. "Best accommodations, first choice in the finest oats, the freshest hay, and I bet you would give it all up for one last ride across the valley."

From around the next corner came a rather loud thump, followed by an exasperated cry of anger from a girl. Both he and Luna turned towards the sound.

When the horse turned back to him, Hector looked her in the eye and said, "Another satisfied patron I wager." Giving Luna one last pat he made for the sound. Turning the corner he was equally horrified, amused, and shocked by the sight that greeted him.

It was a young girl in a fine blue and silver gown. Her face was red with exertion and anger as she was repeatedly kicking a bale of hay. When that did not satisfy her, the young lady reached for a nearby pitchfork and began to repeatedly stab the defenseless hay. Her long blonde hair whipping around her with each forceful stab. Hector recognized the Regent immediately.

After their meeting in the white field, it had been Hector's duty to escort her to the Palace. Normally the escort would have been a full honor guard, but the kingdom was in enough disarray and, even after a century, no one trusted Everfrost. Not to mention the Achelon hating isolationists. To have lost both a King and a Regent within days could have been crippling to the morale of the Kingdom. Secreting in the Lady of Talwoods seemed the best course of action.

"I believe you have succeeded in making the stables safe from that villainous bale of hay," Hector said, after a moment more.

Hearing his voice, Lydia let out a small yelp of surprise. Turning to him, breathing heavily, her face went from one shade of red to another, as her anger faded into embarrassment.

"I have found the stables are normally abandoned this time of day," she said breathlessly.

"It still is," he said. "Well, if I were not on an errand."

"I suppose this is some kind of breach in protocol," Lydia said glancing at the pitchfork in her hands and quickly replacing it.

"Not as severe as mine I am afraid," Hector said, quickly coming to himself and bowing his head. "I should have announced my presence to My Lady Regent."

"Please raise your head and look upon me, such as I am," she said, trying to smooth her hair back into place. "I will not report you to your superiors if you will keep quiet and not inform the Royal Court of my many eccentricities, Lieutenant…Hector, it was, yes?"

"Yes, My Lady," Hector said with yet another short bow of the head. "Of what eccentricities do you refer?"

"Walking barefoot in a field of flowers for one. I understand and appreciate you kept that to yourself. I would be grateful if no one hears of my attempted herbicide upon this poor defenseless hay bale," she said motioning to the bale at her feet.

"You have my word. May I ask though what led to said murder?"

Blushing again Lydia answered, "I was attempting a relaxation technique that was used personally by the wise old General Jovian Aulus of Isaac's Hold. The premise is when you feel overly burdened with responsibilities, you find a quiet place where none can find you so you may breathe and meditate until you feel yourself calm once more."

Looking at the hay bale at her feet, Hector asked, "Failing that?"

"Violence. Specifically against an unfeeling, inanimate object while imagining what vexes you is within. It is rather effective," she said with a nervous smile.

"I understand," he said nodding with approval. He would try it during his forced seven-day holiday.

"You must think that I am severely cracked," she said, tapping herself on the side of the head with the palm of her right hand.

"Not at all," Hector answered. "I have been in service to the Valley for five years now. I understand the need to murder something," he said with a chuckle. "I will leave you with your calming techniques."

"Wait," Lydia called to him as he turned to leave. "The stables will be empty for a little while longer. The stable masters have gone to take their afternoon meal. I would not mind a bit of company." When Hector did not answer right away she added, "I do not mean to take you from your duties, or be an imposition. It is just, I have not had a single conversation since my arrival that has not dealt in Valley politics or someone wishing to sway me to their agenda. I rather enjoyed our conversation that evening on the road and would not mind a few minutes of nonpolitical speech."

Hector nearly declined. His Captain had sent him to find his possessions. But it was obvious he would need one of the stable masters to show him where to look. Then he glanced Lydia's way again. He had thought often of that evening in the field, finding her wading hip-deep through the flowers barefoot. The memory made him feel, he was not sure how to finish that sentence. And she was right, the conversation had been pleasant.

With a smile and yet another quick bow of the head, Hector answered, "I am at Her Lady's service."

Visibly relieved, Lydia smiled and said, "Please take a bale." Sitting down upon the one she had been murdering just a few minutes before, she waited for him to join her. Picking a bale from a tall, nearby stack, Hector set his opposite hers and sat.

Lydia began with, "I suppose a fuller introduction is in order."

"Yes, I suppose," Hector answered. "There was a need in haste upon our first meeting. I am Hector of Green Plains, Son of Felix, High Lieutenant of the Knights of the Valley."

"Lydia of Talwoods," she said laying a hand on her chest. "Daughter of the late Marcus and Anna of Talwoods, Lord, and Lady, House Achelon."

"My condolences."

"Thank you. It has been over eight years now since the fire that claimed my home took them from me. However, there is not a day I could not use their wisdom, not to mention their presence. And your parents?"

"Alive and well. My mother's name is Minerva. They have been farmers their entire lives. I have a sister, Elyssa, who also married a farmer."

"A family of farmers," she said musing.

"Most of my ancestral line, for at least ten generations, is made up of farmers. When the time comes, the men mostly serve their two years service with the Builders Guild and the women spend time with the Healers. Afterward, they all returned to the fields."

"And yet you are a Knight of the Valley? And one who has committed to an apparent life-time of service."

"It did not come with no shortage of controversy within my family, I will admit," he said carefully. "But they understood that this was the path that I needed to take. Admittedly, there are days that I feel the call to put my hands in the soil again. With so many farmers in my ancestry, I would not be shocked if there were literally dirt in my blood."

"So then, what drives Hector, son of Felix," Lydia asked. She leaned forward as if she was fascinated by every word. Strange, no one else outside his small circle of friends and family took this much interest. And even considering them, there had been no one to hang on his every word this way since....

"Service," he said interrupting the thought. "Service to the Valley and all who dwell within."

"Admirable. You have even made one of the tenants of the Blood Oath your own. But is there nothing more," she asked frowning.

"Truly, it is all I need."

Hector could tell by her face that his answer did not sit well with her. He knew he could elaborate further, but it would not have added any more context. Besides, it had become easier not to discuss.

"And friends, you do have them do you not. You are far too kind not to have any," she asked with a note of worry in her voice.

"Those under my command would never feel me too kind," he said jokingly. "Of course, I have friends. Helena, who is a friend from childhood, a much more skilled and capable knight than I. She attained the rank of High Lieutenant a full year before my promotion. I would count Darius as another. He was the knight I was first squired to. He could be the greatest the Valley has ever seen if it were not for his many vices."

"Dangerous and deadly vices," Lydia asked.

"Only to him, and only from the occasional angry husband or betrothed. As the ancient saying goes: wine, women, and song. Though, we try not to let him sing if we can manage," he said with a laugh.

Smiling again she asked, "And is there no wife, or betrothed waiting for the brave Hector?"

A slight catch in his breath at the question but Hector recovered quickly and said, "I am fully married to the Valley and all who dwell within. My life is set aside for them, My Lady."

"It sounds as if you are completely satisfied with the path you have chosen. I only wish I was one-third as satisfied as you," she said, the smile fading.

"Word is that you and the Royal Court are not exactly," Hector paused to think for the right phrase, "dancing in time with the orchestra."

"That is the most delicate way of putting it," Lydia said as Hector noticed her face began to flush again with anger. "Bullish is the word I would choose. The Valley and the sentiments of some people change much slower than is to be believed. No one within the Court was even alive when Achelon acted to save our people. Nearly a century after his death and he is still hated. And by proxy, as his last descendant, I am as well. They wish to drive me away. Like you Hector, I only wish to serve our people. I was on my way home because I had come to my sixteenth year and only wished to serve my two years like everyone else. I was coming to join with the Healer's Guild. I decided long ago to follow in the footsteps of my mother and have studies long to become an alchemist. I was hoping to put my knowledge to use. When word had reached us on the road that my cousin had passed and had, with his dying breath, appointed me Regent, I was shocked twice over. Gaius was still a young man, not even fifty, and to pass over so many more well established and much more learned individuals to hand me the Regency is unthinkable. I know he was like an uncle to me and that I have been told he saw me as a daughter, but he could not have been thinking clearly in his last moments."

"Perhaps he had faith in your abilities," offered Hector.

"Well, it is certainly a faith that is not shared by the Court," Lydia said, her tone very sour. "I do not have a single ally among them."

"You have one, and a strong one. My Captain Vitus stands with you."

Her face softened slightly as she said, "That is at least something.

Sadly, with a session of Court, like many of the Guild Masters, he ranks just below the Wise Men and Moneychangers. Unless we enter a time of war."

"I do not see Everfrost invading anytime soon," Hector said lowering his head and looking down at the floor. "The art of war does seem a rather easy subject to learn as opposed to the many intricacies of politics. At least I had the benefit of being a squire before being asked to serve as a protector. Even the Guilds begin their workers as apprentices. Shame that there are no regency apprenticeships."

Lydia had gone silent. Hector could not blame her. It was not like he was being of any real help. Yet, when he looked up, Lydia was looking right at him. Her eyes wide with excitement and big grin on her face. Somehow it made his heart sink.

"That is it," she exclaimed. "I am in need of a mentor. Someone to help me learn the art of leadership. Hector, be my mentor."

It seemed that destiny had determined it was time for Hector's world to be rocked. Quickly, he said, "That is impossible. I am no politician."

"But you hold a high rank, you do command a regiment of knights do you not?"

"Well yes," Hector was beginning to panic. "But, I am but a lowly knight and you are the Regent."

Raising her hand, she said, "Right here and now, I am no longer the Regent."

"I am not sure I am comfortable with this idea, perhaps I can have my Captain pay you a visit."

"I am not the Regent but a new recruit," she said ignoring him. "I am seeking to be a knight. You are my commanding officer and I am but a lowly squiress."

Hector felt sick as he corrected her, "It is squire and not squiress.

A knight is a knight, there is neither male nor female within our ranks."

"See you have taught me something already," she said over-earnestly, meaning she already knew. Hector, now sitting with his head in his hands, felt as if there were great sharp stones in his stomach. He should have never investigated the commotion, he should have stayed with the horse. Trying to steel his nerves, he looked up and his stomach turned again when he saw her smile.

After a quick one word prayer (help), and a quick glance to see if the Stable Masters had returned he said, "Leadership, or any form of command, requires a firmness. Like a sea captain at the helm of his ship. You are the head that turns the body."

Lydia nodded, but said grimly, "I may be the head but the neck is stiff and it turns me where I wish not to look."

"Become an irresistible force they must reckon with."

"All the while they are an immovable object?"

"Find a common ground."

"They already have a common ground. Seeing me as far away from the Regency as possible," she said, making a shoving motion with her hand.

Hector absently began to scratch the top of his head. He had degenerated quickly into cliché. There had to be something he had personally experienced when he first took command. The problem was the knights under his command had universally accepted him. Then he remembered one who at first had not, one he had to go to Vitus for advice.

"You must both demand and command their respect. If not for you, than for the office you hold."

For the first time Lydia nodded, she seemed pleased with this train of thought.

"Any suggestion on how I do that."

Where Vitus had been genius in his advice, his answer had been "you must find your own way," Hector decided on the less genius course, and answered:

"Think on the reign of Beatrix, the Battle Queen. When history called for an army to defend the Valley, she went out to them as a mother. She went out as a mother and encouraged everyone to come to the defense of their neighbor as if they were of their blood, a brother or a sister. After the first successful defense of the Valley, the people looked up to her as if she were their actual mother."

One glance Lydia's way told Hector he had gone the wrong way. Her eyes were half closed and she was scowling in his direction.

"Your suggestion is that I mother them," her voice strained.

A strained, unintelligible sound was all he could manage.

"Somehow, considering I am of the age to be, at best, their daughter and, at worst, their granddaughter, I do not think this is a group I can mother."

As she stood and walked away from him, Hector tried to speak but found his voice had fled. This had been an exercise in lunacy. How was someone of his position expected to advise a Regent?

Lydia came to a halt, and said, "Actually, you are brilliant."

What?

She turned to him, grinning again, and said, "You are completely wrong, but so completely right at the same time. I cannot mother them. Only a queen or king can be mother or father to the people. I am nothing more than the Regent. What is a Regent but one who stands in authority until the rightful ruler takes their place? When both parents are away, who watches the children?"

Hector still reeling from being called brilliant could do nothing more than a shrug.

"A governess," she said excitedly. "I cannot be a mother to them, but a governess. As with many new governesses, the children test her limits. The children will try to make her break. But in the end, she demands and then commands their respect just as you suggest I do with the Court. A governess' will sets and dictates the pace."

Hector stood as she approached and said, "I appreciate the time you took to sit with me. It was far more effective than murdering hay bales."

"At least the world is safer now that there is one less of those sneaky little bales plotting against it."

She squinted at him in an attempt of looking irritated but that radiant smile never left her face.

"I mean it. Without you, I would not have a new course to set sail for."

"No, you took bad advice and made it into something positive," Hector assured her. "May the Divine protect this Valley if such as I ever attains the rank of Captain."

There was movement somewhere within the stables and voices. The stable masters had returned.

"I need to return to my chambers before I am missed. Next time you are within the Palace be sure to come and see me."

"That may be a long wait, My Lady. I have never set foot inside," he told her.

"May I ask why?"

"I have yet to be sent on official business. I want to earn the right to enter."

"Well then," she said drawing herself up to full height which was just a few inches short of his chin. "You will come and share a meal with me tomorrow after my session with the Court. We will discuss a very important position that you have just been appointed to."

With that, she spun and began to walk back towards the nearest exit, and the Palace beyond.

His mind reeling, Hector asked, "To what position within the Palace could I possibly be qualified?"

She never broke stride. She simply turned her head to the side to briefly glance over her shoulder, and said, "Friend to the Regent, of course." Looking ahead again she added, "It will be a difficult and sometimes thankless task. But you have nerves of steel. Besides, I both like and trust you; you are more than qualified."

Hector stood and could only watch as she walked away. A strange warm feeling began to radiate from his chest. It was almost an echo of long ago, another time. Once the Lady Lydia was no longer in his sights he turned as well, and nearly walked out of the stables before remembering his Captain's saddlebags.

*  *  *  *  *

Hector would not witness the events of the next day personally, but he would hear of them several times. The best telling of the tale would come from his Captain Vitus. Who would relate the events to Hector, after his seven-day holiday:

Vitas was already cursing under his breath long before he had even approached the Palace. He was amazed that her Ladyship had called for another session of the Royal Court so quickly. By protocol, Lydia's Regency still in its infancy, she was allowed to take every fourth day as a recess unless it was followed by a Holy Day. Needless to say, Vitus had hoped she would have taken the day to recover. Considering that the last three days had been so draining. Vitus himself could have used another day. He just prayed he kept his composure and did not draw his sword and run someone through. It was near impossible to get blood out of the ceremonial capes.

The great marble hall that made up the Throne Room, was decked out in full blue and silver banners and tapestries. The room itself was filling quickly with members of the Royal Court. Guild Masters, Wise Men with their acolytes, and lastly the Moneychangers.

"I tell you this my friends, I see good fortune coming our way," said Klytus the Master of the Moneychangers. Vitus hated the mere sight of the man and his long, flowing, shoulder length blonde hair; fine but gaudy clothes, and jewel-encrusted rings on every finger.

"Judging by the frustration and fear in her eyes, I do believe our Regent cried herself to sleep this past night. Poor, lonely little Regent. I can assure you this Lydia will not be in our way much longer," his smooth voice dripping with a cruel type of joy. "Once this pretender has fled back to Isaac's Hold, to seek comfort from those of her kind, I have been assured I will be nominated in her place. That can only mean more profits. Good day Captain Vitus," he added as he noticed Vitus staring him down.

Vitus nodded towards him all the time thinking, *If only you would just fall down dead where you stand. Yes, fall down dead and your soul finds its way to the darkest and hottest abyss in the afterlife. Then perhaps the Divine would scoop that abyss up and cast it into an even hotter abyss.*

Without preamble, the doors opened, and Lydia, dressed in all white, walked out amongst them. Flanked by a pair of Inner Circle Knights in their tar black armor and red capes. She walked with her head held high and her shoulders back. She showed no sign of the frustrations she had to be feeling.

Vitus could only think, *If only politics were something as noble as a battlefield. I would slay them all for you, My Lady.*

As protocol demanded, Lydia stepped up onto the dais and stood to the right of the empty throne. It's blue cushions looked lonely without its king.

*Oh, great King Gaius. You left us too soon.*

Lydia laid her left hand upon the right wooden armrest, becoming the symbolic "Right Hand of Authority," and so began this session of the Court.

"Shall we begin where we left off," she asked those assembled.

*No!* Vitus shouted in his head. *Klytus had the floor when we adjourned.*

"Very well My Lady," Klytus said smoothly. He turned slyly towards his fellows and winked before stepping forward. "Have you by chance had time to review the numbers we laid out yesterday?"

"I have indeed Master Klytus. These new offers for our grains from without the Valley are generous indeed. It would add much gold to our treasuries."

"Indeed it would My Lady."

"I must say that I do fear an order of this size would leave many of the Valley granaries meager in supply. I feel we need more information. I ask that you leave the proposed invoices and ledgers with Master Galen so that he might speak with the Master of the Farmers' Assembly, to determine if such an order would leave enough food for our people. That is if Master Galen has no objections."

Galen, looking pleased with the suggestion, moved forward to agree. Before he could speak, Klytus took two steps ahead of him.

"I am afraid I must object My Lady," he began. Vitus head dropped before Klytus added, "I am afraid this is beyond your scope. Protocol demands...."

"Nothing in this matter."

Vitus head shot up, did Lydia just...?

"Protocol has no bearing on this matter. It is well within my scope as Regent to request more information."

Klytus, laughing nervously, said, "I am afraid this is not entirely accurate. You are young and ignorant of such things, so I will forgive your trespass. But if all you need is more information, than I can provide the figure you seek."

"I understand Master, but I wish for a fresh opinion."

"I am afraid only if I consent. Protocol demands…."

"Please cease in attempting to lecture me on protocol," Lydia said raising her voice sternly. All eyes in the room were darting back between Lydia and Klytus. A small smile was beginning to crease Vitus' lips.

"For weeks now, this entire Court has brought every session to a standstill in attempts to bog me down with lessons of Protocol. How much time have we lost because this council equates my age to ignorance? No one has been more guilty of this than you, Master Klytus. Truly, I would agree that there may be some my age who are under-educated in the working of this government. But, I am the exception."

All eyes were upon Lydia as she continued, "I have known the dictates of protocol since I could read and write. You forget that my father was Lord Marcus; who for a time was not just a cousin to King Gaius, but his chief advisor. My teacher was the great Nicodemus, the oldest and most knowledgeable of any in the Valley. Upon the tragedy of my parents' death, it was my cousin the King who brought me into the Palace. Between accompanying my father to sessions of court and these great halls being my home for a time; I have spent many hours outside these chambers listening to many great debates. Many greater than you are capable of my learned friend. At the King's request, I was sent to study in Isaac's Hold. I lived with our noble ambassador, from whom I learned a great deal more. So, if you will pardon me, Master Klytus, do not presume to lecture me on protocol a moment longer."

Klytus stood seething. For the longest time, all he could do was stare. Vitus believed the Moneychanger was trying his best to look intimidating when in reality he had just been struck speechless.

Once he had sufficiently recovered he said, "I still refuse my consent. Which may not be strictly protocol, but is still my right. Especially if I do not recognize your authority in this matter."

After a moment of tense silence Lydia asked, "Tell me, Master, when you look upon me, what do you see?"

A twisted hateful smile came upon Klytus as he said, "A child. A little girl who playacts as if she has some real authority, when in the end she has nothing. You do not even have a home among us as Talwoods still lies in ruin. You are the last in a line of usurpers. You are nothing more than a placeholder until the rightful King, Lucien, is of age. That is what I see."

"Very well then," she said seemingly undeterred. "I appreciate your candor. Now, let me tell you what you should see. True, I am young. But by the proclamation of Queen Beatrix herself, once I come to my sixteenth year, and agreed to service, I became a full citizen of the Valley and a woman grown. I assure you, when Lucien is of age, I will step aside and allow him to take his throne. But that is little more than five years from today. But in the meantime, Master Klytus, I assure you that I am no mere placeholder. My appointment comes from our late King. With his last breath, he appointed me Regent. That means I do not rule today in Lucien's stead, I rule in the full authority of King Gaius. When you see me you should see the right hand of *his* authority, just as protocol demands. I do not ask that you like me, but you will respect the authority of this throne, you will respect our fallen King's command, and you will respect me. You will not raise your voice in my presence and you will obey my command. If this is too difficult then perhaps you should stand down; allow one more worthy to have your title and position."

The entire Court was holding its breath. It was a major gambit on Lydia's part. If Klytus wished to drag this out, he could find allies and cause a schism within the Court. He could call for a vote of removal. But after this show of strength, the pressure would all be on Klytus to find enough allies to force her out. And if he failed....

Bowing his head, voice devoid of all strength, Klytus said, "Many apologies, My Lady Regent. I am afraid that in my zeal for Valley and Kingdom, I have overstepped my authority in this matter. Please forgive me in this breach of protocol."

Smiling she inclined her head towards him. Vitus could not keep the grin from his face this time. Even as Klytus turned to return to his fellow Moneychangers, and glanced his way. Vitus buried the smile best he could and shrugged. He at least managed to not laugh as one of Klytus' underlings delivered the desired records to Galen.

"Then if all old business be concluded," said Galen finding his voice at last, "Come forward and bring your petitions to the Regent."

Needless to say, Vitus never again exited the Palace cursing in the goblin tongue.

# CHAPTER FIVE

When Hector awoke the next morning in Clovis' stables, he felt refreshed, and his strength renewed. He was still sitting with his back against the wall. Exhaustion must have overtaken him without his realizing. Gingerly he began to stand, sitting in hay all night caused a bit of stiffness.

It was about an hour past dawn, by his recollection. The sun was beaming in through the stable windows. Hector could not remember the last time he had slept this late. His internal clock had always been reliable to wake him before the rooster crowed. A rough and bumpy four-day journey will take its toll, he supposed.

A look around the stable found no Clovis or any other citizen of Bear's Sanctuary. A quick tour about revealed that Lawrence was absent as well. Hector came across what he supposed was Clovis' quarters and found them empty save for a note and another hot meal waiting. Clovis had left the note, Hector found the penmanship remarkable for someone with such large hands. The note read:

**Have taken your horse for a warm up. Eat heartily my friend. We will speak again before your departure.**

Hector quickly finished his meal with regret. Food prepared this well, deserved to be savored; not swallowed whole. Finishing, Hector left the stable to find:

All of Bear's Sanctuary had gathered outside. Hector was taken aback. Why would an entire village take an interest in one lone traveler? All of them were smiling kindly upon him, but their eyes held a completely different expression; sorrow.

Elster and Clovis were standing by Lawrence, who looked just as well-rested. Clovis was unreadable, but Elster held the same expression as the rest of the village.

"Are you well rested M'Lord," Clovis asked.

"Remarkably so," Hector answered. "You honor me with such a title, but I am nothing more than a humble soldier, I hold no nobility."

"Even so," Clovis answered. Hector reached for his money pouch but Clovis stopped him. "It is my honor to serve you in your time of need."

"I hope you do not mind the intrusion," Elster said holding a rolled up parchment. "But we had a look at your map while you slept, and found the route you intend to take. We are sad to report that your map is outdated by at least a millennia."

"That would not be at all surprising," Hector answered.

"Your route called for you to ride around the Great Barrier Forrest," Elster said, unrolling the map and showing Hector. "There is a road now that cuts through the heart of the woods. If you ride due north, by very late afternoon you will come to the waystation at its entrance. By taking this road you will cut three days from your journey at least, probably more" he said handing Hector the map.

Clovis stepped forward and said, "Once you arrive at the waystation, despite your instincts, I recommend you rest and wait for nightfall. When you see the Watchman ride to light the lanterns on the road, count out ten minutes and then ride. By dawn, you will exit the other side and come out on the edge of the marshlands of Katelynn's Woe. Turn your eye east and you will see it in the distance."

"See what?"

"It is difficult to describe. It would almost look like a smudge on glass if you were looking through a window. Do not stare for long, or the pain will overtake you. That will be your first sign of the Desolate Wastes and the Glass Desert at its center. It is important that you arrive to see it by the rising sun. There are no other landmarks to guide you. Duke Belmont ordered all road signs pointing the way be removed eight hundred years ago. Be sure to ignore your compass as it will be useless. You will reach the Wastes at noonday and the Desert by sunset tomorrow."

"Thank you, friend," Hector said as he mounted up upon his horse. The gathered villagers parted to allow him to ride through. The solemn look was still in their eyes and they waved farewell in a very melancholy way. Hector began to feel as if he were part of a funeral procession.

As he began to ride away the sound of Clovis' voice made him come to a halt. Turning in the saddle, he could see the loe standing before the crowds.

"Hector," he called out. "Within the Wastes, ignore the Shadows. They are but an echo of what was."

* * * * *

Refreshed, Hector urged a little more speed from Lawrence. It was just less than an hour later they crossed over onto what must have been one of the merchant roads. For the first time in his journey, he had fellow travelers. This merchant road was loaded with wagons of goods, horsemen, and substantial foot traffic. The road was not congested enough to slow his progress but he had been forced to ride around obstacles. Along the way, he saw the faces of men and a few more goblins. Most turned to observe him. His manner of dress had caught their curiosity. He had once been told Becknor armor was of a one of a kind design. It had certainly caught Clovis' eye.

On the horizon, the Barrier Forrest loomed. A two hundred mile wall of ivory oak trees. The forest itself was ancient, many thousands of years old. It had remained mostly untouched and its borders were still encouraged to grow wild. As the wilds to the north became increasingly violent, the Alliance decided to use this natural buffer to their advantage. An army of men and women were sent to care for the forest. Their task was to trim the dead growth, plant more saplings and thicken the woods even further. In the advent of a fire, this army of caretakers would move in right after and replant. It was said the deep interior was now partitioned off into precincts. Unseen from the ground, these precincts were bordered by empty spaces to limit the harm from a fire. All this work to ensure that any greedy warlord would be forced to ride around the forest to invade.

As Hector approached the towering sentinels of white, he questioned how a road could be cut through these massive monsters. All were impossibly wide, it would take at least thirty men to encircle the smallest. The oldest and tallest were at least two, perhaps even three hundred feet tall.

"'Tis a pity your journey was not a mere two weeks later," a voice called to Hector from the side of the road. Bringing his horse to a stop, Hector looked to see a man sitting at the foot of a small grassy hill. He wore a dark cloak, with the hood pulled down to deflect the hot late-afternoon sun. His walking stick was in the crook of his left arm while he picked apart a piece of crusty bread. "The trees will have leafed by then," the man continued. "The leaves are even more chalky white than the trunks. The woods are so overgrown that a cool breeze issues out even in the hottest summers."

"A magnificent sight and experience I am sure," Hector answered. "Sadly, it is a terrible business that brings me here and not the scenery."

"Yes, very sad," the man said, continuing to work on the bread.

DEFENDERS OF BECKNOR

Turning it over revealed a large moldy section. The hooded man pulled the mold free and tossed it aside before popping the rest into his mouth. "At the very least your eye had the opportunity to take in one of the world's natural wonders. Perhaps it will be a fond memory in better days."

Hector watched as the man finished the last of his bread. His heart hurting to see this man had such meager portions. For the first time, Hector noticed the state of his clothes. The hems of his robe were frayed; his trousers bleached by the sun. His face was hidden, but Hector perceived it would have been just as worn as his clothes.

Reaching into his own provisions, Hector said, "I am near my destination, as such my provisions are well stocked, and are much fresher than yours I wager." With that, Hector tossed a bundle of his own food to the stranger. Without looking up, and showing deft reflexes, the man caught them in midair.

"Thank you for the kindness, good sir."

"You are quite welcome," Hector said smiling. "Good fortune on your journey."

"As to you friend," the hooded man said stowing away the fresh food and standing. "May your quest be victorious and may your troubled heart find peace." With that the man began to walk away, leaning heavily on the staff, the direction Hector had just ridden from.

The gate of the waystation was cleverly camouflaged. Hector's road ended just short of the roots of one of the more massive trees. The oak itself was counterfeit. Even surrounded by a real forest and living trees, it was only upon close inspection that Hector noticed it was constructed of some sort of stone. The entire "tree" had been crafted to fool the eye from a distance. Hector supposed the original purpose of this gate had been to allow entry to the army of caretakers. If the forest was a natural barrier to invasion, you would not want to allow your enemies easy access to the heart of the wood.

Dismounting, Hector found the gatehouse itself and knocked upon the door. He was unsure if he should have been surprised that the gate itself was only a wooden construct. Surely if you could craft stone to resemble oak you could install a cleverer door.

"Who seeks passage," a rather severe looking man of perhaps forty years said looking out through a slot to the side.

"I do," Hector said and then identified himself.

"Your business at the border?"

"I seek the Glass Desert."

"Oh, another one of you lot," the man said with a very bitter laugh. "I wonder if it would not be better if I denied you entry."

"Please sir, I must enter in. I am on…."

"…An important quest," the keeper finished mockingly. "Over my entire adult life, I have made these woods my home. After an injury left me unable to tend properly to the woods, I was given these gates to watch. In the last decade, there have been little more than half a dozen of you adventurers on important quests to the Glass Desert. Seen them all come back horribly broken, I have. One poor woman your age drank a bottle of poison right here at my gate and fell down dead. Go home traveler, you are on a fool's errand. Whoever it is that you are doing this for is dead already."

Hector stood his ground and said, "I am not those people. I have business in the Desert. It does not matter if I pass through your gate or ride around. Either way, I will have the elixir."

"Yes, I'm sure you will," he said with a sneer. "I was just attempting a courtesy young man. But if you wish to be an empty husk of your former self, who am I to stop you? Enter then!"

There had been a number of reactions that Hector had not bargained for. The lamenting looks in the eyes of the people of Bear's

Sanctuary, and now the gatekeeper here was, to say nicely, pessimistic of Hector's chances. As always, to keep his focus, there was but one memory needed to block out the doubt others would place upon him.

The waystation was an open air courtyard. There was troughs for the horses, merchant stalls selling everything from food to weapons, and many other fellow travelers. Hector looked up to see a network of bare branches above them. As the sun's light poured down through them it gave an impression that the entire courtyard was ensnared in a web of shadows. In a few weeks' time, the leaves would provide a nice cool canopy.

As predicted, everything within Hector screamed haste. *It is hours before sundown,* those thoughts said. *Every second you delay brings Lydia closer to death.* Yet, there was no reason for Hector to doubt the words of Clovis. It was now obvious that the loe had knowledge of Hector's destination. As he sat biding his time in the waystation, Hector cursed himself for not seeing it sooner and taking advantage of that knowledge. Yes, he had been exhausted, but information on his destination may have been more important than a few extra hours of sleep.

As much as patience was advised in principle, it was near impossible in practice. It was not long before Hector found himself pacing. To not impede the progress of other travelers, his pacing was confined to a small twenty-foot section. Lawrence watched his progress within this short circuit in apparent boredom and disdain.

"Yes, I know I am wearing myself out and will probably fall from the saddle in exhaustion tonight," he told his horse. "What would you have me do?"

About that time a small family, traveling by foot from the north, stopped and gazed at him quizzically. Their two children pointed and giggled his way. In response, Lawrence took a couple side steps away from Hector as if to say, "I know not this crazy pacing man who speaks to horses."

"Traitor," he said squinting at Lawrence. "See how you like a summer confined to the stables while the mares frolic in the fields."

The smaller of the two children laughed loudly and said as her parents took her away, "But I want to watch the jester and his horse more mama."

Lawrence looked back at the departing family and back to Hector and harrumphed.

"Yes, I understand. I am touched in the head," he said. Dejected, Hector sat upon a nearby bench and looked to the sky. The sun had barely moved. With a sigh, Hector closed his eyes and tried to calm his impatient mind.

In his time as a High Lieutenant, and later as Trusted Hand, Captain Vitus had attempted to teach him, along with his other high officers, an ancient relaxation technique. The purpose was to awaken the part of your mind that he felt true tactical planning rested: instinct. He called the technique the Resting.

In practice, the student sat controlling their breathing in an attempt to free the mind of thought and worry so that they might focus on the world around them. Eyes remained closed, but other senses open. The ears became attuned to the sounds of the surrounding world: the footsteps of man and beast, birdsong, the sound of the wind in the trees. Next, the scents of the world would come into focus. Lastly, sensations of touch were to come alive. The lightest breeze on the skin, the subtle vibrations of the earth under their feet. If done properly, the conscience mind would regress and the student would fall into a kind of semi-sleep. Not a blind trance but a super aware state. Once the Resting was achieved, the eyes would again open and take in the world. But now, free of an over-analytical mind, the world would appear to move at a much slower pace. Allowing instincts to dictate the next move.

In over five years, Hector had never achieved the final rung of the ladder that was the Resting. It seemed to be forever beyond him. His former captain once observed as he attempted to reach the end goal. Hector opened his eyes to find Vitus frowning down upon him.

"All is well until the end," he told Hector once. "Your posture goes rigid and your expression becomes very pained. It is far from resting. It is almost as if you either do not trust your instincts or they no longer trust you."

The failure aside, Hector had found a way to adapt the Resting to his advantage. He found the semi-sleep state an excellent way to allow time to pass unnoticed and maintain his patience.

Hector sat with his back straight, shoulders back, and his hands, palms down, resting upon his knees. Closing his eyes he freed his mind of worry, doubt, and even Lydia; though the latter was painfully difficult. His ears picked up on the clip-clop of horses, the soft footsteps of the people around him, voices far and near. He both heard and did not hear them, beginning with the voice of the gatekeeper.

"There's the fool now. Hope he's praying; for he goes to his doom."

Other fragments of speech drifted in:

"A fortune is to be made plundering the mines of the Dali Mountains."

"With tidings of war, what of the dragons?"

"I tell you the practitioners of the forbidden alchemy in the north will bring Divine judgment to this world."

"You do not understand, the realms east of the Drakemourn do not war with one another. A schism has caused them to war within themselves."

The various aromas of the waystation began to encircle him. The fragrant perfumes of some of the more well-off travelers. The various foods; both carried in and prepared by the opportunistic merchants within the station.

The air, though appearing still to the eye, was alive with the slightest of breezes. It moved and refreshed him just enough that he did not mind the early spring sun beaming down through empty branches.

After what his hyper sensitive senses told him had only been a few minutes, Hector began to feel a change in the air. There was now a steady cool breeze from the north. The scents on the air were farther away and elusive. Finally, the fragments of conversation had fallen away almost to nothing. Hector once again opened his eyes and found the sun had already set and the clouds overhead were reflecting the warm glow of the departed sun. All around the courtyard, torchbearers were going about lighting the many torches round about. One in particular caught Hector's eye as she mounted up on her horse. It was time to continue his journey.

As directed, Hector rode all night. The road to the north was quiet and there had only been a handful of others upon the road. The width of the road was massive. Thirty Horseman could have traveled side by side without difficulty. The torches had been set in the exact center of the road, far away from the massive white trees. The light reflected easily off of the ivory oaks but the forest beyond was pitch black. In Becknor, many of the woods were teaming with wolves and the occasional valley bear, who were very much in danger of extinction. Here, in the Outer World, he wondered what could be in the darkness beyond watching the night travelers. Hector kept his eyes forward. If there was some creature plotting his doom, as determined as he was, Hector would have been far more dangerous than anything in these woods this night.

Hector emerged through the northern gate before the sky had even had a chance to begin to warm. Dismounting he allowed Lawrence some time to rest before the final leg. Stretching his legs, Hector watched the sky towards the east, almost trying to will the sun to rise early.

Slowly the light did come. Looking to the north he took note of the mist covered marshland they had called Katelynn's Woe. Thankfully his journey did not take him by that road. Leagues of soft, sinking ground, only to be greeted by a plain of rocky granite hundreds of miles long and wide.

The moment the sun crested the horizon *it* was visible. Not exactly due east, slightly northeast. Immediately Hector understood. At first, he rubbed his eyes as to clean them of any specks, but the "smudge" was still there. It was as if he were looking through a pristine window and just above the horizon a child had placed a single solitary fingertip. As warned, it hurt to stare for too long, a kind of buzzing pain. It was like there was an insect behind his eyes, gnawing into his brain. There was a wrongness there. A part of him, not cowardice, said, "Turn away. It is unnatural. An abomination that destroys worlds."

Hector's response was Lydia.

* * * * *

The closer to his destination, the more wrong there was with the world. Hector was still a good distance from the Glass Desert but he was beginning to cross over into the eerie wasteland that surrounded it. The lush green fields he had been riding through moments before were now being replaced by brown and wilting tufts of what may have once been grass. The last tree his eyes would take in would induce nightmares.

It was twisted, as if it were writhing in agony. Its long branches were curved back into themselves, actually growing back inside as if searching for an escape. The bark of the tree was just as tormented. The side facing his approach did manage to look healthy. The opposite side was stripped and charred. It looked both living and dead. It bled sap from the tallest branch all the way to its roots. The entire sight brought about a deep feeling of sympathy for it. Somehow, Hector could imagine that if the tree had a voice it would have said, "I would beg, if I could, to be chopped down and bring an end to my miserable existence. But it would be of no use. I will never truly be dead."

Birdsong that had accompanied him all along his journey had vanished completely. So too was the sound of any other creature. There was not one single sign of any other creature but Hector or Lawrence nearby. In a way, he was grateful for that. After the sight of the tormented tree, Hector did not think his heart could take a painfully deformed animal.

Gradually, the air had begun to change as well. The sweet smell of spring had been replaced with...nothing. He would have said the air was stale, but then that would have been something. The air had no scent. If he had not been breathing he would have thought the air had vanished altogether. Sounds on the air were becoming fainter. The sound of the thundering hoof beats of his stead had transformed into a kind of muted thud.

Looking down he began to see changes in the soil. Not long after the last traces of vegetation vanished, the ground began to take an odd pale-like color. Not unlike sand or silt, but it was neither. The surface looked light and grainy but as Lawrence's hooves stamped down upon it there was no dust. It was as if, despite its appearance, it was hard and compact like stone.

Above Hector, the sky, that had been a deep cloudless blue the entire day, was washed out. It was still cloudless but the sky was...white? There was a sudden chill running through him. Not due to the air, for it was exceptionally hot. It was more like a shiver had run deep through his soul at the sight of this wasteland. As a long time warrior he had seen many dead and long decomposed bodies. In his heart, he knew this was what he was looking at now. The carcass of the world stripped clean.

"This is what the world will look like when we are all dead and gone," Hector said out loud. "At the end of time, when the world dies." Fighting another shiver he continued on his way.

An hour later, Hector saw the first shadow.

JACK O CRABTREE

# CHAPTER SIX

Hector pulled back on the reigns as it crossed his path. A moment it was there, and the next it was gone. He cast his gaze to and fro in an attempt to catch sight of its owner, but all he saw was the empty waste. How could that be? He saw the shadow of someone walking in Lawrence's path, just as plainly as he saw the shadow of horse and rider below him now. He looked up into the washed out sky for any sign of birds and found it still empty. Shaking his head, Hector urged Lawrence on.

A league later they passed two more shadows on his right, walking side by side. They were moving. That is to say, he could see the motion of their legs and arms. They both wore robes, as the shadow of them moved with an unseen breeze. One was slightly taller while the shorter walked with a staff. But there was no one to be seen physically. Yet, he saw the movement. As Lawrence moved past them, Hector could hear their footsteps. Each time the shadow staff made contact there was the clicking sound of contact upon the hard desert floor.

A voice called to his left, "Help me. A healer, please." Hector's head snapped in that direction to see a shadow shuffling. He would say shuffling, as the sound of shuffling feet echoed towards him. Then, without warning, the shadow seemed to fall. There was the sound of running feet and Hector looked to see the first two shadows running for the fallen.

"How is this possible," Hector said aloud. One of the shadows shifted towards him at the sound of his words. Was it looking Hector's way?

"You there, horseman," an older woman's voice called out. "Go forth and bring a healer back from the camp. If they are engaged at the very least bring back a tonic-man. Hurry."

Hector's breath caught in his chest. This was impossible. He urged Lawrence faster and away from these apparitions.

"Good man," the voice called out to him.

If Hector had thought he had seen the end of the ghostly shadows he had been mistaken. The closer to the Glass Desert, the more the shadows multiplied. He began to see the shadows of horses, military units marching, and there was a large winged creature he assumed was a dragon. But these shadows were flickering. The closer to his destination the more unstable they became. Almost as if they were phasing through different points of time.

One moment he would see a great force assembling, then a flicker and these same forces were spread apart. He could hear singing and merrymaking. Then a flicker and these same shadows would now be joined by others in conflict. There were battle cries, the clashing of steel, the cries of agony from the wounded, and the far off sound of something he could not readily discern. At one point it sounded melodic, almost a soft singing sound, then it chimed like crystal, finally, it began to build into a familiar hum. Like the sound of the Blooming Death that Lydia had used to defeat the Dread Overlord.

All the while Lawrence continued on steadily, it was as if he had chosen to ignore the chaos around them or was blind to it. But Hector was watching in wide-eyed wonder.

In the distance, the hum grew louder and higher pitched. The battle ceased and Hector could see the shadows upon the ground turn in unison to the east. An eerie foreboding came over Hector, this was precisely how the Ten-Day War had ended. Whatever happened next in the chain of events he would never know. There was one last flicker and Hector would wish he had been struck deaf.

The scene was now chaos. Shadows were running wildly, some were rolling upon the ground, a few others were still caught in combat. It was the sounds of agony that drove the painful wedge into his heart and mind. The painful wails, the calls for help, the anger in the voices of some, but one word was repeated above all others.

"Betrayed."

Over and over again, they cried out that they had been betrayed. Their kings, their generals, their priests, all had betrayed them. Most of all they said, "The alchemist betrayed us."

"Nay, all three," one called back.

"It was *his* design. The alchemist knew this all along."

"Oh, if only Antioch had lived, he would have stopped the Demon, and the Alchemist's true plan would have been discovered."

"Yes," one strong voice called out. "One betrayal was the catalyst of all. The murder of Antioch."

"Cornelius Augusta," another voice called out. A name unfamiliar to Hector, yet, his skin crawled at the sound, not of the name, but the anguish and anger in the voice. Turning in the saddle, he could see a shadow running for him. "Cornelius Augusta betrayed us. We must avenge our General-King!"

To Hector's horror, he watched as the unseen owner of the shadow seemed to leap up towards him. There may not have been a body to be seen but there was one to be felt. The invisible assailant grabbed Hector by his left foot and yanked him from the saddle.

"Yes, justice! Revenge," was beginning to be chanted around him.

Hector felt several sets of hands seize onto him and begin to drag him away. These unseen hands radiated both fire and ice. He could feel the heat blistering his flesh as if began to crack and fall away, just as the ice froze him to the bone. Hector began to hear an agonizing wail and realized it was escaping from him.

Calling and looking about for help; he saw nothing but more shadows swarming his way. He watched helplessly as Lawrence continued to ride away from him, never noticing his absence.

Invisible hands began to punch him, unseen feet began to kick. He felt the fingernails of hands rake across his face. His armor was being yanked away with incredible force. He was being beaten to death by a mob of shadows.

"Enough," the original voice cried out. Hector felt a knee pressing down upon his chest and heard the sound of a sword being unsheathed. "The killing blow is mine."

Deep in his mind, Hector heard the voice of Clovis, "Ignore the shadows. They are but an echo of what was."

Hector closed his eyes and shouted, "You are not here. The sound of your anger is but an echo, directed at another. You are shadows, nothing more than the ill tidings left after the great abomination that fell upon you unjustly. I am on a just and noble quest, leave me be."

The voices mocked him. "None are noble who tread these lands." Hector felt the point of a blade pointed at his now unarmored chest, just above the heart. "All traitors must die."

In his mind, Hector began to close his ears to their voices. He pushed the pain aside and ignored the unseen blade about to take his life. He thought only of Lydia. Lydia, bathed in the golden light of sunset.

And then, all was silent. Slowly, Hector opened his eyes to see he was still in the saddle and Lawrence was galloping forward. The wastes around him were free of shadows.

Looking forward he called Lawrence to a halt. The Glass Desert was before him.

JACK O CRABTREE

# CHAPTER SEVEN

Even after a long and perilous journey, despite the forlorn looks he had received along the way, the undocumented danger of the Wastes, the sight before him was still the more surreal.

Behind him, the sun was setting. It cast a blood red light upon the entire scene. The washed out sky above him reflected none of the sun's last rays. It had already transitioned to a starry black despite the time of day. The strange hard-packed soil of the Waste stopped abruptly and transition into glass. Rolling, jaggedly sharp formations of glass. A desert of glass. And at its center, Hector laid eyes upon an impossible structure. A simple, grey, stone tower. Not unlike one of the many defense towers built into the walls of the Palace back in Becknor. Only this one was attached to no other structure. Beyond that, it was unremarkable. Well, as unremarkable as being the only structure in miles of wasteland and sitting in the middle of a sea of glass. Anywhere else in the world and Hector would have ignored it. Its location made it stand out very much thank you.

Two thousand years ago, that very tower would have been invisible on the bed of the massive lake whose ancient banks now marked the boundary of the Glass Desert. Everything that Hector's eye took in now, the entire length of the Wastes he had ridden through, had once been the most beautiful land in all the world. This country was once the antithesis of the death and horror it was now.

A large crystal clear lake, green rolling hills, and tall, magnificent forests as far as the eye could see. There were no cities, it was outside the borders of every neighboring kingdom and realm. It was said that no other place in the world could match. Travelers sojourned here. All who came, left with a deep peace within them. It was the one pure land in the world that had known perfect peace. Then the war came. The most bloody and destructive war in recorded history since the Breaking. Even every school-aged child in Becknor was taught this moment in history. The war, and what had happened here, was ultimately the cause of Hector's ancestors to migrate to seclusion in the Valley. Kings, queens, and many heroes would die. It would bring about the fall of Kaitlynn Heartstone's great kingdom to the north, help bring about the Alliance, and left this land in ruin. The Blight War.

An ancient evil known only as the Demon King swept in from the eastern seas, and conquered everything east of the mighty Drakemourn Mountains. His true origins were unknown. The histories say he was an immortal, thousands of years old. Though others believed him to be a savvy mortal king who took on the mantle of the Demon to send terror into the hearts of his foes. Regardless, the Demon King proved to be an excellent student in the arts of war and a master strategist. In fact, it was only due to the massive storms that can plague the Drakemourn for years, and the tenacity of the dragon race in their war against him, that the west had years to prepare. It would still prove to be futile. His armies poured off the mountains like a river and began conquering and enslaving.

Then came the man who the world would foolishly trust. An alchemist who had conceived of a weapon that could destroy entire armies. Aldred Zen-Joffa.

What happened next would become unclear, as both history and legend seemed to merge. According to both, Zen-Joffa employed a weapons smith, Coralline Grimmsong, and a wizard, Omni Advantious, to help him build the weapon. Alchemy, magic, weapon-mongery, it was the one and only time the three arts were used in concert. While all three were foremost in their art, it was Zen-Joffa the people listened to. He was the one that stood before numerous crowds, it was his words that gave the world hope. It was his lies that would doom so many.

As the war raged, the trio worked in seclusion for months as the world waited. The pressure mounted upon them as the last of the realms fell and only the five great kingdoms remained. As the Demon King brought his forces to this peaceful lake country to make camp and prepare for the final invasions, the weapon was completed. It was here, on the lake that they had chosen to unleash it.

The kingdoms marched for the lake as a diversion, while the three moved their weapon into place in the cover of night. For days, the two camps hurled insults and challenges towards one another. There were small skirmishes from dawn to dusk. However, The Demon King was no fool. His armies may have been well entrenched but his opponent held a slight advantage in numbers. Whether he intuited that his foe was setting a trap or just grew tired of waiting, the Demon King called for his forces to charge.

Just before Zen-Joffa, Grimmsong, and Advantious brought their weapon forth, the three kings on the field sent out five riders to inform the kingdoms that the hour was at hand. That was the last any news came from the battlefield. Days later, once scouts were dispatched to the desolation, the world discover the truth.

The weapon had been supposedly crafted to obliterate only their enemies, but, as with all doomsday weapons, they found it impossible to control once unleashed. It killed every last living thing on the battlefield. Not just the Demon King and his blight army, but the armies of the alliance as well. It not only killed them but consumed their remains. As for the once perfect land, the trees and grass were burned to ash and dust, and the beautiful lake was boiled away. The sand and silt upon the lakebed melted and boiled until it was a desert of glass.

Remarkably, there were survivors, three in fact. Three out of a million. The scouts found them lamenting by the lakeside praying for death to take them. But the Divine had refused their entry into the afterlife. They were sent back to view their handiwork. Finally, they were cursed with immortality and the knowledge of what they had done. It was said the Divine's final words to them was that they would find no lasting relief, no rest. Only until peace returned and the beautiful land they had made desolate was healed, only then, perhaps, they would be allowed death. Shortly after, the three crafters set out to wander the world and slipped from the pages of history. Of the three, it was Aldred Zen-Joffa that history would label the harshest. Promising much and delivering only death. Scholars would go on to call him the King of Lies. For surely, this Weapon of Desolation was his ultimate plan after all. Priests would write sermons upon avoiding falsehoods and deceits using Zen-Joffa as the archetype. For surely, this evil man would have destroyed the world if given opportunity.

The ultimate irony now was, that in the middle of so much misery and death, this was the only place in the world the rare Blue Orchid could be found. Nowhere in the recorded histories was there even a mention of this wondrous orchid. Miraculously, one lone survivor had endured. One plant in a vast wasteland. According to the words of Galen, just before Hector had departed, it was only centuries after the destruction that the healing properties of the flower were first discovered. And now this miracle wonder resided within the very tower that Hector, now standing on the edge of the Glass Desert, in the dying light, was looking upon.

There were no windows visible anywhere on the structure. It was not overly large in either height or circumference. It had the same feeling of wrongness deep inside Hector's mind. The same sensation that came from looking upon the horizon and seeing the "smudge" that morning. Hector felt less as if it was the location but the structure itself. At once he felt as if it should not be there, followed by the sensation that it was not really there, to a kind of hyper-real, being more vivid than it had any right to be.

Turning aside, Hector began to hitch Lawrence to what was either the remains of some ancient petrified tree or agonizingly deformed rock and stopped. Glancing over the land again, he concluded that the entire landscape looked as if it were in agony. It was almost as if whatever the mythical doomsday weapon had done was still at work in the land.

Patting Lawrence on the side reassuringly, Hector said, "We have been inseparable since the day of my promotion." All Captains of the Valley were issued their own private horse. Hector remembered the day he stood on the field watching the various horses. Most would have pointed to a particular horse to be theirs. Hector had stood still and allowed himself to be chosen. Luna, the King's horse that he had befriended that day in the stable, had sauntered up to him with Lawrence in tow. Lawrence had been Luna's. She had stared into Hector's eyes for a moment as if understanding why he was standing in her field, and then turned and left Lawrence by his side.

"I know not if this land is poison," he continued as he loosened the saddle and then the bridle. "I have no way of knowing the length of these trials, or if I will be successful. But I wager if I am not back by morning, you will never see me again. I do believe horses are in possession of keener minds than most give them credit, but I have no way of knowing if you truly understand my words. On the chance that you do, if I have not returned by the dawn leave this place. There is only death here. A very fell and wicked type of death. A living death. Go back to the Valley if you can, if not, find a new home and be happy there."

Giving Lawrence one last pat, Hector turned from the rotting countryside and began the last leg of his journey.

As he crossed into the remains of the lake bed, the glass began to crack under his feet. Even this had a muffled hollow sound to it. To either side of him were jagged shards of glass. It seemed as if the ancient lake bed itself had still been boiling as the glass solidified. Hector made sure each step was sure. A fall here could prove fatal. Around him, the only sound on the air was the cracking of the desert floor. The pervasive silence made it as if the world was holding its breath as he approached.

A deeper sense of foreboding came upon him as he neared the tower. There were still no signs of life, windows, and by all appearances no door. Yet, Hector knew he was being watched. No, studied. Very intently.

As he approached the tower he pushed it all aside and kept one image in his mind. The reason he had come. The reason he would succeed in besting the three challenges. Lydia, gliding through a windblown field of flowers, smiling.

Coming to a stop before the tower, Hector stretched out his hand to touch the stone, and never made contact.

# CHAPTER Eight

**Year three of the Lydia Regency...**

The Banquet Hall was possibly the second most opulent room within the Palace. Only the Throne Room was more majestic in its decorations. Even though Becknor had always been isolationist in its politics, that did not preclude it from grand gestures of hospitality on the rare occasion of state visits. It was an extension of the tradition of the people. Any Valley-Dweller would rather die an agonizinged, withering death than to be rude to someone from the Outer World. Just as long as the outsider did not expect that they would ever have the opportunity to return said hospitality. When someone of importance did arrive, it was the Banquet Hall they would remember.

From floor to ceiling, a visitor was witness to all things Becknor. The ornate blue carpet, trimmed in silver, was immaculate. The walls were covered in murals depicting the history of the Valley, from the Migration to the coronation of the first king, and the great military victories of the Knights of the Valley. Great tapestries hung all about the room depicting the greatest of the kings and queens of Becknor.

Under Lydia's Regency, the Hall had been used many times, but only once for a state visit. Six months into the Regency, an envoy from Isaac's Hold had come to check on the state of the Valley's one and, thankfully, only dam, Edgar's Folly. The poorly conceived and even more poorly constructed dam was Becknor's second largest threat next to Everfrost. Its inner structure had never been sound. It had not helped that a malcontent had once stored blasting powder inside its corridors, right next to the floodgate mechanisms, and had ignited them in a drunken stupor. When King Gaius had informed the people of the accident everyone downstream nearly panicked. To sooth their fears he asked for assistance from the City-State. Sadly, Edgar's Foley was going to collapse and flood them all out one day, but thankfully, according to the best of Isaac's Hold, that was still many decades from now. And it certainly was not this night. The night Regent Lydia had chosen to honor the courageous Captain Vitus for his years of service.

* * * * *

It had been a celebration months in the planning. Vitus, a very proud and private man, had declined every attempt in honoring him over the years. So Lydia had turned to subterfuge. She had enlisted Hector as her co-conspirator. It had not been a task he had looked forward to with any relish. For a year now, Hector had been serving as one of Vitas' Hands. Making him perfectly placed to gather any information Lydia needed. Which also placed Hector in the unenviable position of incurring his captain's wrath if he caught on to Hector's snooping.

"I was beginning to become accustomed to my rank," Hector said aloud to Lydia shortly before they began planning. "I suppose foot-soldier is still an honorable rank."

"If he strips you of your rank I will just reinstate you the next morning," Lydia said with a wink to reassure him.

His stomach soured as he said, "Then I would only have to endure the public flogging that forcible reinstatement shall surely bring."

"Did I not tell you, that as Friend of the Regent, you would face many difficult and dangerous tasks," she had said grinning. He smiled back when he realized she thought he had been joking. He could feel the edge of the whip now.

Lydia had given Hector a definitive set of instructions. There were only so much she could have accomplished from within the Palace before the gossipmongers among the Court caught wind of what was being planned. Not to say that the responsibilities she had given herself were few. The majority of the "outside" planning and information gathering had been placed upon his shoulders.

Most of Lydia's instructions were straight forward. Seek out friends and family trustworthy enough to glean personal information. Such as preferred foods and drinks, the style of music or any poetry he may enjoy. He was to even ask if his captain fancied a certain color scheme. Hector could not help but cringe each time he asked. It was Vitus' daughter, not much older than Lydia and also a knight, who raised an eyebrow over Hector's mission.

"You really wish to incur my father's wrath this way?"

Hector shrugged, "The Regent made her request. I did not wish to see her ladyship disappointed or find myself locked away because I failed her."

She laughed shortly and answered, "I would have gladly chosen the dungeon mate."

Not feeling much better, Hector's next task was to visit the Archives within Citadel to conduct "research." At least that was what he had told the attendants with each visit. Under the guise of wishing to study ancient strategies, Hector sought out the records of Vitus' greatest deeds. Both militarily and civilian. He was to get the details of these moments, the dates, and relate them to a set of handpicked artisans who would depict them in their chosen venue and style. It was these renderings that Hector was pausing to admire the night of the banquet.

Hector was impressed with the number of artisans Lydia had employed. There were nearly two dozen exhibits on display, most were paintings. Nearly every example depicted Vitus as a larger than life figure, one of the few men in this world Hector believed perfectly fit that description. His favorite of the selections depicted a moment Hector had been present for.

Becknor's greatest danger would always remain invasion from Everfrost, but the threat of raiders and marauders from outside was also constant. One such small band of raiders had ridden in expecting easy picking against the "backward and ignorant isolationists." More than half their number fell by the sword within the first minute of the first engagement. Panicked, they ran to the closest village and locked themselves away, with hostages, in a storehouse of animal feed. Quite by accident, one of the raiders had set the storehouse on fire. When the men at his command proved to be too cowardly, Vitus dismounted drawing his sword and rushed into the engulfed structure, alone. Hector had arrived just as his captain vanished beyond the threshold. Horrified that Vitus was alone, Hector too began to rush the door but was stopped by the steady stream of hostages. Vitus was the last to exit. He walked through the billowing smoke, face merely smudged and hardly a dent in his armor. The remaining raiders had succumbed to his blade long before the flames had a chance.

The artist had chosen to depict the moment the victorious captain exited the structure. She had used bright, vivid colors to contrast the black of the smoke. Hector nodded in approval, and in appreciation of the other great works strewn around the room. Including the somewhat strange wood carved figurine of Vitus upon horseback. It was as if the carver had wished to elevating Vitus to some sort of godhood status. Holding his sword high, with thick muscular arms and legs, a fierce scowl and battle cry on his lips. Riding a horse so muscular, that if a specimen of its like had existed in reality, it would have probably exploded and killed twenty people. It was...different.

. "It is nearly enough to make one sick," a familiar, but unwelcome voice said at Hector's side. Klytus, the soon to be replaced master of the Moneychangers sneered at Hector and said, "Of course you would not think so would you boy? You practically worship the man, both of them actually. That little usurper they call regent, you hold her in just as much esteem."

The last three years had not been exceptionally kind to Klytus. Or rather, he had not been overly kind to himself. After his failed bid for power, his clout, both within the Royal Court as a whole and inside his guild, in particular, had fallen fast. To assuage his shattered ego, Klytus had turned to debauchery. Now that he was to be replaced within a matter of days, there was hardly a time he was sober. Tonight was not one of them.

"I hold my mentors and friends in the highest esteem," Hector said mannerly. He did not wish to set the soon to be replaced master off on a tangent. He still held a high office and could have caused Hector some small measure of grief. But this was also his Captain's night, and he did not wish it to see it marred by a drunken fistfight. Though, as Hector measured the state of the man, fistfight did not exactly cover a one-punch victory. Though tact was the word of the night, Hector still could not help but say, "I have yet to become jaded enough to see everyone around me as stepping stones to power and nothing more."

Klytus' reply was to make a rude noise and quickly down the cup of wine in his hand. The red liquid gushed over the sides and down his soon to be double chin, before making its final resting place on his once fine apparel. There, the wine made a new stain, a new member to join the considerable number of its family already present on Klytus' chest. Once empty he snapped his fingers for his nearby attendant to have it refilled.

When the young man began to protest Klytus growled like a bear, sending the attendant scurrying away.

"You think you are immune because she favors you. Requests your opinion on various matters," the insinuating tone of Klytus' words just then did not sit well with Hector. The moneychanger was trying to start a disruption after all. Hector bit his tongue this time as Klytus continued, "The treachery of Achelon is well remembered, my boy. There will be a judgment day, and it will consume not only our pretty little Regent, but all who consort with her."

The attendant returned with a full cup of wine and Klytus deftly plucked it from his hand. After guzzling half, he sneered at Hector and said, "If one wants to have a future in the Valley, one should keep his distance from the Lady of Talwoods."

Hector smiled viciously and answered in one word, "Never."

"Then she will be your ultimate doom," he said flatly before finally staggering away.

The low murmur of conversation throughout the room became increasingly excited, as everyone turned to the door. Another reason Hector knew Vitus would never have agreed to a ceremony such as this was the style of dress. High ranking knights and their Captains were required to leave their armor at home and attend in formal dress for functions of state. Like the other Knights of the Valley in attendance, Vitus was dressed in a ice-blue jacket with silver buttons. A cravat embroidered with the insignia of his rank. The trousers were white, with a blue stripe running the outer seam of each leg. The boots were polished to a glossy shine. For Vitus, this style of dress still required that he wear the ceremonial cape of his rank. Normally Vitus would have looked about uncomfortable, always feeling that every eye was upon him, mocking him. As Hector glanced his way, he could see that his Captain was uncharacteristically at ease. It seemed Vitus knew all too well, that though this was a night to honor him, at this moment, not a single head was turned his way.

In three years as regent, Lydia had not only proven that she was skilled in surviving, but also thriving in the politics of the Royal Court. She had also shown a penchant for reading and knowing the members of the Court. Upon informing Vitus of tonight's ceremony, and then apparently ordering him to attend, she had made the suggestion that he find someone to accompany him. She had told Hector her hope would be that if he had an escort it would soothe his discomfort. Someone to help him feel that every eye was upon two and not one. Having been a widower for some time, Vitus refused the thought. The only women in his life had been his wife and daughter, and the latter would attend with her betrothed.

Lydia had said his response was, "I am not the easiest of men to befriend. It was the greatest of miracles one could stomach my arrogant, bullheaded nature and return in kind. There were days my wife should have murdered me in my sleep. The night would be a disaster if one of a lesser constitution were to be my companion, even but for the length of the ceremony. And with the greatest of respect to my Regent, this is one thing you cannot order me to do. There is not a single woman you can decree to be my escort that I would agree to."

Lydia's response was to smile and say, "There is one you could not refuse."

Defiantly he asked, "Who?"

Lydia walked, her left arm interlocked with his, side by side with Vitus. Her golden hair in a spiral braid laying upon her right shoulder. Her gown, though mostly conservative, was less in the style of the Valley but, what Hector's imagined, was more Isaac's Hold. It was sleeveless, emerald green, and long flowing. The neckline was inches lower than convention, well compared to the other gowns worn that evening, but still modest. She carried a white wrap draped about her shoulders. Around her neck, she wore a pendant with the emblem of Talwoods upon it.

They paused to be announced. "Lydia, daughter of Marcus, House Achelon, Lady of Talwoods, Regent, and Vitus, son of Pyrrhus, Captain of the Knights of the Valley."

From there, the two slowly made their way through the Banquet Hall, pausing to admire the artwork prepared in Vitus honor. In between they were interrupted many times by high ranking officials wishing to congratulate Vitus. Most eyes were still upon Lydia. Too many as it would turn out. A voice behind Hector made him jump.

"We are here to keep the Kingdom's most precious jewel safe not admire her fashion." Hector felt self-conscience, though later he would not understand why, and twirled around to meet his accuser. It was quickly evident the words had not been meant for him.

The Inner Circle was in full force. With so many of the Valley's most notable dignitaries in attendance, the black armored knights were double their normal numbers. Becknor politics could be heated but was usually more sedate than the Outer World. Though it had not been unheard of for a member of the Royal Court to assassinate a political rival during celebrations such as this. Tonight it would be self-assured suicide with so many knights of the two most prominent orders in attendance.

Most of the Inner Circle, armored head to toe and armed with their staff blades, were standing at attention. The pair behind Hector had obviously been caught by their own captain being less than attentive.

"Keep your eyes within your head or risk having them scooped up and given to chef to flavor his soup," said Aristide as he continued to stare the pair down for a moment longer. He then turned to regard Hector and smiled. "Hector, how is life as a Trusted Hand?"

Aristide was a fifteen year veteran of the Knights of the Valley. It had been a very fruitful career. One that eventually led to his ascension to the rank Hector now held. His record, and a number of quarrels with the other Trusted Hand, Olivia, had led to his appointment as Captain of the Inner Circle. He too was required to attend tonight out of armor. His clothing was jet black with blood red button and cravat. His ceremonial cape was also a deep red. After a year as Captain, Hector noticed he had allowed his blonde hair to grow out considerably. Apparently, Captains were allowed to be lax upon themselves as far as the code was concerned.

"The last year has been, educational," Hector allowed. "Especially these last few months. Both Vitus and Olivia have given me the full benefit of their knowledge."

"And how is old One-eye doing," Aristide asked. Obviously, the feud between him and Olivia was ongoing. The name did not sit well with Hector, but to be honest, Olivia had called Aristide far worse to his face. The thoughtless oaf with the pretty face being the nicest.

"Returning to the valley."

"Retirement," Aristide said thinking it over. "I honestly thought she would have died at post. Run through by one of her knights. But that is the romantic in me," he said with a greasy-slick smile. "Any nominees for the post?"

"Two," Hector said. "Helena and Darius."

"Darius? Who in their right mind would have nominated the inebriated knight?" When Hector did not answer right away Aristide frowned and said, "Not you?"

"I made no nominations this cycle, as I am too close to both. Both highly ranked, but a nomination from a childhood friend or former squire might not help your chances. Olivia nominated both."

"One was a joke of course?"

"Darius is the most senior, I believe Vitus to be taking it seriously."

"Divine save the Valley," Aristide said all at once. "Two deaths away from being de facto captain. May a cooler head prevail and Helena join you as Trusted Hand."

Hector could only watch as Aristide walked away. Darius reputation was difficult to defend him against. There were few knights more dedicated to service. Sadly, there was no one in Becknor more dedicated to their vices either.

The banquet went splendidly. Hector believed it had been more of a success than even Lydia had hoped for. For Hector, what made the night even more special, was the occasional glance Klytus' way. No matter the amount of drink, the man never seemed to get any happier.

There was feasting, the bestowment of gifts and accolades, and many speeches. The most memorable was Vitus' speech. Moreover, the surprise no one had seen coming.

He stood to address all that were gathered, "Thirty-five years. Very few have ever made it this far, even fewer have gone further. Thirteen years as Captain of the Valley. A long tenure such as mine can only be due to peacetime. I am the eleventh Captain of Achelon's peace. Though he is demonized by some, I praise him, and his descendants," he said turning to Lydia and bowing his head, "for the wisdom of their rule and the courage of their conviction that won us this century."

There was a moment of applause. The entire room followed suit but Hector did notice that a sizable fringe only applauded politely. Klytus, his chin resting on his hands as he leaned over the table, looked on half dazed, half bored.

"In my time the Valley has seen many dangers: raiders, marauders, and the occasional starving warlord from the north. But unlike my forefathers, never the threat of Everfrost. My predecessors had the misfortune of seeing many of their brothers and sisters of the Blood Oath fall in battle. Nevertheless, peacetime or war, every captain eventually looks out upon the ranks and is hard pressed to find familiar faces. In the past, they would find the men and women they squired with had taken their place in the Memorial Gardens. I now stand in a familiar place. I look out and see fresher faces every year. Though my generation's foe had not been the goblin hordes but time herself. My fellow squires now tend their farms and some have seen the first of their grandchildren."

"Not too long ago, Olivia," he said as he turned her way, "In great malice, decided it would be great fun to step down so that I might be forced to find a suitable replacement. As I looked out upon the ranks of my army I came to a sudden, dreadful conclusion. It is no longer my army. A younger generation has supplanted my old, beleaguered comrades in arms. Therefore, I have decided to take my second's lead and return to the valley."

The Banquet Hall became alive again in conversation. Vitus retire? How could this be? The man, despite his age, was in fighting form. He was seasoned, wise, and still more than capable. And he was right, Becknor stood at peace. Like it or not, the legions of Isaac's Hold ensured the peace now. Surely the position of Captain was now no more than an honorary title. Vitus could serve another decade and have nothing more than the occasional rabble to deal with.

But none had been more shocked to hear these words than Hector. Long after the banquet, as the last of the guests began to disperse, he sat in the hall pondering his Captain's decision. Darius and Helena had now become candidates for Captain as well as Trusted Hand. Certainly Aristide would be a consideration as well. It was difficult for Hector to imagine anyone else as his commanding officer.

Looking across the room, Hector spied Klytus' attendant; desperately attempting to wake his snoring master. Knowing now that it was well past the time to make his own departure, Hector stood and made his exit. Just through the threshold he found Lydia, still dressed in her extravagant gown, waiting for him.

"Walk with me," she said turning and Hector moved to her side. He was about to speak when she said, "Not within the walls."

She led him silently through the halls of the Palace, avoiding the corridors with high foot traffic. The walls and draperies became less and less ornate, and began to look quite plain. Nearly deserted, the pair only occasionally walked past a servant or two. None of which seemed at all surprised to see their Regent walking amongst them. There were no Inner Circle Knights, no members of the Royal Court, only silence.

Lydia led them down an empty corridor that ended at a simple stone wall. Hector looked upon her silently but with a questioning look. She smiled and turned to the wall. Without preamble she pressed the palms of her hands over two separate sections, right hand high and left low, until there was a hollow clicking sound. She then pressed a section just over her head with both hands and the wall slid away. The passageway beyond was narrow, there was barely enough clearance for him to walk naturally. Shortly after he followed her through, Lydia turned and stopped him with a hand upon his chest. Motioning for him to turn, she moved in closer so she may trip the hidden switch and close the door behind them. She was close enough that the scent of her perfume, jasmine, tickled his nose. For the first time, he noted she had grown an inch or two in height in the past three years.

With the door closed, the passage was only lit by the glow of a single torch that Lydia had apparently prepared herself. Taking it from the wall sconce, she motioned for Hector to follow her again.

The last leg of the journey was short, and the other end of the narrow corridor was open. Halfway, Hector began to hear the trickling of water. Upon exiting, Hector was greeted with the sight of a secret courtyard. The pathway behind seemed to be the only way, no other door or window was visible. They were boxed in on all four sides. Above them was the open sky, a crescent moon and stars twinkled at them. At the center of this hidden wonder was the source of the trickling sound. A fountain of all things. Water lazily poured itself from the center, little more than a trickle.

Lydia busied herself in lighting three more torches hanging from nearby sconces before setting hers in an empty one. She turned and eyed him curiously.

"Remarkable, is it not?"

"Very," he answered with a nod. "Why is this here?"

"I could not tell you. I have searched the records for years and found nothing."

"How did you find it?"

She looked away, a slight frown stole her smile for a moment and said "I suppose I could say, 'Well Hector, this was my home once after all. Even little girls destined to be regents tire of politics and must explore.' And that would be a partial truth. The hallway I took you through, and the empty chamber hiding the door, is where I would come to grieve for my parents. As fate would have it, I looked up through bleary eyes one afternoon and noticed the wall was uneven in three places. Experimentation led me here."

Wordlessly, she moved to the side of the fountain to sit. After a moment, Lydia attempted to use her wrap for warmth.

"I forget how cold it is down here at night. I am going to regret not going back to my chambers for something warmer." Without hesitation, Hector unclasped his coat and offered it to her. She shook her head and smiled, "Always the gallant knight. You are the type of man the poets love to write about."

"You have to be more than a mere mortal for such accolades," he said with a forced smile.

His coat over her shoulders now, she tilted her head to the side and asked, "What troubles you?"

With a laugh, he asked, "Am I that blatant?"

"I do not wish to hurt your ego my friend, but you are an easy book to read."

"So much for my quest to be the man of mystery," he said with a smirk. She motioned for him to sit beside her on the edge of the fountain. As he did he looked upon the water and how the tiniest droplet sent ripples across the fountain.

"You fear the coming change," she asked after a moment of silence.

"Everyone fears the unknown. Almost all of my brothers and sisters of the Oath have had but one captain. But I do not fear the change that is coming. I feel more melancholy than fearful."

"In what way?"

"If Vitus had not been Captain, I would not be sitting here tonight. I would never have been accepted to squire, much less have a chance at knighthood."

He turned to see Lydia eyeing him thoughtfully. The look gave him pause. He worked his next words in his head before he answered.

"A few days before I took the Blood Oath, I was injured. I took a nasty tumble. The worst was my left wrist, it was broken, and that is my dominant hand. I was pleading with the lieutenant tasked with reviewing us when Vitus happened by. He looked me over and told the lieutenant that the first thing a Knight of the Valley must learn is improvisation. As long as I could defend myself upon my first test, I would be allowed to stay.

Sometimes you need a little boost climbing over the wall that is life."

Lydia nodded and said, "Yes. Sometimes that boost comes in the form of a future mentor or a kind knight taking a stroll through a horse stable."

Hector laughed and said, "That was no boost. That was clumsy man tripping with each step and knocking you over the wall."

A moment later Lydia said, "I suppose I have the unenviable task of finding a replacement for a great man. Tell me, who do you foresee as the candidates."

Hector stood and began to pace while his mind began to work. "I imagine that both Darius and Helena, having been nominated to take Olivia's station, are now in play for captain. Darius is both brave and cunning. He has a few eccentricities," he said delicately, "but could be a great leader. Helena is loyal and fierce." Fierce was an understatement.

"I could see Aristide being nominated," he said after another moment of thought. "He has already achieved the rank of Captain. Inner Circle is a fine order but is not as prestigious as the Valley. Though Inner Circle is more visible and…."

"And Aristide is in love with appearance," Lydia finished for him. "Is there no one else you can think of," she asked with a smirking smile.

Hector offered a list of all the capable and highest ranked knights. With each, he made it a point to relate each of their strengths. All were capable but none would ever be the next Vitus. Which Hector realized was unfair, but his soon to be former captain had set a high standard.

"Impressive list," Lydia offered once he had finished. "But I sense we have missed one. One that is more than qualified."

Hector thought it over for a moment and said, "No, I have thought of everyone. Unless you would like an opinion of the junior ranks."

"Not at all. The knight I am thinking of is one of highest ranking and one of the most respected. Hector, son of Felix."

It was as if a bucket of ice water had been thrown into Hector's face. With no breath in his lungs, all he could do was shake his head vigorously.

"And why not," asked Lydia.

"I am the least qualified."

"Shortly you will be the highest ranking Knight of the Valley once Vitus and Olivia return to the valley. Until the nomination and appointment process is finished you will be acting captain."

"But that is a temporary posting," Hector protested. "The Knights of the Valley will need a more capable military mind."

"So Vitus mistakenly appointed you to one of his Trusted Hands?"

Hector had no immediate answer.

"Then what is it?"

"The post needs someone with more experience."

"Who among us has fought an actual war?"

"Someone older then."

Lydia laughed and said, "And yet you mention Helena as a viable option and you are practically of the same age. Perhaps, by your thinking, at the age of nineteen, I am too young to be Regent."

"T-that is not what I mean," Hector stammered. "I am not ready to lead."

"I disagree."

"Then by what virtue do I make the best candidate?"

"Because you already lead. As Trusted Hand, you command half of the Valley. And before you protest again, yes, I understand that you carry out the will of your Captain. But, you are free to improvise if the need arises. Second, your knights respect you. You have acquired the type of reputation that makes others willing to follow you no matter the cost. In a war, there is nothing more important than those under your command having faith in you. Lastly, though there are many more virtues I could offer, you are relentless. If I were to tell you the salvation of Becknor lie on an island in the center of a lake filled with man-eating creatures, you would fell the closest trees and build a boat. Failing that you would build a bridge with nothing more than a spade and the surrounding earth. You are what the Valley needs."

Hector opened his mouth to protest again, but one stern look from Lydia closed it. Defeated, Hector sat down next to her again. In a low voice, he said, "I never dreamed, nor had any ambitions for Captain. My only wish was to serve and be the best knight I could be."

"Which you have been. Sometimes honors come to those who do not seek them," she said laying her hand on his. "Sometimes service requires more than even our dreams and ambitions can take us. It is not greed to accept a good thing as it passes your way. Nor is it noble to refuse an important position because it does not meet your preconceived notion of self-sacrifice. And if you feel service is denying yourself, trust me, you are going to be miserable in your new post. Now you will have daily access to the Royal Court. Not a single day will pass without having to deny yourself the satisfaction of slapping one of your fellow courtiers," she said with a smile.

Smiling in return, Hector said, "I suppose this is something I cannot escape."

"No."

"You fully intend to nominate me."

"I am afraid I can only second your nomination," she said. "You have already been nominated to the post."

"How can I have already been nominated if," Hector trailed off as a thought occurred to him. "You already knew of Vitus' retirement."

"Six months now. The entire reason for your promotion was Vitus wanted a closer look at you and your capabilities. Did you not think it odd that both he and Olivia have been imparting their wisdom to you? You are his choice. With his nomination, the Royal Court will have no choice but to appoint you."

In the absence of a reigning King, all high ranking posts had to be appointed by a Court vote. After the debacle of Klytus' failed power grab, Vitus had become a trusted voice in the Court. Hector was certain it was over now. He would be Captain no matter his objections.

"My only regret is that the nomination process is so slow," Lydia said. "You will miss being the youngest Captain on record by a month."

Deep within the recess of Hector's mind a voice from long ago, its owner long gone, echoed, *I will be the youngest, and bravest, captain Becknor has ever seen.*

Clamping down on the memory, Hector replied, "Let someone else have that honor. Being Captain of the Valley is enough of an honor in of itself."

"As grudgingly as you accept," Lydia said with a chuckle.

Hector smiled and said, "As grudgingly."

# CHAPTER NINE

As fast as a blink, Hector discovered he was no longer standing in the Glass Desert. He was now inside a warmly lit room.

*How is this possible?* Hector was suddenly very dizzy. After leagues of riding through the muted wasteland around the Glass Desert, his senses were being assaulted. Colors were bright and vibrant, sounds, no matter how small, boomed at him, and all the scents and aromas of the room tickled his nose. Even the air itself felt as if it had grown heavier and his lungs momentarily labored to bring each new breath in.

Hector took a moment to close his eyes and settle his senses. Ignoring the sensory overload as best he could, Hector concentrated on his breathing. Deep breaths in, slow and steady exhales followed until his lungs adjusted to the air. For his now aching ears, he concentrated on the sound of his breath only until the pain in his temples eased by half. Finally, Hector slowly opened his eyes again to take in his surroundings.

He was standing in some kind of study. Deep red carpet, pristine bookshelves, colorful tapestries, and some kind of work bench and well-organized shelves stacked with vials, jars, and various utensils. Everything his eye took in said new. The books upon the shelves looked to be the latest volumes on alchemy, magics, histories, even the works of fiction that had trickled into the valley recently, were the latest. The alchemy workshop was clean and looked to be untouched.

*If this place is at least a millennia old, how can it look so immaculate and new,* Hector asked himself.

A crackling fire from the other side of the room caught his attention. He looked that way to find he was not alone. By the fire, there was a table with a silver serving tray and two chairs. One of the chairs was occupied by a man who had not made a single sound since Hector had arrived. He just sat there with a strange, amused look, studying Hector. He was a thin, bald man wearing a green tunic and trousers. It was hard to gauge his age, but Hector would say that he was past his middle years in appearance. His dark brown eyes never left Hector's face; almost as if he were reading him like one might read a book.

After another moment of silence, Hector asked, "Are you the keeper of this place?"

"I am indeed," he said pleasantly, in a warm and friendly voice. "Are you seeking the elixir?"

"Yes."

"Well then, come and join me by the fire and we shall discuss it," he said motioning to the other chair and smiling broadly. As Hector approached he added, "I have to say that you adjusted to the transference quicker than most. You would be surprised by the number of knights and adventurers who fell to the floor and wailed like infants upon their arrival. Some of them quite well known," he said as he steepled his fingers in front of him.

"Is this one of the trials," asked Hector.

"Oh no," the stranger in green said, continuing to smile. "The trials are far more sinister than this. This is just my way of saying, hello."

Hector sat in the offered chair slowly, never taking his eyes off of the stranger. He seemed pleasant enough, but how often in the world did the cleverest traps begin with something pleasant? Upon sitting in the chair, the stranger went silent again. It was almost as if they were participating in some kind of bizarre staring contest. Long uncomfortable minutes past, the only sound in the room was an occasional pop from the roaring fire. That same peculiar feeling began to wash over Hector again, and he reminded himself why he was there.

"I am Hector, son of Felix, Captain of the Knights of the Valley-Kingdom of Becknor," Hector said to bring an end to the silence.

"Becknor? Can't say that I have ever had a Beckish Knight here before," the stranger said more to himself than to Hector.

"You know of Becknor?"

"I know a great many things," the stranger said before falling silent again.

Trying once more to break the silence Hector asked, "And you, you have a name?"

"Yes," he said with a nod and dropped the subject. "Usually the questions that follow are: Is the Orchid real? Or, is the Elixir all that I claim?"

Hector shook his head and said, "I cannot imagine why those would be relevant."

Hector's answer seemed to have caught the man off guard. Cocking one eyebrow he asked, "How so?"

"The journey is perilous enough, the wastes around us seem rather deadly, and this impossible tower rests upon glass. If you were some jester or trickster, this would seem to be an awfully elaborate, and a painfully poor taste of a joke. One that would have gotten old centuries ago for you, if you be immortal, and for the world at large. And if you were not immortal, someone would have run you through by now in indignation."

The stranger smiled and nodded in approval, "Ah, not just a man of brawn but of mind as well. I will confess, that though my life has been extended due to a concentrated dose of the Elixir, I am not immortal. As you see, I have never been run through, but I am sure that there have been, and still are many, who wish death upon me. Sadly for them, my death is far off."

"So you have taken the Elixir yourself," Hector asked.

"Why yes," the Stranger answered. "How else would I know of the Blue Orchid's healing powers? It is a fascinating story, filled with adventure and peril, one I love to tell," the Stranger's eyes lit up. "You must hear it! But first, we must have the proper refreshments. You must be parched after such a long ride. Please join me," he said motioning towards the empty serving tray that was no longer empty.

Hector stared down at the contents, as benign as they seemed, as if they were a coiled, venomous serpent. The silver tray now held a teapot and two cups and saucers, all as silver as the tray. Hector kept his hands by his sides, unwilling to even move.

The Stranger chuckled and said, "If I meant to kill you, do you not think that I would have done so in an extremely more entertaining way than poison?" Shaking his head, the stranger poured what looked to be tea in both cups. After sipping from the one closest to him, he asked, "There, would I harm myself?"

Hector slowly reached for his, all the while thinking of his previous words and praying this man was not a jester or trickster and that this was all a joke in poor taste. Experimentally, he sipped at the liquid and found it to be the most delicious tea he had ever tasted. No bitterness, no hint of poison. He nodded in approval as he took another sip.

"I am originally from the north, and have loved the study of alchemy since childhood," the Stranger began. Hector looked up from his cup and discovered that the study had quietly vanished. He looked about to see that he was still sitting in his chair, the table was still there in front of him and the Stranger was still seated in his place. But they were now inside a small cottage. A small boy of about seven years, with a full head of curly black hair, was excitedly pacing back and forth. He was eyeing a set of glass vials sitting over an open flame. There was a liquid beginning to boil within. Presiding over these was a man with a similar bearing as the Stranger, yet, he had a full head of white hair. Watching the vials closely, he began to jot notes down in a book.

"My father was a master among masters," the Stranger said with pride. "He would have been world famous if it had not been for the shunning of the north by the civilized world."

"He was a practitioner of the forbidden alchemy," Hector interjected still looking about with awe. He could even feel the air of the cottage, smell the sweet aroma of whatever tonic was brewing on that long ago day.

"Fah! Forbidden alchemy. Only the coward would call knowledge evil. But for your purpose and sensibilities, yes, it was among the line of the forbidden. The ancient machines powered by fire and steam held no curiosity for him, but long-forgotten methods did," he said motioning for Hector to watch.

Hector watched as the man in the vision carefully plucked up one of the vials. He then began to measure out the substance, which was now a gel, into a small metal cylinder, no bigger than a man's hand. Once the man was satisfied, he slowly screwed a lid over the top. In the center of the lid was what looked to be a lantern wick. Carefully the man extended a lit candle to the wick. Before the flame even made contact a warm and bright light erupted. The boyhood version of the Stranger began to jump up and down excitedly while clapping his hands.

"The wick would continue to burn continuously for the next thirty days," the Stranger said. "Now tell me, how can such a simple and helpful tool be allowed to be forbidden? Why I even understand a system, not unlike this, is used in the great City-State herself. Now if Isaac's Hold has such courage, then why are the other great miracles forbidden?"

While the Stranger continued to preach the greatness of dangerous alchemy, Hector watched as the scene before them continued to playout. The boy of the past began to inspect one of the other glass vials. As the vial came to close to the open flame beneath it, the entire mixture went up in a spectacular fireball. Both father and son dove for the floor while the cottage became smoky. The Stranger turned from Hector and frowned.

"Oh, yes, of course. I had forgotten that. I usually move on before that little moment. At least you now know what happened to my magnificent head of hair," he said with a chuckle while rubbing the top of his bald head with his right hand.

Hector kept his expression neutral but deep within he was beginning to worry. Worry that, at best, he had gotten himself lost in the Desolate Wastes and was having an elaborate hallucination before death took him, or, at worst, was now at the mercy of a madman. A madman with unheard of powers of illusion and who knew what else.

"But I distract myself with a self-important sermon. Let us move ahead several decades, after I became a skilled alchemist in my own right," he said as the scene around them changed again in the space of a single eye blink. Their tea party had now moved outdoors. They sat on a grassy plane. Hector could feel a gentle breeze upon his skin. High above them, the hot noonday sun shone brightly in a clear blue sky. They were surrounded by a small company of men. A couple of wagons were loaded down with various goods. It appeared to be a merchant's caravan of some sort. Hector took note that only two were carrying any type of armament, both short swords. Just past the table's edge, the Stranger's doppelganger was attending to a sick man laying upon a blanket.

"I always had an unquenchable thirst for knowledge," the Stranger began his narration again. "When I realized there was nothing more to be learned in books, my eyes drifted from home and out upon the horizon. I traded my services as a sort of tonic-man to these fine adventurers of the mercantile. Those two years were some of the best of my life. Sadly, this was the last day I would ever have the privilege of associating with such fine fellows."

As the Stranger went silent, the scene began to play out before them. A young man, not much older than the Becknor Age of Responsibility, came running towards the group raising the alarm. Raiders were charging in from the south. Hector watched as the superior armed bandits made quick work of the merchants and their hired guard. The whole time, something did not ring true for Hector. He could feel the air, hear the death cries, but there was something unreal about it all and it had nothing to do with knowing this was an illusion portraying the past. Like everything else, it was just too real, too detailed. Sure, an event like this could have happened in the Strangers past, but these raiders, their armor was too modern. True, ironmongery changed with the times and stretches of peace allowed for more experimentation. Whole pieces of armor were tailored to an individual smithy's artistic sentiments while the occasional discovery of alloys and craftsmanship moved the art forward. While war demanded a more mass produced, economical set, with little to no extra flare to the design. With a century of peace, Valley smithies had the opportunity to try and mimic the most modern designs of the Alliance. The armor that the raiders wore bared a striking resemblance to the light armor Hector wore now, and not the heavier varieties of the past when the art of metal work had yet to perfect lighter alloys. Lastly, though he recognized no faces, Hector did recognize the branding that each raider had upon their right arm. It was a raider group Hector had faced in his first year as a knight. Surely such a motley crew could not have been at work for centuries.

Focusing on the vision again, the raiders cut the throat of the man the Stranger had been attending. He had attempted to rescue his charge, but was backhanded with such force from an armored hand, that he spun to the ground. All he could do now was watch helplessly as he wiped away the blood from his busted lip. Afterward, the leader of the gang knelt down in front of him.

"Their leader had no intentions of killing me," the Stranger began his narration again. "Once he gleaned that I was a trained alchemist I became his parties' personal slave." The vision changed again, this time, the Stranger's hands were bound and was being led by a chain around his neck. The chain's owner was upon horseback and was coaxing more speed from his horse, nearly dragging the Stranger while the rest laughed.

"They felt the need to break me. Not so much as to break my will but as some perverse sport. Even after several months, I held my pride," the Stranger said with a self-satisfied smile. "Then came the day of my renewed freedom."

The rest of the vision unfolded as a rival raiding party attacked the Stranger's enslavers. Finding the key from his fallen captor, the Stranger unlocked the collar from around his neck and the manacles from his wrists. While the battle raged on, the Stranger next retrieved some of his possession and took off for the horizon.

"Little did I know that I was running straight into this place." Hector recognized the Wastes immediately. On foot, the ill effects of the Desolation had time to do their work. His face flushed, lips pealing, and his eyes were glazed, if not going white in blindness. Slowly, it would seem, he was dying.

"It was then, on the edge of the Glass Desert, I found her," he said as the vision version of the Stranger staggered towards the Blue Orchid. The small plant looked impossible amongst the devastation around it. The Stranger fell upon his knees as he bent down to study the Orchid.

"I was amazed. I had been told life was impossible here. Even my father had warned that the Desolation slowly drains life away. Yet, here she was, alive and well, just as assuredly as death quickly approached to take me. I had not but a mouthful of water left within my canteen. I had my alchemy utensils, but I knew no common potion or tonic could undo what was happening to me. Looking down upon the little miracle, I decided to take a chance. If such a thing could live then perhaps it could restore life."

Gently, the vision version of the Stranger cut away a petal. As he set out to work Hector could see that death was close at hand. His lips were dry and cracked, his eyes were unfocused as he crushed the petal up within a mortar. Without measuring he poured the last of his water in with the powder. Barely stirring the mixture with a few other ingredients from his bag, the Stranger brought the mortar up to his mouth and drank the mixture. For a moment nothing. Then the Stranger fell over as if in death.

"I do not know how long I was there. But life returned to me all at once."

The doppelganger Stranger gasped for breath and sat up. He looked about as if in a momentary daze. His visage had completely changed. No longer was he on death's door but now he looked refreshed and full of vitality.

"I knew it had been the elixir I had mixed from the Orchid. Knew it immediately. It was a miracle I had to share with the world," as the Stranger spoke, slowly the vision dissolved and they were once again sitting in the study. "At first, I tried to find more orchids around the former lakebed and found none. Next, I tried to coax seeds from the original but she never went to seed. Instead, I found that her bloom was, for lack of a better term, immortal. Once I removed a petal, within days a new one took its place. Later I learned a technique to speed up the regrowth."

"At first, my plan was to help as many as I could," he said, his eyes became more intense as they seemed to look out beyond the here and now. "After some time I became fearful for the Orchid. As seemingly invincible as it appeared, the more petals I pulled at once the longer it took for them to regrow. We did some good, but then came the man. A greedy and vile imp of a man. He tried to take her away from me. His plan was to pervert her healing powers into poison. In the dead of night, we escaped the 'civilized world' and came back here. I still believed that she was a gift and my purpose was to help as many as I could, but the key was determining whose cause was the most worthy. Slowly, over many decades, I built this fortress and devised my trials. My three trials. Tests so balanced, I can measure the very soul of the adventurer seeking the elixir. I briefly returned to the trade routes to spread the word of the Blue Orchid Elixir. A few years later, the first of many arrived, which brings us to tonight."

While Hector had much trepidation about the visions the Stranger had conjured before them, he felt there was a level of truth to them. But it was like traveling down a twisting trail of half-truths to avoid an unknown inconvenience. These last words, however, rang truer. Not because there had been no "showy" vision, but because of the sincerity of his words and the intensity of his emotions. Especially when he spoke of this nameless man. Those events happened in some form. Just as the Stranger held much devotion and apparent love for his orchid. If Hector had had any doubts about the validity of the legend of the Blue Orchid and its Elixir, which he did not, those would have been put at ease.

While musing on these things, the man in green asked, "And so, Hector, son of Felix, why have you come here seeking the Elixir?"

The moment had come.

"I have come on behalf of Lydia, Lady of Talwoods, who has fallen victim to the Fever-Sleep Curse."

"A truly dreadful abomination," he said gravely. "This Lady Lydia, she is your queen?"

"Actually, no. Though Lady Lydia is part of the royal family, she is our Regent. She rules for her cousin, Lucien, until he is of age to take the throne."

Nodding the Stranger said, "My memory grows a little long but I do remember that your court politics, like its people, are very unique. Especially for such a small kingdom. Even if it is almost a full step behind the rest of the world. Pardon my interruption. Please continue Hector, Captain of the Knights."

Hector had had days to prepare what he was going to say once he arrived. Since time would be of the essence he knew he would have to be quick and concise. He had worked the entire history of the recent Ten-Day War into a short but informative summary. The stranger in green listened and seemed to be interested. Yet, while Hector spoke he could not tell if he was winning this man over, or if he was just feigning interest.

He finished with the ruminations of the kingdom's Wise Men and said, "And that is what has brought me here. I have come to take on the three trials and prove that our cause is worthy of the Blue Orchid Elixir."

"I see," the stranger said thinking it over. "Are you entirely sure Hector, Captain of the Knights? In the course of the Trials, you may face things you are not ready for."

"I am battle-tested," Hector said proudly. "I fear no danger."

"Ah, but not all dangers deal in physical harm. My trials will strip you of all pretense, all of the various layers you have come to believe is your true self. By the end you will be emptied like a water vessel, and all that will remain will be the true you. Once discovering this truth; none are ever the same. Most would rather die than face who they really are. It is a terrible risk. True, I do not know your Lydia personally, and I'm sure she was very brave, but for all I know she could just be some silly girl. Yes, just a silly girl who doesn't have the good sense to keep her head out of the clouds. Who, for all I know, could always be blundering her way into danger."

Hector could not keep his anger in check at the Stranger's insolence. He was up on his feet in an instant glaring down at the man. He took two calming breaths before speaking.

"You are correct, you do not know her personally. I can assure you that she is not a silly girl. She saw the danger coming from the Everfrost Mountains long before the war came. She was the one that tried to negotiate a peace with the Dread Overlord before he marched. And it was her leadership, strategies, and sacrifice in the last days of the war that saved us. Time and again she put the safety of the people above her own. Including becoming the bait for the trap. So, because you do not know the Lady Lydia personally, I will forgive this little offense. But insult her once more and I will strike you down regardless of any harm you could do to me."

If the Stranger had been surprised by Hector's reaction, or impressed by his response, it did not show. That strange curious smile never left his face. He just seemed to continue to study him. The Stranger's next words were not what Hector was expecting.

"And you love her."

"I am sorry," Hector asked once he had recovered.

"Your Lydia. You love her, yes?"

Hector stood speechless for a moment. The question, or was it the phrasing of it, made him strangely uneasy. After another moment to take a breath, and calm his unexpectedly racing heart, he answered, "She is a wise and just ruler. We all love her."

"Of course," the stranger said with a new wry smile. "Very well Hector, Captain of the Knights. You shall have your opportunity to face the Three Trials for a chance to win the elixir for your Lydia, Lady of Talwoods, Regent of Becknor."

"Thank you."

"Oh do not thank me yet brave knight," the stranger warned darkly.

*When do we start,* is what Hector had started to ask. But in mid-breath, he had blinked and found that the room had once again changed.

"I do not think I am getting used to that," Hector said quietly to himself about the stranger's favorite mode of travel.

Hector had been transported to a dimly lit room. It was rectangular in shape, with a few torches placed about. The air was damp and smelled heavily of freshly dug earth. As his eyes adjusted to the light, he took in his new surroundings.

He was sitting, at the room's center, at the base of a large mound of soil that stopped just short of the ceiling. The sound of water dripping to his left made him turn that way. On that side was a large pool of water that ran from wall to wall and took nearly a quarter of the room's floor. On the opposite side of the room, there was a set of shelves holding rows and rows of jars. Sitting in front of the shelves was a workbench containing all manner of scales and utensils that would have been the envy of any alchemist.

"Before you is the first trial of the three," the stranger's voice said booming all around him. "This room is made up of the thickest stone. There are no windows or common doors. But take heart, for there is a hidden door. As you can see, the room contains the four elements of the world. You must combine them in equal measure to unlock this hidden door."

"A mental puzzle," said Hector.

"After a fashion," the stranger replied, Hector could hear the smile in his voice. "But your mental abilities are not what I'm putting to the test."

"Then what is?"

"May good fortune smile upon you Hector, Captain of the Knights," he said ignoring the question. "Before you begin I wish to put your mind at ease. Do not let the matter of time trouble you. You see, within my walls, time does not flow in the same fashion. In this room in particular, an entire century could pass before one second would tick off the clock in the outside world. Your Lydia's health will not regress any further. You will need all of your mental faculties to solve my puzzle, and I would not have you worry needlessly. But as time is eternal within, and your supplies plentiful, once you have exhausted your resources, the trial ends in failure. And be mindful of this, if at any time this, or any of the other trials become too difficult for you, all you have to do is say, 'I concede,' and you can go home."

With that, Hector heard no more from the Stranger. He was now alone with the puzzle and his thoughts.

# CHAPTER TEN

Throughout the remainder of his life, Hector would never be capable of calculating the length of the first trial. He knew that the Stranger had been a man of his word. Time had to have practically stopped. There was no real way of telling day from night. There were no clocks, he never felt the need to sleep or eat, there was only one clue that time really did pass. At one point, deep in thought, Hector stroked his chin and was shocked to find a nearly full-grown beard. Hours stretched into days and days into weeks in that musty, damp room. How long had he really been down there? Ultimately he would decide it was a question best left unanswered. His entire time in the tower had strained Hector's concepts of time and reality, he feared the answer could have broken him.

Having put the worry of time behind him, upon arriving in the room of the first trial, Hector calmed his mind. He would have rather solved the puzzle early than to go through the process repeatedly. It was a good plan, even if it had quickly proven to be futile.

The puzzle was straightforward enough. Everyone in the known world knew what the four elements of the world were from childhood. They were: earth, water, fire, and air. There were ample supplies of the first two in the pool of water and mound of earth. In the shelves, on the opposite side from the pool, were many examples of fire, both figurative and literal. Starting with Hades Powder, which was a very spicy seasoning used in cooking, to Dragon's Breath. Not to be confused with the flower, this Dragon's Breath was a substance harvested from the glands of recently expired dragons. It was a process that was not for the faint of heart. Only an alchemy master, with intimate knowledge of dragon-kind, was even capable of harvesting it. In a near paradoxical statement, it required a delicate, patient hand and swift action; as the fluids within the glands are absorbed back into the body minutes after death. The scales around the throat had to be removed quickly and a siphon with a long needle inserted. But care had to be taken as the fire glands run side by side. An accidental, premature mixture of the fluids was not only flammable but explosive. Once collected, the fluids would then be carefully mixed by the alchemist with a third fluid that leaves the mixture inert until exposed to air. Once air hit the fluids, it was only a matter of moments before the remaining two mixed into a powerful fireball. Because of the nature of how it is collected, and after several explosive accidents, Dragon's Breath was outlawed by the Alliance. Private ownership held the death penalty if discovered.

Of all the substances organized upon the shelf before Hector, Dragon's Breath was the most dangerous. One drop would be nearly enough to flash burn half the room. Hector swore he would leave it on the shelf the moment he laid eyes upon the label.

As the time approached to begin solving the riddle, the first problem Hector had foreseen was how to measure out air and fire equally with water and earth? There was a full assortment of measuring utensils and scales on the work bench. He supposed that the fire's intensity and heat were what he would have to measure. A flame hot enough to boil away a certain amount of water and bake loose soil into a dry hard substance would be his base of measure. But air? How to weigh or measure the air in a mixture? Having infinite time, he set out to conduct a few small experiments.

Hector's first attempt was to carefully measure out a sampling of dirt and water and combine them in a bowl. Setting a fire underneath the bowl to bring the mud to a simmering boil he began to gently blow on the mixture to add air to it. For a moment, barely long enough to really see, there was the smallest of reactions. It was almost as if the mixture momentarily blinked out of existence. As the moisture began to boil away he began to fan the mixture with his hands, but to no avail. In the end, all he had managed to succeed in doing, not for the last time, was cook dirt and fill the air with an acrid stench. He would reattempt many times and never see the "blink" again.

After much more trial and error, his next experiment was considerably more complicated. He worked for what felt like as least a full day (or was it weeks) taking two of the scales, disassembling and reassembling them into a strange looking four-way scale. Hector immediately hated the monstrosity. A normal set of scales would obviously tip to the heavier side. His four-sided scale did the same; only it had a bad habit of spinning. Not just any spin. No, it had to spin with enough force to dump out whatever was in it. Hector spent another day or two (months?) trying to eliminate the spin only to find it was the only way to ensure that it was sensitive enough to accurately measure all four sides.

Prepared to now live with this hideous contraption of his, Hector began his experiments again. On two sides, he once again attempted to delicately measure out earth and water. Countless times the scale spun out as it was near impossible to perfectly balance out four sides. After losing all sense of time Hector finally did manage to master the earth and water sides. For the longest time, he just stared at the scale, unwilling to believe that it was going to behave. Once he was confident it was not going to throw its contents to every corner of the room he moved on to fire.

From the fire shelves, he plucked up a vessel containing lamp oil.

Carefully, he poured the liquid onto the third side of the scale. He held his breath as the scale began to turn slowly. He moved his hands away and watched as it came to an almost reluctant stop. All four sides were now equal. He had purposely left the fourth side empty as it would be, he hoped, a true measure of the empty air over it. Taking a breath he carefully set fire to the lamp oil. For a handful of heartbeats, the entire four-way scale was perfectly balanced. His heart skipped when something happened, did the mixture yet again blink? He was sure it would work this time. That was until the fire became so hot it burned through its side of the scale and caused a small fire on the work bench. The fire did not last long as the scale spun out of control letting loose the small samples of dirt and water, extinguishing the flames.

Once the foul smelling smoke cleared, Hector appraised his handiwork. The work bench was scorched but otherwise intact. The scale, on the other hand, was destroyed. He cast it to the side. Needless to say, he did not mourn its loss.

After a few weeks more (years?), Hector came across something very odd.

After yet another mixture of dirt and water, with the last of his lamp oil, had been set ablaze, he saw what he perceived to be a mistake in his mixture. Angry with himself, Hector grabbed an empty jar to snuff out the flames, but the exact opposite took place. Within, the fire actually grew larger. The water boiled away and, as if there was a mighty wind inside the jar, the dirt was pulled up into a miniature dust devil. The hairs on the back of Hector's neck stood up as he watched a maelstrom of dirt, steam, and smoke circle about the inside of the jar.

*This has to be it*, he thought to himself. Without warning, the jar exploded, sending glass to all corners of the room. Once again Hector had managed to fill the room with a smoky stench but this time, Hector's spirits were not downtrodden. Even though he had not witnessed the "blink" phenomenon, he felt the solution was at hand. He would just need to recreate it on a larger scale.

In an unknown timespan that followed, Hector tried his best to recapture whatever magic had taken place inside the empty jar. Failing each time. Using larger and larger mixtures of earth, water, and any fire source he could use. Eventually, he used every form of "fire" stored in the room, save for the Dragon's Breath. Hector even broke down some of the empty shelves and used them as kindling.

As the last embers died on his latest failure, Hector sat on the small hill of dwindling earth at the center of the room. Looking glumly through the thick haze that now clung to the room with no hope of ever filtering out, he began to ponder where he had gone wrong. He had been so sure he was close to the solution. Had seen it with his own eyes.

As low as Hector's spirits had fallen, he had no desire to call out to the Stranger that he conceded. He would live out the rest of his days in this room if that were even possible. With very few options left the Stranger could declare the first trial over and expel him from his sight.

Sitting there, his mind exhausted, Hector allowed his thoughts to drift back to that moment five years before. The wind blowing over the fields. The wind blowing through her hair. The wind...

"Wind", he shouted excitedly. "Not just air, wind!" There had been a magical maelstrom of wind inside the glass jar. That had been the clue and he had missed it. He looked about the room once again. The earth had been provided to him in the center, water on one side, and fire on the other. A wind source had to have been provided as well.

Hector began to search the room once again in earnest. He checked the ceiling, the floors, and every wall he could reach. But there was no clue as to where the wind source could be. Just then he saw the tiny symbols on the opposite side of the pool. He would never have seen them in the dimly lit room if he had not been looking. Even now, he could not make them out clearly. Looking about, Hector found no way of walking around the pool to get to them. There was only one way to cross over.

Hector turned and walked to his small hill of soil, picked up his spade, and began to shovel it into the pool. If he couldn't walk around the pool he would build a bridge to the other side. As he dug, he estimated that it would take the majority of what remained to build his bridge. If he was leading himself to another dead end he would not have enough soil left to continue with the trial. He had just made this an all or nothing attempt.

While shoveling more and more in he began to notice that no matter how much dirt he put in the pool it never overflowed. There had to be some kind of mechanism in the pool that ensured the water maintained the same level. Yet, there was no discernible opening for such a mechanism. *An enchanted pool then*, he thought nodding to himself.

After much work, Hector's bridge was finished. A line of mud with water on either side. The mud was a problem. With the water still sloshing at either side, chances were he would sink into the mud long before he made it to the other side. It would need to dry first but he was no longer willing to wait.

Hector made his way back to the last remaining shelf and carefully removed the Dragon's Breath. Unscrewing the lid, his nostrils were assaulted with a strong stench of brimstone. Hector carefully poured one single drop at the foot of his bridge and quickly screwed the end back on the jar. The one drop immediately began to smolder and Hector quickly ran back to the other side of the room. Running to the workbench he quickly turned it over and took shelter behind it. Almost immediately after, the room was lit up by a spectacular fireball.

Hector looked over the table's edge and found the room half

charred, half in flames. Content that the Dragon-fire had extinguished itself, he righted the workbench and set the jar Dragon's Breath upon it. Leaving it behind, he made his way across the room. It was easier to ignore the stench now. His bridge was now good and dry. The water level on either side had dropped by nearly a foot and was still steaming.

Walking across, Hector was now able to examine the carving and discovered a small slot. It was very small, perhaps the size of a man's thumb. On either side were carvings of two men who looked to be exhaling into the slot. A thought occurred to Hector.

"It cannot be that simple," he said. Taking a deep breath, Hector placed his mouth near the opening and blew into it. He heard a click deep inside the wall, and then silence.

The nest instant, a mighty gust blew out from the slot and Hector was blown onto his back. A roaring wind seemed to magically fill the room. Hector found it a struggle to get back to his feet. All the same, he could not keep the smile off his face. Surely this was the final solution.

The smile faded as he heard a troubling noise behind him. The work bench was caught in the wind and vibrating. And so was the jar of Dragon's Breath.

Fighting against the wind, Hector turned and tried to run towards the table. He quickly found running was not an option as it was all he could do to stay on his feet. He watched helplessly as the table and the jar toppled over.

The jar shattered and the Dragon's Breath ignited instantly. The room was filled with flaming death, and the wind was whipping it all around him. Behind him, the water boiled away almost immediately. The earth became dry and brittle and began to fly around the room. A maelstrom of steam, earth, and fire was engulfing him. Hector stood in the eye of this fiery storm with nowhere to run. He watched powerlessly as this wall of certain death began to now quickly encroach upon him. Hector threw up his arms in a hopeless attempt at protecting himself.

Almost instantly, the room went silent. Hector opened his eyes and found he was in a new room. He checked himself for injuries and found that he was once again clean shaven and there was no sign of dirt, mud, or ash anywhere upon him. His armor and clothing were just as clean. He had survived the ordeal.

"Congratulation Hector, son of Felix," said the Stranger from the other side of this new room. "You have passed the first trial. I must apologize for this test was a cheat. I continued to change the solution to the puzzle while you were inside. Several times, you were indeed on the right path. But as I said, your intelligence and mental ability were not what I was putting to the test. You see, if your quest was any less important to you than you claim, you would have lost heart. Within days you would have given up. Instead, you persevered. Most never endure till the end. Their own comfort and well-being meaning more to them than the one lay dying back home."

"Just like that," Hector asked. "They walk away?"

"For them, it was never about the salvation of their fallen comrade, monarch, or supposed love of their life. Unlike you, they only sought to be seen as heroes. Perhaps even a few of them actually went home lauded for their failed attempt. Anointed heroes while practically standing on the graves of the ones they failed."

Hector nodded and then asked, "What now?"

"We go on to the second trial."

"Which is?"

The stranger in green flashed a rather mischievous smile and answered, "All you have to do is walk through the door behind me."

Hector eyed him suspiciously and asked, "Is this another puzzle?"

"No," he said shaking his head. "Come forward Hector, Captain of the Knights."

Hector started walking towards the Stranger and the door. That was until he saw the silver liquid running like a river across the floor in a wide path.

"Quicksilver," Hector exclaimed.

"It is indeed."

"I thought you said this was not another puzzle."

The stranger did not respond. Instead, he pulled from his pocket what looked to be a silver ball bearing. He cupped it in his hands and whispered into it as if he were imparting a secret. He then allowed it to drop to the floor. It landed with a remarkably loud thud and rolled away from the Stranger. Hector watched as it rolled straightway into the quicksilver stream. A moment later a large shape slowly began to rise and move towards Hector. How could something live in a flowing stream of poisonous quicksilver?

Hector watched as it began to rise and waited for the quicksilver to run off so he could get a look at this marvel. Slowly he began to realize that he was not looking at something covered in quicksilver, but a set of armor so silvery and reflective that it looked just like quicksilver. This Quicksilver Knight rose up and stepped out of the stream with a loud metallic clunk.

He stood a good head and shoulders taller than Hector, who was looking over his opponent for weaknesses. He was shocked to find that there was not one single gap or opening anywhere in the armor. There were no hinges at the joints. There was not even a single slot in the helmet to see through. The armor was one solid piece.

His armaments gave Hector another reason to be apprehensive. In his right hand, he was grasping a heavy broadsword. Heavy being an understatement, the blade was three times the length and at least four times as wide. The weight alone could have probably sliced a man in half by just merely falling over. In the knight's left hand was a shield of impressive size. It was less a shield and more a portable barricade. Its dimensions could have held two burly attackers at bay, much less a normal sized Hector. It would take a mere mortal both hands to wield either of these monstrosities, Hector thought. The sword and shield were of the same silvery material as the armor. Hector could see his reflection clearly in all three.

"It is very simple," the Stranger said calmly as his knight came to a halt. "All you have to do is make it through the door behind me and the second trial ends. Getting past my Quicksilver Knight and this small and insignificant stream of running quicksilver should not be that difficult for Hector, Captain of the Knights."

"A test of strength," Hector said quietly, more to himself.

Across the way the man in green smiled, as he somehow heard Hector's mumble, and answered, "After a fashion," and with those words he vanished, leaving Hector alone with the Quicksilver Knight.

At first Hector did nothing. He did not want to draw his sword and anger his opponent. With an opponent this size, a prolonged fight would not end well for Hector. Just a few blows from that heavy blade upon his light armor would be his end. Since the Knight did not seem to be in any hurry himself, Hector began to walk from side to side. There may not have been any eye slots but the knight was watching him. Wherever he walked, the knight turned his head to follow.

Given that they were, for the moment at least, on neutral terms, Hector decided to survey the room of the second trial. Aside from the knight, the river of quicksilver proposed a definite challenge. Even if he had a running start, Hector doubted he would even make it half way. He had no doubts that the poisonous river was probably as deep as is was wide and he would probably drown. Hector shuddered at the thought of the vile liquid invading his lungs.

For the most part, the rest of the room looked to be a replica of the room of the first trial, only wider, and better lit. As he took note of the tall ceilings, Hector noticed a series of some sort of ledges. They were not very wide, perhaps enough space for two or three paces in either direction. He estimated that they would be just within his reach if he were to jump. They were spaced far enough apart that one could have moved from ledge to ledge with a small jump. It seemed that they were strategically placed throughout the room, or rather around his side of the room. There were none over or on the other side of the quicksilver. Ultimately, what purpose the ledges served was a complete mystery as there did not seem to be any windows or doors above them.

"Naturally," Hector said to himself. "Would not want to make it too easy. It would be too bothersome to provide anything helpful in avoiding the knight altogether."

Sighing, Hector set his attention back upon his large opponent. Keeping his hands free of any weapons, Hector began to walk towards the knight.

"I do not suppose that you and I could be friends," Hector asked smiling. "Perhaps I could take a ride upon your shoulders to the other side of the river?" His smile faded as the Quicksilver Knight's head turned to regard him. Hector imagined that if there was a face on the other side of the faceplate, it was scowling angrily at the suggestion. Hector shrugged and said, "It was just a thought."

Hector's optimism was growing, as so far the knight had merely observed. Perhaps if he did nothing to provoke him he would let him pass. Taking another step closer, Hector learned quickly how wrong that thought had been; as he moved within the knight's considerable range.

The Quicksilver Knight moved with incredible speed and swung his sword at Hector's head. Hector barely had time for an unbalanced duck and found himself sitting on the floor; looking up as the Quicksilver Knight glared down upon him. Quickly, Hector set his feet under him and rolled backward just as his opponent attacked again. The sword landed with a loud clang where Hector had been just a heartbeat before. The floor shook from the impact.

"'Just walk through the door and the trial ends,'" Hector repeated the words of the Stranger after he was standing again. "'That should not be too difficult for Hector, Captain of the Knights.' No, not difficult at all," he added sourly.

As his opponent began to advance, Hector drew his sword. Once he had closed the distance, the Quicksilver Knight swung again. This time Hector was ready and sidestepped the swing.

*Time to test your defenses*, Hector thought at his opponent and went on his own offensive. Starting with his blade in a high guard position, Hector slashed downward, then left, right, up, down again, and then a thrust. The Quicksilver Knight's reflexes were sharp and he parried or blocked each attack. As soon as Hector's counter-attack ended, the Knight immediately went back on the offensive and brought his sword down at his head. Hector raised his sword in an attempt to block the blow. The force of the impact knocked him down to his knees. Unyieldingly, the Knight continued to press down, making Hector use both hands. With one hand upon the pommel and the other grasping the blade, it was all that Hector could do to leverage his opponent's sword harmlessly to his right.

Before the Knight could recover, Hector jumped to his feet and slashed down hard on his armored knee. When his sword bounced off harmlessly, Hector slashed again and again, screaming, until he was winded. Hector looked up to see the Knight just staring down at him, it was as if he was amused at his feeble attack. For a moment they just stood gazing at one another. Then the Quicksilver Knight backhanded him as if he was a troublesome fly. The blow landed with such force that Hector found himself flying across the room, landing roughly, face first, on the floor.

His head foggy, ears ringing, Hector slowly came up to a kneeling position. He became aware of a coppery taste in his mouth and swiped at his face with his free hand. He looked down to see his hand was covered in his own blood. As Hector tried to shake the cobwebs from his head, he became aware of a loud clanging to his right. Looking lazily in that direction, Hector found himself looking into the reflection of his own haggard and bleeding face, just before the Knight's shield slammed into him sending him flying again. His back slammed into a wall, knocking the wind from him.

*He is going to kill me*, Hector thought, gasping for air. *He is going to kill me and Lydia will die unless I can get past him.* He looked up and saw he was under one of the ledges. Gathering what remained of his strength, he leapt up and pulled himself on top of it. This seemed to anger the Quicksilver Knight as he began to run towards him. As his opponent followed below, Hector was able to keep ahead by jumping from ledge to ledge. Occasionally his opponent would swing his sword lazily, trying in vain to make contact.

Taking a breath, Hector was confident he was safe for the moment. But if he did not solve the riddle soon he would never make it across the quicksilver river. Hector wished that he had half the strength of his opponent. He could have jumped across with no problem.

Everything clicked into place. Hector looked again to the Quicksilver Knight and smiled.

Hector began jumping from ledge to ledge again, but this time he was not trying to get away from the Knight. Instead, he was trying to position him. Hector laughed inwardly. This was either going to be a brilliant move or he would be dead. At least he would not be alive to hear the ridicule if it were the latter. He just hoped the knight used his shield and not the sword.

"You want me, you slow clanking excuse of a knight," Hector taunted when the Knight was in the right position. Hector backed up against the wall behind him. Pushing off with his feet, he leapt towards the Silver Knight. His sword raised over his head, he flew at the massive knight screaming. His foe raised his shield to protect his head and Hector half landed, half crashed upon it. At the same moment, the Quicksilver Knight pushed off sending Hector flying again, only this time it was the direction of his choosing.

Once again, Hector crashed heavily to the floor. Again, getting up to his knees, he shook his head trying to clear it. The difference this time being, he was on the other side of the quicksilver river.

Groaning, Hector managed to get to his feet once more. Bleeding and bruised, he looked tiredly back across the river at his opponent. He stood on the opposite bank slamming his sword to the floor in anger. Hector offered him a respectful salute and turned for the door. Sheathing his sword, Hector limped through.

Hector was not shocked when his surroundings changed again the moment he crossed the threshold. Glancing behind, he found the door was gone, but so was everything else.

Hector looked down and found he was standing over a void. Although his feet looked to be resting on nothingness, there was no panic within him. There had to be some sort of invisible floor beneath him or he would be falling and not standing. He looked about and saw nothing but blackness all around him. Despite the total darkness, he could see himself just fine. It was as if there was some sort of invisible light source. With the aid of the mystery light, Hector checked and found that his injuries had melted away the moment he had entered the room. He swiped at his mouth and found no blood.

"Remarkable," he said to himself.

"Congratulations," the Stranger's booming voice echoed behind him. Hector turned to face him and saw that he too appeared to be standing in empty space. "You survived the second trial of the three. I suppose you could say that it was a test of the strength of your character. Most warriors who come here cannot stand the thought of backing away from a fight. Their pride will not allow them to acknowledge that there is someone in the world stronger than themselves. Whereas a balanced knight, as yourself, realize that a strategic withdrawal is sometimes necessary for ultimate victory."

"So they just continue until that brute kills them," observed Hector.

"Oh no, I don't let it go that far," explained the Stranger. "True, I do allow them to get roughed up a bit. But, in the end, I send them on their way with a bump on the head to remind them of their shortcomings."

Hector's mind drifted just then to the stable master back in Bear's Sanctuary, Clovis. *This had been where the Loe Warrior had fallen short*, Hector thought to himself. It was not an accusation, or a thought of superiority. The Loe were known to take much pride in their fighting abilities. If they ever met again Hector would never ask if it were true, but somehow, deep within himself, he already knew it was so.

"And now brave Hector," said the man in green, clapping his hands together. "Are you ready for the last of the trials?"

"I am ready."

"Be sure. Only a handful have ever made it this far. I can assure you, this one will be the most difficult."

"I understand," Hector said.

The stranger mischievous smile faded and was replaced with a sad frown. The bravado was gone instantly, there was no mocking laughter in his eyes. He simply said, in a tone that matched his expression, "No, you do not. But you will brave knight. You will."

# CHAPTER ELEVeN

**Three Weeks Before the Ten-Day War...**

An honor guard of one hundred Knights of the Valley escorted the diplomatic procession as they rode up the Mountain Pass towards Everfrost. An unsanctioned mission for peace. Every last one of them, with the exception of Lydia, could find themselves in the dungeon by nightfall. Galen, his order of Wise Men, not to mention the entirety of the Royal Court, had forbidden Lydia's gambit. As Regent, the Lady of Talwoods would be safe from imprisonment for this act of willful treason until Lucien was crowned in seven months. Then her fate would be decided by the king. Despite his bluster, Hector doubted that Galen had the courage to strip them of their rank and lock them away. How would it look if Lydia came home successful with the very first peace treaty between Valley and Mountain, and the first act was to punish all who rode with her. Similarly, if they rode home with the confirmation that their worst fears had been realized and Everfrost was preparing for war, Becknor would need her captain and best knights to defend it.

They came to the section of the Pass that forked off. The road to the left immediately began its decent down and out of the Mountains. The road right began an ascent towards the snow covered peaks of Everfrost. From here one could look back towards the valley and see Becknor in all her glory. Already much of the farmland was being prepared and tilled up.

In just a few more month the view would be green from the Blood Forest to the south and out across the entire valley floor.

Hector rode side by side with Lydia the entire time. Up till now, she had been silent. She had not asked for him to come personally, just assign a hundred of his best. But how could he not? After so many years, not just as Captain, not as the manufactured position of Friend of the Regent, but as a true friend. It was only a few weeks ago that Lydia called to him with the grave news. As they met by the hidden fountain, he could see the weight of worry upon her even before she had even said the words, "We are defenseless." Now, as Isaac's Hold's best marched east, there were no forces to be spared for Becknor's defense, Lydia had only one choice before her. How could he not ride with her this morning?

Unable to ride by carriage, Galen would have spotted it quickly, Lydia rode on horseback. Wearing a heavy coat, for the Mountain was perpetually freezing, her eyes ever forward, her brow furrowed in deep concentration. Hector elected to allow her this time to rehearse her speech to the Dread Overlord.

The entire escort and procession had gone silent as well. The tension around them was thick, as they rode past the ruins of Barricade Garrison. Barricade was strategically planned and built to stymy any invasion from the Mountain. Fear would see it abandoned just eighteen months after it was built. To all, it seemed a bad omen to today's business.

Not far beyond, the path to Everfrost narrowed. It was a mile stretch that was wide enough for but four to pass side by side safely on foot. On horseback, only two could pass easily. Wordlessly the group spaced out into twos and continued to ride without much pause. Hector found himself with a steep drop to his right and Lydia to his left. He could only imagine what she was thinking now.

"I believe Cecilia may be smitten with you," was not the first words he expected to hear from Lydia's lips.

"Sorry," he managed.

"She blushes every time you are near."

"I do not understand."

"I would say that it might be because she let slip a few weeks ago that she was 'Taken with the handsomeness of the Captain.'"

When he regarded her wordlessly, Lydia looked upon him exasperated. "Cecilia, one of the two maidens appointed to see to my needs. She is my political acolyte. The attendant for all of my private audiences." When he remained silent, she sighed and said, "Tall, long black hair, blue eyes, the type of figure artisans love to sculpt."

Finally finding the words, Hector answered, "Yes, I have taken notice of Cecilia, I am not blind. I just would think at a time like this, your mind would be focused to the task at hand, and not attempting to arrange a marriage."

"I am not trying to arrange a marriage. With the exception of my parents, arranged marriages have gone out of fashion. As for the other, what would you have me do, brood the entire trip up the mountain?"

"Perhaps not brood, but have less a mind inclined towards romance. Especially my own."

"It is not just romance," she said with a sigh. "Do you not think of what comes next?"

"After the negotiations?"

Rolling her eyes and groaning, Lydia answered, "Could you just humor me for a moment. I have rehearsed my words many times now, given thought to every conceivable outcome. I am in need of a momentary distraction. I do not wish to go before the Overlord overly tense. He will misread it as fear. So please, give me a normal conversation, Friend of Regent."

"As My Lady commands," he said. "But I am still unsure of what you mean by 'what comes next.'"

Smiling she answered, "I mean after service. I know you have given your life to the Valley. You once told me you were married to service, that still troubles me. But there will come a day when service concludes. Either it is ended for us or time renders us incapable of serving as optimally as we once could, and must retire, like Vitus. May he find peace with the Divine."

Vitus had unexpectedly passed just weeks earlier. Word was he sat by an apple tree his grandfather had planted, admiring a warm day in late winter. He lapsed into sleep and into the world beyond.

"Just as I answered that day in the stables, I have never planned for what is next. But, I assume you have."

Lydia nodded tiredly and said, "Before this," motioning towards the procession around her, "every day for months. In just over half a year my time as Regent will be over. As the leaves change for autumn and are free to fly away, so will I. For the first time Hector, I can choose where I go, how best to spend my time, the decisions I make affect me and me alone."

"Then perhaps, on that day, you can begin to consider your own suitors and not arranging suitors for others," he said meaning it as a joke. When he saw her look away for a moment he knew he has spoken out of turn.

"I would if I had suitors."

"That is impossible."

"I am afraid it is. I am House Achelon. Last of the House. Those of the right age are forbidden by their elders. A courtship or marriage would be political suicide to those Houses. Those that still hate Achelon control the majority of the Court. I have been approached by others. I can see in their eye what they wish to ask, but they ultimately lack the courage.

They feel as if they are below my station and are unworthy of me. I sometimes wish one of two of them would have followed through."

To his own surprise, Hector had never taken notice of Lydia's situation. As he thought back, other than official business, he had visited with her more than any other man in the Kingdom. In the nearly five years of her Regency, their friendship had grown. He had grown quite fond of that time. They had come to the point of knowing what the other was thinking by just glancing across the room. She was always smiling. Her smile was enough most times to get him through a grueling day. Truthfully, he was unsure now what the end of her regency would mean to him. But on the backside of those thoughts was the question on how did he miss her lack of suitors? How had he missed she was always alone? And why did that now make him glad? Perhaps because, in his opinion, very few were worthy of her. This was plainly obvious by what he saw as the blatant discrimination of the Valley Elite. Inwardly, he grumbled at the House Elders and their blind hatred over century old deeds. Who would not wish to see someone as loyal, wise, and courageous as Lydia be a part of their House? Anyone in the Valley should be so lucky.

Looking over he saw Lydia staring at him. Now she had a worried look.

"Please do not worry over me now."

"How could I not be concerned for my friend?"

"Just because there is a lack of suitors does not mean that I am lonely. Nor does that mean I am waiting for a man to sweep me off my feet, take me away, and we live as happily as they do in the old stories. Happiness is a state of mind. Whether you are surrounded by a hundred of your closest friends or alone in chambers. As my mother once said, 'If you cannot be happy in solitude you will never be happy with thousands.' I have my own life to live and it cannot be based upon waiting on a magical courtship. That being said," she began as she smiled sheepishly, "there is someone."

"Really, might I enquire?"

Looking away in embarrassment, she was actually blushing, Lydia answered, "It would be difficult to explain, especially in the time we have now. I do worry as well, that if I were to explain, you might think me mad."

"How could that be possible? It is not as if you like to walk barefoot through fields of flowers or murder hay bales."

She laughed, placed her hand on her heart and said, "Why would I do such things?"

They fell back into silence. Just ahead the path began to widen again and the riders began to fan out. Before their turn, he heard her clear her throat. He turned to see her smile wryly.

"So, Cecilia?"

Hector chuckled. "What if I told you I was quite happy today? All things considered."

Lydia nodded, looking slightly disappointed, "Who am I to stand before your happiness. Or rather your happiness today. What of tomorrow?"

He considered it for a moment. He turned to see her smiling again. The smile that made many things better.

"Let me have today. Today and this very moment, when all is well. Then we will see what happens tomorrow."

\* \* \* \* \*

Back in the moment, the Stranger clapped his hands again and a new world exploded around him. It came rushing in from the horizon like a mighty wind and filled the void with color, light, and a multitude of fragrances, all agonizingly familiar. He and the stranger were still standing the same distance from one other but they were now in a field of white flowers. A large and lone weeping willow stood sentinel over the scene, the golden light of sunset was bathing the windswept fields in warm light. Hector knew exactly where he was.

"What trickery is this," Hector asked unable to keep the edge out of his voice.

"Behold," the stranger motioned for Hector to look behind him.

Hector knew what he would see, even before he turned his head. There she was, in her white gown, hands outstretched running over the tops of the flowers. Lydia's back was to him just as it had been five years ago, walking through the field as the wind blew her golden locks around her.

"Do you love her," the stranger asked quietly.

"I have answered this question."

"You avoided this question."

"This moment has nothing to do why I am here."

"Then why has this moment in time been at the forefront of your thoughts since you arrived outside of my fortress?"

"It calms me."

"She calms you?"

"Yes. I mean no. You are twisting what I say."

"Perhaps you are twisting how you feel."

Hector turned and faced the Stranger angrily and said, "I am a Knight of the Valley. Even before I rose to the rank of captain, I took the Blood Oath. On the penalty of death, I will protect whoever sits on the throne of Becknor. Be it a king, queen, or regent. What I feel is irrelevant, what this day means to me is irrelevant to my task here. How does what I feel have anything to do with my quest?"

"Look again," said the Stranger. As Hector did, Lydia turned like she did five years ago, but this was not the same face he had seen then. It was not even how she looked when he had last seen her. It was Lydia, but an older version. Her hair was still golden but now there were wisps of white at her temples. Once again she smiled as she looked back, the lightest of lines were just now beginning to show. Her blue-green eyes, were still bright and contented, but now carried the weight of years of experiences both difficult and joyous. Hector knew he was looking at an older Lydia, perhaps twenty years or more into the future, though she was still very beautiful.

As she smiled, she turned and began to walk towards him. Could she actually see him? Had he physically been transported into the future? What was she going to say to him? What would he say?

As he began to contemplate how he would explain all of this, Hector was passed by another man. His clothing was regal, red over white, and his ruby red cloak caught in the breeze as he passed by. He and Lydia approached each other slowly at first, almost as if he were a ghost to her. She then ran to him. Hector watched, as this Dream Man scooped her up and twirled her around. They were both laughing and celebrating as if they were reuniting after a long absence. He set her down and playfully acted as if the very act had tired him. She hit him on the shoulder. The man, whose back was to Hector, was staring upon her. Perhaps looking into her eyes. He reached out to move a wayward strand of hair from her face and gently smoothed it back behind her ear. He moved in to embrace her once more as she lifted her head towards him to impart a kiss.

Hector, feeling awkward, began to look away but stopped as he noted that she began to look away again as they parted. Lydia's eyes lit up once more as three children ran to her. A boy, well on his way to becoming a man, a girl, who had her mother's long golden locks, and a small boy of perhaps five or six. The youngest took the lead and Lydia dropped to her knees and threw her arms open to envelop him into a tight embrace. The

DEFENDERS OF BECKNOR

others fell to their knees and so that they may embrace her as well. She kissed them all furiously before holding them at arm's length so that she might look at them. Tears were streaming down her face as she smiled the brightest and grandest smile he had ever seen from her. Hector knew immediately what he was witnessing. This was a family being reunited. Lady Lydia, or, rather perhaps now, Queen Lydia's family.

"I am sorry Hector," the stranger said quietly, now standing at his side. "I know the Beckish royal court is an eccentric one. Unlike most, they do not arrange marriages or always stick closely to the tradition of classes. I know your Lydia is not a queen or a princess but only a regent, but she is still of royal descent, and it is very likely in the years to come that a king, prince, or lord shall come and request her hand. As captain of the knights, moreover, as her friend, you will have to watch all of this unfold in time. Therefore, I need to know your intentions, brave Hector."

He could barely speak, his throat parched, "My intentions?" The Stranger merely nodded solemnly. Hector looked upon the scene again. "You are testing my heart?"

"Yes," he answered. "Be careful of what you say next for it will determine the outcome of the third trial. But be truthful."

The scene before him stung. There was an enexpected, strange aching in his chest. It was all very difficult to put into words, even for himself. Hector had pledged everything the day he took the Blood Oath, so many promises were made. Every aspect of his life, he was prepared to give in service. That day he gave mind, body, and heart. His mind and will bent to his superiors, his body and life ready to give at any moment, and his heart was for the people of the Valley. Nothing had been retained for himself, for there had been nothing to retain. Including love. Had Lydia changed that? But that was impossible. Was it not?

Watching future Lydia interact with her husband and children caused pain where it should not. The thought of watching this unfold over the course of years was not a pleasant prospect. Hector had used the Blood Oath, the welfare of the people of the Valley, as his reasons for riding out here to face these trials. But saying it was his duty was not enough was it? Had he really risked life and sanity on this quest just because it had merely been his duty alone? Would he not have done the same if she had not been the regent and he a knight? Did the image before him hurt because secretly, even to himself, this is what he had wanted since that day in the field? Had he really come because it was Hector that could not live without Lydia?

Hector's mind began to sift through the images of his life as if he were reading a detailed book. It was divided into three: his life before service, his early knighthood, and Lydia. The moments that formed his first sixteen years, the joys and tragedies, triumphs and sorrows. His first five years as a capable but unremarkable knight devoid of a real life. Then there was Lydia. All memory paled in comparison to the years she had called him friend. She had made him better. A better knight, a better citizen, but more importantly, a better man. Yes, she had done many things for Becknor. But he did not do this for them. His quest truly had been for one person and one alone. As painful as it all was for Hector, he had his answer.

*Let me have today.*

Turning from the vision, he looked the Stranger in the eye, and said, "You have shown me her future, but you have not shown my own. I do not know what the days ahead have for me. In truth, I have not given thought towards tomorrow or the day after. I know only what is to be done this day. If I fail in this task then she dies and this future, her future, is lost. If I did feel like you suggest, then it will be hard watching these things unfold, but it would be harder still in knowing my failure caused her death. How could I live with myself? How could I call anyone else friend if I failed the one closest? How can I reject the one who has helped to make me the man that stands before you today, just because our lives will ultimately diverge? She is more important than any feelings I might have. She deserves to have her future, wherever it leads. I came here for Lydia's salvation and I am still here for Lydia. She must live no matter the cost to myself. Even unto death."

The Stranger clasped Hector's shoulder and said, "There are many who come on this journey seeking not the salvation of another but their own glory. To say that they bravely faced the three trials and secured the Blue Orchid Elixir. Once they arrive and find that there will be no glory, no kingdom of their own, and that the one they love will never be theirs, they turn their back on the quest. That is why so few have ever been granted the Elixir. But they are not you Hector, son of Felix, Captain of the Knights. You have answered my question. And you have answered it righteously. If one momentary defeat means your friend's victory you would gladly take the defeat. There are so few of your kind that walk this world, and that makes you the perfect courier. Congratulations, you have passed the third trial."

A blink and they were back in the study. Only now the room was filled with the sweetest aroma that Hector had ever experienced. In the center of the room, on a special pedestal, was the lone Blue Orchid. It was, overall, a fairly ordinary looking flower. Yes, it was pleasant to the eye but visually it harbored no clue that it was special. But beyond the visual, there was something about this little flower. He felt a soothing deep within his own heart. He could not stop staring. For lack of a better term, the Orchid inhabited the room. It was as if there was a third presence among them. Hector turned to see the Stranger smiling as his reaction. The smile seemed to say, "Yes, I know."

The Stranger left Hector's side and walked to the orchid and began to carefully remove one of its petals. As he did, he spoke soothingly to it in a language Hector had never heard.

"I do have to say, brave knight," he said after finishing his cuts and going to the alchemy table. Hector watched as the petal was already beginning to grow back. "You answered well, but you are not the most truthful."

Hector sighed tiredly. He was very tired of arguing with this man. "I have been truthful with you. Part of the Blood Oath is that a knight of Becknor must always be truthful." *Besides, if you can see into my mind you already know,* Hector added silently.

"Even if it is to your own harm," asked the Stranger.

"Even if it means death."

The Stranger chuckled, and said, "And yet, you have yet to speak the truth. Oh, fear not, you have spoken more truth to me than anyone has in centuries. It is yourself you are lying to, about your Lydia. For whatever reason, you have yet to admit what you feel for her to yourself."

"That is your opinion," Hector said gruffly. "I have said all there is to be said. And it matters little, now that I know her future."

The Stranger turned and smiled as he said, "Do you now? Well, in the spirit of being truthful, you see, when I began my quest here so long ago I made my own Blood Oath of sorts. Part of which was that I would always be as truthful as possible. What you saw was not the future but a kind of educated guess. To see into the future is a Divine gift and I am certainly not Divine. Although it was the most likely future, it is not necessarily the real future. There are many choices to be made before that future is certain."

"What Lydia chooses for her future is hers alone."

"Not her choices, yours," the Stranger said, finishing his work and turning to face him. He walked to Hector with three items in each hand. "Be not stubborn young Knight and allow something precious to be lost."

Hector said nothing in reply. His mind was weary of trials and sermons. Seeming to sense this, the Stranger shook his head and smiled.

"This is the Elixir," he said placing a small vial of blue liquid in Hector's right hand. "This will be more than enough to dispel the curse. The fever should break almost immediately. The Elixir will heal her broken mind as well. While the worst of the effects will be cured, she will still occasionally have terrible nightmares, but with time they will become less and less until one day she will be free of them forever."

He then pressed two gummy balls into Hector's left hand. "These are to help quicken your journey home. Give one to your horse and then eat one yourself. They are called Haste Pills. They are more magical than alchemical and will enable you to ride for three days and three nights solid without a break. You can push your horse well beyond what you feel are his natural limits without fear. The magics within will keep him from harm. These should be enough to get you home, but be warned, the moment you stop moving, both of you will sleep for seven days."

Saluting Hector, he said, "It has been a pleasure Hector, Son of Felix, Captain of the Knights of the Valley. In all the years I have guarded the Orchid, I have never met anyone as determined as you."

Hector decided to chance a question. Since the man had pledged to be as truthful as possible, and Hector had felt doubtful of the visions the Stranger had shown him, he asked: "Might I ask just how long you have really been out here?"

"Oh, since the beginning," the Stranger confided. "Almost two thousand years now. Since I found the Orchid." He walked over to the orchid and began to lightly water it with a can. "I make sure I look upon this land at least once a day to be reminded of what evil we three did. What evil I did. Some days it is more than I can bear. But this little one almost makes this cursed immortality worth it."

He looked down upon the Blue Orchid fondly and said, "Sometimes at night, when I can't sleep, she whispers in my mind and soothes my troubles. Sometimes she sings, and all is right again. Truly, this little one is one of the Divine's gifts to the world. One day, when the land is healed and peace reigns, the lakeside will be filled with her brothers and sisters. And then, maybe I will be allowed to move on."

Realization struck Hector, "You are not just any alchemist. You are one of the Three Crafters. You are the alchemist Aldred Zen-Joffa."

The man history had anointed the King of Lies, looked upon Hector sadly, and said, "Be truthful to yourself brave Hector. Always be truthful to yourself."

Hector blinked and was outside standing in the very spot he had dismounted from his horse. The time of day was exactly as it had been when he had begun his journey to the tower fortress. Lawrence was still saddled as if Hector had never removed it. All around was just as lifeless as before. He turned to the Glass Desert and saw nothing. The tower had vanished as if it had never been there. Hector would have believed that the entire incident was just an elaborate hallucination if he had not been holding the three items the alchemist had given him.

Shaking away the suddenness of it all, and the fresh splinter in his mind, Hector moved quickly. He cut a long piece of fabric from his bedroll and wrapped the vial securely inside to cushion it and set it inside his money purse. He fed one of the gummy concoctions to Lawrence, who resisted at first but ate it in the end. He then ate his and realized immediately why Lawrence had tried to refuse. It was beyond sour and had a gritty, dirt-like center.

Mounting up, Hector looked over at the empty spot the tower had sat one last time. The tower had vanished because its keeper had closed the door, but Zen-Joffa was still watching him. Hector could still feel his eyes upon him from that empty spot. Only now he was not being studied. It was as if the alchemist was wishing him farewell. Hector offered a salute towards the unseen tower fortress and the alchemist within, before turning Lawrence and heading for home.

JACK O CRABTREE

# CHAPTER TWELVE

Zen-Joffa had been true to his word. Neither man nor horse ever felt the need to stop to rest or even take a meal. Hector never once had to urge speed from Lawrence. It was as if the horse beneath him was energized with perpetual supernatural power. He could feel the excitement permeating from his horse. For Hector, those three days and nights were like having perpetually just awakened from a long restful sleep.

Hector retraced his path with ease. They rode hard through the night and was well into the Barrier Forest by morning. Hector took a small measure of satisfaction to see the Gate Keeper on duty. He flashed the man a giant grin as all the Keeper could do was vaguely point his direction as his mouth sagged open.

Just past sunset Hector and Lawrence found themselves just on the outskirts of Bear's Sanctuary. A figure stood in the dying light, it was Clovis. Hector supposed he was hunting. Upon seeing them, the loe let out a tremendous roar and began to run beside them. He directed Hector to ride through the village center. Hector complied. As they approached, Clovis took to the front with two massive leaps and began to climb the side of his stables.

Standing upon the rooftop, Clovis called out in a loud voice, "Awake Bear's Sanctuary. Go forth to your windows, come to your front porches, and witness the brave soul who has accomplished a feat of feats. I give you Hector of Becknor! Knight triumphant!" Throwing both fists in the air, Clovis roared once more.

The remainder of his journey went without incident. Having learned from his mistakes, it was easy to avoid the snares that had beset his journey. By noon of the second day, the Dali Mountains came into hazy view. When they arrived in the late hours of that third night, Hector discovered that his perspective of time had also changed, it felt like just a few hours had passed, not days.

Back inside the Valley, Hector began to notice he had picked up an escort. A growing escort. As he passed by, his knights mounted up and followed. Looking to his right he found himself staring into the grinning face of Darius.

"I have heard much of your deeds," Hector called to him. "We must speak of them soon." As soon as he woke from his weeklong slumber, that was. Darius laughed heartily in response.

Arriving at the Royal Palace, Hector dismounted quickly. Removing the Elixir he called to his knights, "Take Lawrence to the stables quickly. He will slumber for a week the moment he stops." At the great door of the Palace, Hector found Galen waiting for him. Hector handed the Grand Master the vial. Cocking an eyebrow, the Grand Master looked from the Elixir to Hector in disbelief. Coming to himself, Galen and Hector hurried to Lydia's chambers.

"I wish to hear every detail," Galen said as they mounted the steps.

"I fear they will have to wait. The moment I am sure Lydia is well I must return to my cottage. Zen-Joffa's alchemy that aided in my swift return will soon cause me to sleep."

"Zen-Joffa," Galen said coming to a stop and twirling towards Hector. "Aldred Zen-Joffa? Surely not."

"We can debate that later Great One. Lydia is in need," Hector said practically shoving Galen to start moving again.

"But Hector, history tells us that the Three were wicked. Are you certain that we can trust this Elixir?"

Hector struggled for an answer. No, there was no real way of saying one way or another that this was not the elaborate hoax he had once worried over. Then he remembered the Blue Orchid. How its presence filled the room.

"The man, I am not sure, but the Orchid. The Orchid we can trust."

With that, they entered Lydia's room. Galen looked upon Hector as if he had lost his mind. Shaking his head he removed the stopper from the vial and moved to Lydia's bedside. She was in the midst of a fitful nightmare. Her skin looked hot and dry. Hector watched as Galen administered the elixir. Almost immediately she went silent. Her eyes who had been darting to and fro began to slow, as she took one extraordinarily deep breath and let it out in a contented sigh. In the same moment, the fever broke. Within moments she was resting comfortably. The first true rest she had had in weeks.

Departing Lydia's chambers, Hector found both Darius and Helena waiting for him. The latter looked relieved to see him home. As he was about to speak he nearly toppled over in extreme drowsiness. They both caught him.

"I must get to my cottage," Hector told them. "We will speak of these things when I wake in seven days."

"Hector," Galen called to him as he walked away. Hector turned his head but kept moving. The Grand Master said the words that Hector already knew were true, "Lydia shall live." As he sat down on the edge of his bed a short time later, these words comforted him.

"Lydia's future is now secure," he said with a yawn.

The energy was now draining from him and he needed sleep. As his groggy mind began to succumb a thought occurred to him. A thought he would never remember having. In the vision, he never did see the face of that future man.

# PART TWO

# AWAKENING

# CHAPTER THIRTEEN

The few surviving victims of the evil Fever-Sleep Curse, the fortunate few who did not have their minds completely shattered, rarely spoke of the nightmares. The handful that did, spoke of random and perilous, nightmarish landscapes. A place where all your worst fears were played out in excruciating detail. There was no logic, no reason, only fear. For Lydia, the nightmare was far more specific. The dawn of Lydia's affliction began at the end of the tenth and final day of the war.

Dressed in light armor and her golden hair pulled back into a single braid, Lydia stood and watched from the Grand Viewing Tower as the streets below were overrun by goblins. She watched as Hector sprung a trap of his own. Feeding through the narrow cobblestone streets, the large Everfrost forces quickly became bottlenecked as archers from above rained down arrows. She watched on as Hector ordered his street level Knights to charge.

Satisfied that Hector had everything, momentarily at least, in hand, Lydia turned from the window to make final preparation for her coming visitor. She had not walked ten paces before the tower shook from a loud clap of thunder behind her. There was no doubt in her mind what she would find as she turned to regard her foe.

He stood before her: pale, frosty skin; black eyes; and long dark hair that laid upon his broad shoulders. His blackish green armor dully reflected the last light of the day coming through the windows. The smile upon his face was more predatory than cordial.

"If death had been your true desire, My Lady, all you needed to do was request it when you came before me weeks ago," he said smoothly. "I would not have had you beg, for very long." All the while he never broke his gaze from her. His seemingly unblinking black eyes gazed deeply into hers.

"Death is the last thing I desire," she answered returning his stare unflinchingly. It would take far more than a look from those soulless eyes to unnerve her. "I wish to see no death at all, yours included. But, because of your lust for land, blood, and glory, and since you will not see reason; for there to be peace, I'm afraid your life's end has become a necessity."

"Perhaps," he conceded. "Though not terribly likely."

For the first time, he broke his stare and strolled towards one of the many long open windows and looked down upon the city. The sounds of clashing swords, battle cries, and screams of agony could be heard clearly through the window. He stood for the longest time, oblivious to the sights and sounds of war. It was as if he were merely a benign visitor admiring the city and landscape beyond.

"My ascension to the throne has been a laborious, decade-long struggle," he continued. "I have faced many open challenges, dueled with exceptional warriors, faced many assassins and done my fair share of assassinating. Someone, such as yourself, who had the throne handed to them to keep warm until the rightful heir comes of age is of no real threat to me. You Beck and your outdated customs."

"And yet we Beck," she spat back the ancient goblin insult for the people of the Valley, "and our outdated customs are still alive and well despite your best efforts. Tell me, just how many of your supposedly dreaded Dread Lords have we outlived now?"

If her words angered him in the slightest, she could not tell. He gave no visible sign of irritation. He continued to smile and look out upon the battle below. His only response was to change the subject.

"Ah, I see your champion down below," he said conversationally. "The Captain of your heroic knights. I was impressed how he stood tall and boldly at your side as you spoke so passionately about the possibility of peace between our peoples. I will confess, if you had not been a descendant of Achelon the Accursed; I may have been dissuaded from my current course."

Lydia frowned, being the last descendant of Achelon was the one and only reason the ruler of Everfrost had come for her. "Achelon only acted in desperation," Lydia said calmly. "He wanted the only thing I ever wanted. A lasting peace."

"Say that to my forbearer who watched helplessly as his people were slaughtered on the floor of this valley by a legion of Isaac's Holds best soldiers," he said darkly as he took notice of the flower pot at his elbow. As he began to inspect it, Lydia tried not to stiffen. Without a word he took a handful of the soil and began to rub it between his hands. If he investigated the contents more closely...

Looking below again he said, "You should see your Champion in action My Lady." He sniffed the soil in his hands and nodded in approval. "A brave one your Hector, good strong name, he faces one of my best even as we speak. Quite the skilled warrior and commander. If it were not for the unfinished business between us, I would have liked the honor of spilling his blood with my own blade."

Dropping the soil and bringing his hands up to his face dramatically he said in a mock sad tone, "Oh, how unfortunate. His shield has shattered. Shoddy craftsmanship no doubt." Turning to regard her with a smile of razor sharp teeth he asked, "That look of concern in your eye, he is more than just a champion to you, yes?"

"He is my friend," she replied calmly.

He shook his head in what looked to be true bewilderment and said, "So strange. I would have thought by now that you would have known that the likes of us can never afford the luxury of friends. Family, friends, lovers, are at best liabilities that place us in harm's way, and at worst rivals and traitors. The ones we trust the most are the very ones who twist the blade as they plunge it into our back. Todays' ally is tomorrow's foe. If you had lived past this day you would have seen for yourself. You would have awakened one day and found that the man that you had put your trust in was nothing more than the stranger you never knew at all."

Lydia held her peace. He was trying to play with her emotions. She would not give him the satisfaction of hearing even the slightest stress in her voice. Yet, his smile deepened at her silence, as if it were a victory.

Turning back towards the window again he continued his commentary, "Quite the show of strength. Your Hector has bested the brute before him and bought himself a few more minutes of life. Tell me, are you really ready to die for every last one of your kingdom? And I do not just speak of the Captain and his extraordinarily brave Knights. Would you also die for the cowards that even now hide in the shadows? Would you end everything you could have been for the weak, the infirm, and all those who have no ambition past what today may offer?"

"Yes," she said almost at once. "I do not expect one who has murdered his way to the throne to understand. These people were given to me to watch over. Every last one is my responsibility."

"What a marvelous backward view of the world," he answered. "Behold the greatest example of why your kingdom is so weak and easy to conquer. The weak were made to serve the strong. This is why their numbers are so great. They live and die to ensure that our greatness survives. We do not bleed for such, they bleed for us."

With that, he turned his back to the window and began to walk towards her. Lydia, backing away, matched each of his steps with a step of her own. The Overlord was much taller than she had remembered upon their last meeting. Then again, he had been seated upon his icy throne that day. Slowly he began to work the fingers of both hands as he whispered to himself. Before long, both hands, from wrist to fingertip, began to glow with a menacing red light. Coming to a stop, he slowly brought them up to chest level.

"But I must say, My Lady, if you truly wish to bleed for your people, then you may bleed for mine as well." The words were barely out of his mouth as angry red energies leapt from his hands and crackled their way across the tower towards her.

Lydia, more out of reflex than design, threw her right arm up to protect herself. The energy swirled around her like a vortex. A moment later, the swirling rays of magic began to be drawn towards the bracelet on her wrist. More accurately, the small walnut sized crystal mounted on top of it. A handful of heartbeats later and the crystal had completely absorbed the goblin's attack. Only a strong acrid stench clinging to the air gave any hint of what had just transpired. Moving quickly, Lydia worked to remove the bracelet before the crystal could burn through to her wrist.

"A focus stone," the Dread Lord said, sounding and looking impressed. "Very time consuming and expensive to make. Most alchemists work their entire lives and never master their many intricacies."

"True," Lydia answered. She held the now scorched and burning remains of her bracelet by the last cool piece. "But this is no mere focus stone," she said hurling the remains towards him. It flew true but the Dread Lord smiled as he put a glowing hand out to catch the gem. Just before the glowing crystal made contact with his hand, it exploded. Lydia turned her face away as the blast sent the Dread Lord flying backwards. She heard a painful groan escape from him. Looking up she found that he had been thrown back into the stone wall behind him, barely missing the very open window he had been standing moments earlier by mere inches. The goblin wobbled on his feet for a moment, but did not go down. The center of his chest piece was dented noticeably by the force of the explosion. The remainder of his armor was pockmarked by the crystal's remains.

Lydia, her ears ringing from the explosion, said, "I have been growing crystals since I was nothing more than days out of the crib. My mother was an accomplished alchemist and a fine mentor in her own right. Now," Lydia said smiling as she drew a short sword hidden at her back with yet another crystal mounted to its hilt, "Shall we see which of us will truly bleed today?"

The Overlord smiled viciously at her from across the room before drawing his own sword and launching his next attack. And so began their duel for the Valley.

Lydia was no master in the art of swordplay. Her tutelage in the matter had emphasized self-defense. If the goblin had been truly content in ending her quickly, the Dread Overlord had needed only to press his superior blade skills and the fight would have ended within minutes. What sword attacks he did employ were well within Lydia's meager knowledge of defensive postures. Easily she parried his swings, used his towering height and size against him to leverage even more powerful blows away. Using the architecture of the Viewing Tower, Lydia did her best to frustrate him by ducking behind stone pillars, vaulting over wooden benches, and using a series of small, hidden inner chambers to recover her strength.

In the end, it seemed the master of the goblins was more intent on drawing out the fight and attempting to inflict as much non-lethal pain upon Lydia as possible. He was toying with her. Either for the sake of taking great joy in her pain or perhaps wear her down and break her spirit before breaking her physically. Maybe both. As more than one of his agonizing spells made its way through her defenses, it was all she could do to push the pain from her mind and stay on her feet. For her trap to work, Lydia had to keep moving.

As night quickly fell, Lydia was forced to counter attack more and more with everything she had left. Alchemical traps and potions delayed the Dread Overlord but did not stop him. If anything it made him angrier, causing him to launch more of his deadly magics. Precisely what Lydia wanted and needed. To win their duel she intended to use his magics against him. The exact same way she had survived the goblin's opening attack.

The Blooming Death. Throughout the top of the viewing tower, Lydia had set clay pots, just like the one that the Dread Overlord had inspected upon his arrival. Each was filled with the richest, but very ordinary, soil from the valley floor. But it was what was had been buried in that soil, a set of special grown flower-like bulbs, that the Overlord's doom had been written.

The bulbs were designed to stay suspended between a state of inert seed and germination until brought into the presence of magical energies. In the presence of a magic user foolish enough to cast spells amongst them, the bulbs would feed upon the magics like a natural fertilizer. Once fully charged, the extra unneeded energy was bounced back randomly and unfocused unless they were in the presence of a radiance stone. Much like the remains of the one now embedded in the armor of the Overlord.

As the moon became visible through the tower windows, the Dread Lord launched a magical attack of sharp ice shards only to see them turn back and strike him in the shoulder.

"What treachery is this," he painfully exclaimed. As he removed the ice, the clay pots began to glow and pulsate with red and white light. The tower began to hum with power as the lights began to pulse quicker and merge. Outside, the sounds of war ceased as all eyes were now undoubtedly upon the Viewing Tower.

Swiftly the power within the bulbs focused on the Dread Overlord. As the red and white light began to envelop him, expand and blossom like a flower, the goblin screamed in agony. Lydia turned and dove to the floor for cover, throwing her arms over her head. Almost immediately the entire room was engulfed in light and a terrific explosion rocked the tower.

As debris crashed around her, Lydia slowly stood. Taking stock of herself, she seemed uninjured, despite the singed and dented armor. At some point during the duel, her hair had come undone and was now hanging limply around her shoulders. Breathing heavily, she rearmed herself with her discarded short sword and took in her surroundings.

The roof of the Viewing Tower had been blown away. The floor seemed intact and sturdy as Lydia gingerly tested each step before moving on. At the room's center, or rather now the roof's center, amongst the smoldering remain of benches was the Dread Overlord. She attempted to observe her nemesis from afar but she could not tell his condition. Cautiously Lydia approached until she was standing almost directly over him. She studied his motionless form. There was no discernable sound or breath coming from him. Death, it seemed, had taken him.

The sound of approaching footsteps caught Lydia's attention and she turned to see Hector. His face was smudged and his short brown hair was soaked with sweat. The armor that had been pristine at their last meeting was now dented and scarred. His helmet was missing, and in its place was a nasty looking bump on the side of his head. Though he and his armor had seen better days, the most important fact was that he was alive and well. But as relieved as she was to see him still among the living, Lydia could not help but smile seeing his grey eyes go wide with both worry and awe as he took in the remains of the Viewing Tower.

"The day is won," she said trying to catch her breath. "Victory is ours."

Without warning, an arm wrapped around her waist painfully tight and she felt herself leaving her feet. Lydia was being pulled back into a tight embrace by the Dread Overlord. She could feel his chin resting on the top of her head as he grabbed onto her right arm with his free hand. Squeezing her wrist, Lydia called out in pain as she dropped her only remaining weapon.

"No, My Lady, victory is mine," he said his voice painfully strained.

Time itself seemed to slow to a crawl. The Goblin moved his head to the side so that he might whisper in her ear. Across the way, Hector, a look of desperation in his eye, went for the dagger at his belt.

Then the Overlord of Everfrost, his voice dripping with venom, whispered, "Sleep and burn." With these words, the Overlord's hands became hot like furnaces. She could feel the heat beginning to seep into her from his hands at her arm and waist. As his grip loosened Hector let loose his blade. Lydia felt her feet once again touch the floor as Hector's dagger found its mark. But Lydia, if there had been time, could have told her friend his attack had been useless. The magic arts were a pathway to power, but at a grave cost. To cast spells drained one of their life force. The more powerful the spell, the less time you have on the back end of your life. The most powerful Abyssal Curses required everything. The Dread Overlord had used the last of his life energies to cast one such curse.

The burning heat began to work its way quickly throughout her body. She felt chilled and feverish all at once. Lydia looked worriedly to Hector but had no time to speak., as a deep unnatural drowsiness was over her. She felt herself beginning to sway in place. Her eyelids had become too heavy, and as they closed, she felt herself fall. Fall into a world of misery and pain.

Lydia had become a victim of the Fever-Sleep Curse.

# CHAPTER FOURTEEN

If Lydia had been of sound mind, she would have not been surprised by the reoccurring nightmare that the Curse brought to her. It was the waking nightmare from which she could never wake. The moment her once secure place in the world had been ripped away and would forever mold her future. It was the day of the fire.

It always began with Lydia opening her eyes. It was truly the most insidious part of the nightmare, the waking. For the semi-aware adult Lydia, each time her eyes opened anew it came with the hope that this time, she had truly awakened. This time, she would be back in her chambers in the Palace. Becknor would be at peace, and she would find Hector later and have a long talk about the strange set of dreams she had that night. But those hopes would be dashed the instant she recognized her surroundings. The moment her eyes took in the home that was now thirteen years gone.

Eight-year-old Lydia, daughter of Marcus, Lord of Talwoods, woke to excited thoughts Thoughts of a day that promised as much excitement that any eight-year-old could absorb. Today was the final day of the Spring Festival. The one day out of the seven that all who dwelled within the valley looked forward to each year. It was the day of the closing ceremonies and Lydia's father would be officiating.

But more importantly, it would be the first time in months she would have seen her parents. Both had departed shortly before the

Mountain Pass had became snow covered to speak with representatives from the Alliance of the Four Greater Kingdoms.

With the help of her governess, Lydia dressed quickly. She wore her best white gown, the one her mother loved so well, with matching ribbons in her hair, ribbons her father had given her. She looked in the mirror and found the little blonde girl with blue-green eyes staring back familiar yet wrong.

*No, this reflection is wrong,* the semi-aware Lydia thought to herself. *I am a woman grown, not a child.*

Looking at her own reflection again, she could not help but see the beads of perspiration spreading across her forehead. The semi-aware Lydia knew this too to be wrong. The day had been a cool one.

The sound of horses in the courtyard broke into her thoughts and little Lydia of the past took over again. The child she had been that day bolted through the door of her chambers, nearly knocking over her governess.

"Sorry," Lydia called back as she ran for the stairs. She could just make out the harsh words of her governess to slow down as she bounded down the curved stairs and made for the double doors.

There, in the courtyard, was the carriage that would take them to the fairgrounds. A team of strong, magnificent white horses were already hitched to the carriage and ready to go. The carriage was in the traditional Becknor color of blue trimmed in silver. On its door was the emblem of Talwoods: two tall and mighty trees on either side, standing guard over a field and a winding river.

For the semi-aware Lydia, everything before her was so vivid. Right down to the sounds of the horses' hoofs on the gravel roadway. The sun gleaming off the top of the carriage, the early spring fragrance of the rain from the day before. The lazy, early spring breeze coming off of the mountains to the west. Everything to the last detail, as if she had actually been transported back to the day itself. Which made the next thing to catch her eye the more heart wrenching.

Standing to the side, grinning, looking tall and magnificent in his dark blue coat with the big gold buttons and trousers was her father. After such a long absence, Lydia was unable to contain her excitement as she ran to him. On her approach, he went down on one knee and scooped her up into his strong arms in one motion.

There were no words to describe what it was like to be held by her father once more. As heartbreaking as the next few weeks would be to have to relive this day over and over, this one moment was special. A moment of respite in a cruel storm. To feel his arms around her, to feel the hairs of his sandy colored beard pressed against her face, a moment in time more precious than any treasure the world had to offer.

"It would appear that someone is excited for the day to begin," he said giving Lydia one more squeeze before setting her down.

"You made it here for the ceremony!"

"Certainly my sweet child," he said. "I had a promise to keep, did I not?"

"The people would be disappointed," she said with a nod.

"That is true my child, but the more important promise was to you. I could never break a promise to my favorite daughter."

Lydia squinted at her father and said shaking her head, "But I am your only daughter."

Grinning broadly he said, "And that is why I can afford to play favorites."

Lydia looked about the Courtyard searching for another familiar face. She could not keep the frown at bay when she did not see her.

"Where is mama?"

"She is not coming today," her father said looking slightly sad at the news himself. "She is feeling poorly from the journey home. She has gone straight to her chambers to rest. But take heart, you will see her tonight for dinner."

Little Lydia suppressed the urge to turn and run for her mother, and greet her properly. As strong as the pull was, she kept her feet planted where they were. Running off would have made them late for the ceremony and if her mother was ill best to let her rest. A decision she would regret forever.

Back on his feet, Lord Marcus could not keep the smile from his face when he added, "I do have a surprise for you this morning. We will not be traveling alone, as an old friend is joining us."

With those words an elderly man stuck his head out of the side of the carriage. He was well past ninety but his brown eyes held as much youth as Lydia's. His white hair was short and his beard neatly trimmed. He smiled brightly, showing off teeth just as white as his hair. Lydia would have recognized his face anywhere. The man she loved just almost as much as her parents.

"Master Nicodemus," she exclaimed running and jumping into the carriage to wrap her arms around his neck. "My very first teacher," she said, her customary greeting.

"Little Lydia, my final student," he whispered his customary retort back to her as he returned the hug.

"You are well again." Nicodemus too had been absent from her life for more than a month. A late winter cold had forced her teacher to stay home at his old farmhouse.

"I may be advanced in years, but no sniffle of the nose could keep me down for long. I hope that you do not mind that it is me and not your mother who is accompanying you today."

"How could I ever mind being in your company teacher," she said, climbing into the seat next to him.

Once they were all aboard the driver urged the horses on. As they drove away Lydia looked back at her home. In just one month Castle Talwoods would have been the most beautiful place in all of Becknor. The flower beds would grow and bloom, the two mighty cedars on either side would be green and full, and the ivy on the castle walls would fully leaf out. Just before they crested the last hill outside the gates, Lydia saw her mother, Lady Anastasia, in one of the upstairs windows. No mistaken her similar white gown and long golden hair. Lydia waved and was pleased to see her mother wave back.

She sat back into her seat and sighed contently. This was going to be a good day after all. Even despite the oppressive heat.

*What heat? It was cool and damp that spring.*

A short while after Talwoods had moved out of sight, Nicodemus asked her father, "Was your journey a success, My Lord?"

The smile that had been ever present on her father's face faded and he answered, "Not entirely. The Affairs of State tied up rather nicely. I dispatched a courier to my cousin the King informing him that Valley wheat and grains will fetch a nice profit for the next decade. Isaac's Hold is stockpiling again. Preparing for wars that never come. Our personal errand was another matter entirely. It was yet another set of fruitless inquiries. I am beginning to believe you and Anna are right. Perhaps it is a riddle best left lost to antiquity."

Breaking eye contact with Nicodemus, Lydia watched her father look out the carriage window. A strange look was upon his face, one she had never seen before, as he watched the rolling hills of the valley move past.

"Our people's thinking may still be backward, but the fact we have changed little in two millennia is, at times, a comfort."

There had been many more words exchanged by her elders, but little Lydia had paid them no mind. The adult world was always weighed down by responsibilities and secrets.

The carriage approached the Becks-Dali River, the mighty river that cut through the entire valley. The river was swollen by the late winter rains. The deep muddy waters moved swiftly around the seat of Becknor power. In the shadow of the eastern slopes of the Dali Mountains, the Becks-Dali River, named for the mountain range and the valley nestled within, split into two branches for several miles before reforming. In the center of these branches was an "island." It was here, that the early Valley-Dwellers moved their center of government once Everfrost began their military campaigns. It was believed that the river would provide some protection. If only they could have seen how wrong that thought would prove to be.

Lydia watched as the carriage passed over the Gateway Bridge, and onto the circular cobblestone road known as the Circuit. It was the only road upon the "island" running through the seat of Becknor power and commerce. The Royal Palace, the Barracks of the Knights of the Valley, the City Citadel, and at the center was the fair grounds.

Long lines of people, horse drawn wagons, and carriages were making their way onto the fairgrounds for the Spring Festival. Tall banners were caught in the breeze, grand colorful tents had been set up for the carnivals, tables and booths lined the way marking the grand bazaar, and games everywhere the eye could see. But of all the attractions and distractions to be offered this day, only one thing was on everyone's mind. The Closing Ceremony.

Lord Marcus strode confidently to the center field flanked by two men wearing bright red long coats and trousers. It would be her father's honor to close the Spring Festival this year. The trio made their way towards a small mound of freshly dug soil. The man on his right was carrying a silver spade and the man on his left was carrying a small ornate box. Marcus came to a stop just behind the small hill and looked over the crowd.

Most of the Royal Family would have taken this time to make long drawn out speeches, before performing what was known as the Ceremonial First Planting. In the ceremony, one single grain of wheat would be planted within this very mound by a selected member of the Royal Family. Afterward, they would take a handful of earth and toss it into the air. If it fell back straight away it would be seen as an ill omen for the coming year and the harvest would be weak. But if the dust was caught by the breeze and flew away, then it would be a good year and the harvest would be Divinely blessed.

The crowd began to murmur excitedly as Lord Marcus elected to forgo the speech, and held out his hand for the spade. He carefully dug a small hole and then, going on one knee, held out his left hand. The man with the box carefully opened it and removed a lone wheat seed and placed it in Marcus' hand. Carefully, he planted the seed and covered it over with one hand. It seemed as everyone on the fairgrounds was holding their breath in anticipation. As Marcus finished patting the soil he scooped up a handful from around the edges. Standing, he looked over the crowds smiling. Lastly, he found his daughter in the front row. Locking eyes on her, he winked and he threw his handful of earth high into the air without breaking eye contact. A deafening cheer went up as a gust of wind blew in, sending the dust throughout the valley. This was to be a good year.

The ceremony now concluded, the crowds began to disperse and make way for the other attractions, well pleased with the results. Lydia waited patiently as her father was stopped frequently to exchange pleasantries with other members of the royal family, nobles, prominent farmers, and merchants. After a few moments more, Marcus successfully detached himself from the crowd and back to his daughter and her teacher. The latter chuckled upon his approach.

"Fine speech," offered Nicodemus.

"I really had no time for one," he said smirking. Cupping a hand to his ear he added, "If you listen closely, my cousin, Stephanos, has yet to finish last year's speech."

Looking down upon his grinning daughter, he asked, "More importantly, did the ceremony meet with little Lydia's approval?"

"It was the greatest," she answered enthusiastically.

Looking towards Nicodemus, Marcus said, "You see. It matters little if you are remembered for your great words or lack of them. You can gain no greater praise than from your own child."

Lydia's father escorted her from one corner of the fairgrounds to the other. The remainder of the day had been for her alone. She had seen the jugglers, the fire eaters, the strange and magnificent animals from the Outer World. She had sampled wonderfully smelling and tasting foods. But it was the closing ceremonies that Lydia would have always remembered. That is if the day had ended differently.

It was on the carriage ride home when all began to see signs that something was amiss. There was a strange thickening haze on the horizon accompanied by an angry orange glow to the south as the sun was just beginning its final descent to the west. As the carriage approached home, the scent of smoke began to waft in from the windows. Silence fell upon the three travelers. A look of deep concern slowly began to crease her father's face the moment the carriage crested the final hill. Talwoods lay before them, engulfed in flames.

The carriage driver came to an immediate stop. The sound of

crashing structure and shattering glass echoed across the countryside. Fire and smoke seemed to be billowing out of every window, the nearby stone scorched. The dry ivy on the outside wall was withered into nothing. Even the cedars themselves were in flames.

Lydia followed as her father stumbled from the carriage and onto the grassy roadside. Behind her, she could hear Nicodemus recounting an ancient prayer.

"No," her father whispered, "Anna." Seemingly forcing his legs to work, Lydia watched as her father ran for the inferno. As she tried to follow a hand grabbed her by the arm and held her in place.

"Let me go, I must follow," she protested then cried out for her father.

Hearing her protests, Marcus turned briefly and called back, "Nicodemus, keep Lydia with the carriage. Keep her safe."

Both little Lydia and Nicodemus watched helplessly as her father made his way inside. Their vigil was short lived, their horror grew as the front of the castle began to fall in upon itself. The double doors fell from their hinges and rolling flames shot immediately from the opening. Lydia tried to call out but had not the voice to do so. Slowly she felt herself being turned away from the carnage by Nicodemus. She would have fought him but the strength had left her. She would always remember the sound of the stone falling in upon itself as Talwoods died.

This was the only nightmare the curse brought to her. The moment Nicodemus turned her away, and the sound of the crumbling walls subsided, the dream would begin anew. Waking, the heat of the fever, the carriage ride, the fair, the ride home, the fire, waking, the carriage ride, the fever increasing, the fair, the ride home, the fire. No relief, no respite.

By the time Hector returned with the Elixir, the Fever-Sleep Curse had nearly finished its work. For weeks Lydia watched as her parents died over and over. How long can one endure so much pain before death becomes preferable to existence? Lydia's mind was nearly broken from grief and the oppressive heat of the fever. She was even beginning to believe she was seeing new details in the memory. Movement in one of the upstairs windows. A kind of reflected light. But it was just her broken psyche, was it not?

Despite the darkness of what she was beginning to pray would be her last hour, regardless the horror and brokenness of her mind, she knew the exact moment the Blue Orchid Elixir had been administered. Her mind interpreted it like this:

As Nicodemus turned her away from the horror one last time, all went dark. She thought, *At last, death has come. I shall now walk the Halls of the Divine and be reunited with my parents.* The moment the thought had finished its journey across her mind she knew it was wrong. For starters, she could still feel her chest expanding and contracting with each new breath. Does a ghost breath? As she lay there in the darkness, a cool breeze began to flow across her. It was the most heavenly thing she had ever felt. And then came the man. The man she loved, or rather, would one day love.

Shortly after the day of the fire, Lydia would begin to have a reoccurring dream. A dream of a future man. He was tall, his arms strong. He was always dressed regally in white trimmed in red. A ruby red cloak always trailed behind him as it hung off his shoulders. There was an air about him that put her in mind of nobility. Never in the dreams was she permitted to see his face, but she knew he always wore a smile upon his hidden features. A smile always meant for her. From the first dream Lydia believed he was a man from her future. Knowing how fantastical it would sound, and so very much a child's dream, it was a revelation she kept to herself. She did not know how she knew he was real, only that he was out there waiting.

This time, he appeared to her carrying a goblet. Its contents produced a cool, blue light. The light was weak and illuminated everything but the face of the Dream Man.

Still lying on the ground, Lydia tried to stand and meet him but there was no strength within her. Placing a hand on her shoulder he silently urged her to sit and rest. He never spoke audibly to her but she always knew what he wished to communicate.

With the other hand, he offered her the goblet. She took it from his hand and sipped from it experimentally. It was the coolest, sweetest water she had ever tasted. Her parched throat opened instantly and she could feel the coolness sweep over her entire body. Quickly, she drained the rest of the goblet and slowly the blue glow began to vanish. A moment later the glow returned but it was now emanating from her as she felt her fever break.

She looked up as the Dream Man's hand reached for the empty goblet and took it away. Without a word he reclined next to her, even this close his face was hidden from her. Running his hands through her hair she felt the strangest sensation. She felt very drowsy. How can one fall asleep while already asleep? Regardless of the unanswered question, Lydia's eyes closed and she seemed to drift away in the Dream Man's arms; both of them caught upon a cool breeze.

* * * * *

An unknown time later, Lydia woke. She looked up to see the face of Galen looking down upon her. His hand at her brow.

"Very good," he whispered. "The fever is gone."

Lydia opened her mouth to ask what had happened but could not make a sound.

"Save your strength, My Lady," he told her. "You have been through quite the ordeal these past weeks. The Dread Overlord meant to kill you with a curse. But you have been saved thanks to a very courageous knight."

With no voice, Lydia mouthed the word, who? Even though she knew the answer before she had even attempted to ask.

Galen laughed lightly as if it were obvious and answered simply, "Hector."

Lydia closed her eyes and smiled. Of course, it was Hector. Who else would move the world to save her? Her mind drifted back to their first meeting five years ago. It was in a field of flowers of all places. There she was, the future Regent of Becknor, walking barefoot in a field with her eyes closed. Letting her hands skim the top of the field and relishing the feel of the breeze upon her face. The carriage driver alone thought she had lost her senses. But no one would have understood even if she had told them the truth of why she was in that field.

And that was how the future Captain found her, she could still see the comically puzzled look upon his face. That was the day their friendship had been born. She thought of it often. Somehow it always made her heart glad. Without fail. Even now as she drifted off to sleep, she thought of Hector and that field. And the wind, that gloriously cool and relaxing wind in her hair.

# CHAPTER FIFTEEN

Elyssa of Green Plaines was rushing through her home packing whatever she felt she would need into her satchel, before returning to her brother's cottage. There was little time. So when the slight, but steady knock persisted; she let out an exasperated sound as she ran to open the door. She was a heartbeat from giving whoever this ill-timed visitor was what for. Instead, once her eye fell upon the frowning face of her neighbor, with Elyssa's son in tow, she let out a tired sigh and joined her in a frown.

"What damage?"

"I dinn'a do it," her son, Myron, exclaimed immediately. Elyssa gave her son a withering stare. Immediately his eyes turned downward. Only five-years-old and he was trying the collective patience of his family to the point that six did not seem terribly likely.

Ellanora, her closest neighbor and mother of Myron's main cohort in crime, merely responded by holding the remains of two of her very own handcrafted flowerpots. Flower pots that Ella made in her own spare time for herself, as neighborly gifts, and sold in the markets for extra coin.

"How many," Elyssa asked.

"All of my latest batch."

"All," she shouted giving her son an even harsher stare.

"Oh, he had help," Ella said looking to either side and seeing nothing. "Sara," she called out shrilly. A few yards behind Ella, from

191

around one of Elyssa's trees, a tiny little head stole a glance and then hid again. "Though it seems that neither can agree on which did the deed.

Looking down at her son again she asked, "What did I tell you this morning?"

Myron answered the question as he always did, "Get out'a bed."

"After that," Elyssa sighed impatiently.

"Go out to the field with papa and stay there because you were too busy visiting uncle Hector." He looked up at their neighbor and said, "He sleeps all day and is very lazy lately. Mama really should stay here and keep an eye on me like papa says."

"Stop trying to change the.... Oh, he says that, does he. You just rewarded your father with a whack from the skillet," she said using her husband', Byron, tired, old joke. Her husband loved to tell people that she regularly abused him with her heaviest skillet. He knew it irritated her and would glance her way each time he told it with a devilish gleam in his eye. It did not help that she had actually knocked him unconscious once by accident when they were courting.

Though she would probably feel guilty later (probably), the words had their desired effect on her very impressionable son. Taking the words to heart, he looked up at his mother with equal parts horror and guilt at the "punishment" he had brought upon his father. Myron at last fell silent.

Looking back to Ella she said, "I will make reparation later, if you do not mind. Today is the seventh day."

Immediately her demeanor changed and Ella asked excitedly, "Hector wakes today?"

"Yes," Elyssa said flashing a big grin. "I would not miss my brother waking for anything in this world. And as for you," she said looking upon her sulking son, "You are coming with me."

\* \* \* \* \*

*I never*, were the first words Hector's groggy mind remembered as he moved towards waking. His mind seemed to repeat them as if they were part of some puzzle. *I never. I never what?* The answer remained elusive. It seemed to be the fragment of a thought. One that had seemed important but was now lost.

As much as his mind seemed to be caught up with the meaning of these two simple words, they were not responsible for bringing him out of sleep. It was his long hardened battle senses that had served him well in his years of service. They were telling him he was not alone. It was then, just on the edge of waking, he heard a voice repeating a set of words that had been spoken to him not that long ago.

"Always be truthful."

Hector's grey eyes shot open and he sat up like a bolt of lightning. His hand grabbing in vain at his side for the sword that was not there. Hector looked down to see his armor missing as well. He was dressed in a simple tunic. He took in his surrounding expecting to catch a glimpse of a mysterious bald man dressed in green, or a musky chamber filled with earth and water, or worse yet, an impossibly tall Quicksilver Knight, bringing his heavy blade down upon his head. Instead, Hector's confused mind found that he was sitting in bed, his bed. He was home, in his cottage not far from the Barracks. The one thing his senses had correctly sensed was that he was not alone.

Seated in a chair at the foot of his bed was a raven hair woman just a few years older than him. She held in her lap a boy of no more than five years. Confused as he was, Hector recognized his sister and nephew right away.

The gears of Hector's mind turned quickly. The event of the last month seemed to replay in a flash.

He remembered the invasion of Everfrost, coming a razor's edge of defeat and death. He remembered the war and the war's explosive conclusion. His mind flashed to Lydia slowly dying in her bed, Galen telling him cautiously of a possible cure. He remembered the long road, the eerie wasteland, the Glass Desert and the impossible tower at its center. He remembered…

Aldred Zen-Joffa. Hector's blood turned cool at the very thought of the name. At the time the legendary, or rather infamous, immortal had kept his name hidden until the end. If Hector had known his true identity, perhaps he would have been more prepared for his three trials.

Hector found it to be a troubling irony that his sister was echoing a variation of the final words of Zen-Joffa before his departure just as he awoke. "Always be truthful to yourself." Quite the joke those words, coming from the so-called King of Lies.

Putting aside the turmoil within his mind, Hector sat in silence. For the moment, it was all he was capable of as he found his throat was desert-like and his tongue heavy. He watched as his sister and nephew sat oblivious to his waking. Elyssa was attempting to speak reason to her stubborn son. At least some things never changed.

"You cannot go around telling lies," she said her voice a little more than a whisper.

"But it was not all a lie," his nephew answered.

"Oh?"

"Sara was really there."

"But it was you who broke all her mother's flower pots."

"No, we both broken them."

"You mean broke," his sister corrected.

"I said broked," he insisted. "We were playing swords with sticks," saying sword with a hard w, "and she hit me on the head with her stick," he said rubbing the top of his head indicating the less than mortal blow. "I hit her back, then she shoved me, I shoved her, and then we shoved each other. Then we fell into her mother's pots. But I told the truth."

"And how is that, love?"

"I told her mother that Sara did it. I just did'na tell her I helped."

"But that was only part of the truth," his sister sighed. "A half truth is still a full lie. A single falsehood has the power to destroy entire kingdoms, commit murder and the victim yet live. And a half-truth may be the worst of all. While the world goes on believing the lie you will always remember the part held back. Slowly, it will eat away at your heart until the person you were is gone forever."

"Because you will die," his nephew said grimly.

"Pardon," she asked him frowning.

"If something eats your heart you die."

Smiling she answered, "No dear, I meant figuratively."

"Figuring? Is that like when papa's 'figuring numbers?'"

His sister opened her mouth and closed it again. Hector would have laughed but he could not seem to make a sound. His throat was so dry it was nearly shut. He supposed a seven-day slumber would make one dry. Again he attempted to speak.

"Elyssa," Hector attempted to say but could only make out, "Lys."

Both turned to regard him. His sister's eyes lit up as she smiled. Getting to her feet and setting her son down, she quickly moved towards him.

"Look who decided to join us at long last," she said reaching for the flagon that had been set by his bed. Handing it to him his sister sat on the edge of the bed with him.

"Magical spells and alchemical potions aside, over a week in bed and ignoring your family is unacceptable."

"Unasseptable," his nephew agreed in tone if not quite able to manage the word itself. With a grunt, he climbed up onto the bed beside him.

Hector drank until his throat was soothed and asked, "How long have you been here?"

"Shortly after you nodded off apparently," she said in playful ill temper. "Not that you could have at least waited for us, lazy bones."

"Lazy," his nephew agreed trying to look angry and failing. Hector squinted at his nephew and then ruffled his hair with his free hand causing him to giggle.

After another long drink emptied the flagon Hector asked, "You have been here this whole time?"

"Where else would I be," she asked almost tearing up as she began to stroke the top of his head. "Papa and mama are here as well. That reminds me," she said turning towards her son, "Myron, be a dear and go tell your grandparents their son is finally awake."

Nodding enthusiastically the young boy vaulted himself off the bed and ran from the room. A moment later the sound of an opening and closing door. They could hear his exclamations as he ran away screaming Hector was awake.

"You are in favor of more visitors?"

"After a seven day nap, I would be ready for anything," Hector said smiling.

"So you are feeling well. No ill effects," she asked cautiously.

"Aside from a parched throat, never felt better my whole life."

"Wide awake? No weariness?"

"Not at all. Possibly the best sleep of my life."

"Good," she said, sounding relieved, still stroking his hair fondly. "Then I will not feel guilty for this," she said slapping him on the back of the head with such force he nearly went face-first into his covers.

"I swear to all that is sacred and holy in this world that if you ever ride out like that again, to some Divine-forsaken wasteland, with not so much as a word, you will not have to wait for a goblin horde to march off the Mountain to kill you, I will do it for them."

"Time was short," Hector said apologetically.

"Blazes, don't you think we know that," Elyssa said with fire in her eyes. She delivered a slightly less forceful slap to the back of the head, it didn't hurt any less, and added, "It was not as if we expected you to come and have one last meal with us. You could have at least said a quick farewell as you rode out. Our farm is on the Valley Road, you had to ride right through Green Plains to get to the Mountain Pass, you could not spare a moment? You could have at least circled the house and called out, 'I am leaving on a perilous journey, might return, may die, one never knows with quests, farewell.'"

Hector dropped the empty flagon, crossed his arms and asked, "And a statement like that would not have been welcomed with a slap to the head upon my return?"

"Well, the number of slaps would have been limited to two at least."

"You have only slapped me twice."

With lightning fast reflexes Elyssa's hand made contact once more.

"I never said I was finished hitting you now did I?"

Hector began to massage the back of his head with his right hand. The punishment inflicted upon him by the Quicksilver Knight was beginning to feel light in comparison to this.

"What a welcome home," he said shaking his head. "I am beginning to think I would have found a better welcome if I had awakened to find the Valley was now ruled by Everfrost. Or even better, Iracundia the...."

"Stop," Elyssa said throwing her hands up. "You are in enough trouble with me as it is. Now you go and try and summon," she paused, "fire and death by naming one so hastily."

"That is an ancient, disproved, superstition."

"So help me, Hector, if you summon a," again she paused, "a Child Thief to this valley, I will skin you alive myself." There was much venom in her voice. Hector was beginning to believe there was something else afoot aside from superstition and his lack of farewell upon his departure.

"How else have I crossed you?"

His sister's eyes went distant for a moment as she said, "I had to deal with the aftermath of your departure. You did not see the pain that your absence caused. Our mother was in tears Hector. Tears! The woman didn't even cry in childbirth. At least that's what papa says."

"Probably threatened to kill him if he ever said otherwise," Hector said with a smile.

He watched as his sister's expression softened slightly. "You will understand soon enough," she finished.

Abruptly, the sound of Hector's door flying open and the sound of little running feet, interrupted them. Myron reentered the room just as quickly as he had exited. Again he climbed up beside Hector and looked to his mother.

"They coming," he said offering a near knight-like salute. Elyssa rolled her eyes in response.

"And words cannot express how grateful we are for that. It was not as if we needed a gnome-sized Knight of the Valley."

"Yet something else you wish to give me credit for," Hector asked.

"He comes home one day after listening to the older children speak of their families and the reputation of others. He asks us what family reputation means, although he pronounces it…."

As if on cue, Myron said proudly, "Reprentation."

"My well-meaning, but not very thoughtful, husband explained simply as being known by the deeds of your most prominent or infamous relatives. So you will be happy to know that your nephew now believes you alone have shaped our families reputation and we must now live up to said reputation. Even though he ignores what I tell him and then single-handedly destroys our neighbor's property."

"Sara help-ed," Myron insisted.

All further discussion of family "reprentation" was tabled as they were joined by the two elder members of their family. Felix and Minerva moved to their son's bedside, nearly squashing their grandson in the process.

"Welcome home, brave warrior," Felix, whose hair was long gone and farmer's physique giving way to age, said laying a hand on his shoulder and giving it a squeeze. "Tis a shame that we all cannot be here to welcome you home."

"Bryan sends his regards," Elyssa said of her husband. "He would have been here but he had no choice but to work the fields."

"I understand," Hector said nodding while still rubbing the exceedingly painful place on the back of his head. "Glad to see he has finally recovered from the incident with the skillet." He could not keep the smile off his face as she turned to regard him coolly.

The smile faded as he looked and saw the haunted look in his mother's grey eyes. Her face still wore an expression of pain and worry that made her look older than she was. Her hair, which had already begun making its own transition from brown to white a few years before, looked aged a number of years too early as well. Instantly he saw what his sister had seen and was immediately sorry for being so cavalier.

"Hector, we are exceedingly proud of you," she said after a

moment. "We all understand the Blood Oath. We all understand you chose the sword over the plow and that keeping everyone safe was your calling. Nothing has made us happier than to watch as you quickly moved up the ranks to become one of the youngest captains the Knights of the Valley has ever seen."

"We know that yours is not the easiest task," his father added. "We are well aware that at any moment you may be called upon to ride out and meet any danger."

"But you have to promise us," his mother said. "That you will get word to us if this ever happens again. We know the need was great, but we cannot live like that again."

Hector's eyes never left his mother's. For all the words that had been spoken, it was the ones left unspoken that held the most weight.

After a moment he answered, "If ever there is cause for my departure from the valley. you will be the first I tell. I will not leave in silence again. Never."

Suddenly, his nephew began to laugh. In-between chuckles, he said, "I never! Never, never, never. I never."

The hairs on the back of Hector's neck stood on end in an instant. With a forced laughed he asked, "What's he going on about?"

"You were talking in your sleep today," Elyssa said. "You kept repeating two words, 'I never.'"

"We were hoping you could tell us when you woke," his mother said optimistically.

*I never,* again his mind was troubled by these words. He could not help but feel that these two words had held some special significance. Hector worked the words through his mind like one would examine a foreign object with their hands.

"There was a thought just before sleeping," he said out loud, almost as if he were trying to make it materialize in front of him. Shaking his head he said, "But I have no memory of what it could have been. Sorry."

His father shrugged and said, "Then worry no more. If it had been important it would have stayed with you."

Hector nodded. Deep down though, he knew the thought had been more important to him than that. Laughing it away inwardly, he cast the matter aside in his mind. His quest had been successful, Lydia's future secure, and he was home. More importantly, he was home for good. Never again would the road take him away. That was all he truly needed to know.

"Now, get dressed Captain," his mother ordered. "There is someone outside who wishes to see you." With that, all turned and left the room to give him some privacy.

Hector washed up in the basin of water that had been prepared for him. He glanced in the mirror to see that he had a week's worth of beard growth to deal with later. At the very least it was not several years worth. Hopefully, whoever had come calling would not be offended by his slightly unkempt look. Dressing in a fresh tunic and trousers, Hector slipped on his clean boots, Elyssa must have cleaned them as he slumbered, and made for his front door.

The door was open and Hector stepped out into the bright sunlight, his eyes watered at the brilliance. As they readjusted to the waking world, he was taken aback by what was before him. Ranks upon ranks of the Knights of the Valley, standing at a silent attention. Their armor was clean and gleaming in the midday sun. The blue and silver banners of Becknor caught in the breeze. In the front ranks was Darius and Helena. Darius, dark haired with a mustache and goatee and quite a few extra inches around the middle from years of great merrymaking, was, as usual, grinning ear to ear. Even the usually ironed faced Helena, could not keep a smile from her face.

On Darius' cue, the entirety of the knights saluted at once and proclaimed, "Hail Becknor! Hail, Hector the Triumphant! Hail, The Knights of the Valley!"

Their voices thundered around him. A cheer erupted from the assembly that was so loud he was sure it could be heard as far away as the Palace. Afterward, the entire company moved to greet their captain. The first had been Darius who wrapped his arms around Hector, squeezing tightly, and lifting him off the ground laughing.

"Hail, Hector the triumphant," Darius proclaimed.

"Help, says Hector the suffocating," Hector groaned. With a laugh, Darius dropped him to his feet. Hector put his hands on his knees and feigned catching his breath.

"We will have none of that my Captain," Darius said clamping his hand on Hector's shoulders. "We have put off the grand celebration long enough. There shall be great feasting, so much wine and ale shall flow; we will drown in it. And lest I forget, there shall be many starry-eyed maiden, wishing to hear the tales of Hector the Great!"

"Is that all you know, debauchery," Helena spoke up at Hector's left. Hector turned to see she was regarding Darius with one of her very stern and cold expressions.

"Is there anything else worth living for," Darius asked loudly to the cheers of some of the gathered knights.

"Celebrations will have to wait a little longer, my depraved friend," she said. Turning to Hector with yet another uncharacteristic smile she said, "The Lady Lydia has decreed that you are to be honored in a special ceremony at the Palace. She said the very same day you awoke, you would be honored that night."

Hector's mind turned quickly and he asked, "The state of her

202

health?"

"Recovering," Helena assured him. "No one has been permitted to see her as of yet, but Galen assures us all that she is well and in her right mind."

"Then all is well," Darius proclaimed loudly. "And who am I to get in the way of our Regents wishes? Tonight the Palace, later tonight; much drunkness. But, If our Captain is to be honored then let it begin here properly, as it should." Raising his arms and turning to the gathered company, "My Brothers and Sisters of the Oath, I give Hector the Triumphant."

Another deafening cheer erupted as one by one the rest began to welcomed him home. While they cheered him, Hector glanced towards his mother. While the other members of his family were grinning at the sight of Hector's knights honoring him, he could still see the unsaid words in his mother's eyes. They needed no translation.

*You promised.*

Hector remembered. He remembered that day, and those that preceded it, all too well. And his sister had been wrong. Their mother had been moved to tears once before. The day she had been moved to tears for Hector's sake. It was the same day he had made the promise. One that Hector now realized he had nearly broken.

\* \* \* \* \*

Elyssa took in the scene from Hector's porch while holding her son back by his shoulders. Though she, like everyone else in the family, had never approved of Hector's choice, seeing his men gathered around him, celebrating his accomplishment, made her heart a little glad. There were so many back in Green Plains mourning the loss of husbands, wives, siblings, and children. Her brother was not among the dead. And he was one of the reasons so many yet lived. She would have been willing to finally give

Hector his due; if it were not for the next words from her mother.

"It is happening again." Both Elyssa and her father turned almost immediately.

"Surely not," her father said in a strained voice.

"Mama, you overreact. It was his duty," Elyssa spoke quickly.

"I do not speak of this," she said motioning towards the gathered knights. "In my own way, I am proud of him. He saved our Regent and countless more. For the first time, I see good fruit from his poor decision. But, I see it in his eyes. He regresses."

"He seems to be Hector to me," her father said.

"For now. But I tell you the truth, he will backslide. Whatever solace he found these last five years in the service to our Regent has left him. I pray that I am wrong. You do not know how much I wish that his heart had died that day with his spirit."

Elyssa turned her head and regarded her mother scornfully. How could she say such a thing?

Her mother raised a finger and said, "Do not rebuke me child, I already regret the words. But we all know it to be true. I would rather my boy be at peace with a dead heart than to actively seek death in a contrived suicide by service. His path is laid out now. Only in the grave will our Hector truly know peace. But my greatest fear is how many more will he drag to an early grave with him." Then her mother turned to her and warned gravely, "This madness has already claimed your son. He will follow your brother into madness."

Elyssa tried to think of a counter argument. Her son would never take up the sword, never. As for Hector, he was a different man now. The events of the past held no sway. But each time she attempted to speak, the words would not come. For her mother spoke what she already feared was true.

# CHAPTER SIXTEEN

Galen stood by the window in his meditation chamber and watched the crowds below. Stroking his long grey beard thoughtfully, he watched the merry making. It had only been a few days since the Regent had awakened and now Hector too was awake. Tonight had been the time of their first appearance.

Lydia had demanded that a full honor ceremony be performed for the brave knight that had rescued her. With Lydia still in a slightly weakened condition, the officiating of the ceremony had fallen upon Galen. Against his wishes, Lydia had insisted upon being present. Galen relented, but only long enough for her to witness the honor. The curse had preserved her, for the most part. From Galen's observance, the curse had fought the dispel to the last moment. It was completely defeated, but it had taken a small portion of Lydia's strength upon its retreat. She would be fully recovered within a matter of weeks. Though, last night, he took note that, for the first time in a week, her sleep had become fitful as she had yet a nightmare for the first time since the Elixir. From what Hector had told him this evening, this was to be expected. But Aldred Zen-Joffa, no, the imposter claiming to be the King of Lies; as far as Galen was concerned, had said this was to be a temporary affliction. Still, Galen would have been happy if the Regent had listened to his wisdom. On second thought, perhaps he would allow more than a few weeks recovery for her Ladyship.

As for the ceremony, he was sure the historians would write long, flowing, eloquent dispatches of this day. Surely some future playwright would be destined to turn what was a simple ceremony into an overlong, epic poem of countless soliloquies that were never spoken. Though beautiful the ceremony was to most, the fact of the day would never live up to the legend.

Only the very elite were present for the ceremony itself. The Palace could only hold so many, after all. That did not stop the many thousands of villagers, farmers, and knights from crowding around the walls outside for just a glimpse of the man of the hour. There had been no need in formally announcing the Captain's arrival. The roar from the outer gate had rattled the window within Galen's private chamber the moment Hector was in sight. He was told that Lydia had watched from the window of her chambers, again against Galen's wishes, and had applauded him from afar.

Inside the throne room, all members of the Royal Court, every last Wise Man, and the highest ranking Knights of the Valley were present. They all stood waiting within the room's white marble walls and pillars. A long and luxurious blue carpet had been laid out from the doors; all the way up to the dais at the room's center. Standing at her place by the throne, wearing a long blue gown, was Lydia. It took most of her strength to stand. By protocol, the Regent of Becknor must never sit. Instead, they must stand with their left hand upon the right armrest of the throne. Symbolically, standing as the strong right hand of the kingdom until the high monarch was of age. Galen stood to her right and with a silent nod from Lydia, whose voice had yet to fully recover, called Hector forth.

Hector, son of Felix, marched in, head high and in full ceremonial armor, the usual ice-blue with silver flowing cape. On either side, he was flanked by his two highest Lieutenants. Darius, son of Cyrus, and Helena, daughter of Heron. The trio came to the base of the dais and stopped.

Lydia motioned for Hector to approach. Leaving his comrades, he ascended the steps and, as protocol demanded, stopped and knelt in front of the throne.

The Ceremony of Recognition of Valorous Service to the Valley, as it was known, was one of the longest known ceremonies in Becknor protocol. A choir was present to sing the Grand Anthem of the Valley, a scribe would come forward and read the great deeds of the honored, the choir would sing *Rise Battle Queen Rise,* in honor of Queen Beatrice, who instituted the law of required service, then there would be speech by the High Monarch or Regent, the honored would rise and take the ceremonial blade presented to them, then the choir would close with *For the Valley I Serve* in closing. Today, so Lydia could retire to her chambers the more quickly, the ceremony was greatly abbreviated.

There was no choir, there was no scribe to recount the deeds of the honored, and there would be no speech from Lydia. The reading of the great deeds, the speech and awarding of the ceremonial blade would be combined in one motion. All of which had fallen to Galen. Blade in hand, Galen moved before the kneeling Hector and began.

"There are two words that are synonymous within the Kingdom of Becknor. The most prominent would be farming. The fruit of our fields is well known even in the Outer World. The second is the true backbone of our Kingdom. That word is, service. Without required service our defenses would be weak, our roads and bridges would have crumbled long ago, and our master healers would be overrun by the sick and injured. Many have given their lives, and many great deeds have passed into legend; all in the name of service. But I tell you the truth, no words can be spoken to match the great service this brave Brother of the Oath has bestowed upon our Kingdom. Surely, Queen Beatrice herself, if she could have seen into the future, would have pointed towards this brave Captain as the prime example of the selflessness she wished to inspire in the indoctrination of her Two Years Service Edict. That those who would serve their Valley, whether by Knighthood, Healer, or Builder; would continue to serve their Brothers and Sisters long after their required service was concluded. Truly, many of our youth return to work the fields as better men and women, after their years of service. Thankfully, for some of us gathered here today," Galen paused to quickly glance in the direction of the Regent, "our best remain to lead us to a better future."

Looking down upon Hector he commanded, "Now rise, Hector, son of Felix, and take your place in history."

As Hector stood, Galen presented the Ceremonial Blade, hilt first. Carefully, Hector took the blade and held it close to his chest. Then with a smile, he inclined his head in respect to Galen's position and took a step backwards.

Galen then witnessed something rather curious. Despite protocol, the captain turned his head slightly to look towards her Ladyship. No one but those standing upon the dais would ever be aware of the breach. Considering the extraordinary events of the last month, Galen saw no harm in allowing protocol to slide for the moment. But the curious part was the immediate moment that followed.

As Hector's eyes met Lydia's, the latter could not keep the grin from her face. For a moment, the captain's smile faded slightly and he averted his eyes. Then just as quickly the smile was back but it almost seemed as if he were unwilling or unable to look upon her further and turned to regard the crowd.

A thunderous cheer had gone up, easily heard by the crowds standing outside the gate who let loose a cheer of their own. Now, as the day waned, there was great feasting and celebrating to commence. Part of him hoped the sounds of joy would make its way up to the very peaks of

Everfrost. *Break our spirits will you,* he thought towards them.

Just then, there was a boom overhead. Someone had apparently found the kingdom's supply of fireworks and began to use them quite liberally. At this rate, there would be very few to remain for the Harvest Festivals this year. But then, why not? The people had nearly been murdered by the Armies of Everforst. They had suffered great personal losses in the victory. Then, in said victory, had nearly lost the one woman who had been responsible for saving them.

*Let them have their celebrations then,* he thought. Rarely did life offer moments such as these.

After such a beautiful ceremony, after surviving a fierce Ten-Day War, and being the man responsible for finding the references to the Blue Orchid Elixir that had saved the Valley's savior, one would think that person would be just as pleased as the rest. But the High Master of the Wise Men was the exact opposite. He stood watching the celebration, as his soul felt twisted and tormented.

From an early age, Galen's father and grandfather had instilled within him a strong moral code of right and wrong. Chief among that code, a safe Valley was an isolated Valley. Even now, well into his seventh decade, those principles were a guiding force in nearly every decision. What would they say to him now, if they knew that the last of Achelon's line had been at death's door, and he had played a hand in saving her life? What would they say now, seeing that she was not only celebrated as the savior of the kingdom, but Galen had facilitated the ceremony that had honored the man responsible for rescuing her? They would not have had to say a single word. Their disapproving gaze would have burned a hole in his soul.

Till their dying days, they had insisted that Achelon's medaling, his usurping of his brother, the king, would prove to be Becknor's downfall. The recent war had nearly proven them right. While the Valley had enjoyed a century of peace, Everfrost had prepared for war and had nearly overwhelmed them.

Galen winced as one of his earliest memories floated up before him. Only once had he dared to question the wisdom of their hatred for a man long dead. After all, the Valley had known forty years of peace by that point. The back of his father's hand taught him to never question them again.

It was his grandfather, gnarled by old age and leaning heavily on a staff, who explained the reason for their hate.

"The world outside this valley is ruin and decay. Every dealing with outsiders has had dire consequences for us all. Look to the ignorant kings of old who dared break the ancient Isolationist Covenant. Janus the Greedy, after seeing our granary surpluses, thought he saw and opportunities to increase the treasury and sent forth merchants to the Outer World. Once our existence was known, bandits and marauders began raiding us for grain and gold. A plague upon us for more than five centuries."

"Look upon Edgar the Fool. The first king to travel out of Becknor. His curiosity led him to the City-State of Isaac's Hold and their great military and engineering feats. Foolishly he was inspired to dam up the northern branch of the Becks-Dali for 'better irrigation.' Instead, Edgar's Folly nearly flooded the entire circuit, the Palace, and the valley beyond."

"Just because the seeds that Achelon sowed have yet to sprout, does not mean his actions have not harmed us, my foolish grandson. Our valley is now wide open to the Outer World and that will be our undoing. That is why we will forever hate him and his line. That is why we celebrate the death of each of his descendants. It will be a happy day indeed, when the last of his line is in their grave."

And so Galen hated the line of Achelon as it had been instilled in him. From the very beginning of his public service within the Healers'

Guild, to the day he was accepted into the ranks of the Wise Men, he vowed that his skills would never benefit the Lords and Ladies of Talwoods.

The day the fire consumed that ancient castle, taking Lord Marcus and his wife, had been met with celebration. He had poured a drink and toasted his long dead fathers.

"Nearly finished," he had told them. "Achelon's stain is nearly gone." Then came the turning, and the dilemma of his heart.

All the Wise Men had been summoned to the Palace by the King Gaius that night. Almost giddy with anticipation for the details as he walked the halls, he noticed Nicodemus to the side. Galen had always despised him for his association with Lord Marcus. Turning aside with every intention of gloating, even if it was silent, he stopped short when he saw the child.

Lydia had heard his approaching footsteps and had turned to regard him. It was not the slump in her posture, or how she clung to her teacher, that affected him. It was the eyes. One look from her red tear-streamed eyes, the vacancy behind them, that had stabbed his heart. Eyes that never looked away. Even the days that immediately followed, he was haunted by those eyes.

It was more the memory of those eyes, more than the sight of Lydia lay dying of the Fever-Sleep, or the multitudes beyond the gate, that spurred him into action. Despite the teaching of his father and grandfather, their admonishment to hate Talwoods more than even the goblin hordes of Everfrost, Galen worked tirelessly till he found the cure to save the last of Achelon's line.

So while the Kingdom celebrated their victories, Galen could only stand by his window and watch. Stand and try to convince himself that his actions had been just despite what he had been taught and always believed. That is why the very last thing he desired was the knock at his chamber door.

At first, Galen ignored it. He had ordered no interruptions, to be alone with his thoughts. Self-loathing and self-justification were disciplines that required solitude. After a second, more insistent knock, he sighed heavily and turned towards the door.

"Well, come then," he ordered. The ancient hinges squealed in protest, as the wooden door opened to reveal the scarred visage of another of his order. "Cassius, do you not care to join the Valley in celebration."

"My appetites for merriment are as diminished as yours, High One," Cassius's rattling voice spat.

"Perhaps," said Galen, "Yet, I believe our appetites are diminished for separate reasons."

"Whether by old age or the scourge of life, the result is the same I am afraid. The loss of joy," he said trying to smile sadly but looking hideous thanks to the long scar running from his forehead and through his missing right eye and down his cheek.

If there was a man that was the walking embodiment of an enigma, it was Cassius. For all that was known about the man, there was an equally gaping void of mystery. A former Knight of the Valley, at age thirty he transferred to the Inner Circle. Within two years he was Captain of that order. He would serve a handful of years before retiring to private life fifteen years ago. His retirement came shortly before a time when the Valley could have used his services the most.

From the Seven-Year Bandit Wars, to the burning of Talwoods; leadership and bravery had been in short supply. Perhaps, in the end, Cassius would have been a better candidate for Captain of the Valley over Vitus. Vitus had proved to be capable but his judgment of character was far lacking. Prime example was how could one such as Darius rise so high in rank? Perhaps, a Captain Cassius would not be standing before him scarred and forever injured. In his retirement, Cassius had been called to defend his very own farmhouse as it was attacked by bandits more than a decade ago. Though no one had witnessed it, word was that he had defended his home magnificently, but to no avail. The bandits took his eye and left him to die within his burning home. While badly injured, he crawled away from the inferno. Beyond the loss of his eye, and the scars, Cassius felt no sensation. His skin forever numb and the senses of taste and smell would never return.

Beyond the records of his service, and the incident with the bandits, the remainder of Cassius life was a mystery. He did not speak of his parents, he seemed to have very few comrades from his years as a knight, and mostly refused to speak of the day he was injured. The man was a blank slate beyond his devotion to the people of Becknor and love of the Valley.

After convalescing for years, Cassius had sought membership within the ranks of the Wise Men a year before the death of the king, just as Galen was about to ascend to the highest rank of the order. While not always agreeing, Galen had found that he and Cassius were usually of common thought. Eventually, Galen trusted him enough to make him his second.

As much as Galen had come to rely on Cassius' council these past years, he was the very reason Galen had wished to retire to his chambers undisturbed. For within the words of his second, was the echo of the sentiments of his forefathers. Galen was already torn and had no need to hear Cassius next words:

"The only real joy left to men like us is the joy of service to our people," Cassius continued. "Who we have failed."

"Not this again," he said turning back to the window.

"You know it to be true," he hissed behind him. "We had our chance to end the Usurper's line and our brothers lost their nerve."

*You lost your nerve.* Cassius may not have spoken the words but Galen heard them nonetheless.

"Some would call it, doing that which is right," Galen answered.

"Is that so? When a soldier is gravely wounded in battle and a healer's only choice to save his or her life is to amputate a limb, does the warrior think it is right? Of course not. It is up to the more learned individual to make the decision for him. Then, years later, when the warrior has had years to live his life; he sees the wisdom of it all. The people would have mourned the loss of Lydia, but as the years passed their hearts would have healed. They would have built statues and even the likes of us may have one day believed she was a hero. We have failed to act accordingly, and we, the more learned individuals, have failed our people." Taking a breath and letting it out as a sigh Cassius added, "I fear we have left the kingdom gravely injured."

"Strange, our kingdom does not seem gravely injured to me," Galen said motioning towards the celebration out his window. He heard footsteps as Cassius moved to his side.

"We both know appearances can be deceiving, High One," he whispered. "Some foolish ones would think what Achelon did a century ago strengthened our people. But we both know; looking to outside the valley for help weakened us. We lost something. Reclamation must commence. To do so, Achelon's line must die out; sooner rather than later. The Kingdom must go back to the very principle that had guided us for over two millennia. An isolated Valley is a strong Valley. And it must begin with the death of the Lady of Talwoods."

Galen answered with silence. Yet his mind within motion. This was madness.

"Lydia saved our people," Galen protested, turning to his second.

"The Knights of the Valley saved our people."

"It was Lydia's strategy that put them in the proper place for that victory. And if she had not slain the Dread Overlord, we may still have lost," he said turning away again to look out the window. "I think you worry over nothing my second. She is merely the Regent. It is only a matter of months before Lucien takes his throne. Once upon the throne, she will be dismissed and she can go tend her gardens."

"You truly believe it will be that simple," Cassius asked mockingly. "Have you truly forgotten the influence Lord Marcus had over King Gaius? His words held more sway than anyone within the Royal Court, including your predecessor. The last two years of his life, Marcus spent far too much time outside the Valley. Bringing back dangerous ideas with him. Ideas he would whisper into the King's ear. Do you think Lydia will be any different? Lydia held the favor of the King, after the fire, when he took her in. It was his short-sightedness that sent her to Isaac's Hold for tutelage. Filling her head with even more dangerous Outsider ideas than her father. When Lucien takes the Throne, to whom will he listen? Lydia will have an ear in the Royal Court long after her regency. Then High One, whose words will hold more sway, ours or the woman who is like a sister? Where will it end? The dissolution of our sovereignty as a kingdom? A full member of the Alliance of the Four Greater Kingdoms? Perhaps an even worse fate. We wake one morning to find we have been fully absorbed into the dominion of Isaac's Hold? No, High One, for the Kingdom, Lydia must die," Cassius hissed. "And if not by the hands of our enemies, then it must be by ours."

Galen was torn. He heard Cassius words, in his minds eye he could see the disapproving stares of his forefathers, the wisdom of how Achelon had weakened their Valley-Kingdom, the pain of young Lydia's eyes. To even entertain such thoughts was high treason. What if a Knight of the Inner Circle, loyal to Lydia, was within earshot? He and his second would be executed by morning.

Galen knew exactly what he should do next. Dismiss Cassius at once. Strip him of his rank and call for his immediate arrest. Then, for entertaining such ideas, Galen would step down from his position, so a more balanced and tolerant individual could guide the kingdom. That was precisely the course of action required.

Instead, as he watched Cassius' reflection in the window, he heard himself ask, "What do you suggest, my Second?"

Attempting to smile cruelly, and succeeding, he answered, "Nothing, for now. A death now would look suspicious. But her Ladyship is a meddler. I guarantee you she will find herself in danger again in time. On that day, we do what is right for the Kingdom and ensure that her life ends. Only then High One, can our people be truly safe, and begin to take back their true destiny. An isolated Valley is a strong Valley."

Galen reluctantly nodded and said, "Then let us keep our eyes open my Second. When destiny calls, we will act."

Cassius saluted him and said "Hail Becknor." With that, he turned and left Galen alone with his thoughts and eyes that never looked away.

# CHAPTER SEVENTEEN

The celebration was a truly joyous one. The sounds of the collective merrymaking of the people reverberated across the valley. From the Circuit to Green Plains, between the Blood Forest and the Mountain Pass, wherever there was people, there was dancing, feasting, and singing. There was not a single inch of the valley that did not feel the excitement. Even deep underground, in the abandoned caverns below the valley floor. The ancient caverns and abandoned mine shafts shook.

Deep down one particular cavern, under the unsteady ground of Green Plains, the sounds of celebration was causing the walls to rattle. Some loose stones began to shake away. One such stone, no larger than an average pumpkin, found its way loose and rolled down a lonely stone corridor. Its movements echoed loudly as it traveled long and far. Unobstructed, it reached its final destination, a deep pond of cool, mineral-rich, spring water. It splashed down displacing the water; sending a small wave to every last nook and corner of the pond. The water lapped over the edge and splashed upon the nose of the cavern's lone sleeping occupant. He awoke with a snarl, and brought himself up to full height.

"**I awaken**," he said growling deeply within his sizeable chest. "**Woe to you and to all you hold dear!**"

Stomping and snarling he looked about the place of his hibernation, he saw not one living soul. How strange. Was he awakened by the simple splash of water? Impossible! He, like the rest of his kind, was not known for sleeping so lightly. A full hurricane could have blown into his face and it would never have troubled him. Something else was afoot.

Raising his head higher, he listened carefully. The sounds of the celebrating people were high above him.

"**Yet another festival,**" he growled to himself with a sigh. The people of Becknor seemed to love to celebrate. Twice before, he had been awakened by one of their many festivals. On both occasions, he had cursed himself for choosing this valley for his hibernation. Who knew a society of farmers could be so loud?

"**No doubt one of you has, at last, learned to grow tomatoes to the size of a grapefruit. Or better yet, a pumpkin the size of a horse and carriage. Imagine the pies you could bake,**" he mocked them.

In disgust, he lowered his head to settle in for another round of sleep. He was still drowsy. Perhaps another decade would prove beneficial. One thing was certain, he would never make the mistake again of picking such a loud people to hibernate next to.

He had traveled far and wide throughout the world before his current hibernation. He had taken much into consideration before his centuries sleep. He had been born far to the east near the seaside realm of Endlan. A peaceful, but small realm of fisherman and explorers. It would have probably been a much better pick for hibernation but his mother had cautioned not to pick a place too peaceful. The danger would have been to close his eyes and never open them again. Sleep for thousands of years, until his life force was spent and his bones merged within the stone of some forgotten cave.

The remaining twelve realms of the east were fully occupied with the others of his kind. It was doubtful that his cousins would have been willing to share their hibernation chambers, and nests with him. So he had migrated west, over the tall and magnificent Drakemourn Mountains. For a time he considered sleeping deep within them, but he thought of the terrible winter storms of snow and ice. Even deep within their roots, the cold was said to travel deep. Then there was the yearlies, the powerful wind storms that moved through the mountains every decade. Yearlies took their name for the sheer length of the storm. Did he really want to hear the constant howling winds for two or three years? Again he moved on.

He considered the great deserts of the Kingdom of Mar'Gev in the south. The great stretches of glorious sand dunes to bath in. The long scorching days of heat that permeated deep underground. Ah, that would have been more than sufficient to give him a nice warm sleep. Even as he looked longingly upon those sandy dunes, he knew that Mar'Gev was one of the Four Greater Kingdoms of the Alliance. If his presence was discovered they would have sent for the Vanguard Knights and they would have surely murdered him in his sleep.

Next, he traveled to the Wild Country of the North. Stretches of untamed forests, the marshes of Kaitlyn's Woe, the Great Granite Plain, all ideal but too busy. Bandits, marauders, despotic warlords, and cut throats roamed those lands too frequently. How often would he have been awakened by some overly optimistic brigand? Probably not as often as the tripled cursed, celebration-loving farmers above him now, he realized. At least he could have eaten the brigands. Though, he did tarry for a time in the North. Even as he began to feel the first stirring of drowsiness, he stayed long enough to observe the practitioners of the so-called "Forbidden Alchemy." He had to confess, he did marvel at the machines that ran on fire and steam. The warmbloods were a creative lot when they put their mind to something other than war.

So finally he had moved down and inspected the Dali Mountains. Nestled amongst them was this lush, green valley cut off from the rest of the world. He could see what the early Valley-Dwellers saw when they migrated here. A nice and peaceful way of life. But not too peaceful. The threat of war from the goblins in the Everfrost Mountains would be enough to keep his senses open and he would not have to worry about sleeping forever. But these Becknor celebrations! Did one people need to celebrate this often and loudly? Eighty years he had rested now, but had he even had a full continues decade of sleep?

Grumbling to himself, he curled up to settle back into hibernation. Just then, there was a new scent tickling his nose. It was not fresh, perhaps as much as a month old. His head came back up to take in a lung-full of air and get a stronger sample of the scent. The coppery smell of blood. It was followed by the stench of smoke and burnt flesh. Not just of man, but goblin as well. The scents would have taken a great amount of time to reach him. Doubtful any other than his kind would have had the ability to detect scents this old.

Celebrations? Much spilled blood and burnt flesh? Realization donned and he again brought himself up to full height.

"**Ho, Ho,**" he laughed growled. "**War has returned to the Mountain and Valley!**" So not just any celebration, but a victory celebration.

"**So my Beckish and Everfrost friends, you have once again turned to studying war! What plunders, I wonder, have been taken?**"

Now he was fully awake with the holy bloodlust of his kind. He savored it, allowed it to course its way through his entire being. The righteousness of it.

He looked up towards the ceiling of his place of hibernation, imagining the people beyond. Had the victorious Valley-Dwellers filled their coffers with goblin gold, and precious gems, while he slumbered? His only wish was that the drums of war had awakened him sooner.

If war had returned here then surely it was raging elsewhere in the world. Perhaps the time had finally come to build his first nest and attract a mate. War begat war. So it was with the warmbloods of this world. It would not be long before the females took flight. He would need to be ready.

But there would be time enough for that. First, he felt a great hunger within. He was far too weakened to deal with the warmbloods properly. Soon he would feed. Then he would raze the Valley and storm the halls of Everfrost. He would shatter their shields, melt their weapons of war, cleanse their dwelling in fire, and then finally raid their strongholds of gold.

Launching himself from his resting place, the great beast moved through the crumbling tunnels and caverns. Making for the first opening to the surface he took flight and soared high into the moonless sky. Up and up he went so that he might look down upon all that would shortly be his prey. Not one single eye took notice of his flight for Becknor was too focused on celebration and Everfrost was still licking her wounds.

As he looked down, he did not see the world that was, but, in his mind's eye, he saw what would be. The fire, the smoke, the dead and the dying. After all, such was the judgment awaiting all who study war.

# CHAPTER EIGHTEEN

**Two months later...**

*It is but a dream; look to the window.*

Once again, in the nightmare landscape that the small remnant of the curse brought, Talwoods was engulfed in flames.

*It is but a dream; look to the window.*

Nicodemus was an unrelenting snare upon her shoulder. Her father turned and once again instructed her first teacher to keep her safe.

*It is but a dream; look to the window.*

Flames shot from the front door as it fell, moments before that section of the outer wall collapsed. As her world followed suit, Nicodemus slowly turned her away from the horror. The fully aware Lydia tried to turn and look in the still intact window and the moving light beyond. But it was no use. She should have realized long before, one cannot redirect the eyes of memory to look where they never had before.

Despite reminding herself it was only a dream, once the terrible sound of Talwoods collapsing reached her ears, Lydia awoke all at once. Gasping for breath, her heart thundering, her eyes darted about the room to ensure she was truly awake in her bedchamber, inside the Palace. From her bedside table, covered in papers and books, to across the room, where she could see her own full-grown adult reflection in the wall mounted mirror. She barely recognized the woman in the mirror. The look of terror in her eyes, her entire body soaking with sweat, and both hands balled up into fists desperately holding onto her blankets.

Willing her hands to loosen, Lydia dropped the blankets. Her right hand went to her chest as if it would calm her heart and wiped the sweat from her brow with her left. Beginning to feel slightly calm again, she rubbed her face with both hands to wipe the tears away. At least she had managed to not call out. Lydia had lost track of the number of times the pair of Inner Circle Knights, station outside the door, had come bursting through, as if bandits had scaled the thirty-foot smooth stone wall and through her window to kidnap her. At least Aristide had corrected his initial mistake and had ensured that both knights at her door were women after that first night.

Despite her quietness, there was a knock at the door and a girl's voice calling out, "Is all well My Lady?" It was the voice of Brenna. Lydia rolled her eyes despite her shaky insides. A month ago, Galen had dismissed the two maidens that had been her assistance, Cecilia, and Fenella. She had yet to speak with them, or anyone else for that matter since waking.

She looked towards her window and saw that the world beyond was still dark. Of course it was. Had she really expected to have slept through the night? The one light source within her chamber was a lone candle, perched on the table on the other side of her bed. Only a few inches of the wax had melted away. She laughed humorlessly.

"I suppose an hour of sleep is all anyone really needs," she said as she kicked her blankets away. Her gown was soaking with sweat. She made a mental note to leave the blankets off next attempt. If there was one.

"My Lady," Brenna called again.

With a sigh, Lydia rolled over and threw her feet over the side of the bed. "You may enter," she called out.

Brenna, dressed for bed herself, entered the room and eyed her warily. "Are you in need of Galen or one of the healers My Lady?" That was the last thing Lydia wished. Galen was the only constant in her life and she did not need a late night visit.

"I am well, thank you. I was just settling down to sleep, but the room is stifling. Thought I might open the window and let in some air."

"Oh, I would be more than glad to open it for you," the girl said in a tone so over-helpful it bordered on condescending.

"That will not be necessary."

"It is no trouble at all My Lady," she said already moving for the window. "Master Galen would not want you to strain yourself. You need to recover your strength."

Mentally Lydia thought many ill things towards Galen, all very un-ladylike. Aloud she said, "Considering I am now allowed unescorted excursion up to the battlements, and tomorrow I will be allowed to hold court for the first time, I would think a window is within my abilities."

"All the same, My Lady," Brenna said.

*All the same, My Lady,* Lydia mocked in her head. If she heard those five words again from the girl, Lydia waged that she might actually say a few of those choice curses out loud.

Pleased with herself, Brenna turned and asked, "Can I be of further service?"

Silently Lydia answered, *You could ask me what no one else seems to have the courage to ask. You can ask the question that Galen forbids and allow me to say the words. Perhaps I could unburden myself and not worry that I truly have lost my senses. If only I could coax Hector into coming to see me; he would ask.*

Smiling politely, Lydia dismissed her. Brenna curtsied and left the room for the comforts of her own bed, leaving Lydia alone with her own dark thoughts.

With Brenna gone, Lydia stood and went to the window, praying for a cool breeze on the night air to wash over her, and flow through her hair. Instead, the night air was calm, though much cooler than her stagnant bedchamber. Disappointed, Lydia still took what was offered. She sat on the window seal and took long even breaths to finish calming herself. If Galen had been present he would probably admonish her for sitting on the seal. Especially when there was a readily available chair tucked beneath her private dining table. She thought many more un-Ladylike words towards Galen, this time in goblin. A bad habit she had acquired from the late Captain Vitus.

It was a mystery why Galen was treating her so. He had become more protective of her health since the night of the ceremony in Hector's honor. She sighed. At least there was now an end in sight. Unlike tonight's experiment.

Another night, another failure. Aldred Zen-Joffa had been correct in his warning that Lydia would still suffer from the nightmares for a time. Mercifully, they did not reoccur until a week later. From what little Galen was wishing to tell her, the very few who had survived their ordeal, shortly succumbed to sleep deprivation. Apparently, once the crazed victims closed their eyes their nightmares reemerged in an instant. They began to practice forced insomnia. Not one had ever voluntarily slept again. Yet, something else that differed in Lydia's case as she had begun to force herself to sleep for the past month. A fact she was most assuredly hiding from Galen. She had been forcing sleep to intentionally dream. For Lydia believed there was something more to the day of the fire.

That light upstairs was the key. A tiny spec that seemed to dance through the air. It could have just been a flying ember, but in her heart, she suspected differently. That was why, for the last month, Lydia had been taking sleeping tonics to ensure she dozed long enough to dream. The nightmare did not come every night but it did come often enough. She knew she would have but a limited time from Hector's report to Galen. Soon the nightmare would be gone for good and she would have no way of revisiting the past. Not that she found it particularly helpful. No matter how much she tried to force herself, she could not make her past self turn her head.

*The past is but a shadow,* she mentally repeated the words of Nicodemus from her childhood. *Learn from it what you can, and let it guide you into the light of today. Dwell on yesterday too long, allow it to envelop you into its darkness, and you risk being caught in the abyss of what if.*

It was these very words that Lydia was attempting to use as a guide post. She had come so far in her recovery that she did not wish to cause herself further harm. She especially did not want to give Galen another opportunity to curtail her life further. If he had the slightest inkling that she was seriously attempting to sleep to uncover details from the past, he would end her regency immediately. How could he not declare her insane?

Lydia might not be as vain as others, but she did not want the histories to read: "Lydia, Lady of Talwoods, served as Regent five years, one month, and eighteen days before quitting the post due to insanity." It would be worded more politely, and there would be a footnote, at best, that informed the student that Lydia had cracked due to the Fever-Sleep Curse. But once insanity was used as a label that would be all the world would remember. Even children would be taught little rhymes to sing while at play. "Shall we sing Crazy Lydia?"

But then, Lydia herself was beginning to have the occasional doubt of her own sanity. What if she truly was caught in a personal abyss? She was desperate to speak with someone, anyone at this point. All she wished to do was explain her nightmares, have help sharing the burden, and then they could say the words she longed to hear. "It was only a curse induced nightmare, distorting the past to torment you. That little light was nothing and the fire was accidental. Your parents were not murdered." But, conversation was the one thing Galen had expressly forbidden, above all else. No one was to ask about her nightmares and she was to never speak them aloud. Galen believed if it was ignored, it would drift harmlessly away into memory. That was why Lydia wished to see Hector so desperately. Hector, the Ever Absent.

Lydia missed her friend desperately. As soon as she felt rested enough, she began to conspire a meeting. For years they had been having private and secret meetings ranging from the state of the Valley to the latest atrocity the palace chefs had bestowed upon them. She truly should have replaced them but they were Gaius favorite cooks and she felt terrible each time she attempted to dismiss them. Hector had shared a laugh or two with her about the state of the kitchen. How she missed him.

Each time she had sent a message out to him, his reply was that he was bowing to the wisdom of Galen. He would not wish to cause her harm. Even when Galen had allowed her to travel to the battlements she had attempted to see her friend. Again he declined, this time it was his lack of time due to rebuilding the ranks. Which she supposed could be true, but in the back of her mind she began to wonder, *Is Hector avoiding me?* Each time she thought the words she dismissed them as being paranoid and seeing conspiracies. But it was beginning to be increasingly difficult to dismiss.

It was not only for the sake of unburdening herself to Hector, but she wished to hear the account of his journey, in his own words. So far Lydia had been forced to read his account from his meeting with the Wise Men. A copy was secreted to her from one of her many allies within the Palace. She had read it over during one of her sleepless nights. It was fascinating, harrowing, and…incomplete. Oblivious to the Wise Men, who argued among themselves the validity of the claim by the alchemist that he was Aldred Zen-Joffa, the usually meticulous Hector was rather vague in more than one area. But most specifically, the third trial. There had been some sort of vision of the future, her future. But his details were sketchy at best. It was one of the reasons she could not wait to speak with him, whenever he deemed her worthy again of friendship. A fresh pain erupted and she did her best to push it away. They would speak again.

With no one to speak with, and attempting to prove her irrational fears were just that, Lydia spent her waking hours trying to remember every detail of her childhood within Talwoods for clues. She found it remarkable the number of details that she had long forgotten in thirteen years. So many happy memories had been suppressed to chase away the pain. Now, thanks to a curse and a mind full of questions, she could recall them all vividly.

How the sounds of her footsteps echoed loudly back to her when she ran through the halls of Talwoods. How the early morning sunshine cast long shadows just outside her chamber door. Lydia remembered standing at that window pretending to be a giant walking over mountains.

The aromas that made their way from the kitchens as the cooks were hard at work preparing one of the seasonal banquets her father hosted. There was much boiling, stewing, chopping, and baking as she walked through the kitchens. The head cook, tall and lean Quintis, was a master at everything, but mostly Lydia was fascinated by his chopping skills. She would watch, wide eyed, as he sliced and chopped with speed and accuracy. His hands were nearly a pair of blurry images he was so quick. Lydia once joked to him that he was more skilled with the knife than any one knight in the Kingdom was with any blade.

He had smiled that gloriously toothy grin and replied, "I mourn for any hapless knight who dares steal food from my kitchen." He finished by twirling his knife and making stabbing motions with it making her giggle in response.

She remembered the one great snow, a rare thing inside the valley.

Even though there are cold rains and ice in the winter, snow seldom seemed to move down from Everfrost and the Mountain Pass. There were two snowstorms that Lydia could remember vividly. The latter was but a few inches the winter before the fire. Enough to build a snowman at least. But the first was two years before. A snow came that piled so high it came over her head and up to her father's waist. From her window, she watched as this white fluffy blanket of cold settled over everything. It was her first snow and she remembered becoming giddy at the prospect. Though when it kept her indoors for weeks she became far less pleased.

Lydia remembered her days under the tutelage of the great master Nicodemus inside the library. The library itself was the largest private collection in the Valley. It was nearly a quarter the size of the Record Vaults within City Citadel. Towering bookshelves from floor to ceiling containing histories, fictions, plays, works of poetry, everything a curious child needed to keep her mind occupied. Every morning she would arrive for her lesson to find the tables laid out with books, maps, or whatever the day's lessons called for. At the beginning of every week of study, Nicodemus would lead her to one of the many bookshelves and motion towards a section in particular to select a book for her own private reading. By week's end he would expect to hear her thoughts about her selection.

So many things, once forgotten, were flowing back to her now. But Lydia remembered no clue, if there had been any, that would help solve the present mystery. But no matter how much she attempted to tell herself that just because she did not remember anything sinister did not mean it was not there. It was not impossible that she had seen something but had been too young or of a childish mindset to recognize danger when it was afoot. That was when Lydia, to prove to herself once and for all, turned to the magistrate's investigations.

Lydia looked over towards her bedside and the papers and books laying on the table. Retrieving these documents had proven to be more of a chore than they should have. All investigation journals would be stored within the Record Vaults of the City Citadel. Being confined to the Palace, and forbidden by Galen to read official state documents, made getting her hands upon them difficult but not impossible. It was fortunate that Lydia had learned years before how to get things accomplished without the aid or approval of either the Wise Men or the Royal Court. She had found it easy to run the kingdom without either one, as did most of the monarchs of history. Yet, it was always best to go through them in most matters, if not for protocol sake but to be polite.

Over her five years as Regent, Lydia had cultivated friendships with the truly indispensable servants of the kingdom, the Palace staff. Maids, butlers, cooks, stable workers, all of whom the Palace would be a terrible wreck without.

"Never make the mistake that a title makes you more than what you are," her father had told her once. "Our forbearers were given these titles as a reward for their service to the Kingdom. The Kingdom is nothing more than the people that live within its borders. Never treat your brother as your slave only because you inherited a title you yourself never earned. Today you are royalty, a revolution tonight and you find yourself the slave tomorrow."

While the majority of the Royal Court looked upon the Palace servants as nothing more than furniture, Lydia took the time to speak with them, to learn their names, their hopes, their dreams, their families. Over the years Lydia learned that most of those who served, especially the young maidens that had been tasked to see to her needs, were an exceptional and bright lot. Many had become trusted co-conspirators over the years. Not necessarily spies but an extra set of ears that moved about the Palace that would occasionally hear the odd word. Certainly not traitors to their oaths, but occasionally they could fetch desired items in secure locations. All Lydia had to do was make a simple request, a note quickly slipped into the hand of a passing maid, while making her way up to the battlements, and the records were within her hands the same day.

The High Magistrate of the day of the fire was Gower son of Gavin, who felt it necessary to begin the record with a notation. He wished it to be known to all future generations that it had been Lord Marcus who had nominated him to the position of High Magistrate. And while the tragedy had affected him deeply, it had in no way swayed the thoroughness of his investigation. Meaning he was just as dedicated to the other investigations as he was to the death of his benefactor.

Lydia had no real reason to not trust that the Magistrate was a man of his word. Yet, it seemed that Hector was not the only master of vague reports. Oh yes, Gower had conducted countless interviews with the surviving house staff, which it seemed was nearly everyone. Lydia's mother had dismissed the staff shortly after the departure of the carriage carrying her, her father, and Nicodemus. Only her mother's personal maiden, Keara, remained behind. Keara too died in the destruction, but exactly how was either never concluded upon or reported. The rest of the staff had intended to rest within their own quarters but her Ladyship strongly urged them to leave the grounds altogether. On two occasions she even gifted a surprising amount of coins so that the youngest could go visit their families for a few days in nearby villages. Beyond this somewhat out of the ordinary behavior, not one member of the staff could report on anything else. They met no travelers but those heading for the fairgrounds, there were no strangers milling about, the house was quiet upon their departure, and not one was close by when the fire destroyed Talwoods.

Next Lydia was shocked to see she had given her own eyewitness account. As much as she tried to think back, she had no memory of Gower speaking with her. Though looking over the record, it seemed to be her words. Her account was sparse, had very few details to add, and painful to read. Lydia could see her own misery in what was recorded. Lydia's second shock came as she found that her words consisted of the final interview in the investigation. There were no mentions of political rivals or any names belonging to the men and women of rival houses who had openly hated the Lord and Lady of Talwoods for Achelon's sake. Had he never interview them, or had they spoken only off the record? She looked over the pages to see if any were missing. But no, Gower had only interviewed Lydia and the staff.

"Where are the words of Nicodemus," Lydia had asked herself upon finishing the witness record. "He had been an eyewitness as well."

Next Gower walked the grounds of Talwoods looking to find anything that might have been out of place. He made his way through the ruins and found nothing out of the ordinary. Lydia found the wording to be strange itself. How can a structure destroyed by fire be ordinary?

Gower's final ruling was that the fire had been accidental. That her mother, according to the last two maids to leave, had been ill and seemed distracted. Lady Anastasia had retired to her alchemy chambers, presumably to mix a tonic for whatever her ailment might have been. While there, she had probably fainted and accidently knocked over a flammable mixture and the fire quickly moved out of control. He listed hers as the first death. By the time her father had rushed in she was already gone. The Magistrate had ruled that Lord Marcus had died when the interior had collapsed upon him and death was instantaneous.

Lydia read the final ruling over and over. It was a reasonable conclusion. Lydia had followed in her mother's footsteps into alchemy and some mixtures were immensely unstable. And Lydia remembered that there was a private chamber inside Talwoods that her mother had worked in, but there was never anything unstable. And she knew this to be true as her mother had taken her to a secret cottage on the grounds of Talwoods. It was a half hour walk away and hidden deep within the neighboring forest. It was a simple and ancient looking stone hut with a faded wooden door, open air windows, and a thatched roof. Her mother had brought Lydia to it the very day she began to teach her the beginnings of Alchemy.

"If we accidently destroy this place, it will not be a great loss," she had said. "I would rather perform unsafe work here away from home. Lesson one my daughter, which is a good rule for life and alchemy, never conduct volatile experiments under your own roof; unless you wish to be homeless."

Furthermore, Gower's timing was considerably lacking. If her mother had gone to mix a tonic, fainted, and had accidentally caused the fire shortly after the last two maidens had departed, why did it take the fire hours to consume Talwoods? Surely everything would have been in ruins upon their return. And what of Keara? Would she have let a fire that slow burning consume everything? Would she not have tried to save her mother at least?

Upon completing the records, instead of Lydia' fears being laid to rest, they were now magnified. Gower's ruling, as incomplete as it seemed to Lydia, would be his final words on the subject. He died a year before she had become Regent.

It was apparent now to Lydia that there was only one person that could help her questioning heart. She would need to speak with Nicodemus. With her duties as Regent, she had not seen her old mentor for a number of years. He was well advanced in age now, over a century. He continued to live in retirement at his old farmhouse in Amethyst Grove. Perhaps it was time to have a visit with him. What better time to make her request to see him then tomorrow at her first meeting of the Royal Court.

Surly Galen could see no harm in a meeting with Nicodemus. If she was now well enough to take up her old duties then how could he object? Having someone to talk with about matters outside of affairs of state might do her good. Where was the harm?

And then perhaps, afterwards, she could have a private word with Hector. Tomorrow she could finally begin put some of her fears, and questions, aside. Nicodemus would explain it all away and she would find Hector and they could both have a laugh at her sleep deprived fueled paranoia. Tomorrow everything would be set right and the world would make sense again.

# CHAPTER NINETEEN

Cassius, by training, had always been the lightest of sleepers. As a former Knight of both the Valley and Inner Circle, one needed to be ready for action within a heartbeat. It was one of the chief tenants of the Blood Oath after all. Due to the injuries that had left most of his senses dulled: smell, taste, and touch; his vision and hearing had increased in efficiency many times over. By consequence, he became and even lighter sleeper. A moth against the window might as well be an entire flock of birds smashing into the glass. The full moon was as the noonday sun. So when his contact helped himself into his home, left the sealed envelope on his nightstand, and then made his way out again without waking him, it was more than a little disconcerting.

Cassius was never sure exactly what it was that woke him. He would just wake and find all as it was as he had drifted away with the exception of the envelope.

Throwing away the covers he did not feel, Cassius moved to the edge of the bed and sat looking upon the nightstand. He laughed humorously. They even managed to approach on the side of his one good eye. Reaching over to the nightstand, Cassius raised the wick on the burning lamp by his bed, he had hoped to cast more light in the room in an attempt to see a passing shadow. Plucking up the envelope he took the time to turn it over and study it as he always did.

Just like all the others, there were no discernable clues as to who had sent the dispatch. The paper was of fine quality but old and yellowing, it could have been decades or centuries old. The wax seal bore no insignia. Even if he had been a practitioner of the forbidden alchemy of the north; he knew there would be no extra clues to discover.

The first order of a conspiracy was secrecy. The less known by the majority the less likely one could give up his compatriots. This, he would say, his co-conspirators had raised to an art form. Even now, years later, he had yet to meet face to face with any of his allies. The only communication was one way. There were no secret drops, no moonless rendezvous in empty fields, only the letters. Just as the day he was recruited, when he was nothing more than a shattered shell of his former self. Sitting in a Healer's Hut, begging death to take him, he turned to find the first letter waiting upon his pillow.

It was evident from the beginning that The Plan, as they called themselves, were of a kindred spirit. They shared with him a concern that the Valley had become corrupted and held a deep mistrust of the Becknor's rulers. From the lowest ranks of the Royal Court to King Gaius himself, The Plan sought a change. Their mission was to take the Valley back to her former glory. A strong Valley is an isolated Valley and all that.

It pleased Cassius to no end when their mistrust would eventually include the Lady of Talwoods. The day she was proclaimed Regent, it seemed as if they understood that Lydia too was a threat to all. All those years ago, when they approached him anonymously, Cassius had pledged his allegiance almost immediately despite his many injuries. It had given him a purpose once again. And when Lydia came into play, he saw them as a means to an end.

The members of the conspiracy may have wished to remain unknown but Cassius had not lived this long to be played the complete fool. The contact had to be someone close at hand. Many times the letters had touched upon conversations among the Wise Men and Royal Court that were not for public ears. On two occasions there was mention of Cassius' own history, which told him that one of his allies was within his very limited circle of acquaintances.

A year ago, he would have wagered that the chief architect of the conspiracy was none other than the Grand Master himself. Even if they did not agree on all matters, Cassius believed they shared a vision. That was, until the day Galen had failed all of Becknor. It was Galen who had found the writings on the legend of the Blue Orchid and its healing properties. Cassius was at his side when he discovered it. He had advised his Master to ignore what he had found.

"This is the moment history has brought to us High One," Cassius had said when his superior began to waver. "Our enemies have given us a gift. Let Lydia die! Let Achelon's line fall."

But it had been to no avail. The people calling out for a cure and the sight of the girl dying in her bed was too much for him and he weakened. The moment Galen had laid eyes upon Hector, that accursed villainous knight, it gave him the only ray of hope that he needed.

Cassius now feared if Galen would ever have the resolve to follow through. Lydia had some sway over him now. Perhaps the time was coming for Galen to be replaced? Perhaps that was the subject of tonight's message. Surely the Conspiracy had become disenfranchised with his master.

Cassius broke the seal and read the latest epistle. The words on the paper were not what he had been expecting. Cassius read and read again with mounting confusion.

*The ill-timed Ten Day War with Everfrost has caused a schism within The Plan. Some of our founders now walk the Halls of the Divine. For now, all activities are to halt until the end of the Regency.*

*It will take time to recover, but there is hope. A new benefactor has come to our movement. Our goals are one in the same. With but one exception, Lydia. The Lady of Talwoods is to live. Our new benefactor has need of her outside the walls of our Valley. Beforehand she is to be the chief centerpiece to bring about Change. If she is to die let her serve her people one last time and then let her fall somewhere out in the Outer World, far away from the eyes of the people. Be patient. Change is coming!*

*Hail Becknor!*

"Madness," Cassius growled as he threw the paper aside and stood. He began to pace around his bedchamber in an attempt to calm his anger. It was of little use. He would have laughed if there had been any humor left within him.

So the Plan now sought to restore the Valley to its former self by turning to a new benefactor who has ties to the Outside? Surely Everfrost could not have depleted their ranks of the Plan so severely. And what had brought forth this schism? Had Lydia's so called heroics softened their hearts? Or was it this new benefactor? Had the very thing that Cassius had worried over for all his adult life begun? Was the storm coming?

But what distressed Cassius the most, was that he alone truly understood the real danger Lydia posed. *Our new benefactor has need of her outside the walls of our Valley.* Lydia outside the valley was potentially more dangerous than Lydia at the King's ear.

Plucking up the crumpled paper on the second attempt, his numb hand failed the first, he sat on the edge of his bed in sad contemplation. The Plan to which he owed the resurgence of his life was now proving to be nothing more than wasted years.

*It falls to me then,* he thought bitterly to himself. *I must act where others lack the courage or the vision to do so.*

So was the course of his life, as if it had been ordained since the beginning. This was not the first time Cassius had been forced by events to act alone. He still remembered the day he had killed for the first time. It was the same day the seeds of mistrust for Talwoods were planted and his true purpose had been revealed to him.

Thirty years ago, when he was just weeks removed from his promotion to full knight, a large raiding party had come down the Mountain Pass pillaging the local farmers.

Raiding parties had never been as great a threat as Everfrost. Mostly they would consist of small outlaw groups that dare not go to any civilized villages due to the bounty on their heads. For whatever reason, they liked their chances against the civilian Watch of Becknor and the Knights of the Valley. But on occasion warlords from the north, with starving private armies of a few hundred, would raid. These were far more dangerous as they were not only battle tested, including skirmishes with the armies of the Alliance, but desperate.

The day Cassius remembered so vividly was one of these invading armies. They had come in riding hard, destroying each watch post and slaughtering the men and women stationed there. Once inside the valley, they split in two. One sizeable group guarded their one and only exit, the rest fanned out raiding storehouses and farms, burning as they went.

Cassius and his group had been on the heels of one such party. Somehow the marauders managed to stay a step ahead. Their commanding-lieutenant, a dull-witted officer who had maintained the same rank for twenty years, kept splitting his forces to attempt a capture. By the time they arrived at a large burning farmhouse there was but eight of them still together.

"This mayhem is very recent," their commanding-lieutenant said. "The scum cannot be far. Fan out by twos in all direction. Call out when you find them."

Cassius glanced worriedly to Roland, the last man he ever had call friend, then replied, "With respect, all signs point to a sizeable force. If we go out by twos we could be overwhelmed."

"I did not peg you for cowardice boy," his superiors said with a sneer. "Still wish you were a lowly squire? You are a Knight of the Valley, now is the time you prove you have the mettle for the post." With that, he motioned for them to disperse and rode off to his ultimate doom. They found him later, his throat cut from ear to ear.

A crackle of thunder overhead had not helped Cassius' mood.

Roland laughed and said, "Fits the moment rather smashingly, no?" A heavy overcast was blotting out the sun and a strong wind from the south was making the tall fields of wheat before them dance. "Shall we take the center," he said motioning towards the wide path down the middle of the wheat.

Cassius rode side by side with Roland. Both had taken the Blood Oath the same day. Though they had never met until that day they had been inseparable during their training. It had not been by design at first, they had been partnered by the trainers for combat sparring the first two weeks. Compared to Roland, Cassius combat skills had been nonexistent. Before entering the Knights of the Valley, Roland had been conditioning himself for a year. His family held a long legacy of knighthood, a legacy of success and honor. It was said that Roland was the best of all.

Seeing Cassius' own skills were fleeting, Roland had taken him under his wing and began to secretly train him when time allowed. Within a month, Cassius was proficient enough to pass the first tests. Roland also started Cassius on the path of mental discipline.

"Like the foot soldiers of an army, a well-trained body must have a knowledgeable and wise mind to command it," Roland had told him. A proficient fighter and quickly becoming a masterful tactician, the trainers and lieutenants took notice of their gifted squire. If fate had allowed,

Cassius knew it would have been Roland, and not Hector, in the captaincy.

Midway down the path, movement on the opposite side caught their eye. A boy a few years younger than Cassius, in the garb of Becknor Nobility, and a tall man with long white hair wearing battle worn armor seemed to be arguing.

"That mismatched armor is not Valley forged," Cassius had said.

"But the boy is of one of the houses," Roland said squinting. "The colors, the dark blue and gold piping, is that House Achelon? What is Talwoods doing out here?"

Without warning, a volley of arrows flew from the wheat field to their right. Three flew directly for Cassius. The first flew safely over his head, the second was a glancing blow off his armored shoulder, the third was a mortal blow to his horse, who fell dead almost instantly. Cassius tumbled away as the animal fell. Falling hard to the ground he heard the thud of his horse hitting right by him. Flailing for his shield to protect himself he heard Roland's horse galloping away. Chancing a glance over his shield he noted the horse was without a rider. Not far from him, his eyes found Roland. Lying upon the ground, a river of blood rushing away.

Forgetting the threat of another volley, Cassius scrambled to his feet and had run to his dying friend's side. An arrow had taken him in the throat. His eyes locked with Cassius' as he gurgled his last breath away.

As Cassius closed his friend's eyes for the last time, someone called out in pain in the field where the archers had ambushed them. Leaving his now dead comrade, Cassius drew his sword and made his way through the grain. In a clearing not far away, he found a boy with red hair staring back at him. He looked to be the same age as Cassius. His armor had been dented and rusty. It was quite evident that the unfortunate raider had managed to break his ankle. His sword was drawn and in hand. When he saw Cassius his eyes went wide in horror.

"Please, good sir. Help me before they come back," he begged. "They hold me against my will, they raided my farm three seasons ago and have forced me to fight with them."

Cassius did not hear a single word. His eyes were transfixed on the red stained blade the boy held in his right hand. Noticing this, the boy threw the blade away as Cassius moved towards him. His cries for mercy died quickly.

Filled with bloodlust, Cassius took no notice of the two archers that had crept up behind him until he had heard the clink of their light armor. Twirling around, he was greeted by a fist to the jaw. Staggering back he attempted to bring his sword around but it was intercepted low by an ax wielded by his compatriot. Already off balance, Cassius lost the grip on his sword and could only watch as it flew away. The first attacker kicked at his knee bringing him down. Cassius then felt as one of them grabbed him by the shoulders, lifted him up, and then pressed a knife to his throat.

The second walked into view, sneering. Cassius looked up defiantly, he meant to meet his end staring into the eye of his executioner.

"Hold," a voice had called out. Shortly, the silver-haired man and the boy came into view.

"Release him," the boy demanded.

"You would leave a witness to your own treachery," Silver Hair had asked cocking a similar silvery eyebrow. Despite the color of his shoulder length hair, the man looked no older than his early middle years.

The boy had brought himself to full height, apparently bristling at the word treachery. "My father even now rides to the Palace to inform the King of the settlement he has reached with you. If there is no secret there can be no treachery."

"Settlement? He sends you to negotiate but rides on without knowing if I would agree."

243

The boy had smiled and said, "He knows your greed well, and that you could not possibly turn away from such a lucrative offer."

"Yes, ten thousand gold coins and an entire storehouse of goods is too good an offer," Silver Hair smiled. "But tell me, young man, does he intend to tell the king of the true nature of his negotiations? Does he plan to explain this to him?"

From a pouch on his belt, Silver Hair had produced a small wooden box. It was slightly bigger than hand sized, old and worn. The Boy's eyes went to it immediately but he remained silent.

"I thought not. Lord Magnus is no fool." The name had clicked immediately for Cassius. Roland had been right. Magnus was Lord of Talwoods, which means the boy was his son, Marcus. "But, what if I decide to keep this little heirloom for myself?"

"Then there would be no agreement, and you would have to face the full brunt of the Knights of the Valley," Marcus had said sternly.

"Yes, your splendid Knights that lose as many wars as they win. But by the time their full force is ready I will be far from your little insignificant valley. And I know your forces would never give chase for that would give Everforst all the more incentive to strike. Plus I would have a bargaining chip of my own."

"What makes you believe you could use that as a bargaining chip," Marcus had asked motioning towards the box.

"Oh, I do not speak of this. I would use the son that Lord Magnus has left behind to be my hostage," Silver Hair had said grinning.

Cassius did admit he had admired the boy's courage. He held his feet firm but there was no shortage of worry in his eyes.

Bursting out into laughter, Silver Hair had said, "Relax my boy, I do not believe in hostages. Kidnapping is a nasty business that ends badly for everyone. Besides, I like your father. Lord Magnus has a keen mind, I have enjoyed our conversations. Here take your item," with that he had pitched the box to Marcus who caught it carefully in both hands.

"Next time tell the mother of your betrothed to keep such valuable enigmatic items secure," Silver Hair had said once he had stopped laughing. "Speaking of which, I thought despite your people's many peculiarities you didn't arrange marriages."

Grumpily, Marcus had looked at the box in his hand and back up to Silver Hair, and said, "It has not been arranged in the old fashioned sense. Our parents arranged our courtship but we decided on our own to marry after our required services."

Silver Hair laughed again and then said, "Fourteen, and already wishing to marry. Though I am not one to talk. I married my first wife when I was not much older than you. I like weddings, I believe in having them as often as possible."

"I do not understand, how many weddings?"

"O dozens my boy, dozens."

"Did you not love your first wife?"

"I still do. I love all thirty-seven of my wives but she has a special place in my heart that cannot be touched by the others. And if she thought another had taken her special place she would cut my heart out with a dull blade and keep it in a box so no one could touch it again. But we waste time," Silver Hair said as he had put his arm around Marcus' shoulder. "Now you will take me to my gold and food, or should it be food then gold? I cannot decide if I am greedier than I am hungry. Along the way, I shall give you advice for your, um, wedding."

With a hand signal from Silver Hair, the two restraining Cassius let him go free. Though one of them had given him one last backhand across the face upon departure. Marcus had looked over his shoulder briefly to consider him. Cassius averted his gaze. His comrades and friend were dead, and there was strong evidence that Talwoods had been at fault. His heart hardened that day.

Cassius retrieved his sword. Once again he looked down upon the lifeless form of the man he had killed. For the first time, he noticed the sword he had been wielding was indeed red. Not from blood, but rust. But Cassius felt no remorse for his deed. Sheathing his sword, he turned his back on the grisly scene he had created and back out to bury the dead.

Sitting on the edge of his bed, still clutching the dispatch in his fist, Cassius bitterly reviewed his life from that day till now. For his deeds that day he was rewarded with a medal of solemn recognition, meaning he alone had survived. He never mentioned the truth of what happened that day. That Talwoods was still actively consorting with forces outside the Valley long after Achelon's death. There had been no record of the settlement. If Lord Magnus had reported it to King Gaius they both took their knowledge to the grave. But Cassius never forgot. He suspected the true nature of the raid had been over the contents of that mystery box, and that Talwoods was responsible for so much more misery than even he could imagine.

Refolding the crumpled paper he set it over the edge of his bedside lamp and set it ablaze as he always had. Only this time the burning paper was a symbolic gesture of breaking all bonds. He was no longer a part of the Plan. Just as he had now set aside all allegiances to the Wise Men, the Royal Court, both knightly orders, and Becknor herself. As far as Cassius was concerned they all either stood with Lydia or were an obstacle to her. The entire world was his enemy now.

Sitting there on the edge of the bed he smiled grimly to himself. Let the fools on both sides make their plans and counter plans. Cassius would ensure that Lydia died before she could take up the work of her fathers and add to their dark legacy. Soon the malignancy of House Achelon would be removed forever more.

# CHAPTER TWENTY

Doran of Amethyst Grove was a rather good distance from home. It was approaching that in-between time of night where one could have said that he was either out very late or an exceptionally early riser. But for those who knew Doran well, the less than savory dwellers of the Valley, the strange hours would have been no surprise. If a random passerby would have caught sight of him, they would have shrugged off the rather plain looking man if it were not for his armaments. Being armed with a bow, and a quiver full of arrows would be quite difficult to explain in the dead of night on the edge of a forest. It would have been a generous clue to his profession, poacher. Doran was one of the most successful in Becknor.

Poaching carried a heavy penalty. Take down a stag without a license and one could find themselves a guest of the Regent or ruling Monarch in one of the many stately dungeons for a month or more. But the quarry that Doran sought carried an even deadlier sentence if caught. Especially in the southern edges, deep within the Blood Forest.

All hunting was forbidden within the forest. It was considered as sacred as any of the many remembrance fields. Eight hundred years ago, King Straton, a paranoid and slow-witted king; a most dangerous combination, feared that the Captains of the Valley and Inner Circle were plotting against him. So he murdered them and their officers in their sleep in one bloody night. Assuming command, Straton intended to turn his eye towards the remainder of the Royal Court, but Everfrost had other ideas.

Seeing from afar that the Valley was in clear disarray, the Dread Overlord of the day boldly attacked with every last warrior. Having never bothered to study tactics, Straton ordered his knights into the forest in an attempt to ambush his opponent. The result was a slaughter of nearly every Knight of the Valley and twenty years of goblin oppression. To this day, the trees were still stained with the blood of the dead.

Forbidden as it was, Doran found this the best hunting ground for the highest profits. His clients, usually the wealthiest of Becknor, paid handsomely for the most forbidden prey. To some, it was a dangerous status symbol to show off to like-minded guests. For others, it was the opportunity to feast on rare meats. The more endangered the animal, the higher the pay.

Whether it was here in the Blood Forest, or another hunting ground altogether, it was Doran's custom to spend a few days in the area he planned to poach. He would observe the patrol patterns of the Valley Knights or get to know and befriend members of the local Night Watch. In the local taverns and public houses he became a familiar and popular face as he would spend a generous amount of both time and coin. There would be big cheers and grinning faces to greet him each night. Drinking and gambling always loosened the lips of the locals. It was especially helpful finding the weakest links within the Watch. Once that man or woman was identified he became their best friend. And it always began with:

"This would appear to be the loneliest of tasks," he would say smoothly. "Might I not join you for a spell and keep you company?"

The usual reply, as it came from the disheveled Watchmen that had stood before him three nights ago, was, "Ah, if only I could. It can be dangerous with highwaymen and poachers."

"Highwaymen, in Blood Forest," Doran scoffed. "There are no

goods or money wagons that travel these roads. And have you ever been attacked by a poacher?"

The man paused to think it over and said, "Usually they run the other way." He had a slight hiccup at the end and begged his pardon. Doran had bought him several rounds before his shift and smiled to see that he was not much of a drinking man.

"Aye, obviously they would run away. Just look how you fill out that Watch Unifrom. They see your imposing figure and run away frightened."

The Watchmen looked down upon himself frowning as if to say, really?

"I doubt I would be safer in my own humble cottage tonight," Doran said. Again the man looked down and up confused, but with a shrug, he motioned for him to follow.

That night was like so many before it, feigning interest in conversation while memorizing the patrol route. The weakest links were always talkers, not state secrets but personal details. The unsuspecting constable would go on for hours about a string of bad luck. There was gambling, occasional too much drink, but a solid four out of five were having troubles of the heart. Doran considered it a service really. For a night they were able to talk out their hard lives with a total stranger who would never judge them. How could he judge them? He was not even listening.

The dull-witted Watchmen of three days ago was experiencing less than marital bliss. By torchlight he explained his wife did not understand him, all she did was complain that he was out all hours. He was on Night Watch; where else would he be? He regretted marrying at all. Doran was waiting for the classic, "and there is this beautiful maiden" story. As chance would have it, they never made it that far. The seemingly blind, self-obsessed dullard walked them right into a bear. If it had not been for Doran's quick action they would have both been mauled. Well, the Watchmen would have.

Doran turned to run. Glancing over his shoulder he saw the Watchmen was standing firm and screaming his head off as the bear roared down upon him. Grabbing the man by the arm and turning him, Doran pulled him into a run. As they ran, the poacher kept his eyes ahead looking for an escape. He could almost feel the bear's breath on the back of his neck as he saw what he hoped would be their refuge.

There was a steep hill just ahead. His hope at the time was that they could roll down to the bottom and the bear would be too lazy to attempt chase. Coming to the edge, the Watchmen gave protest just before Doran shoved him over the edge and then joined him. The both went tumbling down, the Watchmen's torch and sword went flying away, Doran kept a firm hand on his money pouch to prevent it from joining them.

Once at the bottom, Doran turned to look up the hill. There was the bear, nearly four times the size of a man. It looked down at them and growling to itself. After a moment of indecision, it turned and went back the way it had come.

As Doran breathed out a sigh of relief, the Watchmen wrapped his arms around his neck and exclaimed, "You are a blessing from above." This close to the man, a whiff of his breath told Doran yet something else the man's wife did not appreciate.

"Yes, yes, you are welcome," he said trying to untangle himself from the Watchmen and his pungent breath.

"How can I ever repay you?"

"Trust me friend," Doran said looking back up the hill grinning. "We are already even."

* * * * *

Treasure hunters had their hidden vaults of gold, scholars discovered long forgotten manuscripts, and poachers of Becknor had bears. The most endangered animal in the Kingdom was the most profitable. There were less than two hundred that made the valley home. With sheer cliff faces on three sides, a river and a well-trodden mountain pass on the other, there was very little migration in or out by the animal. The moment Doran had laid eyes upon the beauty he could see the mountain of gold coins before him. Immediately, he had thought of half a dozen extremely wealthy individuals, including one highly ranked Royal Court official, who would pay handsomely. This one hunt could set him up till next spring. Unless he gambled it away by autumn. The latter was more likely.

For generations now, the Monarchs and the Regent had continued to deepen the penalties in an effort to save the animal. Doran knew that the hunt for them would end one day when the last had fallen. Even he might shed a tear that day, for his sake and not the animal's.

Now that Doran was sure of the exact whereabouts of the locals at any given time, it was time to hunt. Some would say that his preferred nighttime hunting was a handicap but he saw it as a challenge. His archery skills were second to none. He had honed them in his two years of service to King and Valley. Having never had to use them against a living breathing enemy, he had found a suitable hideaway during the recent war, he turned to archery contests and hunting. There was only so much riches to be had in contests and the hunting kept him fed. Eventually, boredom took him and he decided upon poaching and selling his wares on the black market. Doran found that he was quite adept at both but, again, after a few years the boredom returned. He found excitement again by testing his skills in a pure nocturnal exercise. The reduced field of vision, stalking his prey, never knowing if a wild boar or a large predator was stalking him. Now, with the prospect of a bear hiding in the night, he was absolutely giddy.

251

The joy was destined to fade as the hours and days began to tick away and there was no sight of the bear. Rarely did Doran hunt more than two nights in any given area. Even if he was intimately familiar with his hunting grounds. Patrols could shift unexpectedly or a member of the Watch could become ill and the roster would be rotated. But in making the bear his sole priority, Doran had willfully passed on several trophy kills that would have been profitable in their own right, he was in danger of losing money this round. With little choice, Doran went out one last night.

He did not understand. He had found the trail of the bear quite easily that first night. Had tracked him over hills and through streams. Not once did the animal show signs of leaving the Blood Forest. Somehow it managed to keep a perpetual distance between them. An hour before sunrise, just as Doran had given up all hope, something large moved just behind a thick grove of trees.

He smiled and whispered, "There you are my pretty beasty. You are going to keep me in food and wine for some time."

Carefully, Doran moved slowly through the underbrush. The bear was in the shadows. No good way of aiming for a vital spot. Doran knelt down on one knee when he was certain he was close enough. He pulled three arrows from his quiver. The first two he set, head down, into the soft earth in front of him. The third he quietly knocked to the bow and drew back. His first shot would be to startle it. If it ran to either side or charged him he would have a clearer shot. Once in the open he would rearm and let loose again. It there was time for a third he would take it but by that point, he knew he would likely need to turn and run. If he aimed properly the bear would be dead in moments, but there would still be enough rage for it to give chase.

As Doran took aim, he took note in the oddity of the shadow it seemed to cast. It was much larger than he would have thought. Mentally shrugging it off as a trick of the moon and trees, he drew back again and let fly.

His arrow sang into the night and true. But when it reached its target there was the oddest of sounds. I kind of thwacking, as if the arrow had broken on impact. The shadow began to move slowly, its owner was beginning to turn. Rearming, Doran took aim. Beginning to draw back he stopped, something was wrong. The size. This was not the bear or any other bear. Nothing in the valley was this large.

His blood froze as the form before him raised its head and Doran caught sight of it in the moonlight. His spine became like ice, his arms and legs numb, and his bow fell from his grip.

*This is impossible*, Doran thought to himself. *Never in the history of Becknor. This is impossible!*

Doran ran. There was no measure of time, he ran until there was no longer in breath in his lungs. Falling to his knees in exhaustion he listened to the sounds of the forest around him as he took great gulps of air.

To the east, the very first faint glow of sunrise was crossing the sky. In the distance, he could hear the forest coming alive with the sound of birdsong and then…silence. Not just the birds but every single creature in the Blood Forest seemed to have gone silent all at once.

Doran cast his gaze from left to right and behind and saw nothing. Then all around him, every nearby bird seemed to take flight in frantic escape. Still, he saw nothing. A frightening thought crossed his mind just then. What if it can see me?

Looking about, he was in a sparse area. Only a few trees round about. Perhaps if he climbed one he would be hidden from the creature.

Seeing a tall stained oak to his right, Doran staggered for it. Still exhausted from the run, he found climbing challenging but just manageable. He sat on a thick branch surrounded by a canopy of leaves to catch his breath. He listened carefully but could hear nothing. Satisfied that he was well hid, Doran delicately moved the branches around him so that he might see the fields. There was still nothing. Surely he had lost the creature.

Just as Doran was beginning to feel safe he felt a burst of hot breath upon his back. He turned to see a pair of large, amused eyes looking back at him. Doran took a breath to let out a scream, but the scream never came. Death took him quickly.

# CHAPTER TWENTY-ONE

If Lydia had been honest with herself and had honestly expected a different answer to her request, then her faculties really were diminished. Still, there had been a hope. As her mother had tried to instill in her, always leave room for hope. So with that hope in mind, she had let her reasonable request be known. Galen's reaction was predictable and less than enthusiastic.

"I am afraid that is not a possibility at this time My Lady," Galen answered. It was the only answer the Grand Master of the Wise Men seemed capable of. Lydia knew the words by heart, she had heard them daily for weeks now.

They had gathered in the Throne Room for Lydia's audience with the Royal Court as protocol demanded. Though in her "weakened condition," as Galen continued to call it, only a select few were allowed audience. Until such time as, again in Galen's second favorite set of words, "Her Ladyship was sufficiently recovered from her ordeal." In the meantime, most of the Kingdom was to be left to its own devices or was being overseen by, again, select senior members of the Wise Men. Which was not protocol. If Lydia had been more than the Regent she would have complemented them on their neat and tidy, bloodless coup.

So as Lydia stood by the throne wearing her customary white gown, her left hand resting on the right arm rest of the Throne, she looked down upon the "select" Royal Court. Today it consisted of the ever present in her life Galen. He was dressed in his silver and blue ceremonial robes. He held in the crook of his left arm the book for today's agenda. Normally this was a stack of books carried by one or more acolytes. To Galen's left was Aristide, in the traditional armor of his rank, black armor and blood red cape, and armed with his staff blade. His blonde hair perpetually centimeters from out of code.

The third and final member of today's Royal Court was the ever absent in her life, Hector. Even now he was looking towards her but not upon her. It was almost as if he could not will his eyes to turn in her direction. Lydia was amazed he had even bothered to attend. By his posture and the occasional glances towards the door, it seemed he was asking himself the same question.

*I am sure if you would have asked nicely, Galen would have dismissed you,* Lydia thought bitterly towards him. Surely the Wise Man would have been overjoyed at the prospect of an even smaller Court.

So here Lydia was, standing by the Throne within a room meant to hold hundreds, asking for permission to regain a small portion of her life from a trio meant to represent the thoughts, wisdom, and wishes of the Kingdom. Had she really expect for this to end well?

Bringing her irritation back squarely on Galen's shoulders she asked, "May I enquire as to why?"

"Aside from the fact that I still believe that granting personal audiences would do more harm than good," somehow Galen feared dinner conversation would bring about a relapse of the curse, "I am afraid that Master Nicodemus himself is not well. His advanced years have caught up with him, I am sorry to say. After more than a century of life, his mind is not what it once was. At my personal behest, the Healer's Guild has dispatched a maiden to see to his needs. He does not venture any further than his front door now," he said apologetically.

"How long has his health been in decline?"

Beginning to look trapped, Galen's face went pale as he answered, "More than a year now."

"Why was I not informed," she demanded with an edge creeping into her voice.

"You were engaged in important affairs of state at the time and shortly after was the invasion."

"Master Nicodemus is like family to me. The last of my family, in fact. My first teacher is all I have left from my childhood. No affair of the state, no matter how pressing, should have taken precedence over this news. I should have been informed."

"Yes," Galen said inclining his head apologetically. "You are right My Lady."

Lydia felt a pain radiating from her chest. The last time they spoke face to face was during the ceremony to honor Captain Vitus. Numerous times he had tried to speak with her but the itinerary of the night and Galen's second, Cassius wishing to confer with him, had kept them apart.

"Very well then," Lydia said after a moment of thought. "It is fairly evident that I have neglected my old friend and mentor too long. If he cannot come to me I will go to him."

"At that I must object," Aristide spoke up before Galen could even open his mouth. "Even at this late date the Knights of the Valley are still rounding up Everfrost stragglers," he said turning to regard Hector.

"This is correct," Hector agreed. Even as he addressed her, he would not look her in the eye. "We have received troubling news of missing livestock across the Valley in alarming numbers. Add in a series of random disappearances and all signs point to a much larger force at work in the valley than we thought."

Aristide nodded and added, "There is much open country between here and Amethyst Grove. One lone goblin archer, looking to make a name for himself," he left the last unsaid. "I cannot guarantee your safety outside these Palace walls. We nearly lost you once My Lady; I refuse to give that bloodthirsty horde a second chance."

Lydia could not believe how this was beginning to spiral even further down into the depths of the extraordinary. Galen was keeping her in perpetual solitude over his fears that she could break, and now Aristide wished to keep her a prisoner over the possibility of what could happen. She was surrounded by madness. When had there not been a monarch or regent who was perpetually in danger? Was that not why the Inner Circle had been commissioned? There had been many instances of illnesses and attempted assassination with varying degrees of success. She was no safer in solitude from a relapse nor did the Palace walls afford any extra protection. If the illness was terminal and the assassin persistent enough, death was assured.

Lydia had one play left, one last hope. She looked to Hector and prayed that he would be the voice of reason.

"I am sure, noble Aristide, that the Knights of the Valley are more than capable of seeing to my welfare," she said motioning towards Hector. Silently, she urged him to follow her lead, break whatever spell he seemed to be under and be the man she had known all these years.

Hector glanced nervously at the others as they turned to regard him. "I am sure we are My Lady. However," he said and then stopped, seeming to be overcome by a sudden bought of discomfort or guilt.

Hope failing, Lydia asked, "However, what?"

"May I enquire how much rest My Lady has had this past night? Moreover, the past fortnight?"

Stung, she said frostily, "Enough."

Visibly wincing Hector replied, "My Knights are more than capable of seeing to your safety upon the road. Amethyst Grove may not be the greatest of distances, but it is a long enough journey on its own. I do not think it is wise, or healthy to escort you across the valley on less than an hour's sleep."

"I see," Lydia said, no longer willing to keep the anger from her voice. "So now you have tasked the maiden at my door to watch my activities through the keyhole. Is it not enough that you all look upon me as if I am some delicate porcelain doll who may fall off her shelf and shatter, but now you will not allow me the common decency of the privacy of my own bedchamber?"

Galen and Aristide began speaking over one another in an instant. A long string of apologies and excuses. All the while Hector looking away. *You have been avoiding me after all,* she thought disappointedly. *What has happened to you?*

Tired of hearing the disjointed double argument from Galen and Aristide, Lydia threw up her right hand calling for silence. As protocol demanded, as laughable as that word was at the moment, silence fell. Her eyes fell upon the wincing Galen, she used her best withering stare. With a nod she allowed him to speak.

"Please forgive us this small trespass, My Lady."

"I should not think it small, High One," she said. "I am the Regent of this Kingdom. That comes with it the high price of a highly visible life. I would think the invasion of what little privacy I have not a small trespass."

Holding up his hand nervously Galen said quickly, "We have the utmost respect for you but we are still concerned for your wellbeing. At this point, you are the longest living survivor of the Fever-Sleep Curse and the first to survive thanks to the Blue Orchid Elixir."

"Which has worked magnificently," She reminded him.

"Yes, My Lady, it has. But we do not know of what lasting effects this or the Elixir will have upon you. Even the legendary alchemist Aldred Zen-Joffa, if that be who he truly was," he said glancing towards Hector with a frown, "warned that it would be some time before the nightmares leave you. As for the Elixir, our own books, and histories are so incomplete that I have found no record of it ever being administered. It conceivably is every ounce the miracle cure we prayed for, and I have no doubt that it is by the results," he said motioning towards her. "But if our actions are out of line, it is only out of caution. You have given much in service to our Kingdom. Do you truly wish to risk your life as well?"

Lydia had grown tired of arguing. While she may have wanted to lay into all three of them, Hector especially, she held her tongue. Not because she saw the wisdom of the argument. She wanted to maintain all appearances of etiquette and protocol within the Royal Court. Most of all she wanted them to believe that they were winning the argument. Deep down she had no intention of giving in. As Galen spoke she could not help but feel she had yet to hear his true reasons and intentions. He was making too much of a show of calmness; while there was much anxiety in his gestures. After so many years of officiating the Royal Court, Lydia had become adept at reading body language; and the secret language of Valley Politics. While Aristide was his usual showy "all for the honor of Becknor" demeanor and Hector was an empty shell, Galen was speaking in half truths. And she did not believe for one moment that the spying maiden had been to benefit her health. Fortunately, as she had become quite skilled in understanding the secret language; she was even better at speaking it herself. She knew exactly how to tell the Royal Court precisely what it wanted to hear.

"You are right of course," she said, even managing a gracious smile. "I suppose my lack of sleep has impaired my judgment. I see now that I have acted foolishly and without any regard to my own safety. I am truly blessed to have so many wise and caring individuals looking after me in my time of need. I can forgive this, as you say, small intrusion, as long as you promise that something like this will never be done again."

"I assure you My Lady, we only had your best interests at heart," Galen spoke soothingly to her. "We will never act as foolishly again."

"Just as I promise to put off this foolish notion of riding out to Amethyst Grove," she lied. She smirked inwardly as all three had the nerve to look relieved. Amazing no one in the court had learned to read her. Hector knew her best and even he seemed to be taken in by her act. Another sign that something was terribly amiss. Or was it that he too believed she was impaired? Regardless, it all worked to her advantage.

"I have no objections of personally escorting you to Amethyst Grove," Hector spoke up. "I would just like to see you in better health before attempting the journey."

*Oh, you do not get off that easily,* she thought at him.

"Thank you, captain," she answered with a false but seemingly believable smile. "Since a decision has been reached I see no reason to hold things up any further. Shall we move on to today's agenda High One?"

Galen nodded and opened the book at his arm. The session was as brief as the Galen approved Royal Court was limited. The agenda itself was so truncated it neared the border of vulgarity. For months Lydia had been within a vacuum of news and by the end of the session she almost knew less. She did learn that the farms were on track despite the war. There would be food enough for the Valley and plenty left to fulfill all Outsider agreements. This included a surprising bump in the request for grain by Isaac's Hold. With a true war to fight, the City-State had doubled its order and tripled its payments. As for new details on the war, here Galen did not have to hold back. Becknor knew as much today as it had months ago.

According to a courier, the Alliance had gone forth to keep the peace as a series of civil wars had broken out in a small handful of the thirteen realms. Which begged the question, why were seven of Isaac's Hold's ten legions needed to keep the peace. Especially when Greater Ortivan had already sent a sizable force. And why would the High King of the Alliance, along with many of the Vanguard Knights, march with them?

Lastly, there were no petitions, no rulings brought before her. She thought to ask Galen how could the Kingdom go months without a regency decree? Knowing that the answer would only make her angrier, Lydia decided to bite her tongue.

And so ended Lydia's session with the "Royal Court." The entire proceedings lasting not even an hour. Galen closed the book within his grasp with a note of finality and as protocol demanded, laughable on a day that had seen ample breaches in said protocol, Lydia thanked them for their service to the Valley and dismissed them. Removing her hand from the Throne, Lydia fixed her gaze on her next target.

"Captain Hector, I would have a word with you before you leave."

"I have many pressing matters to see to My Lady. Perhaps another time."

"It will take only a moment," she said walking towards him. "I shall escort you to the gates." The words were barely out of her mouth before a concerned Galen turned and raised his hand.

Turning towards him, Lydia smiled and said as curtly as possible, "I do not intend to walk through the gate itself. But seeing as I have more than survived the stresses of today's session and that I am now allowed unsupervised trips up onto the battlements, I can see no harm in escorting the Captain through the gardens of the outer courtyard."

Turning quickly to Aristide she added, "And if by chance I am struck within the courtyard by a very fortunate goblin's arrow, then you will know that our impressively tall walls need to be built a few spans higher."

Again she turned to Hector, offered him one of her best "you will say yes if you know what is good for you" grins, and motion for him to lead the way.

"Very well My Lady," he said looking miserable. They walked in silence side by side until she was sure the rest could not hear.

"I am rather perturbed with you," she said right away.

"Sorry My Lady, but I do agree with the rest. You are not ready for such a long journey."

"I am not speaking of that, but I am seriously cross with you on that account as well. Just tell me you at least pretended to argue against the spying."

The uncomfortable silence was all the answer she needed.

"Of all the people to agree to this," she said disappointedly. "If you truly wished to know the state of my health why did you not come and ask."

"Galen had forbidden any visitation," he said. He continued to walk forward without turning to regard her. "For what it is worth, I did not voice my support."

"But obviously you did not voice your descent either," she said sighing. "We will speak of it later. Today I just want to know why you seem to be avoiding me. Ever since you awoke from your seven-day sleep and the ceremony, you have made numerous excuses to my requests."

"Sorry My Lady, my duties have kept me busy since my return."

"So busy that you could not spend time with a friend? That never seemed to stop you before."

"I am sorry."

"And why are you so formal with me again in private? It took years for you to agree to call me by name and not by title when we were alone.

Now every other sentence ends in 'My Lady.'"

"Sorry."

"Stop apologizing Hector," she said exasperatedly. "Why will you not look upon me? Did I offend you by not informing you of my real plans during the war? Has anger so engulfed you to the point that we are no longer friends?" For the first time, he stopped and turned to her.

"Of course, we are friends. And there is nothing in this world you could do to ever offend me," he said but she could see an inner turmoil in his eyes. What harm had the quest for the Elixir done to him? For a moment she could not decide whether to be angry with him or concerned for him.

He did not give her a chance to decide as he was once again on the move.

"Much has happened since we last spoke in the Viewing Tower that night," she said trying to match his pace. "I only thought we could catch up."

"Perhaps another day."

At first, Lydia did not realize that they had stepped beyond the threshold and into the courtyard. A few steps into the sunlight was all it took to distract her. She was on ground level and outside. For a moment she knew how the maiden's felt in those fanciful tales of old, when they were finally freed from their prisons in the highest towers. Her pace faltered and she began to drink it all in. The green grass, the decorative flower beds; the flowery aromas that never quite made it up to the top of the Palace was now tickling her nose. Even the sun seemed brighter here on ground level. It all called to her and she wished she could just kick off her shoes and walk through the grass.

Snapping back to herself, Lydia glanced back to see Hector making for the gate. Seeing his opportunity he was making every effort to escape.

Catching him she asked, "No escort from the barracks?"

"I have taken to walking the distance in solitude. It is less than half an hour on foot. Good for meditation."

"I see, I am glad that your duties at least allow you extra time to meditate but no time for visiting," she said and he did not answer. "May I ask how long now you have been taking the extra time to clear your mind?"

"Some time now," he admitted as they neared the gate.

"Hector stop," she said so loudly that her voice echoed across the courtyard.

He obeyed wordlessly.

"Please, look my way," she said in little more than a whisper, realizing all eyes were now upon them.

He again obeyed wordlessly.

"What has he done to you," she asked, very concerned now.

"Who?"

Irritation growing again, she said, "The King of Lies."

"I thought it was the opinion of the Kingdom that I met an imposter and not Aldred Zen-Joffa."

"The opinion of the Wise Men, not mine. They may have the privilege of writing our history, but if my friend tells me he met with Aldred Zen-Joffa, then he very well met the notorious immortal."

There was the briefest change in Hector's eyes at her words. A moment of gratitude perhaps, but also the man she had known. But it was only a fleeting shadow and he was gone again.

"I have read the account of your quest. I find it all remarkable. I would like to discuss it with you at length one day."

"Nothing really to tell," he said. "It was all rather boring."

"Not to me," Lydia assured him. "It was to my benefit."

"I cannot see where hearing the words from my lips would alter the story in any way."

"Perhaps I would like to know why you seem to be so vague about your telling of the third trial."

His posture stiffened as he said, "There is no vagueness about it. It is the full account."

"I do not believe that for one moment. You and I have sat for hours and even in the simplest matters you recount everything to the greatest detail. I know when you are holding back."

"It was the simplest of the three trials really."

"The simplest, a vision of my future and you cannot elaborate beyond simplest?"

The pained look had now returned to him. Worse yet, it was now accompanied by a hollowness in his eyes. His mind was elsewhere.

A short bitter laugh escaped from her as she asked, "Who are you?"

"I am your friend," he said with a pained smile.

"Are you? Are you really," she said doubtfully. "Then take a few moment and let us walk the grounds. One circuit around the outer court and you can be on your way. There is no need to discuss Aldred Zen-Joffa or his Three Trials. We will pretend as if the past three months never happened. No Everfrost, quests, or curses. We will be two old friends reuniting after a long absence. Just a little time to talk."

"I understand, but unfortunately, that is what I do not have," he said looking away again. "The ranks of the Knights of the Valley are still depleted. We are still working our way through the reserve rosters to ensure that even our basic defenses are at full strength. Perhaps another day, My Lady."

*My Lady again,* she thought bitterly to herself. It was those two words, after being shoved to the side once again, that stoked her anger to the breaking point, and bruised her heart. Emotionally, she could no longer stand the sight of him and maintain control. She felt her hands balling into fists so tightly that her fingernails dug into the flesh of her palms.

"Very well," she said sternly. "Go and see to your duties, *Captain*," with that she turned and left him by the gate. She could feel his eyes upon her back but she refused to turn and look. She sincerely hoped her tone stung him as much as his poor choice of words had her.

* * * * *

Lydia made her way quickly back into the Palace and up to the western facing battlement seeking some small refuge. At least there would be no Wise Men, no Knight Captains, or spying maidens. Pacing from side to side, Lydia took deep long breaths, attempting to calm her anger. How could one person change so much? It was incomprehensible to her how someone could one day be responsible for so much good in one's life and the next bring so much misery.

The words of the Dread Overlord floated back to her just then, almost as if he were there listening to her thoughts. "The ones we trust the most are the very ones who twist the blade as they plunge it into our back." It was his response to Lydia admitted that Hector was a friend. His last words to her about Hector was that she would wake one day and find, "the man that you had put your trust in was nothing more than the stranger you never knew at all."

Lydia had refused to listen to his words then and she was just as inclined to ignore them now. But Hector's behavior was beginning to make the goblin ruler sound prophetic.

Letting out another sigh, Lydia finished her pacing and leaned against one of the, still cool, stone walls. It was still early enough in the morning for the western side of the Palace to be in the shade. Soon the summer heat would build and the stone would begin to bake. And again the air was still. *Where is a breeze when I need it?*

Her mind turned again to Nicodemus and again her heart ached. The situation with Hector, and her hurt feelings aside, there was still work to be done. Her instincts, like a small voice within her heart, were telling her she needed to ride out and speak with Nicodemus that very day. If nothing else, she needed to see the state of his health for herself. Call it paranoia, but Lydia was no longer willing to take anyone's word on face value.

*Perhaps Galen is right. My mind is impaired. Seeing conspiracies and murder where there may be none.* But being spied upon by the Court did little to downplay her doubts. *Only Nicodemus can put my fears to rest.*

There had to be a way to get to Nicodemus. Getting out of the Palace would not be as hard as Galen and the Royal Court would believe. Lydia's network of allies would be more than capable of finding an exit. But outside the walls, she would be recognized within moments. She needed a disguise, but one that could blend in without notice.

As Lydia contemplated and plotted, her eye began to take in the beauty of the valley, the lush green fields, and trees surrounding the Palace until movement caught her attention. Frowning she could not believe her bad choice and luck.

"I should have chosen the eastern side," she growled to herself. "I would rather have suffered heatstroke than to see more armor."

But did she really expect to not see knights? There was no place within the circuit that the Knights of the Valley did not march or conduct training exercises upon. Before Lydia's eyes now were a group of heavy cavalry knights riding upon horseback. Their heavy, dull, metallic armor reflected no sunlight but one hundred horsemen riding in formation were not hard to find in the noonday sun.

Again her mind went back to Hector and her mood threatened to sour further. At least this group was faceless, armored head to toe with heavy iron helms. Helms with fully obscuring face plates that protected the wearer from flying debris. A group of faceless knights. Faceless.

Lydia stood upright and smiled.

# CHAPTER TWENTY-TWO

All Hector could do, as he watched Lydia walk away, was to once again questioned his actions. He knew all too well that he was endangering his friendship. And why? Just so that he did not have to explain.

He could see the anger in her posture, but he knew it was more than that. Her last words to him had stung not because of the anger in her voice, but the hurt. Hurt he had caused. He stood at the gate and watched until she was out of his sight. He continued to look on for a moment more before turning away as well.

Hector began his journey on foot to the Barracks. Just as he told Lydia, he begun to use this time for meditation. Meditation was a loose term for what it he was actually attempting. Self-contemplation sometimes turned to self-loathing and both required solitude to be done properly.

His self-conflict had opened up with an assault on two fronts. The first being Aldred Zen-Joffa's question, "Do you love her?" Why this question continued to bring him so much misery he could not say. Though, Zen-Joffa was also of the opinion that Hector was lying to himself about Lydia. Hector was at odds with that last statement. How could one lie to himself and believe that lie?

*When your life is a half-truth.*

The second offensive came to him each night just as he was beginning to close his eyes. The look from his mother, that haunted and tired glance. All families have that nonverbal language of knowing looks and glances. "You promised," that look said. "You promised you were not seeking death. You promised to live." That look and those unspoken words were what he could not lie to. They were the doorway to the memories and failures he condemned himself for. The moments that had led him down his current path and his promise. He had promised and yet, when he traveled to win Lydia's salvation, had he not promised to himself he would return victorious or not at all? Was that not the true reason he was avoiding Lydia? That Lydia had become more important than a tearful promise from long ago. Or was his misery even deeper, was it because of another, more secret promise. The promise within the promise.

*Do you love her?*

Hector knew all too well that he was like an open book to Lydia. What she did not intuit herself she outright asked. And whatever Lydia asked, Hector answered. Remarkably in five years, she had never strayed close to the subject of his promises. Even accidently. Even that day in the stables, all those years ago, never did she follow up her questions with, "Why did you choose knighthood?" But now, thanks to Aldred Zen-Joffa, the path would be wide.

He could see it all unfolding in his mind. Telling her the true and accurate account, not the one he had given to the Wise Men. He could see her listening attentively, drinking in every word. At the end, she would cock her head to the side and ask, "Why would he ask you this?" This time, the answer he had given to Zen-Joffa would be appreciated but he could hear her ask, "Do you?" His answer would then lead to more questions and each answer would bring him closer to the promise given.

*Would that be so terrible? Being your friend, would she not understand?*

Yes, and yes. She would know everything. Including the life that he now lived was not his own but another's. Would she be as accepting of him then? Would their friendship survive such a revelation? And....

How long had he been back inside the Barracks? How long had he been in the war room? And just how long had Darius and Helena been speaking?

Hector stood in the middle of the room looking upon his two Trusted Hands as they looked back at him expectantly. Their next reactions were as different as their personalities. Helena's eye narrowed as she began to look concerned. Darius began to look confused just before his features began contorting into a big grin just as his distinct booming laughter began.

"Aye now, this is certainly a first," Darius said as he caught his breath. "Between the three of us, it is usually myself that comes stumbling into the Barracks oblivious to my surroundings. Although for me, the cause is usually due to being distracted by the recent memory of a beautiful maiden from the previous night," Darius added wistfully.

Helena laughed shortly and said, "No, with you, it is usually the entire barrel of ale you consumed the night before and passing out face first in some puddle."

"Aye, that too love," he said with a chuckle.

"Do not call me that. You know I detest that. I have not nor shall I ever be 'your love.'"

Darius clutched at his chest dramatically and moaned, "Oh, thou hast injured me with thine cruel words. However shall I go on?"

"If you keep going on you will be injured," Helena promised.

"Now, now fair Helena. Why are you forever playing the cold heart? You know I caught thine eye the day of our first meeting."

"I am surprised you could remember yesterday considering the lifetime of ale and wine that has gone to your head by now."

"Ah, but you do not deny being smitten with me," he said smiling devilishly.

"My apologies," Hector said raising his hand before Helena threatened to draw her sword and lop off Darius' head, again. "I was lost in thought."

"No doubt," Darius said with another chuckle. "We have been at your side since the gate."

"Truly," Hector asked. Looking towards Helena, still the look of concern in her eye, as she nodded in agreement. "Well then, shall we discuss our depleted ranks?"

The smile faded slightly from Darius' face as he answered, "That is precisely what we have been doing."

Hector closed his eyes and began to massage the bridge of his nose. *Focus Knight of Becknor, Focus,* he admonished himself before looking up at them again.

"Then we shall discuss it again," he said motioning them to the map table. "So what is the good word on our efforts?"

Darius frowned and said, "The reserve rosters are brimming with the names of many, still living candidates. On the good side of the scale, there are enough able bodies in the rosters to bring us back up to full strength. Though on the counter side we will all die of hunger this winter because there will be no one left to work the fields."

"So this is all," Hector asked unable to keep the disappointment from his voice. "Nothing more?"

Darius shrugged and said, "Truth be told, there is another, rather large group of seasoned knights. Some would say over-seasoned. I am sure they would be more than willing to volunteer. Yet, once we fitted them with proper armor and weapons their hearts would fail within ten paces."

Hector turned from Darius while he was still speaking and said to Helena, "And I am hesitant to ask about the possibility of new squires."

"Over the next two months more than five hundred will reach the

Age of Responsibility and be ready for their two years' service," Helena said raising Hector's hopes slightly.

"Five Hundred is a start," Hector mused.

"Of which, only a handful have stated their intentions of joining our ranks," Helena added knocking Hector's slight hopes to an all new low.

"Bringing all five hundred to the Knights is possible," Darius spoke up. "We would need a special conscription decree from the Regent to make it work. Surely your friendship with the Lady Lydia could go a long way to securing that decree."

"And if we did," Helena interrupted, "I am sure that the Guild Masters will take out assassination contracts and have us murdered in our sleep. The Builders especially. Some of their number threw in with us to help evacuate the people to Citadel. They suffered nearly as many losses. Now with so much yet to be repaired and so little hands to spare," she said with a shrug leaving the rest unsaid.

Hector sighed. He did not see any chances of getting any special decrees from Lydia anytime soon, nor was he in a rush to be murdered by his countrymen. Rubbing the back of his neck, Hector looked down and regarded the map of the Valley.

Thankfully, the routes into Becknor were limited. One could make an argument that there were two ways in. The Mountain Pass, which was a stone's throw distance from the Dominion of Everfrost, hence the goblin kingdom's preferred route of invasion, and the River Pass on the southwestern boundary of the valley. The River Pass was a pass in name only. Once outside the valley and into the remainder of the mountain range, the Becks-Dali River quickly turned from a gentle stream and into a swift moving, giant boulder strewn, raging river of certain death. In the last century, only two small invasions had come from that direction. Both times it had been a small team of desperate and starving bandits. By the time they made it to Becknor proper there were only one or two survivors.

Hector's eye fell to the south of the map and he asked, "How many encampments still operate in and around the Blood Forest?"

"Only two," Helena answered.

"Close them, and bring those Knights north of the river."

"The commanders there have reported some sort of increase in activity in the wood. Animals are disappearing at an alarming rate."

"That is now the exclusive problem of the Watch," Hector said firmly. "In peacetime, I give no second thought in hunting down poachers but not with these numbers."

Running his hand along the eastern edge of the map Hector ordered, "Also close the fort and outposts at the foot of The Giant's Teeth in the east. It has never been more than a place for our people to run to when all hope has failed. In our entire history, no one has ever invaded from the east for they know it to be certain suicide."

"There is always a first time," Darius said with a shrug.

"Any army brave enough to climb down those sheer cliffs deserves to take us," Hector answered. The Giant's Teeth was a tall, steep and craggy mountain range that made the eastern border of Becknor.

"So we leave the south utterly empty and weaken our eastern side," Helena said looking Hector in the eye. "May we know what you are planning?"

"We have very little choice," Hector said as his eye fell back to the map and the Mountain Pass. "It is the one solution. The only move available that has been glaring right at us. We have no choice but to reopen Barricade Garrison."

"Our ancestors closed that garrison for a reason," Darius argued a few moments later as the trio was making their way through the stables.

"Yes, fear," Hector said flatly.

The stables were quickly filling with heavy cavalry and horse masters. Making up nearly a quarter of the barracks' size, more than two hundred horses were housed within. Nearly half of Becknor's heavy cavalry and the few select personal horses set aside for the officers of the Knights of the Valley were cared for here.

Hector, minus his ridiculous ceremonial cape, moved deftly through the stables sidestepping obstacles as men and women, knights and squires, were running to and fro through the chaos, as his two Hands followed close behind. Hector had ordered a training exercise this morning and apparently the day's activities were concluded. He made a mental note to speak with their commander once he returned.

"Perhaps they saw the folly," Darius offered trailing just behind Hector's right shoulder. "To properly man Barricade is to send a substantial force."

"Two thousand Knights," Hector supplied the figure.

"Aye, two thousand. And when our ranks are at full it is a drain; even in peacetime. With our numbers this depleted it is madness."

"Yet, Barricade Garrison has never been used in a time of war," Hector said stepping aside to allow a stable master leading a horse to pass by. "Not once did Everfrost invade while it was in use. The simple fact is Barricade sits in the middle of the Mountain Pass, between Becknor and Everfrost. Our forefathers saw how the pass grows so narrow that only a few side by side, unarmed, travelers can move through cleanly. It has always taken Everfrost time to move through their side of the Pass. Two thousand Knights lying in wait could bottleneck an entire invasion force for weeks, perhaps even indefinitely."

"The descendants of those forefathers you noted saw the weakness of Barricade," Darius continued to argue. "A sufficiently planned sneak attack, using barrels of blasting powder, could collapse the Pass and then those Knights would be cut off. It would be a slaughter."

"This is true," Hector admitted. "But such an attack could only be on our side of the Pass. To work, it would require a small force carrying nothing but blasting powder, be stealthy enough to not be seen by our Eyes upon the mountain, regular patrols, and anyone looking out one of the garrison's windows or the front gate."

"Aye, of course, how silly of me," Darius said as they parted to make way for a trio of cavalry knights. "Because the pages of history are not filled with the tales of small but determined groups carrying out the impossible."

"You also forget Barricade is built partially inside the mountain," Hector said refusing to be dissuaded. "Even if the Pass collapsed, they could withdraw within and wait for reinforcements."

"Which will come from where precisely," Darius asked. "With all due respect my Captain, this exercise will prove to be foolhardy. Helena, make him see reason."

"I have to side with the Captain this time," Helena said from his left. "I do not think we have much of a choice."

Darius made an indignant sound and said, "'Tis madness. All of it. It will be our doom. And furthermore…."

"And furthermore this is not a final order," Hector interrupted. "That is why we are riding out first to inspect Barricade. I want to see how far it has fallen into disrepair. No point in sending a force if there is no viable garrison to house it. And stop worrying," Hector turned his head towards Darius and smiled. "I have someone else in mind for command."

"Thank you," he said looking, and sounding, relieved. "Surely I would not live a month without an ample supply of ale and wine. And the lack of, shall I say, companionship would drive me mad."

"That life of debauchery is going to," Hector was going to finish with "shorten your days" but found himself knocked onto his back instead. As his head made a sudden introduction to the hard stable floor he admonished himself for not watching his path. As he looked up at the strong wood beams that made up the ceiling he thought, *If I make it through the day without killing myself it will be a miracle.* Turning his head to his left he saw the crumpled heap of the cavalry knight to his left. Helena's shouting did not much help his throbbing head.

"Get on your feet this instant," Helena was shouting down at the fallen knight as Darius was helping Hector back to his feet. "You do not just casually run through the stables like an errand boy. A cavalry knight, most of all, should know better."

"It is fine Helena," Hector said once he was back up. "I am just as much at fault." He offered his hand to the fallen knight. For a moment they just seemed to stare at it a moment before accepting it. With a nod to the faceless knight, he said, "Go about your business, and keep an eye out for more absentminded commanders."

"Yes, Captain," a strained but feminine voice answered from behind the faceplate and then marched away.

"Mine might be a life of debauchery, but at least I can walk in a straight line while sober," said Darius with a chuckle.

"That is lovely for you," Hector said rubbing the back of his sore head. "I can rest easy knowing that my knights have perfect balance. Go ahead please and see to our horses."

Darius, chuckling, turned and walked away. Helena remained by his side expectantly.

Once Darius was out of earshot Hector said, "Speak your mind, and before you protest we have too much history together, so I know that face when it is troubled. Not to mention you have been too agreeable with my plan."

"Perhaps I just do not wish to be seen agreeing with Darius, it would go to his head," she said. After a moment of patiently staring she added, "I see the wisdom of Barricade."

"But?"

"I am worried that the wisdom of my captain, my friend, has been compromised."

"I assure you I am in complete control of my faculties."

"Are you?"

Taken aback. Hector asked, "You think otherwise?"

"It is hard to put into words," she said uncomfortably. "You seem, distracted."

"I run into one knight in the stables and now I am distracted?"

"You know precisely what I mean," she said briskly. Now that they were speaking as a friend to friend and not subordinate to commander, Helena was letting her emotions free. "It is as if you have lost your focus. You have been this way since the Glass Desert. It is almost as if," she stopped seemingly reluctant to finish.

"Go on," he said nodding. "If one cannot take criticism from a friend then they are not your friend."

"It is as if you are empty. That this Zen-Joffa took away the very thing you were living for."

*Do you love her?*

The twisting pain in Hector's chest flared again for just a moment and then was gone. Smiling sadly he asked, "You worry that Zen-Joffa has emptied me of my will to live?"

"You forget, I have seen you like this before. For years you excelled within the ranks of the Valley but you took no joy in it. You had your duty, you performed it, was highly commended for your skill, but you had nothing else."

Hector opened his mouth to respond but Helena stopped him with a raised hand and offered him a rare smile and said, "No this is not an accusation or criticism. I was there, remember? You had a fair reason. It did not stop us from worrying over you. Then one day, like a miracle, you snapped out of it. For the past four or five years you have been like the boy I once knew, but more. You carried yourself as one who looked upon the world ready to accept the challenges ahead. You became an even better Knight and warrior. Your wisdom and strategies grew well beyond your years, far beyond anything I had ever seen from you. Lastly, you actually had a zeal that had never been part of you, even before."

Again Helena's features became stone as she continued, "Then, this bloody war came and the Regent needed you. You rode out upon this grand quest and bested it as only Hector, the best and greatest of us, ever could. But then you awoke, and at first, everything was as it was, but shortly after you began to regress. Slowly, you have again become the man who merely exists, biding his time until his days have ended. I cannot help but be worried that Aldred Zen-Joffa has harmed you in some unfathomable way."

Hector at first stared back in stunned silence. Twice, within an hour, Lydia and Helena had voice nearly the same fear.

Smiling, Hector put his hand on her shoulder and said, "I assure you, I am neither under some spell or incantation. The trials were indeed a harrowing ordeal. The ancient alchemist has a way of stripping away the barriers around your heart and getting to your very center. But trust me, he holds no sway over me. Once I departed his tower our interaction ended. I sense no ill effects as a result of my time with him. I will admit, despite my week-long slumber, the entire exercise was somewhat fatiguing. As is the task of rebuilding the Order. I grow weary from my duties, not of life. It is nothing a nice long furlough would not remedy when the chance presents itself."

Cocking one eyebrow she said, "You? Take a furlough? Now I know something is wrong. In ten years you have never taken rest unless forced to."

"Well then it will be a well-earned rest," he said smiling. "Come now, we have left Darius alone far too long. Chances are a beautiful maiden has turned his head and he has wandered off."

Helena laughed shortly, "Unless a barmaid has sauntered in I am sure we are safe."

"Unless he has smuggled one into the Barracks."

"Again," Helena agreed sourly.

As they went in search for Darius, Hector's mind began to puzzle over not just the last few months, but years. So strange that he was blind when it came to the changes within himself. Especially considering he had noticed no such change. His mother had to remind him wordlessly of his promise, he was purposefully hiding from Lydia so that she might not ask too many questions, and now Helena had become worried he was becoming an older version of himself he never knew had gone away. By Helena's account, Hector had made this supposed change for the better when Lydia had come home to become Regent and a change for the worse after he had seen her future. Could Zen-Joffa have been right? Could Hector be lying to himself?

*Always be truthful to yourself?*

Hector set it all to the side for now. There was a task at hand. Rubbing the back of his head again he discovered a lump already growing. He sighed. There was going to be a sizeable knot before the day was over. Could the day get much worse?

# CHAPTER TWENTY-THREE

"Hector will be barred from the next session of the Court," Galen said as he moved grumpily through the halls of the Palace.

"It was a slip of the tongue Master," Aristide said at his side. "Who would have thought that Lydia would have deduced a deeper meaning?"

"Hector," Galen growled back. Finally coming to an empty hall devoid of Palace staff, Galen always feared that there were too many ears listening. It was a long hallway with every door to the left of them closed and the windows on their right shut tight. The curtains were pulled back, allowing the late morning rays of sunlight to filter in. Galen observed that they were alone.

"Their friendship is well known. After years together he would know how to phrase his words to drop clues."

"Surly Hector would have voiced his displeasure when we decided upon the spy."

"He did not voice his support either," Galen reminded him through gritted teeth. "Does he not know that we only wish to keep her safe? The watchful maiden was a key cog in the machine."

For the first time, Galen took a breath to calm his nerves. He knew he should have postponed her return. No, he should have kept her bedrest until Lucien claimed his throne. How was he supposed to keep her safe if he did not know her whereabouts at all hours?

Galen took notice of Aristide now that he was calmer. He seemed to wish to speak but was uncomfortable doing so.

"You have words to speak?"

"Master Galen, I would never second guess your wisdom. After all, it was you who nominated me for this post. Whatever it is that you advise I will do without hesitation."

"That is a lot of preamble for the coming nevertheless."

"This business is beginning to feel very distressing."

"In what way?"

Aristide looked to their surroundings again and said, "I am beginning to feel less like a protector and more like a dungeon master. This is beginning to take on the appearances of a thinly veiled insurrection."

Galen laughed and said, "I spent too much time trying to save the Regent than to attempt supplanting her."

"I did not say that you were," Aristide said in little more than a whisper. "I have served my Valley for twenty years High One. To reach a position this high, cannot be done without attaining a certain level of wisdom. Plainly speaking, I am not a fool. And I would ask you to cease treating me as such. Master," he added inclining his head.

That was it then. Galen thought he had been clever in hiding his true intentions. Most of the other Wise Men seemed content in believing every decision Galen had made was out of fear of relapse. Perhaps Cassius suspected otherwise, but he had kept those musings to himself. Speaking of which, where was his Second?

Out loud, Galen asked, "You think I have an ulterior motive?"

"This is Becknor High One. When it comes to Court politics, the cows being milked in the Palace barns have ulterior motives."

Galen could not help but smile at the image as he asked, "Then noble Aristide, what say you of my motives."

"I do not believe you seek the throne. You are, I say sorry beforehand, much too old to seek that type of power. Now if it were a younger member of your order, someone as young as Cassius, then I would be greatly worried indeed."

Galen was unsure if he was naming his Second at random or if the Captain of the Inner Circle had genuine suspicions. Regardless, Galen kept his face as unreadable as possible. Suspicions of Cassius could easily lead to suspicions of Galen himself. Especially if he were to echo Aristide's sentiments. Then the next question would have been, "And why did you not report this immediately High One?"

Aristide continued, "I think you move upon the path you wish to project to the world, but not for the reasons you give. You wish to protect her Ladyship but not from relapse. I am a simpleton in the fields of magics, wizardry, and alchemy, but even I know the curse is broken. You may not believe that the alchemist in the Glass Desert is Aldred Zen-Joffa, but you believe his words. Your overprotectiveness comes not from the wisdom of your profession but instead in the form of doting parent or guardian."

His words elicited the image of Lydia that solemn night. The image of those haunted eyes. Eyes that never look away.

Aristide continued, "Which is contrary to the previous five years. Yes, you and the Regent have been allies against the more radical members of the Royal Court, especially the Moneychangers, but you also have had many heated debates. So heated I have seen you look upon her with much resent. So why the change in heart?"

Galen stood impressed with Aristide. He was a master tactician in his days with the Knights of the Valley. A cunning warrior who knew when to be the hammer of war and the olive branch of peace. A dedicated member of the Inner Circle who would die to protect his ruler, whether they be monarch or regent. These were the reason Aristide had been his nominee for Captain. But now Galen saw in the man a master observer and quiet wisdom that would serve him well long after his time in the Inner Circle was finished. Perhaps Galen was looking upon the man who would hold his position one day.

Galen shrugged and said, "Perhaps it is merely an old man feeling guilty. Guilt from the fact that I had given up so easily when she was near death."

"I am sure that is a portion of the truth," Aristide said. "But that is not the why."

Galen thought for a moment then asked, "May I have your staff blade for a moment." After Aristide complied he continued, "A rather unremarkable piece of weaponry, would you not agree. Perhaps even appearing as nothing more than an innocent looking staff."

"For those who are not regular attendees of the Palace. I would imagine so," Aristide agreed.

"Say a man such as yourself takes a walk with this in his possession. The hour grows late and he is still a distance from home. He takes a shorter but far less safe route. This man comes across a pair of highwaymen. Seeing him 'unarmed' they draw their weapons, daggers or short swords, and advance. Today they have an easy mark. Surely he is still dangerous with the staff, but between them, they can get in past his nonlethal defense and bury their blades in him. Never knowing the entire time...."

With that, Galen held the staff away from him and pressed the four hidden buttons under his grip. With a sound of springs coming free, two long hooked blades on either end came forth in an instant.

"Never knowing the true danger they were in," Aristide finished for him. Taking back the staff with both hands, twisting the staff in two directions at the middle to sheath the blades, he asked, "Hidden threats, this is your worry?"

*Yes and no, my friend. I worry that my Second will slip beyond my control and murder Lydia before her regency has ended,* Galen thought to himself.

"That is precisely what I mean," Galen lied.

"Is there a direction my gaze should fall towards?"

Galen nearly gave up Cassius' name. He found he was still torn. Though he was doing what he could to keep Lydia safe, it was only for the sake of the Kingdom. The death of a beloved Regent would cause untold harm to the people. Lucien deserved to take his throne in the bright light of a glorious future, not in the shadow of a tortured past. As much as he had come to respect Lydia, the words of his fathers were still upon his heart. The line of Achelon must be hated and shunned.

"There is no specifics Captain," Galen said. "Perhaps just the paranoia of an old man."

"Regardless, if you feel there is a threat, then I shall charge my knights to be extra vigilant," Aristide said nodding. "But if I may suggest, High One, if it is truly the latter, then please allow Lydia more freedom to move about and govern. She has very little time left as regent. Let her take the full joy of the journey's end. Let Lydia have the glory she deserves."

"I will consider it," Galen offered. With that, both men went their separate ways.

Perhaps tomorrow he would allow Lydia more privilege. He could conceivably give her back full latitude in the Royal Court within a week. The continued nightmares could be a problem but then there was nothing wrong with letting her dictate the pace.

Galen felt a little more at ease now that he had warned Aristide. If Cassius did make a move it was more likely to be seen. Chances were that his Second would follow his lead. His hatred for Talwoods was genuine, but did he have the capability to follow through? His body was broken, as a member of the Wise Men he was highly recognizable, and now the Inner

Circle would be watching.

The sound of Aristide's departure echoed through the hall behind Galen, just as he came to his own exit. Suddenly a chill went up his back. *We were not alone*, his mind panicked. Cassius was here, he had heard! Galen twirled around to find:

The empty hall behind him. Galen laughed at his own foolishness. Conspiracies and counter-conspiracies were taking their toll. He had made Lydia safe. The Inner Circle was vigilant and Cassius would now be powerless to harm her. Feeling more relieved, Galen let the door close behind him as he walked away.

* * * * *

The two Inner Circle Knights stationed by Lydia's door eyed him curiously. Both women knew precisely who he was. His rank as Second Master of the Wise Men garnered him much visibility, but his time as Captain of the Inner Circle left him respected. Both made him the ideal assassin.

*So this was the great plan? Did you truly think I would not recognize your tactics, High One,* Cassius thought mockingly towards his master. *The Inner Circle keeping extra watch by the door of our sick Regent, her movements restricted to highly guarded areas of the Palace; I only lost one eye, Galen.* The former Captain of the Palace Guard recognized extra measures to hold internal threats at bay when he saw it. He smiled, only if his former Master would have been more vigilant, he would have anticipated Cassius' next move.

"May we be of assistance Master Cassius," the knight to his right asked.

"I have come to inform you that you are dismissed from your extra duties," Cassius said smiling as he handed the knight the decree he held in his hands. "Master Galen is satisfied that there is no further threat of harm to her Ladyship."

The knight unrolled the scroll and read the words herself. It was all in order, it even bore Galen's personal seal. Some time ago, Cassius had observed a certain habit of laziness on the part of the Grand Master. When pressed for time, Galen would lay his seal to several orders at once. He would stack them together and fan out the bottom of the pages. Without bothering to read each one, he would quickly set his seal to all. One day Cassius had managed to slip a blank parchment into the stack. Galen never notice. Later, when Aristide investigated the Regent's assassination, Galen would seem complicit by ordering Lydia's extra level of protection away. It was very likely Cassius would not live past the day, but he took joy in the knowledge he would be responsible for dragging Galen to the executioner's block and the abyss beyond.

*You should have let her die.*

After reading, the knight nodded to her companion. They both offered Cassius a salute, he returned it and thanked them for their service. He departed with them, trailing behind. As they turned right, he feigned a turn to the left before retracing his steps back to Lydia's chambers. Pausing at the door, he drew the small curved dagger hidden within his robes and knocked upon the door. No answer came. Quietly he inched to door open and looked within. Empty. Perhaps she had gone up to the battlements.

Cassius shrugged. It was just as well. He could surprise her upon her return. A thought occurred to him. Death was his destiny, perhaps this would be his last chance to solve the riddle. Surely Lydia would have the box.

After that fateful day in the field, Cassius had dedicated his life to not only unraveling the treachery of Talwoods but discover what was so special about the contents of that small box. The search consumed nearly thirty years of his life.

For a time Cassius remained with the Knights of the Valley. As he moved up through the ranks it moved him closer to the type of authority to look within the records of the knightly order without suspicion. He would eventually learn that Silver Hair was a terrible War Lord named Maksim Berengar. He was highly sought after by the Four Greater Kingdoms as a war criminal. But the Alliance did not dare send a force after him, he was far to the north and well entrenched. To go that far risked war with every faction in the Lawless Lands. Cassius also learned that Berengar was of the nymlus race. A tribe of man with life spans three times that of all others. All nymlus were known for their silver hair.

After he had learned all he could, and that the path for advancement had narrowed, Cassius found favor with the Captain of the Inner Circle and left the Valley Knights behind. Within the Palace, he could begin to investigate Talwoods up close. Quickly Cassius learned what everyone within the Royal Court knew, Talwoods kept their family business behind closed doors. All the other Houses could not help but brag about their great deeds or gossip about their political rivals. But the Lords of Talwoods kept to themselves. Even as Marcus took over the lordship after the death of Magnus, they remained a mystery. As Cassius attained the rank of Captain of the Inner Circle, he became shocked at how frequently the King sent Lord Marcus on errands outside the valley.

Cassius did all he could to unravel the mystery of the box. A frustrating endeavor of riddles and half-truths that did not entirely escape attention. As quiet as Lord Marcus was, the keenness of his awareness was without question. Eventually, he learned of Cassius' lurking in the shadows of his life and Marcus' profound memory helped him to remember Cassius from that day in the field. It led to a very brief encounter one night outside the Palace Gates as Cassius was going out to his then home in City Citadel.

"I am glad to see that you have prospered indeed," Marcus had spoken from the shadows. Cassius turned to see the Lord of Talwoods step into the moonlight. "Becknor would have lost a valuable asset that day in that field, if we had not intervened."

"Yes, I suppose I should be grateful that a murdering war criminal and a traitor were so close at hand," Cassius said with a fake gracious smile. There was not the slightest change of expression from the other. Marcus took a few steps closer, close enough that Cassius could have lopped off his head if he had wanted to.

"What your eyes have seen is only a fraction of what you know. Your service to King and Valley have been admirable and have served your interests well. Know this, I will do what I must to ensure the safety of my wife and daughter. Even if it means forfeiting my freedom and title in the removal of a threat."

Cassius laughed a low, menacing laugh as he said, "Then it should be a comfort to you that I, the Captain of the Inner Circle, perceive that there is no such threat to you and your house. Tonight."

"See that it remains so tomorrow and all the days that follow," Marcus said then turned and moved back into the shadows.

*If only you could see me now, rifling through your family's possessions as I lay in wait to kill your daughter.*

Cassius decided then and there, that he was too visible for such investigations. He retired from service a month later.

After an appropriate time, Cassius began to search again for the truth of that small enigma. He retired to an old farmhouse in a secluded section of the valley. Having made no friends in his time of service it made it easy for him to leave the valley on his own secret fact-finding mission. From Isaac's Hold to the Northern Expanse he searched for clues as to the business of Talwoods. Twice he followed Lord Marcus and Lady Anastasia on their business for the King. Both times Marcus made for the Alliance and Anastasia made for the north. Both times Cassius followed her. Little by little he was getting closer to the truth. It was only a matter of time, he felt, until he had the full answer. But then fire took Talwoods, the answers he needed, and the location of the box. Then, there was the question of his own injuries that had kept him bedrest for years. As consequence, this was as close as he had been in years to anyone in Talwoods.

There was nothing extraordinary about Lydia's chambers. There were fewer momentous than one would have thought. The one time Cassius had been allowed within King Gaius' chambers he remembered the great number of hunting trophies and family portraits that hung upon the walls. In contrast, Lydia's walls were nearly bare but for one full-length mirror, a family portrait, and the Talwoods Crest above the fireplace. It was almost as if he was looking upon the temporary living quarters of a guest. Which in a way, he supposed Lydia was. Her position as Regent was but a few short years, but the palace had been her home once before and was her home now. It reminded Cassius of his own dwelling. That was the one thing he had in common with her ladyship. Their ancestral homes were destroyed over a decade ago, hers was the more opulent to be sure, and his had burned for more complicated reasons. But Cassius wagered where the sparseness of his dwelling was to keep himself free of distraction and focused. It appeared as if Lydia had no intentions of living inside the Palace Walls past Lucien's coronation.

The box was nowhere to be found. Either it had been destroyed in the fire or Lydia was guarding it in a more secure location. Perhaps it was in a vault inside the Valley Embassy within the City-State. Another thought struck him. Was her Ladyship even aware of its existence? Nonsense! If the box was valuable enough for a Warlord to blackmail the Kingdom with, Lord Marcus would make sure his daughter was aware and made her its keeper. Perhaps he would enquire about it as she bled to death.

While the chambers were sparse in decorations, and the answers

Cassius wanted missing, something did catch his eye. A stack of journals on the bedside table. Selecting one Cassius leafed through the pages.

"So, you have a sudden interest in the fire," he whispered to himself. What had brought this about? Could this explain Lydia's sudden desire to speak with Nicodemus? Cassius had been listening from behind the door as she made her request. He was not shocked to hear Galen's refusal. Cassius had suspected Nicodemus knew much. But how much?

The sound of quickly approaching footsteps caught the attention of his super sensitive ears. Dropping the book, Cassius took station behind the door. As Lydia entered he would fall upon her.

"My Lady," a voice called out from the other side. It was Galen's spy. The door flew open and the young girl sprinted through. "Oh no," she said breathlessly.

Cassius stepped from his hiding place and backed to the doorway. "What is the trouble child," he asked when he was in place.

The girl whirled around and flinched involuntarily. It was a reaction he had long become accustomed to. His scarred visage and missing eye caught many off guard. At first, he cursed his scars until he realized it helped to keep most off balance. It made the task of gleaning information easier. It was harder to be lied to when the quarry before him was doing everything in their power to be polite and not stare.

"The Regent has vanished," the girl answered all at once. Her hair was matted with sweat and her cheeks flushed. "I have run from one corner of the Palace to the other. From the battlements to the kitchen, and out to the gardens. She is nowhere in the Palace."

Incredible! Cassius could not believe his ears. The most recognizable woman in all the Kingdom and she simply walks away without a trace. Could there have actually been a separate threat to Lydia than himself? Kidnapping? A group of Everfrost sympathizers? It would not have been the first time a Valley-Dweller had turned traitor for goblin gold.

Then a thought occurred to him. His eye fell again upon the Magistrate Records. She has gone to Nicodemus. For a brief moment, he panicked. Nicodemus had always been loyal to Talwoods. What if Cassius had been right and the old man was in possession of some knowledge? Now that Lydia was of the right age he would tell her everything and then…. And then, what? By all reports Nicodemus' mind was gone. Even if he had a lucid moment; would there be enough time to tell Lydia everything? And even if Lydia knew, she would have no time to act upon it.

All of this ran through Cassius' mind in an instant. His face remained expressionless. Coming to himself again he smiled upon the maiden and she again flinched.

"All is well child," he said trying to sound kindly. "You see, Master Galen has been impressed with Lydia's recovery. Her session of the Royal Court has gone exceptionally. He has recalled the guard at her door," he said motioning behind him, "and now he has granted her time outside the Palace walls. She had gone to inspect the City Citadel. Captain Hector is escorting her."

A look of relief came across the maiden's face. Especially with the mention of Hector. Always plant your lies as close to the truth as possible, this had always been Cassius tactic. Hector and Lydia had been inseparable for her entire Regency. Strange that it was only Cassius that believed there was more to their closeness. One only had to look upon the devotion of Hector. Only a man following the passions of his heart would risk everything.

"Thank you Master Cassius," she said smiling. "I shall ride to Citadel so that I may continue my observations."

"That will not be necessary," Cassius said raising his hand to stop her. "Galen is allowing her this time of privacy. If anything is amiss, Hector will inform the Master. Might I suggest you see this as an opportunity to recover your strength? You have shown your devotion quite clearly. The Regent shall not return until late afternoon. Surely you can retire to your own chambers. Becknor thanks you for your service," he said quickly as she was about to protest again.

Finally, the girl smiled and nodded as she departed, leaving Cassius alone again with his thoughts. For decades Cassius had despised Talwoods. Lords Magnus and Marcus. He learned to hate Marcus' wife the Lady Anastasia as well. But Lydia had managed something new. For the first time, Cassius had found respect for a descendant of Achelon. To sneak away while an entire Palace, no, an entire Kingdom was watching. That was skill. There was no doubt in his mind now. Lydia had to die before sunset.

# CHAPTER TWENTY-FOUR

Lydia felt very conspicuous as her horse clip-clopped its way loudly over the cobblestone path of the Circuit. Even though she was completely unrecognizable in the full armor of a heavy cavalry knight, she felt as if all eyes were upon her. Hector had told her on many occasion that being a Knight in Becknor did not garner you any special recognition. The Knights of the Valley were ever-present, seen upon every road within the Kingdom at all hours. Between acting as high-level couriers, assisting in the occasional Village Watch Patrols, or riding out to the various forts and barracks; a knight was as noticeable as crops in the field or a tree in the forest.

"The absence of armor upon the road would be noticed quicker than its presence," he had said once. It was these words she was trying to remember instead of mentally calling out to her horse to stomp quietly.

Between feeling conspicuous and the determination to see her former mentor, Lydia could not keep her growing anger with Hector in check. She supposed she should have felt guilty, but supposing and actually feeling were two different things. But if one was wanting to make a stealthy exit, you did not knock over the highest ranking officer in the stables. Much less the highest military commander in the Valley. Like Hector, she too had not been watching the path in front of her. Though she had landed in a heap beside of Hector, the armor had absorbed most of the landing. At first, she had been mortified of her mistake, but once she had discovered it was Hector she had knocked over she was actually glad. Even if it had meant her plan of escape would have been forfeit.

She was not clear yet. Lydia had never seen any of the "Heavies," as Hector had called them once, on the open road before. Nor did she see any other riding along the Circuit now. A knight on the road may be invisible to the populace but would a fully armored cavalry knight riding alone be an acceptable sight to a seasoned warrior?

There was but one way off the Circuit and that was the Gateway Bridge. In peace time both sides of the bridge was guarded by two knights on the ground and an archer above. It was these six that Lydia would have to convince to let her pass.

An argument could have been made that there was a second, possibly less watched, route off the Circuit. Edgar's Folly. The dam had always meant to have a secondary purpose as a bridge off of the Circuit. The road on the other side, with huge boulders strewn along the side, was too narrow for a large army to march across. It would have added miles, and much more time to her journey than Lydia felt she had. And, the Folly was also slowly collapsing as a number of its flood gates were stuck open and the structure within was slowly washing away. Although they had been assured by Isaac's Hold it should stand for centuries, Lydia did not wish to take the chance that today was the day.

Electing to stick with the known imp, as the saying went, it was not long before the Gateway Bridge came into view. It was the third largest structure in Becknor. Not surprising considering the Generals of Isaac's Hold were neither minimalists or subtle. Every building project was a monument and a statement of their military might.

As the bridge grew larger upon the horizon her racing heart's pace continually quickened. At this rate, she feared she was going to pass out and prove Galen right about her health. Lydia turned her horse and began her approach to the bridge. She could not help but feel the eyes of the waiting Knights upon her. They stood watching her, their armor gleaming in the midday sun. The two on the ground began to motion her way in an apparent conversation with one another. Any moment now she knew they would order her to halt and demand to know why a lone Heavy was making their way off the Circuit and into the valley.

Lydia had to fight the sudden urge to turn and go back. Instead, she made herself keep tight hold of the reigns and take a deep breath. Turning back now would raise suspicion. All she could do was watch as the knight to her left removed his helmet and looked up at her. Holding up his hand he motioned for her to halt. This was it.

"I do not envy you on a hot day such as this friend," the helmetless knight said, his face covered in perspiration and his dark hair ringing wet. Smiling he wiped the sweat from his brow and returned his helmet to its place.

"What we must endure for the glory of Becknor," the Knight to the right said with a snarky laugh.

"You speak the truth my brothers," called the female voice of the archer above. Her helmet was by her feet while her hair hung loosely around her shoulder. Most assuredly two major breaches in protocol. With both hands at the neck of her armor pulling at it for air, she said, "At least you don't have to stand atop hot stone for your watch."

Lydia, knowing it was her turn, said loudly, "Yea, but you are just upon the stove top, I must sit in the oven with the roast."

The archer nodded with a laugh and gave a halfhearted salute. "Hail Becknor," she said, with even less enthusiasm.

As the two knights below offer their stale salutes, Lydia offered her own less than enthusiastic reply. With that, she crossed the threshold and the sound of the horse's hooves went from the clip-clop of stone to the heavy footfalls upon wood.

While the floor of the bridge was wood, the outer layer of the bridge was heavy stone to protect the mechanisms inside. Above Lydia was one of two massive wood and iron gates. Even though they had chosen to not use the gates during the Ten-Day War in order to lure Everfrost to their doom, the gates would swing down on either side of the bridge and meet at the center. The thinking was that your enemy would spend days attempting to break down one gate, only to be demoralized as they found a second gate waiting for them. While covered from above, the bridge was left open to the sides so that archers could harry those working to break the gate.

The bridge itself was a bustle of activity while Lydia rode across. Carriages, horseman, and foot traffic had quickly surrounded her but did not crowd or impede her progress. Yet another of Isaac's Hold's building measurement. Any structure built had to meet a strict military code. All roads and bridges must be wide enough for a regiment of fully armed troops to pass through easily and quickly. An Isaac's Hold regiment always marched thirty across.

Passing numerous knights who paid her no mind, Lydia's nerves and heart rate began to ease considerably. As she exited the bridge she found the knights on the other end far less conversational. Then again, their side was shaded by a pair of tall trees marking the beginning of the main road into the valley proper.

A short time later, Lydia glanced to her right and then to her left. She was alone on the road. Despite the stifling and claustrophobic nature of a full-faced helmet, Lydia felt free. For a moment she wondered what it felt like to live the type of life where one could go as they pleased and not be watched and fretted over constantly? Perhaps one day she would be blessed enough to find out for herself. Perhaps she was even living a portion of that life now.

Before the fire, all trips outside of Talwoods were in the company of her parents or Nicodemus. Each journey was an immeasurably different experience depending on her companion. Nicodemus believed everything was a teachable moment, even in moments of leisure. Not that there was much leisure within his excursions. Nicodemus had taken her to many historical locations within the valley: birthplaces of kings or lords, the sights of battles as he described step by step the strategies and counter-strategies.

When her mother was not teaching Lydia the beginning of alchemy, or her governess the manners and protocols of being a lady of royal descent, her father introduced her to the Royal Court. The summer before the fire, Lord Marcus brought her into the Palace so she might learn of his duties there. At just over seven years of age, Lydia became bored quickly with the old men arguing what seemed like the most unimportant of matters. Regardless, she would sit patiently by the door until her father had had his say. She found his portions to be at least a little exciting. He was the Lord Emissary of the Kingdom and Ambassador at large, when he spoke it was often of the world outside.

The same day Lydia's world had shattered, her cousin, King Gaius, moved her to the palace where she was treated like any other member of his family. Though she did come to love him like an uncle, those days were never as special. How could they be?

In those days, time spent outside the Palace walls was accompanied by her governess and a pair of Inner Circle Knights. The Inner Circle Knights were a constant companion. The moment she exited her chambers in the morning until she returned to them at night, a pair of knights would always be trailing three paces behind her. Eventually, growing tired one day of their constant presence, Lydia would learn ways to escape their watchful gaze. That was when she began her exploration of the Palace and eventually found her hidden fountain.

Over that time she began to see less and less of Nicodemus. He retired as a tutor and began to dedicate his time to study. Now as Lydia thought back to those days when her former teacher did visit, Nicodemus seemed to keep a wary eye on the Inner Circle Knights. Almost as if he were unwilling to speak in their presence. A habit that would not change when he came to the Palace during the first few years of her Regency. Only then he seemed to have grown weary of nearly everyone in the Palace.

*What if what they say about his mind is true? What if it was a clue, not to dangerous conspiracies, but the beginning of the breaking of his mind*, a questioning voice surged to the front of her thoughts. Lydia quickly banished it away as nonsense.

Then came the day that Gaius sent her away to Isaac's Hold. At first, she begged him tearfully not to send her away. Leaving the Valley would kill her. Now she would say, excluding the time before the fire, it was the best five and a half years of her life. The Becknor Ambassador to Isaac's Hold, Myrrine, who was just twenty-five and already a seasoned diplomat. Myrrine was unflinching in her beliefs, full of bravery, and brilliant. Lydia loved her almost instantly.

Though very little changed living in the ambassador's home over the Palace. Every journey to the schools and universities, or to the nearby street market was accompanied by a pair of the Ambassador's Guard, always following three steps behind. The only saving grace was that they were not allowed inside while she was at study. The military leaders of Isaac's Hold seemed to bristle at the idea that they could not be trusted to keep the students safe. The one concession granted, due to much whining from the delegation of Greater Ortivan, was for public events and state dinners. However, they were ordered to keep their distance and be dressed in the common attire of the people. They could accompany their charges but had to blend in with the other guests or household staff. Though Lydia smiled at the memory now, there was one occasion her constant companions were quite welcome.

It was just a few days before Lydia was to turn fifteen. She was in attendance for the Day of Antioch celebration within the High General's massive dwelling. Dignitaries from every corner of the Alliance were present. Including a young prince, the nephew of the reigning Duchess of Greater Ortivan, Eldric Alsvaldo. Tall and lean, a head of thick brown hair, dark eyes, bright toothy grin, devastatingly handsome. Sadly, his handsomeness was greatly overshadowed by his chief character trait, extreme arrogance. Coupled with all the charm of a garden slug, any attraction Lydia might have had for the prince was short lived the moment he had opened his mouth to greet her.

Alsvaldo had acquired the reputation for romancing nearly every young maiden he laid eyes upon. The fact that he was handsome and many maidens were instantly smitten by his charming smile was not lost on him. A long string of broken promises and hearts were left in his wake. Lydia had been formally introduced to him a few days earlier. His father, hoping to make him a great military mind, had sent him to Isaac's Hold to finalize his study of the war arts. It was a chance encounter in the corridors of the Great Academia that Prince Alsvaldo had set his desires upon Lydia.

After the High General's banquet, most of the evening had been spent finding somewhere else to be in avoiding the smitten prince and his less than savory ambitions. In between hiding places, Lydia had managed to catch the eye of one of the Ambassador's Guard. The fact that it was one of the women guards made it all so much better and sweeter. Lydia informed her that she feared someone was following her and they conspired to set a trap.

Lydia stepped out onto the High General's personal garden that overlooked the City-State. Her only wish was that she could have had more

time to admire the spectacular view. A starry night overhead, the city below
was alight with alchemical lanterns. Wicks that burned continually with
nothing more than a small vile of an oily mixture for fuel. With not much
more than a small cup of liquid, the fuel and wick could burn for weeks
without changing. Its secret mixture was said to borderline on the
forbidden alchemy, but the Generals of Isaac's Hold cherished efficiency
over superstition. It was while Lydia studied one of these lanterns within
the High General's garden that she heard the approaching prince's
footsteps.

The sound of running footsteps quickly drowned out his. There
was a yelp of surprise and the sound of bodies tumbling to the ground. To
Lydia's momentary horror, the exercise escalated as the woman guard drew
her hidden blade and held it to the prince's throat. The scuffle quickly drew
a crowd, including the High General and Myrrine. The look of anger in the
former's eyes and the bewilderment in the latter's quickened Lydia's heart.
As Alsvaldo got to his feet, he loudly demanded satisfaction for this
diplomatic incident.

Fortunately for Lydia and all of Becknor, Alsvaldo's reputation had
not escaped the notice of his Excellency. A string of unpopular run-ins with
various higher class citizens, especially the fathers of several daughters, had
brought him to the attention of the High General. Combined with what
Myrrine had called, Lydia's earnest fear that her wellbeing had been
threatened, was all the High General needed. Taking the prince aside,
whose flawless chin was scraped and bloodied, and asked if he would not
be more comfortable within his guest house the remainder of the evening?
Lydia never laid eyes upon Alsvaldo again. The incident did not go without
reporting back to King Gaius. For the remainder of her time in Isaac's
Hold, Lydia found herself under double guard escort.

Now, years later, Lydia found herself in the constant company of two knightly orders, maidens that seemed tasked in reporting on her every move, and no small number of bodyguards that were trained to blend in with the "common folk." Perhaps now she had a word for the peculiar feeling that had been growing since the bridge. Freedom.

* * * * *

The road to Amethyst Grove snaked its way through farmland and farming communities such as Green Plains. By midday, the roads were empty with the exception of Green Plains. As Lydia rode through, it seemed everyone there was gathering for some sort of celebration. Its purpose a complete mystery to her. Apparently yet another item that Galen felt was unnecessary to report. She was glad for the people of Green Plains. Whatever they were celebrating she hoped it would be a memorable one. There had been enough darkness this year, everyone deserved to enjoy a day of peace.

Between Green Plains and Amethyst Grove were miles of farmland upon the rolling hills of the valley. Though there were other crops, the majority of the land was covered in wheat. Becknor wheat was a staple throughout the region. The fertile soil of the valley had provided more than enough food for all of Becknor for countless generations. The remainder was sold to merchants from across the Alliance. Even in the days of deep isolationism, the farmers gladly sold their overabundance to the Outer World. A strong Valley being an isolated Valley was one thing but gold was gold. And it seemed everyone was wanting Becknor grains and goods. Even the goblins of Everfrost, in between wars of conquest, bought Becknor goods. Though always through third parties, no self-respecting Overlord would dare lower himself to negotiate with the lowly Valley-Dwellers.

Finally, after a long ride in the hot sun, Lydia had come to the outskirts of Amethyst Grove and the rock formations that gave the village its name. Here the land gave way to large, jagged rock formations rising up from the ground. The rocks themselves varied in size. Some were roughly the size of a common dwelling, while others were nearly half as tall as the Palace walls. All were covered in a thick colony of purple lichen. The lichen seemed to thrive on the rock and nowhere else. The effect gave the illusion that giant amethysts were growing from the ground in a thick grouping.

The most direct way into the village, Amethyst Pass, was a tight and narrow winding road through the rock formations. So tight in places, only a single horse and cart could pass unscathed by the jagged purple rocks. Bunched so closely together, very little sunlight made its way to the road within. As Lydia began to pass through, she was greeted by refreshingly cool air. She began to remove her helmet and cool herself but thought better of it. No telling if someone was approaching around a blind corner. She promised herself that she would be free of the helmet soon. Not far from Nicodemus now.

Lydia was sure that the stories of her teacher's ill health were just that, stories. Just an excuse concocted by Galen to keep her isolated and within the Palace. The need for answers aside, she could not wait to see her old master. She felt like a child again, almost giddy. Just another mile or two and she would be there.

# CHAPTER TWENTY-FIVE

A slight, but steady knock at the door was demanding Elyssa's attention. She had been so busy preparing for the celebration she had nearly missed it. Besides, Myron was usually very prompt at answering every single knock of the door. Her son had declared himself "Keeper of the Door" a few weeks ago. Yet another example of her brother's influence. Another reason to flog him. When Elyssa finally opened the door and saw the faces before her everything clicked into place.

"I have something of yours," Ellanora said with a firm grip on the shoulders of Myron.

Elyssa sighed heavily and closed her eyes. Trying to remain calm she began to massage her temples.

Finally, she addressed her son by asking, "What did I tell you this morning?"

"Get out'a bed."

"After that!"

"Feed the chickens."

"After that. No, wait, did you at least feed the poor things or are they half starved?"

"I did, I promise," he said raising his little right hand to the sky and placing his left over his heart. Though, the hand didn't quite make it that high up as it sat on his stomach. "I did everything you tolded me."

307

"How," she demanded. "If you did everything I tolded you, I mean told you, then why did you not stay on the farm?"

"You did not say stay on the farm."

"What did I tell you about lying," she warned her son darkly.

"I am not," he said waving his little arms excitedly.

"Yes, you are, I told you to stay put."

"Not dis morning," he said. "You said, 'stay close to the farm,' and I did."

"No, you did not! Ella's farm is half a mile that way," she said motioning towards her neighbor.

"It is closer than a whole mile, and their farm is right next to ours, so I was staying close."

Elyssa had no reply. She looked up to see Ellanora actually laughing.

"This is not funny Ella," she said chuckling herself.

"I agree," she said nodding. "I made a discovery of my own just outside your front door. Sara," she said calling her daughter's name. For a moment there was nothing and then, ever so slightly, a small shape began to peak around the folds of Ellanora's skirt. Big brown eyes underneath a massive head of brown hair stole a glance up at Elyssa, just before ducking behind her mother again.

"I found her seeing to your chickens when I got here," she explained. "Just after I found Myron feeding our pigs."

"You go to their farm to work Sara's chores and send her to do yours," Elyssa asked her son exasperated.

"She asked for my help," he said with a shrug. "Sara is afraid of the pigs, so I fed them. I had the family reprentation to uphold."

Elyssa closed her eyes and sighed to keep from muttering a curse meant for her brother. Despite her best efforts, she could not break her son of his hero worship of her brother. If anything, it was getting worse. The family reputation nonsense had begun to include everything from escorting a mother duck and her ducklings to a nearby pond, whether that was their intended course or not, to making the barn safe from mice and spiders. Now apparently it was giving aid to little Sara, who he took turns tormenting when she was not tormenting him.

"I like pigs," he continued. "They do not peck at me and they make funny noises."

Elyssa looked up at her neighbor, who looked just as perplexed.

"Well then, there is our solution," Elyssa said once her voice returned to her. "We will just trade children."

* * * * *

All of Green Plains had set the day aside to rest and celebrate their accomplishments. The Ten-Day War had hit the valley hard but not as nearly as bad as Green Plains. Having the High and Merchant's Roads converging in the middle of their village made it an important staging post for Everfrost. The lands had been trampled and the heart of the village had been burned along with several homes. Some of the community had also renewed their Blood Oath and assisted in the battle of Citadel. There were many casualties. No one would have blamed them if they had been forced to give up on this season. So much to rebuild, many dead or wounded. But Green Plains came together and supported one another. Everyone helped work his neighbor's land as if it were his own. The village center was still in need of repairs but Green Plains was once again beginning to prosper.

Elyssa looked out upon the fields. The grains were growing well. Despite the rough start, all the farmers were more than pleased with the progress. If all continued to go well, there was a good chance of a record harvest.

The moment they arrived at the celebration, the crowds began to press in and around the husbands of Elyssa and Ellanora. It had been their initiative and leadership that had led to the salvation of Green Plains. Both men, used to lives of quiet obscurity, seemed to be taken aback by the attention. There was talk among the people to nominate them as the village's representatives in the Farmer's Guild. There were some who wished to see them leading the Guild.

As proud and happy as Elyssa was to see her husband receive the recognition he deserved, she could not help but worry what effect this would have on their very impressionable son. Myron's world view was becoming increasingly skewed. As laughable as her husband thought it was, and as adorable as her neighbors viewed it, she was becoming ever fearful for her son. Yes, Hector was a model of service but she now feared his reckless life was leading her only child down his path, just as her mother had warned. For more than ten generation their family line had consisted of farmers and builders. Not men of violence. Elyssa knew her brother's reasons for his dedication. But in her view, it should have dissuaded his life's course, not informed it.

Setting her fears aside, it would be a decade before Myron's service, Elyssa took a walk with Ellanora far from the crowds. Together they spoke of everything that had nothing to do with farming, rebuilding, or goblins. Ellanora was like the sister that Elyssa never had. Yet another thing Hector was to be blamed for; how dare he be born male! Her neighbor was several years older and the mother of three children, Sara the youngest. It was because of their closeness that their husbands' friendship had begun. It was also the reason for whatever the proper name was for the tormented, stressful relationship between Myron and Sara.

As the heat of the day was approaching its height, Elyssa and Ellanora began to search for refuge in the shade. They had no more than sat on the remains of a felled tree when the shriek of an angry child pierced the air. Looking out, Elyssa saw her son running towards her holding a flower high over his head. Trailing him was a very angry Sara. It seemed that the time of cooperation was now at an end.

"It would seem our children have found yet something else to disagree about," Ellanora said sighing.

"It is mine," he was shouting as they approached.

"You stole it," the little girl squealed.

"I saw it first," he replied as he jumped into Elyssa's lap. Holding the flower up into her face he said to her, "See what I found."

"I see," she replied to her son. Elyssa recognized it instantly. About the size of an adult's fist, the petals were arranged in a starburst pattern with a deep orange in the center that faded into a light yellow towards its edges.

"It is a rare find you have there," she said knowing full well the nearby hillside, and half the valley was covered with them. "It is called Divine's Providence. It is the only flower hearty enough to grow in rocky soil."

"Divine's Proudness," her son said experimentally.

"Providence," Elyssa corrected. "It is said that it was created for the sole purpose to seal the world's wounds after the Breaking."

"The Breaking," Sara asked. Ellanora flashed a smile her way as if to say, well you have done it now. If there was one thing the two children were in agreement about, they both loved a good story and they were about to get one.

"The breaking of the world, the event that brought about the end of the war that bears its name. The War of Breaking," Elyssa began.

"Who fought this war, Becknor," asked Myron.

"Becknor would not exist for another six thousand years, but everyone fought in the war. Every people, every race, every corner of the world blood was shed."

"What started it?"

"No one knows because those responsible all died, and their books did not survive the war. We just know how it ended and that it was a useless war. There are legends of strange and beautiful creatures that were slaughtered for their land, their gold, or both. The war ended in one day. After more than a century of conflict, the world cracked. It was as if the world could take no more. The ground opened up and spread for thousands of miles. From deep within, a monstrous roar could be heard. Those that stood on both sides watched as Hostimentum and Vindicta flew free."

"Who were they," Myron asked. Elyssa paused for a moment. Not too long ago she admonished her brother for nearly mentioning their proper name. It was not a mistake she would make willingly. But surely in teaching a child the history of the world would keep any such curses away. But still, her voice was unwilling to call them out.

"Judgment," Ella said for her. "Divine judgment upon those who coveted their brother's wealth and went to war to take what was not theirs."

Elyssa took the flower from her son's hand and said, "To seal the Rift, the Divine brought forth the Providence, and used these same flowers to knit the world back together stone by stone. Not unlike a master healer would use thread to seal a deep wound. A scar in the world was left at the point of the Rift, the towering mountains of rock far to the east known as the Drakemourn."

An idea came to Elyssa's mind, "The flower, the mountains, Hostimentum and Vindicta, they were all set forth as a reminder and a warning. That we should all try to be people of peace, not war, and share with one another. And now, my son did you steal this from our friend," Elyssa asked.

"No," he exclaimed. "I saw it first. How can I steal what I saw first?"

"I picked it," the little girl protested. "And he stole it from my hand."

"And you could not have picked another," asked Ellanora.

"Let him pick another," Sara said pouting.

"Why should I picked another when I foundeded this one," Myron said looking at Sara.

"So you learned nothing from the story I just told you? How the world was broken because of greed and you still will not share," Elyssa asked. When the children remained silent she added, "Well then, I think I know just how to correct this." Elyssa eased her son off her lap and flashed a mischievous smile towards Ellanora. She should have felt ashamed for what she was about to do. But as far as she was concerned they deserved it.

"You are both going to share this flower and I know the perfect way. Come here love," she motioned for Sara to approach. Parting the little girl's hair on the right side she slid the Divine's Providence in above the ear.

"How dis sharing if she has the flower," her son protested.

"Because she is now your betrothed," Elyssa said, and Ellanora began to laugh.

"What is be-loathed?"

"Betrothed," she corrected. "It means that she is your future wife."

Both their little eyes went wide with shock. Quickly, Sara's hand went to remove the flower.

"Now, now," Ellanora protested. "You wanted the flower, you have to keep it. You do not want to upset your future husband."

Both children looked towards each other in horror. Neither it seemed could find the proper words for how life had so cruelly turned.

"Now I have had quite enough of your stubbornness today. Go to the clearing and play with the other children," Elyssa commanded. "And take your wife with you and decide which of your friends you want to attend the wedding."

"But I don't want a wife," Myron protested as he looked up at his mother pleading.

"I remember saying the same thing," said Bryan who, along with Ella's husband, had come to join them. "Said it over and over. Until your mother hit me in the face with a skillet."

With one last forlorn look towards their parents, both children slowly walked away. Shoulders slumped and head down.

"And do not go blundering into the caverns to run away again," Elyssa called out to them just before they passed out of sight. Turning to her husband she said sternly, "I just shewed away two annoying children do I have to send off a third and fourth? And will you please stop telling our son I hit you with a skillet. You act like it is a common occurrence."

"Is it not?"

"Of course not," she said. Turning to Elanora she added, "Twice in ten years is not common."

"Three times," he corrected. "Or did you forget about last year?"

"That does not count and besides it was your fault." Turning to Ella she added, "A mouse had managed to get into our pantry and I was on the hunt with a skillet in hand. He hid behind a corner and jumped out. It was all reflex."

"She hit me in the face and flattened my nose," he said running a hand over his perfectly fine nose. "When she saw it was me she hit me again and now I have wooden teeth. See," he said motioning his hand in front of his face and sucking in his lips to hide his well intact teeth.

"Your teeth are all in their place," Elyssa said sharply. "Stop telling everyone I knocked them out, someone will believe you eventually and then I really will hit you."

"Speaking of unfair punishments, should we torture our children like that," he asked.

"Yes, we should," Elyssa answered him. "Our children have taken to torturing us every day of their lives so far. Where is the harm?"

"None I suppose," said Ellanora. "But perhaps ten years from now we could be in the midst of preparing for an actual marriage."

"I can see your point," Elyssa said. "Who would want Bryan in their family?"

"Your parents did not seem to mind," he protested.

"That is because they did not know better."

"Either way," Ellanora said interrupting them before the argument could start. "There are darker things than can happen then having Bryan as my daughter's father-in-law. At least having Hector in the family balances it all out."

"I am unsure how to take that," Bryan said with a laugh.

The conversation between Bryan and Elanora faded into the back of Elyssa's awareness. Fresh worry flowed over her with the words "Hector in the family." Many thoughts: a tragic past, an uncertain present, and the worrisome future sprung to mind. Would the day come that, like her mother, she would wish her son a dead heart?

*Yes, there are worse things,* she thought to herself.

# CHAPTER TWENTY-SIX

In the space of just a few short hours, Titus of Green Plaines' day had gone from bad to worst case. Now, within just a handful of heartbeats, it had gone from worst case to hell on earth. As he stood with his back pressed against a wide tree, sweating; Titus tried to control his breathing to stay as quiet as a mouse. The great beast was moving about behind him, with each massive footstep, the ground beneath him quaked. The terror was growing within him as the quaking under his feet grew stronger.

When Titus had opened his eyes to the first light of dawn he knew something was wrong. Everything within his humble home seemed to be in perfect order. From top to bottom, from bed to pantry all was in its place. But something had awakened him early. Not far from his normal time of waking but early.

Dressing and grabbing his staff from the front door he went out to check on his animals and found the barn was all in order. His cow and chickens were all in their homes. The barn door was in full working order, it even managed to not squeal loudly when he opened it. His horse was still stabled where he had left her and his wagon was in one piece. All the feed and hay were right where they should have been. So what had awakened him?

As the skies to the east began to lighten and night retreated from the world around him, realization struck and his heart fell into his stomach.

Quickly, Titus made for the hill and his sheep. What he saw stirred a great anger within him, rather what he did not see.

His sheep pen was empty. Not one remained. He listened carefully for the sound of his noisy flock and heard nothing.

At first, Titus thought, Bandits! Bandits have made off with my flock! But as his anger cooled somewhat, and some rational thought returned, he realized it would have taken more than a couple bandits to move more than fifty sheep. Even in a deep sleep down at the house, he would have heard that commotion. And they had never been the quietest animals in all of Becknor. Twice he had been forced to move the pen because of the complaints of his neighbors.

He began to walk the perimeter of the fence. It did not take long to find the sizable gap between two of the posts. Some fool had dismantled his fence and allowed them to escape. He thought very violent curses towards those responsible. After all the fence had not been in place to protect them from roving predators but to keep them from wandering off as they were apt to do.

With a sigh that was closer to a mournful cry, Titus set off in the direction beyond the gap. There was nothing to do now but search the countryside and pray. Pray they were close by and had not destroyed anything else.

\* \* \* \* \*

This one flock of sheep, sheep Titus had never wanted, loved to roam. It was not that they did not like the valley, just Titus' little corner of it. It seemed now to Titus that he had spent his entire adult life chasing down this triple-cursed flock of stubborn, dull-witted sheep. He had never wanted to be a shepherd. His father and siblings had taken to it naturally.

No, Titus plan had always been to buy his own farm. Once that was established and he was making a fine little profit for himself, selling his

318

grains to the merchants outside the valley, he would take a wife. He would go and search out the most beautiful maiden in all of Becknor to woo and marry. They would have many sons that would work the land and require very little hired help. He would take his profits, buy more land, work that land, make bigger profits, buy even bigger parcels of land, and eventually die the largest land baron in the Valley next to the Monarchy. The plan was perfect. Too perfect.

Shortly after Titus had completed his required years of service with the Builders Guild, word had come to him that his father had unexpectedly passed. The family had all gathered for the Remembrance Ceremonies and to hear the final instructions that his father had left for them and their inheritance. Titus, the youngest, was the last to be mentioned.

"To my youngest son Titus," the document read. "There is nothing in this world that had made me prouder than to see the man you have become. Very early, your intelligence and tenacity were greatly apparent. Your time with the Builders has served you well and it does my heart good to see that you continue to be an excellent worker. You have set a plan for your life and you have never deviated from it. It is because of this great persistence that I leave you my most beloved of possessions. My sheep."

While all of his brothers and sisters nodded with great approval, and out of relief; Titus' heart sank to his feet. Had his father forgotten just how much those creatures tormented him as a child?

If it were possible for something as simple minded as sheep to love one man it was his father. But, if it were possible that same sheep to hate, despise, and spitefully misbehave a single person, it was Titus.

His first memory of the devilish flock was when he was just a small boy. Titus had accompanied his father to the fields one bright and sunny late-summer day. The flock, much larger in those days, gathered in around him and followed him wherever he led. There was a good-humored joke back then that his father spoke fluent sheep and had befriended them. He would laugh it off and say that there was no difference in herding sheep and raising a family. "If you show them love and earn their respect, they will follow you to the ends of the world."

The day young Titus first met the flock ended with his father stepping aside for a moment and leaving him in charge. As he left, it seemed every sheep turned to watch him leave before turning their attention to Titus. One of them approached him. Titus smiled innocently at the "lead" sheep. It stood looking deeply into his eyes, blinked twice, then turned and walked away. Almost in unison, the rest of the flock turned and left him there alone in the field.

The moment Titus collected his now inherited flock of sheep he had a deep sense of déjà vu and foreboding. Just like that day as a boy they all gathered around him, one ventured forward, blinked, and the flock slowly scattered away from him. So began a life of playing the game, Titus Go and Fetch Your Sheep.

"Titus, I saw your flock wandering the countryside." "Titus, your sheep are down in the Blood Forest." "Titus, we heard baying from the foot of the Mountain Pass and found the sheep grazing on flowers." "Titus, no one can cross the Gateway Bridge." "Titus, I saw your sheep at the mouth of Everfrost." The last had been an exaggeration but close enough to reality. After thinking it over, he could see where it might actually have been a blessing if a horde of goblins would have run off with his flock. But, he knew they would just have brought them back to him in the end.

There was not a single aspect of his life that had not been infiltrated by these sheep. In chasing them across fields, countless meals had been missed, time with friends in the local tavern was nonexistent, even sleep apparently was forbidden when it came to the flock. Several times they had somehow worked the door to his cottage and let themselves in and gathered around Titus as he slept. "Baa," they called into his ear causing him to jump off his bed so high he nearly managed to bump his head on the low ceiling of his home.

"Leave me be you dull, fell devils from the deepest pits of the Abyss," Titus screamed after being startled awake. Satisfied that their work was finished they would happily stroll out again in single file.

Farming had proven impossible. Between fetching them back home and little to no sleep or food, most seasons he was too exhausted to plow and plant. The two seasons he managed to work the fields, ended when he found the flock trampling and grazing on the grains.

All things considered, that was probably why Titus took much pleasure, some would say too much pleasure, in shearing season. Making it a point to learn the technique himself, he often laughed like a madman as he held them down and shaved them bald. Every year, the flock being so big at first, Titus would hire new hands for the purpose of shearing. Strangely enough, he was forced to hire new hands every year. No one was willing to stay after one season.

The one area of Titus life he could not blame on the sheep was his constant bachelorhood. With the exception of the night he met a beautiful maiden with very bright green eyes. That night, the flock apparently became lonely and went in search of him. As he sat there in the tavern, back to the door, across from the maiden, his sheep found him. One by one they walked in and gathered around him and began to nuzzle up to him like cats. Having been born and raised in City Citadel the maiden was not the greatest admirer of farm animals. Which in hindsight meant she probably was not the best maiden to attempt to woo.

If he were honest with himself, there was but one party to which blame for his perpetual solitude. Obviously, it was the women of the Valley.

Scholars and teachers throughout the history of Becknor had

always encouraged free thinking among the youth of the Valley. The women possibly were encouraged a wee bit too much in Titus' opinion. He could not make a single maiden see the privilege he was offering them. A home with a big kitchen to feed him and his many future sons. None seemed impressed that they would one day be the widow of a wealthy and famous land baron, provided they outlived him of course. No, all the women of the Valley seemed hung up on some antiquated sense of romance and love. Could they not see the honor he wished to bestow upon them?

Supposedly the second detractor was his features. Admittedly he was probably not the best to look at. His years of walking the Valley in search of his sheep and missed meals had made him a bit scrawny. His oval shaped face with a very small thatch of red hair on the very top of his head gave him the appearance of a scarecrow with a pale, flaming eggplant on top. However, he rather thought of his look as rugged. A great adventurer who had conquered both land and beast. Sadly, most maiden's used the phrase "ugly as sin."

He paid them no mind and their shortsightedness. It was their loss.

* * * * *

It was now well past midday and on to early afternoon, Titus was distressed. There had been no sign of his sheep. Not really a surprise in such a short time and over uneven terrain. After all, Green Plaines was not a plain or even remotely flat.

The ancient forefathers had possessed a rather perverse sense of humor when it came to naming the great stretches of land. It was either that or they ran out of names. Although early farmers had transformed swaths of land into farms, Green Plaines was a hilly, forest dotted, obstacle course. It did not help that there were so many gaping holes in the ground leading to the various abandoned underground chambers below. Some kind of ancient mining system was eroding away beneath them. Strangely, that had been the one place his sheep had yet to run to. Even they knew it was too dangerous to be traipsing around down there.

Titus' spirits may have been failing him but his sense of direction had not. He recognized the landmarks around him quite clearly and sighed.

"They are going to make their way into Maxis' crops again," he said grumpily to himself. "He will kill me this time and no mistake. Kill me, bury me in one of his fields and no one will ever know."

The last time his sheep had escaped his land they travel for four miles trampling crops and grazing on grass set aside for cattle. The worst of the damage had been a wide swath across the fields of his neighbor Maxis. Maxis, the crassest and most ill-tempered man in Becknor, if not the world. Well past seventy years, and the largest land owner in Green Plaines, Maxis was well known and to be avoided as much as possible.

Titus remembered, not very fondly, the last time he had crossed paths with Maxis over the sheep. The moment Maxis had laid eyes upon him, the small, balding man turned several shades of red. A rather spry man for his age; he had run up to Titus to curse at him. With each breath, every curse known to man, goblin, and every other race, alive or extinct, exploded from him. To add emphasis he poked Titus in the chest with such force he feared he would actually burrow through with his fingers and remove his still beating heart.

Maxis had taken him to the local magistrate seeking recompense for the damages. There was not much Titus could say in his defense, especially when all his neighbors came forth presenting the damage they had incurred. His sheep had trampled down a large crop of Maxis' wheat. But Titus took exception with the charge his sheep had destroyed Maxis' fences. Even his turncoat neighbors took exception to the term "fence." There were rotting, felled trees in any random forest of the world that were in better shape than the logs Maxis called a fence. If one of his sheep were responsible at all, it would have merely taken a weak yawn towards a random post and it would have crumbled.

The magistrate ultimately ordered Titus to pay hefty fines and spend an exuberant fee for not one but two new fences. One to replace Maxis' ancient rotted logs and a fence to hold his sheep on his property. To afford such punishment, he was forced to sell much of the flock. Not that he was sad to see the wretched things go but it was the principle of the matter.

Titus' spirits dropped as he neared Maxis' land and saw the new fence he had paid for. Just like his, well not exactly. There was a wide gap in the fence, but where his had neatly been dismantled, Maxis' looked splintered. Titus muttered a curse of his own. Somewhere there was a jester laughing hysterically and Titus was going to be in debtor's prison before sundown.

Taking a breath, Titus resigned himself to his fate and stepped onto Maxis land. Perhaps they would not have damaged too much this time. Maybe they would not have had time to graze on his crops. And there was always the chance the hole in the fence was a coincidence and his sheep truly were in the hands of bandits, marauders, or goblins. Then again, perhaps the Lady Lydia would ride by and be taken by his rugged handsomeness and offer him marriage. Titus always believed if one was going to hope for fantasies one might as well hope for the biggest.

It was not long before the angry voice of Maxis echoed in the distance. It was too far to make out any discernable words but the emotion was quite clear. Just as Titus was calculating the cost of the damage by the tone of his voice, he came to a gory scene.

Oblivious to the world at large, Titus very nearly stepped into a puddle of blood. A small pond was more like it. Snapping back into the moment Titus' nostrils were assaulted to the pervasive, festering stench coming from all around him. Judging by the amount of blood, he knew this did not just come from one creature. Someone or something had been slaughtered on the spot.

His eyes fell upon something in the gore. His stomach began to turn as he began to see that it had many mates strewn around the ground. Inspecting the first piece closely he found in the midst of the blood a leg. A leg belonging to a sheep. Letting his eyes drifts again he began to make out the tufts of wool soaking in the blood.

"He is killing my sheep," Titus said almost as a question. "He is slaughtering my sheep!"

Quickly, Titus anger was stoked and he set out for the direction of the old man's angry voice. It was one thing to demand coin for damages imagined, but no one had the right to slaughter animals in revenge. Maxis had gone too far and needed to be put in his place or his grave.

Quickening his pace, imagining what he was going to do to the man when he caught up with him. Along the way, he found more blood and gore. Titus did not bother with checking the remains. Only sparing a glance he could tell they had been hacked to pieces.

"I will see the old man dead," he promised. By the sounds, Maxis was just on the other side of the next hill. Now he could make out the words quite plainly. Strange, instead of angry they now sounded strained and pleading.

As Titus rounded the next hill he found yet another gory scene. This time, Maxis was standing in the midst of it all. It was then that he realized more than his sheep had been slaughtered this morning. Then his eyes looked up and his mouth fell open now seeing the true cause of the massacre.

"Please, I have much more cattle and livestock," Maxis was

...

pleading to the massive creature before him. Titus could not believe his eyes. How could such a thing found its way into Becknor?

**"Are you truly ignorant of what I am,"** it asked

"N-no, I am fully aware M-my Lord," Maxis answered. When the creature seemed unimpressed with the honorific title Maxis continued, "My Prince, m-my Liege, my…."

**"Then why would you believe my hunger so easily satiated, my thirst slaked, by the flesh and blood of cattle?"**

"I employ many farmhands," Maxis said quickly and gesturing back towards his farm and towards Titus. Quickly, Titus jumped behind a large tree to hide before Maxis got him killed.

"There are many young men and women," Maxis continued. "Dozens and dozens. I am an old man. Take them, leave me!"

Chancing a glance around the tree, Titus watched as the creature's lip curled back in disgust. The beast seemed to actually be angered by Maxis' blatant disregard for those in his employ.

**"Behold, the very example of why the Divine created my kind. To bring swift and perfect judgment down upon yours."**

It ended Maxis quickly.

A whimper escaped Titus just then. Remembering himself he clamped a hand to his mouth and closed his eyes. He could hear the beast sniffing at the air.

The ground beneath him began to thunder as the great beast moved towards him. Its massive shadow was already moving past him upon the ground. Titus stood watching the shadow of its head as it cast it from side to side and continued to sniff. Titus heart hammered within his chest as the shadow of its head moved lower to the ground and in his direction. Each thundering footstep was the herald of his impending doom.

Then, it stopped. Raising its head into the air again to sniff the air.

He watched as the head of the shadow turned to this side. Was it listening?

**"Hmm, and so begins the Reckoning of Becknor,"** its booming voice rattled Titus chest as it spoke to itself.

Titus dared not move from his tree. Even as the shadow moved quickly away and as its footsteps became lighter. A little time passed before Titus could will his legs to work again.

Looking all around, Titus found he was alone. The only signs of the creature's existence at all was the gore, what remained of Maxis, and the footprints of the creature. Titus knew not what had caught its attention but he was grateful that he had escaped unharmed. At least for the moment.

He needed to find a knight or a member of the Watch. Someone needed to know. In midstride a chilling recollection came to Titus' mind. Whirling around, he again looked to the footprints of the creature.

"No," he said turning to follow. "Not that way."

# CHAPTER TWENTY-SEVEN

Hector and his two Trusted Hands rode quietly for the Mountain Pass. No, that was a lie, Hector and Helena rode quietly as Darius serenaded them with one song after another. As the ancient saying went: wine, women, and song, Darius had a passion for all three. Usually, his passion for the last came after much consumption of the first. Only when he was pleased with himself did he break out in song. Seemingly, today, Darius was exceptionally pleased. After traversing the Gateway Bridge, Helena had yet another opportunity to shout at undisciplined knights on duty there, and crossing onto the High Road, Darius had begun to dabble fully into his considerable repertoire of songs.

It was not the number of songs he knew that was impressive. Nor was it the passion he poured into each, though that did not help. It was just how badly his voice cracked as he sang. Birds took flight, dogs ran away yelping, and rodents took cover in their burrows at the mere sound of his approaching caterwauling. And all of it, Hector suspected, was for the benefit, rather torment, of one person.

After miles of pretending it did not bother her in the slightest, Helena finally broke and demanded, "Just give the word and I will cut him down!"

"Now, now Helena," Hector said trying to smile despite his song induced headache. "Tongues would wag if we rode back as two instead of three."

"I did not say we would leave the body on the road for all to see. We would drag him off to the woods, and let the poor, starving wolves have his body. Later we could blame highwaymen."

Darius, finally no longer singing, said, "Now that would be a tragedy love. Just imagine the wail that would be heard throughout the Valley, as the maidens of Becknor mourned my passing."

"It would be drowned out by the cheers of husbands everywhere. Not to mention the applause of the Kingdom's minstrels and lovers of music," Helena added sourly. "Please my Captain, if I may not kill him at least order an end to his songs."

"Darius," ordered Hector calmly.

"As you wish. But let it be known, you can order away the song on my lips but you cannot touch the one upon my heart," Darius said over dramatically, as he laid his hand upon his brow and feigned tears.

Out of the corner of his eye, Hector could see Helena's hand go for the hilt of her sword, as she said, "If you wish something to cry over...."

"Helena," ordered Hector calmly.

"Yes, sir."

Now that one of his senses was no longer being assaulted by ear shattering singing, Hector's other senses, and headache were easing back to normalcy. Though, at least the singing had helped him ignore the stifling heat of his armor. The sun was high and he was beginning to bake. At least he was not wearing a helm.

After a few more moments of silence, Hector slowly became aware of a rather pleasant fragrance. It was not persistent, just a whiff every now and again to remind him of its presence. It was slightly flowery, but it was not coming from the wild flowers on the roadside. It was too nearby and slightly artificial.

Perfume! Hector's mind clicked into place. The overly jovial mood, the singing, and now the fragrance.

Hector shook his head, and with a sigh said, "You are going to get yourself run through one of these days."

Darius, with a big toothy grin, said, "Oh Helena is all scary barks and growls, she would never finish the job."

"Try me," Helena growled, bringing a chuckle from Darius.

"Not Helena," Hector said. "The new maiden at the pub. The one you have spoken of frequently."

"Ah, yes. A true beauty," said Darius wistfully, his eyes glazing over. "Hair as black as freshly tilled soil, big blue eyes, the figure of an hour glass, long swirling skirts." Shaking his head away from the daydream he added, "Not her I am afraid. Despite my best efforts, she has gone and forgiven her betrothed. The pair has gone off to elope this very day."

"Come now," Hector said. "How else do you explain your mood, the singing, and the smell of perfume emanating from you?"

Darius looked at him oddly. "My excellent mood is due to the excellence of the day," he said, raising a hand towards the world around them. "I sing because it irritates the fair Helena, who looks exceptionally becoming when the veins of her neck stand out when she is angry."

"They do not," Helena said clutching at her own throat discreetly.

"As for the fragrance, I am afraid my Captain is mistaken."

"I can smell the aroma from here my friend," Hector insisted.

Darius laughed and said, "I assure you it is not me. You may send Helena to smell for you."

"I would rather throw myself into a swine's pin," she said with great venom eliciting a hearty laugh from Darius.

Hector sat upon his horse confused. Darius was not the type of man to deny his actions. The man loved to share his exploits to the last scandalous detail. Yet, here he was denying the perfume. Perfume Hector could smell clearly. It could not be coming from him. Could it? How could it be coming from him? He had had no close contact with anyone, especially close enough for a woman's fragrance to cling to him. The only woman, other than Helena, he had come in contact with had been Lydia. Come to think of it, the fragrance was the same as Lydia's preferred perfume. Jasmine. But he had never come that close to her today.

Hector then realized he was forgetting about his collision with the Heavy. One who had answered with a strained but feminine voice. One who had been faceless behind her mask. Who had been shorter than him.

Hector slumped grumpily in the saddle. He was a blind man.

"Continue to Barricade," he said bringing Lawrence to a halt and turning him around. "Begin inspecting it. I will be with you shortly." With that, he urged Lawrence back the way they had come.

"Where will you be," he heard Helena's confused voice call to him.

"Retrieving a set of armor."

\* \* \* \* \*

When Nicodemus entered his seventh decade of life, the king and nobles of the day sought to honor the wisest man in the Valley. Having devoted his entire adult life to study and passing that knowledge to the younger generation, the great master had no time for land or houses. All that knew him well, also knew of his great fondness for the old farmhouse that his grandfather had built. The century had not been kind to the old house and it had fallen into disrepair. Quietly, the Kingdom worked to repair Nicodemus' ancestral home. From the ground up they installed new doors, glass windows, and a new thatched roof. The King's personal gardeners had tended the shrubs and flower beds. Once completed, it was presented to the old master. It was said that he nearly wept at seeing the house not only restored, but restored to a greater glory than it had ever known. Thirty years later, Lydia too was moved emotionally. For this was not the house that her eyes laid upon.

Lydia brought her horse to a halt in front of an old ruin of a farmhouse. The lawns and hedges had been allowed to grow wild for years. Sections of the roof looked as if it could give way at any moment. Save from some smoke from one of the chimneys, probably the kitchen, she would have believed the wreck abandoned. Lydia could feel the heat rising within her. To think of one of the most senior and wisest of Becknor living in such disarray.

*How could this have gone unnoticed,* she thought to herself bitterly. *Where is Galen and the rest of the Wise Men? Where is the Royal Court? Where,* she stopped as the guilt began to wash over her like a sea tide. *Where was I?*

Dismounting and tying her horse to a section of the severely leaning fence, Lydia made her way to the front door. She removed the heavy helmet and, for the first time since leaving the stables, felt as if she could breathe. The air was no cooler, but being free from the helmet made it feel like a cool spring morning.

The farm house's aesthetic was by no means improving upon closer inspection. Most of the wood had taken that dull, grey just before rotting look of too many rain storms. Half of the windows were still shuttered. The broken glass laying on the ground below one such shutter gave clue as to why. What few unbroken windows remained were cloudy and dull. Lydia's cheer fell further at the thought of her mentor in such conditions.

There was a knocker on the front door and she reached for it. It was encrusted in what looked like a century of rust. Lydia was afraid to touch it for fear it would fall off or that a single knock could cause the ancient battered door to come loose of its hinges. Finally taking hold of the knocker, Lydia grimaced and held her breath as a terrible squeaking sound escaped its hinges as she began to knock.

Silence greeted her. Pressing her ear to the door she heard no movement. Reluctantly Lydia moved her hand to knock again when something clicked behind the door. After a moment more, the door slowly squeaked open and a young girl stepped out onto the threshold. This was the maiden the healers had sent. She barely looked old enough to be allowed out of her parent's home unchaperoned, much less have reached the Age of Responsibility. The small girl before her wore the simple white dress of her guild. Upon her head was the large and overly elaborate kerchief that all apprenticed healers were required to wear while tending their duties. It too was white and covered in red symbols. Each symbol represented what level of apprenticeship the wearer had achieved. The two largest symbols at the temples were the primary marks of the two master healers responsible for her training. Both men and women were required to wear the kerchief, which completely covered their hair, until their two years service be completed or unless the apprentice wished to make the art of healing their profession. Then the kerchief would be worn until their masters considered them full healers. The symbols embroidered on the kerchief showed that the girl had already committed herself to lifelong service.

She eyed Lydia suspiciously and asked, "Can I be of service Lady Knight?" Her face and hands were pale, as if she had not seen the sun in months. Her emerald eyes stared up impatiently waiting for Lydia's answer.

"I have come to visit Master Nicodemus," Lydia announced. "Might I come in?"

"I am terribly sorry. But I have been instructed to," stopping midsentence, the maiden's eyes went wide as she recognized the visitor before her.

*Of course she does*, Lydia thought. It was another of Lydia's duties to administer the Blood Oath once a quarter to all beginning their Two Years. It had also become Lydia's custom to greet each young man and woman taking the oath personally. As she viewed her time as Regent as an extended service to Kingdom, Lydia wanted to wish them well in whatever service they had chosen.

Before the girl could say anything Lydia raised her hand to try and keep her calm and quiet. Yet, the child seemed to barely have the ability to contain herself.

"I-I am sorry My Lady," she stammered. "You are hardly recognizable in armor. I would never have thought I would actually meet with you again. It is an honor." With that, the poor girl could not decide if it were appropriate to curtsey, bow, or incline her head. Shaking her head, Lydia reached out with both hands to stop the poor girl as she was in the middle of all three at once.

"The honor is mine. May I," Lydia asked motioning towards the door.

"Oh yes, Please enter."

The house smelled as old and musky as its outer appearance would suggest. The interior of the house was dimly lit. But what stuck Lydia was the number of books. There were books and parchments on all sides. Stacks and stacks, at every wall and corner. Some were nearly tall enough to reach the ceiling. Lydia turned to the maiden quizzically.

The now recovered maiden answered the unspoken question, "The Master Teacher has a great love for books, as I am sure you know My Lady. Many of the maidens that have served him, myself included, have offered to reorganize the clutter, so to speak. He rebuffs us on each occasion. One girl took it upon herself to act without his permission."

"I imagine that did not go well," Lydia said.

"You would be right. He locked her out of the house and never let her in again. It was all the Masters could do to talk him into another maiden to see to his needs. And as the fates have decided, that would be me."

"He loves his books. Always has, but this," Lydia trailed off at a loss for words as she looked around her. The sheer number of volumes around her could have rivaled the Palace Libraries, the Hall of Records, and possibly the Archives in Citadel. "Have you served him long?"

"A little more than a season My Lady. But I have served him the longest. Most girls only last a week or two."

"He must like you then."

The girl frowned as she said, "More likely the stews I cook for him."

Lydia could not help but grin and said, "One in the same. Is my master well enough to receive visitors?"

Ominously, she answered, "As well as he is going to be. I must warn you that this might not be the man you remember. There is nothing wrong with his body aside from advanced age. It is his mind, My Lady. It is as if, well, you will see," she said turning and guiding Lydia through the old library of a home.

The maiden escorted her into what was the farmhouse's kitchen. It was the one room where the windows all remained intact. The room was well lit, with the light from the windows and the numbers of lit candles strewn about. The room was filled with the aroma of a now simmering stew upon the fire. But all of these were on the periphery of Lydia's awareness as she stopped just within the doorway. Immediately she understood. Truly, there were no words that could have prepared Lydia for what she saw.

Nicodemus, old and hunched over, seated at a table covered in books. His old gnarled hands were turning the pages of some ancient text. His white hair and beard had grown as wild as the shrubbery outside. His robes were frayed and faded with age.

It was as if Lydia's heart had fallen to the floor. The last tether to her childhood sat before her. How had she not known his state? She understood all too well his advanced years but could someone age this much in two years? But the worst for Lydia was to come.

"Master Nicodemus," she called to him.

Setting a finger down on the page to not lose his place, he looked up at her dully. Lydia's breath caught in her chest as his eyes met hers and there was nothing. It was not as if the man was missing, it was his recognition of her that was. With a massive sigh and frown, he turned his head and began to read again.

"Just as I told the last brave knight they sent, I have no intentions of leaving," he answered gruffly. "I am far too old to be running from the goblin hordes. At worst I would slow your retreat, at best I would die upon the road from the strain of travel. If it is my time then let Everfrost find me doing what I love and let my life end that way."

"I have not come to evacuate you but only to speak," Lydia answered back. His answer was silence. "Master do you not recognize me?"

When he did not as much look up at her this time, she went to him. Setting the helmet aside she knelt down beside him. Gently she took up his right hand and held it in both of hers.

Stroking his hand fondly she asked, "Do you not remember me, my first teacher?"

Slowly he turned his attention towards her. He looked deeply into her eyes searching. Slowly a smile creased his lips.

"Little Lydia, my final student," he said as if it were a question.

"Yes, Master, little Lydia," she assured him offering him her own smile. His eyes brightened, and then, just as quick, was replaced with a frantic look.

"Oh dear, this will never do," he said agitatedly. "We are so ever behind in your studies. His Lordship will be very cross with us. Here it is past midday and we have not even had our first lesson."

"Sorry," she asked unable to keep the worry from her voice.

"Your studies. Come, come child. I know that I am sometimes quite liberal with your free time but this will never do. Lord Marcus will have my hide!"

"But Master, the fire," Lydia began.

"It is chilly in here, we will make up a fire," he interrupted. "I have always been naturally warm-blooded and always seem to forget it is winter. All that snow and cold. Now, did you finish all the reading I gave you last night? Well of course you did. Such a remarkable child that you are. Such intelligence, and so well behaved. But, dear me child, what have you done to your beautiful hair?"

He took the single braid of her hair and began to study it as if it were some foreign entity.

"I thought I would try something different," she said softly. It was all Lydia could do to keep the smile upon her face. But deep within, her heart was breaking by the moment.

"Well, I guess there is no harm in new things," he said dubiously. "However, your mother will not approve I think."

"I agree," was all Lydia could manage. "She always wanted my hair to flow freely."

"Do not worry little one," he said with a wink, "The secret is safe with me. Now, dear me, where to begin," he said taking his hand back and looking through the text before him as it were a study plan.

Lydia, back on her feet, watched him working. She silently cursed herself. One of the most important people from her past and she had neglected him. She should have been here sooner and not for her own selfish purposes.

"My Lady," a soft voice spoke from her side. Lydia turned to see the young maiden. "I was about to serve him his midday meal. There is plenty if you would wish to stay."

Lydia looked back at her old teacher nodding and said, "Of course I would." This could very well be her last chance to sit with him. And she would take it.

Nothing mattered now. The Kingdom, the day of the fire, her questions, even her anger with Hector was so distant. Though she wished momentarily he was with her now. The old Hector that was, not the imposter. The only thing that mattered to Lydia right now was Nicodemus, and sharing one last meal with him.

# CHAPTER TWENTY-EIGHT

Myron shuffled his feet as he walked, sulking. How could his mother go and marry him like that? His life was ruined. Worse yet, his "wife" had yet to leave his side.

"I blamed you for this," he said, pronouncing it blame-ed.

"It was my flower," Sara grumbled yet again.

"Stupid flower. Useless flower."

Myron looked about and watched as the other children happily ran about the field in the shade of the big trees. The green leafy canopy overhead kept most of the sun's heat at bay. They all had reasonable parents. He wagered that none of them were married yet. Even the really old ones who had been alive a decade now.

He moved closer to the opening of one of the caverns. He glanced towards it. It seemed to be deep and dark down there and he did not need his mom to tell him to stay away. Yes, he had tried to run away once to live in the caverns. But he found that nasty little things lived in the dark and he wanted no part of it. The caverns were crawling with hideous, little spiders. Myron did not trust anything that had more than four legs.

Myron did find the cool damp air drifting from the cavern to be "refreshonable." Finding a nice big rock he sat to ponder the unfairness of life. Starting with Sara, who plopped herself down beside him, uninvited. He gave her the angriest look he was capable of. For a moment he thought of saying one of the words his father used when he would accidently injure himself or was angry, but he remember the last time he had done so. His mother had been quite cross with him. Who knew some words were so troublesome. Like the double cursed flower in Sara's hair right now.

"**Such long faces,**" a strange, deep, growling voice spoke. "**One would think the fate of the world hangs upon thy shoulders.**"

Myron looked about but could see no one near them. For a moment he thought he had imagined it until he looked and saw the wide-eyed surprise on Sara's face.

"You hear it too," he asked.

Sara nodded and said, "But I see nothin'."

"**I am over here child,**" the voice called again and Myron turned towards the cavern. "**Yes, that is correct.**"

"What are you doing in there," he asked.

"**Why I live here my boy. Have for nearly a century.**"

"You must be old," Sara chimed in.

There was a sound just then that came from the owner of the voice. Myron supposed it was a chuckle but it made his spine feel icy. It sounded wrong.

The voice answered, "**By the reckoning of man, in the way he marks the passage of time, I would be quite old. But in the reckoning of my kind, I have yet to even begin.**"

Something told Myron that he needed to get up and walk away. The wrongness of the voice. The way it growled and sounded menacing even when it was trying to sound friendly. But Myron stayed fast to his rock. His curiosity was piqued. He would never have forgiven himself if he did not stay and at least hear what the strange creature had to say.☐

\* \* \* \* \*

Titus had become skilled at tracking over the last decade. Every time his sheep went off into the woods he had learned to look for broken branches, disturbed leaves on the forest floor, and small tufts of wool caught on anything sharp. Even so, with the size of the beast he was trailing, there was very little difficulty following the trail before him. This time around, the trick was to follow in silence and find a way to get ahead and warn its next target. Titus knew he had to get to the clearing first. He could now hear the sounds that were attracting the beast. They were both getting too close.

Twice now the creature had stopped and sniffed the air. Both times Titus moved closer to a tree or dove into some nearby bushes. *He can hear me*, Titus thought to himself. *If his ears are keen enough to hear the celebration miles away, he can hear every twig I step on or even the movement of every blade of grass that I rustle through.*

Titus knew he was going to have to take a chance if he were to have even the slightest chance. But after seeing the quick work it had made of Maxis, his courage was trapped by fear. That was until he became aware that something had changed. He could no longer hear the powerful footfalls of his quarry.

*You have to do this now*, he told himself. *What is the point of surviving if you cannot live with your conscience later?*

Risking everything, Titus left his safely overgrown route, and crossed over to the beast's path and found…nothing. There was not even the slightest hint the creature had even come this way.

A thought struck him, It knows. It knows I am here and has doubled back to circle around and kill me. He cast his gaze quickly all around him. Turning this way and that expecting to see certain death fall upon him. Again Titus found nothing. Could it have taken flight and he not seen? How could he have not seen the creature's massive shadow as it flew overhead? Screwing up his courage, Titus began to move back along the path. It was not long before he discovered the opening that led into one of the caverns. His heart froze. It was using the caverns below.

Walking up to the mouth of the cave, Titus peered in. Nothing. Cocking his head to the side he listened for movement. The only sound he heard was his own heavy breathing. Not even the birds above him seemed willing to offer a single chirp. The entire world around him was silent.

Titus stood straight. There was no longer any sound coming from the clearing, where the children of Green Plains had gathered.

"Divine have mercy upon us in the valley," he prayed quickly and turned. If he was right, he was already too late.

* * * * *

The other children had now gathered around Myron and Sara as they stood just outside the cavern. The owner of the voice had yet to come out and greet them. While the other children had taken turns asking the voice question, the hidden creature always turned the conversation back toward Myron. Almost as if he had a singular fascination with him.

**"You seem to be a rather bright child Myron,"** he said in a way that made Myron feel sickly. It brought to mind one day he had been walking through the forest and caught sight of a deer being stalked by a hunter. At first, the animal took no notice of them, only continued to graze lazily while looking down. Though the hunter had never made one noise, even when he had drawn back on his bow, the deer looked about frightened and ran before the hunter could act. Right now, Myron felt as if he were the hunted and wondered if he were better off running to his mother, even if the others laughed at him.

"I fear there is nothin' brightly about me," he said unable to keep his voice from quivering slightly. Sara was still by his side, she had taken his hand without realizing. One glance her way told him she wished to go as well.

"**Now Myron**," it said, causing him to regret every giving his name so freely. "**I think you sell yourself cheaply.**"

"No, I am afraid Myron is correct. He and his family are cheaply made," one of the older boys spoke up. Myron turned to see Rufus coming up alongside, scowling at him. Myron returned the look and tried to be all the more severe with his. Rufus, tall for his age and owner of a mass of long, curly, dark hair, despised Myron almost as much as every other child in Green Plains hated Rufus. Myron was the only other child willing to stand his ground, the other children had been victims of Rufus' cruelty and had lost their will to stand up for themselves. Myron was the last to refuse to give in, had taken a punch or two for his trouble but did not back down.

"Myron likes to believe he is some kind of brave Knight of the Valley. All because his uncle is a Captain of the Knights. He thinks he is better than all of us. Says so every day," he lied.

"**Is this true about your uncle,**" the strange creature below asked with a new tone. Curiosity?

"He is Hector," Myron answered. "A great hero. He saved the Regent single-handedly."

"**My, a mighty man of valor by the sound of it. I would hear more of this great Hector. I know, why not join me down here for a spell, and we will discuss your mighty uncle. In fact, your friends can join me down below as well. There are great wonders to be seen by all.**"

"My mother said not to, many times," Myron said quickly eliciting groans and snickers from the other children. The others now seemed eager to follow, but Myron's feet felt glued to the ground below him. "She said it was dangerous."

"**A wise and most observant woman. Truly, many dangers are** below," a new tone, delight? **"And yet, I am sure she would not fret if you had a guide who had called these caverns his home for such a long time. Someone who could keep you from the perils of the underground."**

"I do not know," Myron began but was interrupted.

"Behold the true family reputation," Rufus said loudly to be heard by all. Myron was finding himself in the minority. Either curiosity about the creature or out of fear of being bullied and tormented later, the rest of the children were now siding with Rufus. All but one, Sara shook her head in a silent plea.

Another horrible chuckle came from the cave as the voice said, **"Come now children. Let us not make a fuss. Be it upon my head if something tragic were to befall you. Yet, I shall let Myron have the final say. If he says it is too dangerous, then I shall be on my way."**

Silence fell upon the clearing as every eye was now upon him. All things being equal, he would have gladly walked away and let the others tease him for the remainder of his days. But one glance in Rufus' direction, and seeing that smug smile, he knew he had no choice. The family "reprentation" was at stake.

Taking his future wife by the hand, Myron took the first step. He could not let his uncle, or even his parents, suffer shame because of his cowardice.

* * * * *

Titus hit the clearing just as the last child crossed the threshold into darkness.

"No," he cried out. "Come back!"

**"Ah, so you are the rodent that has been nipping at my heels for the last hour,"** the beast bellowed from the darkness.

Titus' legs failed him and he came to an abrupt stop and fell back into a sitting position. He knew he was already dead.

"Leave the children be," he called to the beast. "They are but innocents."

**"This is true, my heroic pest. But would you really have me leave them for last? Would you really have their little hearts broken as they watch their parents die horribly? What you and your kind see as murder, my kind sees as mercy. This is why we always begin with the children and why you call us Child Thieves."**

"Please," Titus began, "The people of the Valley do not study war. Our ancestors came here to escape its horrors thousands of years ago. We are nothing more than farmers, such as myself."

**"Good! Then your warriors shall be no more difficult to dispatch than you."**

With that, the beast launched himself from his hiding place within the cave. Titus had no time for contemplation, no time or place to run, only time enough for one scream.

* * * * *

Deep down in her heart, something began to trouble Elyssa. As Bryan began to tell one of his terrible ancient jokes, she ignored him and began to ponder her troubled heart. Something was terribly amiss. Realization struck and she was up on her feet in a heartbeat.

"What is it," Bryan asked all levity gone from his voice.

"I do not hear the children," she said worriedly.

A man's gurgling scream came from the direction she had sent her son. Without waiting for the others she pulled up on her skirts and ran. She cut through the farmland not worrying about the grain she was flattening as she went. She had to get to the children.

Elyssa came to the clearing just ahead of Bryan. They both froze at the horror. They were quickly joined by others coming to their children's aid.

The clearing before them was mangled. There were deep gouges in the earth as if something very large had propelled itself along the ground by digging in. Not one single child was to be seen. But at the center was one mangled body.

Elyssa had chosen the Healer's Guild when her two years of service had come due. She had seen many horrible injuries. Witnessed heartbreaking illnesses. But nothing could quite match the body before her. It looked as if he had been ground up, no, chewed up and spat back out upon the earth. Her heart ached when she realized the man was still living. Though that would not be for much longer.

Going to the man's side, she thought it was perhaps Titus, a very kind, yet greatly eccentric man. There was little she could do for him. He was gurgling his lasts breaths. She took him by the hand so that he would know that he was not alone in his final moments.

All around, the others were calling for their children. But she already suspected what had happened. It was her fault after all? It was considered bad form to even mention the ancient names. She had conjured this upon them. So when Titus' eyes opened, and as he silently urged her to come closer, in her heart she knew his last words be. It was only one explanation for his injuries. As he spoke the word, her whole being froze.

Unable to will her body to move, she slowly became aware that Bryan and Ellenora were speaking. She became aware that strong hands were grabbing her by the arms and lifting her up. She looked up at the imploring eyes of her husband. Even forcing herself to speak, she still could not manage the creature's true name, only one of the many names given to their kind by legend.

"Child Thief."

# CHAPTER TWENTY-NINE

Lydia sat looking down upon her bowl of stew, lightly stirring it. It had arrived in front of her steaming and now it was little more than tepid. It might have been the best vegetable stew in all of Becknor, but she would never have known. A heavy heart rested squarely on her stomach, and each glance towards her first teacher only added to the weight. His voice was strong, his recollection of things long past was quite remarkable, but his place in the here and now was far askew.

Not once did he seem to notice that she was no longer the little girl that had sat before him for many lessons. Their entire meal together was like the teaching sessions of the past. He had her recite old rhymes and tested her knowledge of history.

"Finally, who was Kiron," he asked taking his last crust of bread and running it through his empty bowl before chewing it thoughtfully.

"Kiron was the tutor of Beatrice the Battle Queen."

"And what is considered to be his best-known philosophy?"

Lydia perked up in her seat. While she was sitting across from her teacher, cursing herself, was he attempting to subtly get her attention? Was her teacher still in there?

She answered, "Kiron is best known for the saying, 'Do not concern yourself in what may have been but instead ask what may be?'"

Lydia thought for a moment. Another of Kiron's famous quotes had been, the question that is left unasked, is knowledge left unlearned.

"I always marvel teacher, at the depths of your knowledge," she chanced.

"I remember nearly everything that I have ever read, all that mine eyes have taken in as if in an art gallery, and many conversations as if they were still ongoing. Have since childhood," he said a whimsical smile creasing his lips. "My mother sent me to the scholars earlier than most children. I plagued her with many questions from the moment I learned the art of speech. I am distressed that you have not called upon my knowledge more."

"I am sorry. I guess you could say, I was feeling poorly for some time, yet I am now much better," Lydia said watching him closely.

Nicodemus looked up quizzically and said, "Yes, I remember your mother coming to me and telling me you had a rather nasty fever. What was the ailment again?"

"The Fever-Sleep."

"Ah yes, horrid it is," he said as his eyes seemed to lose focus again. "Glad to see you are all better now. We will have to make up for lost time. Your father would be furious at me if you slipped too far behind. There is still much that I have been tasked to teach you."

Lydia frowned, was he speaking cryptically so only she would understand or was he down another trail entirely?

"Yes, we have not seen you at the house for some time," said Lydia.

"I am afraid some of the Wise Men have kept me busy," he answered. "Many mysteries they would wish to know. Sadly, they feel the only path to true wisdom is not by study but by observation."

Being watched? Lydia glanced towards the maiden at work. "I have served him the longest," the girl had said and that Nicodemus liked her stews more than herself.

*No, you are more trustworthy than the other girls*, Lydia thought. The other girl who had been locked out for "reorganizing the clutter." Spying more like it. Not unlike a spying maiden back in the Palace.

"Have you some special knowledge they do not already possess," she asked.

"I suspect that they suspect that I do. Yet, do they suspect that I suspect that they suspect I do," he said with a laugh and leaving Lydia just as uncertain. "In the end, those few who wish to know probably know more on the subject than I ever will. I suppose your father was the true scholar of the matter."

"They came to my father as they have come to you?"

"Oh yes, many have come to your father for advice. Quite the learned man, Lord Marcus. Wise beyond his years. Some days I just love to listen to him and your mother laps into the conversations philosophical. A trusted advisor to the king. He should have been in the ranks of the Wise Men years ago despite his youth. Sadly, many of the more senior members have long memories. Or rather they possess the memories of their fathers. Still too much anger towards Achelon and his progeny. Such sentiment is not limited to the ranks of the Wise Men either. Makes one wonder where such blind hatred will lead."

"Why would the Wise Men seek knowledge from my father if they hated him so?"

"Fear," he said bluntly. "Fear that perhaps he alone had some secret knowledge or wisdom that would see the downfall of their position. Perhaps the fear of this secret knowledge was being used as leverage to curry favor with King Gaius. A load of nonsense that last. If there is such secret wisdom only a very small number would even be aware. Sometimes secrets are necessary. They are best guarded even from the knowledge of kings."

Deciding to chance that he was indeed lucid, Lydia asked quietly, "Would such secret knowledge have any relation to the day of the fire?"

Shaking his head he said, "Goodness child. I know it's the dead of winter but you cannot be that cold." Turning to attract the attention of the maiden he said, "Stoke the fires, will you? Young, little Lydia seems to have caught a chill. We would not want her health to decline and her illness return."

"No, that is quite alright," she said more in response to the maiden's quizzical look. "I am quite warm." Back to her former master, "Do you remember the last Spring Festival we attended?"

"Oh yes, the Spring Festival," he said his eyes lighting up. "You have been looking forward to it all winter? I hear your father will be officiating the closing ceremonies this year. Tell you the truth, I am rather looking forward to it myself," he said with a twinkle in his eye, "Cannot wait to see what he has in store for us."

So that was it then. Her teacher had not been speaking in riddles after all. Lydia had been following the musings of a mind that had grown long. Nicodemus' mind was now trapped in the past with more pleasant memories. Surely she could not begrudge him that. It might prove to be a terrible thing to have one's mind leave but if it also filtered out the tragedies and left only the pleasant, then perhaps it would be worth it.

"Well, I suppose that is enough for now," he announced as the maiden collected their bowls. "You should go and have some free time since you have done so well in your studies. Perhaps, if you do not tarry too long in the cold, you should go build a snowman or some such in the courtyard."

"Perhaps I will," she said getting up and helping the maiden carry away the bowls.

"Is he always like this," Lydia asked the girl.

"Mostly," she said turning to offer Lydia an apologetic look. "He lapses into the past most days. Thinking I am one of his students. Quizzing me on everything from The Great Migration to naming the seven regents who have served in the stead of the monarchs."

"Strange, I am the seventh regent," Lydia said, taken aback.

"Your Regency seems to be his one tether to the present My Lady. In those moments he speaks of your accomplishments with pride. Mentions repeatedly that you were his final student. Then without warning, he lapses into the past and retires to work on a study plan for the following day."

"During these lapses to the past, does he ever mention the fire," Lydia asked. "The fire that claimed Talwoods?"

"I think the fires are hot enough already," he called out behind her.

Both women turned to regard him and Lydia offered, "I only wish to see you comfortable master."

"By roasting me like a leg of lamb? I think not."

Turning back to one another the girl answered in a hushed tone, "Not that I can remember."

"Nothing about any strange movements or lights in the upstairs windows or odd sightings about that time? Perhaps even strangers about or secret meetings?"

"I am afraid not. He seems to perpetually believe it is winter thirteen years ago."

Lydia sighed. It had been worth the try. If nothing else she had the opportunity to see Nicodemus one last time. Spending an hour with him was the least she could have done.

"Have there be many visitors," Lydia asked more out of curiosity.

"Not many my Lady. Though as I have said, I have only been here a season. Those that have come have been Wise Men."

"I suppose one does not see many familiar faces when you are confined to your house," Lydia said thinking out loud. Though the thought could also apply to herself.

"He is not confined to the house."

Now that was a revelation.

Frowning Lydia asked, "I was under the impression that with the state of his health that travel was forbidden."

"On the contrary, the Healing Masters feel as long as his physical health holds, he is allowed to travel anywhere within the Valley as long as he is escorted. To my knowledge, his movements were only restricted once."

"When was this?"

"When you fell ill, My Lady," said the maiden. "The moment word had come to him that you were under the Fever-Sleep Curse he had a moment of lucidity. He requested a carriage from the Palace so that he might aid the other Wise Men in a search for the cure. He was denied and commanded to stay here for fear of goblin stragglers upon the road."

"Who denied his request," Lydia asked already knowing the name she would hear.

"Grand Master Galen, by way of his second Cassius."

Galen. What game was the Grand Master of the Wise Men playing? Lydia thought back now to how many times she had actually seen Nicodemus since her Regency had begun. Even early on, her teacher had been missing at the strangest moments. Slowly their face to face encounters had grown further and further apart until it had been two full years since speaking. Many times, it had been Galen that had passed along Nicodemus' "apologise" for being absent. Coincidence or plan? This would be something to meditate upon.

As the maiden left the room to fetch water, Lydia gathered her borrowed helmet. With Nicodemus' mind splintered there was no real way of knowing now what it was that she had seen. Perhaps she could inquire of the other witnesses. Perchance one of them neglected to say something. Deeming what they had seen as meaningless and not important enough to mention. Or perhaps, at the behest of the Wise Men, some of the details had been suppressed.

She turned to regard her former teacher. He had gone back to reading the manuscript before him, oblivious to the rest of the world. A fresh pain moved through her heart. As soon as her regency ended she promised herself she would become a regular visitor.

Once more she went to his side. Stroking the top of his head fondly she bent down and kissed his brow.

"Good bye my teacher," she whispered. As she started to move away his hand caught hers with more strength then she would have thought he possessed. Turning in his seat he brought her closer.

"I know not what has caused the past to awaken within you," he whispered, "but you must keep it to yourself. I saw no such movement that you speak of, but that does not mean it was not there. You are correct in supposing that there was more to the fire. It is a riddle that I have pondered since the day itself. One, sadly, I have yet to fully solve. Perhaps, you are in a better position to ferret out the truth. But you must be cautious and go quietly. Careful who you trust child. The people may love you but you already know there are many thorns among them. They would see you dead just for your ancestry alone."

Then looking up and giving her a wry wink he added, "If there is time, I will speak with you again before the end."

Grateful as Lydia was that her master was still with her, panic struck with his last words and she asked, "Are you unwell master?"

He offered her one of his big smiles and said reassuringly, "No child, I am a man of more than a century. As blessed as I am with long life the Divine shall be calling my name soon I think. Now go with my love. Quickly, before you are missed."

Smiling, she once again kissed his brow and gave him a wink of her own. Helmet in the crook of her arm, Lydia turned to go back the way the maiden had brought her. Her heart was now glad. Not that she had learned she had been right about the fire but that Nicodemus had been in his right mind after all.

Reaching for the door and pulling it open she looked up to see the frowning face of Hector. He stood with his arms folded across his chest and his eyes glaring.

"You are late," she said pushing past him. "I expected you a quarter of an hour ago."

# CHAPTER THIRTY

Hector's anger was boiling hot. Though he was greatly cross with Lydia, his anger was directed towards himself. Helena had been right, his focus was askew. No, it was missing altogether. For the realization to dawn so slowly that it had been Lydia in the stables was testament. He should have known the moment she had knocked him over.

From the farmhouse, through the Amethyst Pass, and back upon the open road, they rode side by side in tense silence. Lydia had not uttered a single word since she had pushed past him to her horse. For the first mile this suited Hector just fine. This entire episode had been an exercise in foolishness. At least he was not alone in absent focus. Barely recovered, not only risking relapse, but chance as well. Here she was, Regent of Becknor, with many dangers upon the road, and she sat in the saddle with her helmet resting upon the pommel of the saddle. No, he would bite his tongue. There was nothing to be said.

Over the next two miles, his anger began to cool. Her Ladyship was not thinking clearly. Could he really blame her? Long sleepless nights, nearly succumbing to a terrible curse, unspeakable nightmares when sleep did come, how could she be of right mind? Then the strain of learning that her mentor had fallen ill. If Hector had been in the same position would he not have acted the same?

Halfway through the next mile, Hector tried to work up the

courage to speak. Occasionally he would steal a glance over towards her. She sat ever rigid atop her horse. Her gaze was steady on the road, and her face was like stone. Each time he looked over, he could not think of a single word to say. Finally, after screwing up his courage, he said the first thing that came to mind.

"I am...."

"So help me Hector if the next word to follow is 'sorry,' I shall knock you off your horse, and run you through with your own sword," she snapped. For the first time, she was looking at him and Hector wished she had not. There was so much fire in her eyes that he feared he might combust any second.

"What do you want me to say," Hector asked.

"Nothing," she snapped again and looked forward. After a few yards, "Or perhaps you could start treating me like I am your friend again."

"You are my friend."

"No," she snapped again. "That is the one thing I can say for certain. I think I would almost prefer you looked upon me as your enemy, or even a complete stranger, rather than how you have been treating me."

"And just how have I wronged you," Hector asked. He felt the heat again rising.

Laughing bitterly she said, "I have to answer?" When Hector did not respond, "Fine then. Why is this the longest, most private conversation we have had since the night in the Viewing Tower?"

"Galen had forbidden. It would have been a breach of protocol."

"Oh send protocol to the Abyss," she said waving her hand dismissively. "How often have you and I already breached protocol? How many times in the past year, as Everfrost stoked the fires of war, did you and I have private consultations, in the dead of night, without the Wise Men? How many months did you spend bolstering our defenses when

Galen advised patience? And was it not you and I, who stood side by side inside the belly of the beast, attempting one last negotiation with the Dread Overlord, against the direct order of the Royal Court? You worry about a simple breach of protocol when we together, have by the letter of the law, committed treason time and again in defense of our people."

"You nearly died," he said sternly. "Perhaps I only wish to be cautious."

Looking forward again she answered, "You are like the rest of the Royal Court. You place me in a prison and tell me it is for my safety. I am denied the courtesy of common conversation and I am to believe it is for my own good health: both physically and mentally. I can expect it of Galen, but not you. Never you."

"Perhaps we act out of caution and bow to Galen's good judgment," Hector offered.

"I would think that I am the best judge of how far my recovery has come. And I would think this afternoon more than proves the state of my health," Lydia said through clenched teeth.

Hector's anger boiled over and he shouted, "Taking a ride across country, alone, on some frivolous whim is a very poor measure of recovery." Hector immediately regretted the words. Her head snapped in his direction, her mouth fell open but no words came at first and she again closed it. But there was something in her expression just then. It was not that the fire had gone out of her eyes, it still burned hot, it was something much deeper. So many emotions played across her face that Hector hardly could register them. Something within had broken and she turned from him with a look of grim resignation.

"A frivolous whim," she breathed the words heavily and for the first time since Hector first knew her, Lydia's voice nearly cracked. "I can see how you would think that, knowing me for so long. Certainly, because I have lived my life to whatever the slightest flights of fancy has dictated. Barefoot in white fields, hay bales, an unknown list of private moments and jokes used against me. So my life has brought me to even this," she said looking up into the heavens. "My state of mind doubted, concern for my health makes me a prisoner, and now this new outrage." She turned and looked at him sadly and said, "You, my greatest friend and ally, think me a silly girl."

Hector's mind flashed back months ago to the Glass Desert. As he set his petition before Aldred Zen-Joffa, that his cause for Lydia had been just and worth of the trials, and that he would face any danger, the alchemist had answered:

"I don't know your Lydia personally, and I am sure she was very brave, but she also could just be some silly girl. Yes, just a silly girl who does not have the good sense to keep her head out of the clouds. Who, for all I know, could always be blundering her way into danger."

Zen-Joffa's answer had angered Hector so greatly that it was all he could do not to draw his weapon. Now, he had just accused Lydia of the very same thing himself.

"Do you know that no one has ever asked," she said a moment later. Hector turned to her but she was looking ahead again. No, her head was facing the road but her eyes were staring off into nothing.

"I have been asked are you comfortable, are you hungry, cold, hot. Yet, not one person has asked, what did you dream? That is almost the hardest reality to live with since waking. Not one healer, wise man, friend, or even chambermaid have asked 'what did you see?' I would have willingly told them. I would have confided to my worst enemy if they would have asked. You see I needed to tell someone. But no one cared to listen."

"It is a terrible thing, having to relive the day your world ended. Presented to you, time and again, in the form of a nightmare that you can never wake from. It is a terrible thing watching your parents die as your home is consumed by fire. It is something no one should see once, much less repeatedly. One person willing to listen would have been enough. Perhaps then, I might not have had to shoulder the pain alone. But no one seemed to care."

"Harder still was the sitting and waiting, then praying that someone I trusted would come to talk with me. Maybe in the space of nothing more than a quarter hour, I would have felt a fraction of my former self again. Then I could have confided in them, 'I believe my parents were murdered.' Recount the long forgotten details that the Curse brought before me so vividly. I could have told this friend of my investigation and the inconsistencies within the Magistrate's ruling. Then perhaps they would have gladly followed me on a 'frivolous whim.'"

"But, I tell you the truth, there is one fate even more unbearable to live with. You see, there was this man, the trusted friend I spoke of. His name was Hector. Our friendship meant more to me than the entire Kingdom. I could have lost it all: my position, my title, my home in the Valley, just as long as I could have called him friend; I would still have the world. Hector was brave, intelligent, and kind. There was not a selfish bone within him. He lived for service and that was his downfall. When I fell ill, he rode out to win the cure to free me of my affliction. This, gloriously noble man, faced many dangers and won my cure. Yet the most heartbreaking tragedy occurred. He never returned from the Glass Desert. A stranger wearing his face returned, but my Hector is lost to me. It is, in my eye, an unfair trade. I would have rather died in my bed than to have faced such a cruel reality."

Again silence fell on the road. Only the sound of the hoof beats of their horses were between them.

It was done then. Hector had been the frivolous one. He had been a fool. Worst yet, he had congratulated himself on his foolishness. What harm would have there been, in the end, if she had asked him of Zen-Joffa's third trial and his ultimate question? Was there a reason to be ashamed of why he could not answer the question directly?

*You know the true reason*, the constant inner voice spoke up again.

Hector chanced one more glance Lydia's way to see she had turned her head away from him. *How do I make this right*, he asked himself. But deep down there was no answer. The inner challenging voice had too fled. Or was its purpose complete? Just as the ruination of Hector's life, by his own hand, was now complete.

So Hector turned his head towards the road and rode on. He could think of nothing more to say to Lydia. There were no words that he could put together to mend what he had just rendered asunder. He had no words at all. Fortunately for Hector, Lydia did.

"Not that I am surprised," she said her tone slightly warmer but still chilled. "And not that I really care, mind you. But how did you work out it was me?"

"Jasmine," he said smiling slightly.

"My perfume," she asked turning towards him.

Turning to look her way he answered, "I and my lieutenants were riding out to Barricade Garrison today. On the road, I kept getting a whiff of jasmine on the air. At first, I thought it was Darius."

"Darius," she said looking over to him confused. "Not Helena but Darius?"

"Helena wears no perfume while on duty. I am not entirely sure she has ever worn any scent at any time. However, as you know, Darius has many," he paused looking for the right term, "lady friends. So I confronted him on the road and he denied it. Shortly after I realized the scent was coming from me. I worked back to when I first began to smell the jasmine and realized it was after you knocked me over."

"And it never occurred to you that this knight might have had plans later," she asked.

"You would never wear perfume before riding out on maneuvers. You could bathe in a tub of perfume and still smell of horse an hour later."

"Yet, you traced the scent of jasmine to me. Surely the valley must be filled with young maidens that wear the scent as well."

"None that I have dealings with on daily basis," he said. She nodded thoughtfully and looked ahead once more.

The door is open, she wants you to make this right. What are you going to do now?

He added after a moment, "I would not apologize, for it might prove to be my end at your hand, but I do apologize. I should have come to you."

She did not answer him but instead inclined her head towards him as a silent thank you.

"You truly believe your parents were murdered?"

"After today, more than certain," she answered before falling silent again. He knew she was not going to make it easy for him but he could not help but grimace. There was but one thing to say now.

"Ask."

"And what precisely am I asking." There was a devilish twinkle in her eye. She was enjoying this.

"The very thing you inquired about at the gate."

"Oh, you mean Zen-Joffa and the boring third trial. Perhaps I am worried if I do, you will hide behind titles, or Valley business, and then run away."

Hector gestured toward the open fields around them and said, "Not many places to hide out here."

"So what is the legendary Aldred Zen-Joffa like?"

"A remarkable hard man to read. I suppose after two millennia any man would be. Very observant and deep thinking. As brilliant as the legends have always said, just judging by the crafting of his trials. But filled with grief. He is very sorrowful for what he and the other had done. And yet," he stopped there.

"What?"

"I do not think his grief comes from the death that he caused on that battlefield alone," Hector said thinking back now. There was a great sadness in his eyes once he had revealed who he was. "He did not offer many insights into who he was. He is the King of Lies after all."

"So he lived up to his title," Lydia asked.

Hector thought it over for a moment and said, "The curious thing is, I would never have guessed he was outright lying to me. He had even said he had taken an oath long ago, his own Blood Oath of sorts, that he would be as truthful as possible. But then, would not a skilled liar be able to put you at ease about his own falsehoods?"

"So you do believe he lied to you?"

Without hesitation, "Yes and no. As he recounted the story of his life he felt more like a play-actor performing for my entertainment. But, portions of the story felt true as if they were based in something real. Ferreting out the truth would be impossible considering angry mobs destroyed all of his journals and papers after the use of the weapon. But it was the passion in which he spoke at certain points that makes me believe. But in the end, I will admit that it was I that was not entirely truthful."

"About the third trial?"

"Yes."

Then the question Hector dreaded, "And in this third trial; he showed you the future?"

"A possible, but most likely future, Yes."

"But not your future."

"No," he said feeling the pain of that vision coming back. "I was nowhere present."

"And it was, for certain, my future that you saw?"

"Yes. I saw you standing in the field where we first met. You turned but did not see me. It was then I realized I was seeing the future. You were older, perhaps twenty or more years from now."

"I am sorry Hector," she said interrupting him, "but as of yet, I see no reason as to why this vision troubled you."

"I suppose," he said uncomfortably, "You will understand at the end."

Seeing his discomfort she offered a smile, and said, "It is alright Hector. No one else is out here. Whatever you saw stays with me."

Her smile and kind words had the opposite of what she had intended. Offering a false smile he continued.

"I then realized something else had caught your vision. Your eyes were looking upon a man who would pass just to my left."

The curiosity upon her face seemed to grow as Lydia asked for a description.

As the twisting blade feeling worked its way back he said, "He was nearly my height I suppose. Dressed regally in white and red. No doubt a Lord, Prince, or perhaps even a King. A cloak trailed behind him, ruby red. He quickened his pace towards you. In a single motion, he scooped you up and twirled you around. Jugding by what happened next, I believe I was seeing your future husband."

Glancing towards the road and back again she seemed to be speechless. He could see her mind working behind her eyes as she began to ponder his words. As they passed into Green Plaines, Hector's misery lightened. Lydia had gone silent. Perhaps this was it. She would ask no more.

The pain returned in a flash when she asked, "Was there anything else?"

"I saw three children. Your children. Two boys, one small and the other nearly a man, and a girl with your long, golden hair."

Again silence. Hector imagined it was quite the shock to hear what your life will probably be like in twenty years.

"But this makes little sense Hector. To what purpose would he show you my future?" she asked.

Hector's mind was back again in Zen-Joffa's workshop as he had finished mixing the Elixir and was about to send him on his way:

*Be truthful to yourself, brave Hector. Always be truthful to yourself.*

He glanced over to see Lydia waiting expectantly for an answer. He took a useless breath that failed to calm him before speaking.

"The purpose was two-fold I imagine," he started shakily. "One was to show what would be lost if I failed."

"And the other?"

"To ask a question."

"What was the question?"

"Do you...."

"Hector," a frantic voice called out behind him. Before he turned he knew the owner of the voice was Bryan. Hector turned in his saddle to look behind and saw him running towards them. One look at his pale face and Hector knew immediately something was wrong.

"Hector," he said as he approached, "I was running to the barracks for help."

"What has happened?"

"The children," he said gulping for breath. "The children have been taken. One of our neighbors has been mauled to death. It was...a Child Thief."

Hector was astonished at his brother-in-law's words. *A Child Thief, here in Becknor?*

"My Lady, I think it would be best if," before he could finish he saw that Lydia had replaced her helmet and had helped Bryan up upon her horse.

"Show us the way," she said. For a moment he watched dumbfounded as they both rode away.

"My heart cannot take much more," he grumbled to himself before turning his horse to follow. Lawrence harrumphed at him.

"Yes! I know, I only have myself to blame. Less observation and more speed."

# CHAPTER THIRTY-ONE

The scene before them was chaos. A group of men and women were quickly gathering around the small opening in the side of a hill leading down into the caverns. Lydia could see that many had armed themselves with farming tools, bows, and at least two carried swords. The group was beginning to pass out lit torches. They were about to raid the caverns, they were all about to die.

"Halt," Hector called out to the mob as he came in riding hard past Lydia and Bryan. "Stay this foolishness," he said as he dismounted.

"There is no time," an angry voice called out from the group. "The longer the children are below; the sooner they will be eaten," cried another.

"And just how were you expecting to retrieve your children," Hector asked them. "Sheers and scythes have been pressed into wartime weapons in the past, but that was against flesh. The creature's hide is made of scales wound tighter than chainmail, and harder than a shield molded from pure steel."

Lydia made her way quickly to the crowd and added, "None of you possess the armor necessary to survive. The beast's teeth and claws alone are sharper than any blade forged by man. Be hasty and you will face the same fate as your friend and neighbor," she said motioning to the now covered body of the fallen man. "Your children will need living parents to comfort them once this ordeal is over."

369

A dark haired woman broke away from the group and made her way towards Hector and Lydia. Even though she had never met Hector's sister face to face, Lydia would not have had much difficulty identifying her. It was not the family resemblance per se, but the fire behind the eyes. Especially when driven by purpose.

"Has anyone gone in," Lydia asked as she approached. The woman eyed Lydia suspiciously as if to ask why a knight would speak up before her captain. Lydia had nearly forgotten she had replaced the faceless helmet. It was amazing how quickly it had become nearly comfortable for a stifling hunk of ironmongery.

"Not as yet," she answered Hector and not Lydia. "Some of us have cautioned patience until Bryan could make it to the local garrison. But now that he has returned," she said glaring at the man standing at Lydia side.

The mob was now glaring their way. It would seem now that half were impatiently waiting to go below while the others seemed to be contemplating flogging the newcomers for their interruption. Seeing this, Hector moved closer to Lydia so he could whisper.

"We too are woefully ill-equipped. I doubt even our entire armories are stocked for such a threat. Someone needs to go back to the Palace and raise the alarm," he said. Lydia knew all too well that Hector was going to insist she be the one to go back. Hector, always the selfless one, would go below the moment she was out of sight and attempt to rescue of the children, knowing it would be his end. Meanwhile, Lydia would be supposedly safely away while the Knights of the Valley waged yet another war. No doubt Galen would find some dank locked basement for her to hide away in. As always, Lydia's plan was very different.

Turning to the man who had shown her the way, she said, "You there, take my horse and ride for the Palace. Ask to speak with Galen, Chief

Wiseman. Inform him of all that has happened and that we shall need reinforcements." Immediately Hector began to protest.

"My Lady, that is not what I," was all he could manage. Slowly she turned to regard him. Even with her face obscured he took her meaning pretty clearly.

With a heavy sigh, to the man Hector said, "The word of the day is maelstrom. Speak it at the gate and they will let you pass."

The man stood his ground confused. Like Hector's sister, his head swiveled back and forth. She could hear the questioning silent thoughts of everyone gathered.

Hector's sister spoke up and asked, "I am sorry but why would the Chief Wiseman trade words with a simple farmer? No offense love," she added in the direction of her husband who had turned to frown at her.

Lydia removed her helmet and for a moment there was nothing. Then an excited murmur went through the crowd. An audible groan escaped Hector. She glanced over apologetically as she saw the misery in his eyes.

"So much for returning to the Palace unnoticed," Hector said with a halfhearted, crooked smile. "Perhaps Galen will only strip me of my rank. A hear the dungeons are a comfortable cool and damp in the summer."

Overcome, the man before her began to bow down. Quickly, Lydia grabbed him by the arm and righted him on his feet.

"I am honored but we have no time. Galen will speak with you once you tell him where I am, and that I intend to go below and negotiate with the beast. Now, take my horse and go." Wasting no time he made for the horse and rode away.

Lydia turned to see Hector staring towards her, frowning. "Negotiate?"

"Why not," she said moving past him and towards the cavern.

"I can think of a litany of reasons."

"There are many instances of successful negotiations throughout history," she said. "Some were effective enough at stalling the creature, while others were able to change its mind entirely."

"And there are just as many instances throughout history of everything ending in fire," Hector protested. "The first stage of their reign of terror is the thievery of children. We may already be beyond any such negotiations."

"Let us hope not," she said stopping short of the cave's entrance. "I understand your trepidations, and I know your concerns for my safety, but I have to try. Even if it proves to be a frivolous whim," Lydia said and took no small satisfaction at seeing his face take a painful turn.

"I did not mean that," Hector said.

"Yes you did," Lydia said calmly. "I might have said the same words if I had been in your place. Though I would hope I would never have let silence come between us. I am not going to pretend that I understand these past months, but I will take on faith that you had your reason. And that somewhere in there is my Hector waiting to come back to me."

Visibly stung, Hector nodded to her gravely and turned to leave. With a hand on his shoulder she stopped him and said, "And if I were honest with myself, instead of having narrow vision, I should have explained why my need was great in seeing Nicodemus as we stood by the gate."

"I wish I could say that I would have listened and been supportive, but I am not sure of myself right now," Hector admitted.

Smiling kindly Lydia said, "We will speak of these things later. Provided death does not take us," she added darkly. "But if you will please allow one request: If this is destined to be the day of our departure, let us at least do so as the friends we have always been."

"Agreed," Hector said with a nod. With that, Lydia replaced the helm upon her head and made for the cavern. Standing just on the outside waiting was Hector's sister. She held two lit torches for them. She locked eyes upon Hector as she handed him his.

"I fear that I may have brought this upon us," she said.

"How so," he asked.

"Myron and his friend Sara were tormenting each other over a flower, and I thought I would talk sense into them by telling them of the Breaking."

Hector laughed and said, "So you thought you would tell your stubborn son of the greed of people eight thousand years ago, thought he would take it to heart, and see his own faults."

"There is always a first time," she protested. "But in the course of the tale, I said their names." When Hector did not respond she continued, "It has always been said to mention them was a bad portent. I thought the names would be safe."

Hector shook his head and said, "Coincidence. A superstition born out of fear. Unless you have recently been granted the powers of conjuration and have summoned Hostimentum or Vindicta to the Valley by accident. If so, then I heartily apologize for every time I booby-trapped the floor around your bed as you slept."

In return she offered him a very cross look as if to say, could you not joke at this moment.

He continued, "I also remember a very wise young woman once told me that ill tidings, and fell deeds have run rampant throughout history, and sometimes they come about regardless of our actions. Mostly we are powerless to stop them, but can only watch as the driverless carriage careens into the abyss."

"Those words were meant to dissuade you from your choice," she said after a moment.

"Perhaps today it will be fortunate that I did not listen. I will not come back without him," he assured her.

"Just make sure you both come back," she said darkly.

"Worry not, I remember my promises well."

Looking to Lydia, as she took her torch, she said, "You are a witness to this. He remembers his promises. Be sure to remind him of this if he tries anything foolish, My Lady."

Lydia bowed her head in agreement. Hector moved to her side and they shared one last glance at one another.

"Your sister," Lydia whispered.

"Yes," Hector said.

"Does all your family have that stern look?"

"When we are driven," Hector said nodding. "My nephew is one that has been taken."

"I am sorry."

"Do not be. If fortune favors us, we still may yet save them. But promise me this, if I should fall, be sure that you and the children make it to safety."

"We shall bring them all to safety," she said sternly.

Taking a breath, they took their first step into the darkness.

*   *   *   *   *

The children found themselves being herded into a chamber somewhere deep within the caverns. The strange giant creature that had seemed benign to most, with the exception of Myron, had stuck to the shadows behind them. Any time one of the children began to wander down one of the side chambers, the creature stomped or growled.

Their final destination was a large domed chamber of smooth and cracked rock. Myron could see slivers of daylight beaming down through small gaps in the ceiling. He supposed if every child were somehow to climb up on each other's shoulder, and not fall, they would still be too short to reach freedom.

The rays of light coming from the ceiling illuminated a large underground pond at the room's center. A pond created by the water collected from the numerous spring rainstorms. The children were being forced to walk around the pond to the back of the chamber, far from the only exit.

Myron took notice of two large rock deposits on their side of the pond. Both deposits were loose and crumbling as if they had been carried into the chamber. The first was easy to identify, coal. The black rock had many uses within Becknor, from smithies, to furnaces, to ovens. The second was a yellow stone of some sort that Myron had never seen. Venturing over to take a closer look, he quickly pinched his nose shut. He never knew rocks could smell so bad.

Sara had never left his side during the entirety of the journey. Unlike some of the children, who were even now crying and whimpering, she was just as calm as he.

Looking about Myron addressed the other children, "We have nothing to worry. My uncle will be here with thousandses of Knights."

"**My, such confidence,**" their captor growled behind them. Myron was beginning to make out the size of the monster, as his eyes were adjusting to the dimness. The beast was large. Nearly half the height of the chamber. It walked on all fours and had a long neck and tail. Its length nearly matched its height. Its forelegs were oddly shaped, almost as if they were more arm-like with clawed hands. There was something tucked under these "arms," were those wings?

"**What makes you so sure,**" it asked. "**Tell me, is your uncle as** great as these little urchins, and you, believe?"

Myron walked to the edge of the pond and said, "My uncle, the great Hector, Captain of the Valley," valley pronounced with a b. "He faced the bestest of Everfrost, he traveled to the Glass Desert and returned. He fears nothing and he will slay you."

"**A mighty warrior indeed then,**" the creature said with a nod of its large head. "**I have heard that very few can traverse the Glass Desert and the Desolation that surrounds it. It has claimed many over the millennia. Excellent, the story of Talio the Bold should begin like the days of old. When the greatest of my kind did duel with warriors of great renowned. I hope he is up to the challenge, we would not want this to be completely tiresome. But tell me little one, is your uncle prepared for one of my kind? Is he ready to test his worth against a dragon?**"

With that Talio the Bold stepped forth into one of the beams of light. His scales were a greenish brown. He had large, almost bat like ears and a long snout. Opening his mouth, the dragon showed off a row of razor sharp teeth, nearly as large as Myron, and a mouth big enough to swallow a man whole.

At the sight of such a beast, the chamber filled with the screams of fearful children. Myron, though longed to join them, refused the dragon any such satisfaction. If he was willing to meet his mother's gaze when she was angry with him, then how could a dragon's ever match?

Standing defiantly Myron replied, "My uncle will face your worstest, and match it."

Talio sneered, or was it a smile, and bellowed, "**Well then, let us gather the greatest minstrels of your kingdom. For only a feet of bravery worthy of song will best the likes of me. Only one of unmatched cunning, and bravery, could hope to best Talio the Bold!**"

# CHAPTER THIRTY-TWO

Galen watched as the farmer departed the Throne Room. The Grand Master of the Wise Men could only shake his head in disbelief. There was much information to contemplate and no time to do so. A second invasion of Everfrost, though dire, would have been easier to strategize than a dragon at their doorstep.

"In the entire two thousand year history of our Valley, there is not one writing of dragons nesting in these mountains," he said once the power of speech had returned to him. "How could there be one now, and we not know it?"

"The Dali Mountains are filled with ancient caverns High One," Aristide answered. The Inner Circle Captain was the last remaining, highly ranked Royal Court officer within the Circuit. "It is quite possibly that the beast entered the valley through an outer chamber."

"And what is her Ladyship thinking," Galen continued exasperated. "It was just this morning that she was so reasonable in seeing the wisdom of staying within the walls of the Palace. How did she manage to slip away?"

"We will discover the weakness High One, and correct it," Aristide assured him.

Galen waved away the sentiment and said, "We have no time for face-saving platitudes Captain. As foolish and act as it was, it would seem that fate may have placed our Regent precisely where she is needed. Perhaps she can stall the creature long enough for us to respond."

Turning to Aristide he said, "With Hector by Lydia's side, and his highest-ranking lieutenants off to Barricade Garrison, I am temporarily placing you over the Knights of the Valley. Assemble a force large enough to deal with the problem at hand."

"Apologies High One," said Aristide uncomfortably. "But there is not one weapon within our armories formidable enough. We must dispatch a courier at once to the Alliance. Only the Vanguard have the weapons and experience necessary for such a foe."

"A courier, riding at full speed, would still take days to reach Isaac's Hold," Galen told him. "By the time they would return, we will be nothing more than ash and dust. No, my friend, we must find a way to slay this creature ourselves."

Aristide nodded grimly before turning and making way for the barracks. Galen turned too and motioned towards an acolyte that had been standing nearby. The young man, wide-eyed in terror, ran to him quickly.

"Noble Aristide is correct in the need of a courier." Galen could see the question forming in the young man's mind and added, "I know what I told the Captain. The courier is not for our benefit. Our fate will be decided this day. The Alliance must be warned that a dragon has awakened. Their armies are marching to war, if a dragon here is on the move then it might mean others are rousing from slumber. Not all dragons hold to the Treaty of Vindicta and Heartstone. Many still hold to the ancient ways."

"Go and bring back the fastest horse and rider. I will write a dispatch for them to carry away. Tell them that they are to post themselves at the top of the Mountain Pass and watch. If the dragon takes flight, so will they. Go with haste."

Galen quickly moved through the halls of the Palace. His next destination was to be his chambers. He would write the message for the courier quickly. He was no warrior but he had every intention of meeting the Knights of the Valley at the Gateway Bridge and riding to the scene. His chosen service was still as a healer, his skill would be needed. And if things went badly, he would rather meet death head on instead of waiting for it to come to him. What he did not need was to find Cassius waiting for him by his chamber door.

"It would seem, High One ,that our patience has paid off rather quickly. Quicker than even I could have hoped for," he said turning his good eye to regard him.

"What do you mean?"

"Lydia has provided us with the proper method for disposing of her."

"Surely you cannot be plotting her assassination with the specter of death over us all," Galen asked.

"If the plan is shrewd enough, and executed with great care, there is no reason both cannot be dealt with. Perhaps Lydia can still die the hero and be forever loved by the people."

"And how do you propose we go about this?"

"We seal the caverns with blasting powder."

Galen laughed shortly and said, "The caverns crisscross the entire valley. There is not enough powder to seal every exit."

"But the caverns near Green Plaines are notoriously weak. A large enough explosion could collapse the entire section, effectively burying both of our problems."

"And the children?"

Cassius shrugged and asked, "What of the children?"

"You kill them as well?"

"There will be more children High One. So a few die this day, a million more shall be born over the centuries. To make safe the rest of the Valley does it really matter?"

"And just how are we any better than the dragon? We murder the innocent to execute the guilty?"

"What you see as murder, I see as a sacrifice for the common good. Our history with Everfrost is replete with multiple incidents of commanders sending knights to certain death to secure victory and freedom. How is sacrificing a handful of children any different?"

"They are not knights."

"A decade from now they very well may be," Cassius countered immediately. Galen turned from him. His soul was torn in two. Again, his own warring soul brought the memory of child Lydia looking up at him, with vacant eyes.

"What crime is Lydia guilty of that warrants so much death," he asked closing his eyes in an attempt to shut out the vision.

"I concede, High One, that Lydia may be innocent today," Cassius answered, his tone low but somehow more menacing. "We could sit here in the Palace and pray that it all works out to our good. Perhaps Lydia is up to the task and the dragon, who perhaps is our only enemy today, will not burn our world to the ground. But what of all the tomorrows that follow. We know that the meddling of tradition did not just end with Achelon. It continued all the way to Lord Marcus and his wife. How many journeys did they take, separately and together, to parts unknown? It is no secret that your predecessor as Grand Master, and his contemporaries, openly question Lord Marcus before King Gaius. What if they had been conspiring with powers outside the Valley? What if their daughter picks up where they left off?"

Still looking away, his eyes still shut tightly, Galen felt a hand land on his shoulder and Cassius voice in his ear, "We must act while we can.

Not just to snuff out Lydia but the dragon as well. Regrettably, yes, some children shall die. But we will have made the day safe and bought future generation peace plus security. It is sound wisdom, my friend. Only have the courage to act this time."

Galen's mind was whirling. Again he could hear the words of his father and grandfather. Of the dangers of Achelon and how his entire line needed dealing with. Perhaps they would have agreed with Cassius. Maybe they would have seen the logic in this argument. If they could have stood in Galen's stead, he knew that they too would have sacrificed the innocent to execute one they perceived as guilty. But Galen was not his fathers and he knew of no crime that Lydia was guilty of, or could think of no crime ever committed, where the death of innocents was acceptable in the execution of one.

"This is madness," Galen growled wrenching his shoulder away from Cassius' grip.

"Do I sense a change of heart," Cassius asked.

"Perhaps," Galen admitted. "Perhaps I was an old fool for listening to your ravings and for seeing them as sound wisdom."

"Do not turn a blind eye to our plight out of false sentiment."

"Enough Cassius," Galen shouted, no longer willing to keep his temper under control. "Achelon may very well have taken too much upon himself, but it did leave us with a century of peace. Perhaps it is time we applauded his wisdom instead of assassinating his character. As for Lord Marcus, there was not a man alive who loved this Kingdom more. As for my predecessor, there was no small amount of jealousy that guided his actions. The King favored Marcus' word over nearly every other Wise Man. Gaius put his faith in the wisdom of the Lord of Talwoods. Just as I will gladly yoke my fate with that of Lydia's. She shall have her chance to stop this dragon. And be warned, once this day is over you will no longer have a place with us."

"Do not be foolish Galen," Cassius said breaching protocol by dropping the title and stepping in Galen's way. "You can remove me from your council, but you know there are many others within the Kingdom that feel as I. Some are even among the Royal Court. You may quickly find yourself in the minority."

"Better in the minority of the righteous than in the majority of political schemers and murderers of children. Becknor thanks you for your service, such as it was. Get out of my sight," he said pushing past him and into his chambers.

Immediately Galen sat and began to write out his message to the Alliance. Cassius had taken up far too much of his time. Not just today, but his entire time as his Second. He prayed now that there was still something that could be done for Lydia and those trapped with her.

* * * * *

For just a moment Cassius stared at the closed door before him. He should have acted quicker. He should have had the foresight to remove the old fool years ago. At the very least he should have acted the very day the Grand Master had lacked the fortitude to keep the Blue Orchid Elixir secret from Hector and the rest of the Kingdom. Cassius had even purchased an untraceable poison by the direction of the Plan. A nice painful concoction that he had been directed to give to Vitus once his usefulness was at an end. He was still in possession of a good amount. Perhaps it was time for new leadership. He would find time to slip it to Galen once the dragon was dealt with.

The dragon! No time left for personal vengeance, there was still time to deal with both Lydia and the dragon. Precisely in the manner he had described to the Grand Master. It would take time for Galen to strip him of his privileges, time he did not have while organizing and ill-conceived rescue mission. He would use what time he had left as Galen's second wisely.

Working his way to the stables, destiny was on his side. Two Knights of the Valley passed him on an errand of their own. He allowed himself a small smile before adopting a worried look.

"You there, Knights," he called out just before they disappeared around a nearby corner. As they returned, one recognized him and saluted.

"How may we be of service to the Wise Men, Master Cassius?"

"I am on a special assignment for Grand Master Galen. There is death and ruin in our midst." He told them of the dragon and watched as their eyes went wide with fear. This pleased him. He explained it all, conveniently leaving Hector and Lydia out.

"We have little time. Go now to the armory and requisition blasting powder. Enough to fill the back of a wagon. I will go to the stables and see to the wagon myself. We shall save our brothers and sisters this day. Hail Becknor!"

Both Knights saluted enthusiastically and departed. It amazed Cassius how required service seemed to dull the intellect. So happy to do what was needed, they never once asking for a single extra detail.

Likewise, the stable master was equally enthusiastic to give him a wagon and a pair of his strongest horses. The journey to the Barracks was quick. The Knights he had sent ahead were already waiting for him. From inside the walls, Cassius could hear Aristide marshaling the Knights.

"Captain Aristide has called all Knights of the Valley to assemble," the knight that had recognized him said as they began to load the wagon.

"Aristide's order are separate from mine," he said not exactly lying. As they finished loading, he ordered, "Under the authority of Grand Master Galen, I order you to escort me to the scene. I shall arrive quicker with an escort clearing my way." Again, the pair of knights never questioned his countermand of Aristide's orders.

Everything worked splendidly with one exception. As they rode past the Palace once more, Cassius noticed the acolyte. Galen's personal attendant was standing by a young maiden on horseback. As she dismounted and began to follow the acolyte through the gate, the young man turned and eyed Cassius and his cargo suspiciously. For a moment he thought of ordering their arrest, but that would have cost too much time.

*It does not matter*, he thought to himself. *There is nothing Galen can do to stop my crusade.*

Strange, in everything he had lost due to his injuries, Cassius was amazed at how much clearer his moral vision had become. *Let Galen and the others label me as they wish*, Cassius thought with a satisfied smile. *I will do as Aldred Zen-Joffa and his allies did so many millennia ago. Let history call me a traitor. It is sufficient that I know this moment that I am Becknor's true savior. I saved her from the oncoming storm of blood and death.*

# CHAPTER THIRTY-THREE

For the second time in her life, and both in the same day, Lydia found herself taking an extraordinary journey. The first had been a solitary ride across Becknor, and now she was walking underneath it.

"Be sure to keep your torch as low as you can," Hector ordered softly. "A dragon's eye does not see light as much as it sees the heat. Our one chance to approach is to keep it blind to our presence. But it is still as likely to hear us with its magnificent ears. or smell our approach with that near perfect sense of smell."

Lydia nodded, and heard every word, but her eyes were drinking in the wonder around her. Whatever she had been expecting, this was certainly not it. The tunnels and chambers under Green Plaines were towering. No wonder the dragon could navigate them so easily. It was quite well known that an ancient mining operation had taken place long before the first Valley-Dwellers, many of tunnels were still squared off. Over time, water had eroded most of the smooth walls, and stalactites dotted the ceilings. Finally, she had expected total darkness aside from the light of the torches, only to find that there was light filtering down from the outside. A point she relayed to Hector.

"The caverns here are the weakest," he said. "A few centuries ago, the farmers began to notice small sinkholes plaguing their fields. By their request, the Royal Court sent men down here to map the worst areas and found that the ground above was slowly sinking down into here. Some of the farms were abandoned and the forest was allowed to take over. I believe someone thought the roots would act as support."

"Over mining," Lydia asked.

"Most certainly, but not by Beckish hands. These caverns predate the Migration by at least thousands of years. The Dali Mountains have always been mineral rich. That is what brought the first goblins to Everfrost. Legend has it that there are whole mountains deep within the chain that are practically hollow."

"I have always liked the thought that these are the remains of an old dwarvish stronghold. A place of importance before they became extinct."

"A very romantic notion," Hector said with a nod. "A place that was carved out for something noble and not for greed."

"Though dwarven greed was known to be exceptional, and is still famous after nearly eight millennia."

For the fourth time since the beginning of their journey underground, Hector stopped and drew his dagger and carved an X and an arrow pointing the way they had come into the wall. Once they had started moving again she said, "Good idea, marking our way."

"Actually, I am marking your way. This can become quite the labyrinth, and if we get separated you need to find your way."

"And I suppose you have a keen skill of direction and can never be lost."

Hector turned and smiled, "Something like that. I memorize each turn by constantly repeating them in my head. The longer I go, and the more moves I make, I turn them into sing-song like lyrics, with the very first turn last and the last first. A trick I learned as a child on my many underground wanderings."

"You would come here as a child?"

With a chuckle, he said, "Many times. Not always by choice. My sister was always dragging me down here. She would take me further and further down attempting to confuse me. Once we were far enough down to satisfy her, she would distract me and then run away."

"Seems rather extreme for play."

"Oh, it was not playtime. I had offended her greatly and she demanded restitution."

"What could you ever have done to offend her so," Lydia asked puzzled.

Hector tried to suppress a laugh and said, "I was born male. You see, Elyssa had always wanted a baby sister, a brother would never do. She claimed I stole her sister. This went on for years until our mother found out."

"What did your mother do?"

"She had me hide from her for a whole day. When I did not come home after a few hours, Elyssa panicked and searched for hours calling my name. All the time I was hiding in a tree with," he hesitated for a moment, "a friend. Later, when Elyssa found me near sunset, she yanked me from the tree and gave me a rather nice thrashing."

"I wager that is what led to the promise you both spoke of," she asked simply. For a moment Hector paused as his body stiffened. She feared she had somehow offended him until he answered:

"No, the promise would come much later," he said as he began moving again. "As you know I am the first of our family in generations to choose the sword over the plow. Let us just say that there was much discussion within our home when I made my choice. So," again a pause, "under the circumstances, a promise was required. A promise that I would not do anything...overly foolish."

"What would be considered overly foolish?"

Again he smiled and said, "Oh, no doubt leaving the valley without a word, riding to a desert of glass, and facing a dangerous immortal. I would think taking a stroll underground, with the Regent of the Kingdom, in search of a dragon to negotiate with, would come a close second."

They fell into silence after that. Lydia, her curiosity beginning to grow, started to ask more but she remained silent. For just over five years, the man at her side had been the one she trusted most. For the first time in the history of their friendship, she was beginning to feel as if Hector was purposefully hiding something. He had been attempting to hide the real details of Aldred Zen-Joffa's third trial for some unknown reason. Could he be hiding yet more?

Frowning, Lydia quickly chastised herself. Until recently Hector had been an open book. Whatever the ancient alchemist had done to Hector was obviously very personal and painful and her probing was adding to his misery. In question everything, because she had been awakened to the true tragedy of her past, was she now seeing conspiracies among her closest friends? No, she needed to stop this moment, or risk becoming what she had accused Hector of not even an hour ago, a complete stranger.

Changing the subject she said, "Once I request a council, protocol demands that no harm come to us until negotiations are complete," Lydia said. They were speaking in little more than whispers and yet their voices seemed to echo off every wall.

"That is when the creature is one of the more honorable of its people," Hector pointed out. "We have no clue as to which dragon we are dealing. There are only twenty-three left in the world, and some of them have very long memories."

"Then let us hope ours is one of the more ancient, and is still loyal to Vindicta the Terrible."

"Amen," he said stopping to carve another marking into the wall.

The next hour would find them searching one corridor after another. Lydia was glad that Hector had his own underground compass because it felt as if they were moving in circles. Some of the side corridors seemed to bend back the direction they had come. To add to the confusion, twice they entered large chambers where several of the corridors seemed to crisscross through. All the while, Hector would occasionally glance her way with a reassuring smile, as if reading her thoughts.

As Lydia began to fear that they would never find the children in time, Hector came to a stop. He had closed his eyes and tilted his head from side to side.

"Listen," he whispered. Closing her eyes she could just make out the dripping of water into a large pull of water somewhere down their right. There was another sound as well. Was it a whimper? Just then, there was a deep growling roar and the scream of children. Lydia's eyes flew open just as Hector's did, and they both ran towards the sounds of the screams.

They came across a chamber with a high domed ceiling. At the top was a small opening large enough to let a tiny ray of sunlight through. With the aid of the light, she could see the children. They were huddled together between two large piles of rock, on the other side of an underground pond. Just as she was about to run to their rescue, she saw it.

Lydia, like most alive in the world, had never laid eyes upon a dragon before. The vast majority of people that had ever lived had never seen them in their legendary glory. The dragon had been created by the Divine to bring an end to the terrible, genocidal War of Breaking. As long as peace reigned, dragon kind hibernated. Their sleep could last for centuries, or even a thousand years. It was, for a time, a great deterrent to war. March on your neighbor to sack his kingdom and you could have a dragon to answer to. First, your armies and cities would be ash, and then

2

your treasures raided of its gold to create legendary dragon-stone so that the dragon could use it to build a nest and attract a mate. Today, a dragon, though fearsome, was not unbeatable. A schism within their ranks had caused a culling of their numbers, and the Alliance had a few dragon-slaying weapons within their arsenals.

Lydia was frozen in place as she looked upon their formidable foe. She found that it was as impressive in size as all the histories and legends said. It moved in and out of the shadows pacing around the children. Its long neck pointed down so that it might look upon the children on their level.

Lydia felt a strong arm wrap around her shoulders and pull her away. It was Hector moving them both into hiding behind a large boulder. By the look on his face, he too was taken aback by the size of the dragon. After a moment to catch his breath he looked at her expectantly. His crooked smile seemed to say, "Well, this was your idea. Say something."

Lydia removed her helmet so that she might be heard clearly. Remembering what Hector had said about the ears of the dragon, she turned her back to the boulder and faced the way they had come. She would call out and away from the dragon and hope the echo would confuse it.

Taking one last deep breath she called out loudly, "Under the Concordance of Mutual Understanding, set down by Queen Kaitlyn Heartstone and Vindicta the Terrible, I seek to negotiate terms with the keeper of these caverns."

A growl of surprise came from the other side of the room. Lydia chanced a look around the corner of her boulder to see the dragon frantically moving its head from side to side. It sniffed the air trying to get their scent.

**"Who dares to interrupt my rights to exact retribution,"** it growled.

"I am Lydia, Lady of Talwoods, and Regent of the Valley-Kingdom of Becknor."

"**Ho, Ho,**" it growled laughed. "**You are a bold one Lady of Talwoods. Come to die with the first of the young ones have you?**"

"Under the Concordance of Mutual Understanding you are to respectfully address me, identify yourself, and guarantee my safety until our discussions are concluded," Lydia said sternly.

Silence. Hector's hopes that this was one of the more honorable dragons of history rang through her mind. Granted, the ancient protocol Lydia was evoking was nearly two thousand years old, but it was set forth by the oldest and first of dragons. Surely even the most dishonorable of dragons would not go against the will of Vindicta.

"**Respectfully address you,**" it mocked. "**Why should one of my kind show any respect for your kind? Especially when history shows your kind has no respect for any kind. Especially here, west of the Drakemourn. For centuries, it was the warmbloods of your Four Greater Kingdoms who murdered my kind whilst they slept, in order to rob their nests of the precious dragon stone. A council with scoundrels and murders can only have one true outcome.**"

Lydia could sense Hector's posture go rigid as his free hand moved for his sword. She began to fear that he had been right.

"**And yet, who am I to go against the wishes and wisdom of the First. It is said her ears are everywhere and that the Divine gifted her with prophecy. If I were to betray her wishes, would I not incur her wrath? Would not Vindicta wake and seek my execution?**" A strange sound just then, did it sigh?

"**So be it, Lady Regent. I am Talio, the Bold.**"

Talio the Bold, Lydia's mind raced through the list of known dragons. It was not a name listed in the census of dragon-kind. Though the dragon-count was never to be believed to be absolute. Dragons never volunteered to be counted in an official census. Nevertheless, the number of known living dragons had just grown by one.

**"And you have my word, for the duration of our negotiations, you will be safe. Now, why not come out into the open."**

As reassuring as it was that Talio respected Vindicta's Concordance of Understanding, the way he had requested her to come forth set off a warning bell deep in her mind. One glance at Hector confirmed the warning.

"I think I am quite comfortable where I am right now," Lydia answered.

**"Suit yourself, Lady Regent,"** he said seemingly amused. **"Do not think your misdirection will fool me for long. If I were to seek your harm it would be over quickly."**

Another strange sound, perhaps laughter, as it asked, **"By chance, that noble and mighty man of valor, the slayer of goblins, conqueror of impossible trials, and friend of mythological alchemists, the great Hector, does he accompany you?"**

Lydia looked to Hector quizzically as he answered, "I am here."

**"Excellent! I have heard much about you from these children. I believe most aspire to be just as you are, especially your nephew."**

Lydia watched as several emotions played across Hector's features. He seemed both relieved and terrified that his nephew was nearby. Lastly, there was a look Lydia had seen many times before, and it was never good for the obstacle in his way. Defiance. Especially as Talio added:

**"I look forward to besting you in front of them."**

Hector remained silent and wisely so. This Talio was only trying to goad him into foolishness.

**"So now, Lady Regent, bring forth your petition."**

"Under the authority given me as the protector of the Throne of Becknor, I ask by what right have you opened hostilities with the people of the Valley," Lydia asked purposefully, putting a fire into her voice.

**"The only right that I need,"** Talio growled. **"My Divine purpose."**

"How can that be so? There is no war in the Valley. The people of Becknor are at peace."

**"You cannot lie to such as I, Lady Regent. The nose of a dragon is very sensitive. I have smelled the blood and burnt flesh. I have heard the revelry of your people. You and your Goblin foe have been at war. Oh yes Lady Regent, dragon-kind knows all too well of the wars that have waged here. Curious, that you have escaped our judgment till now. But now I will correct that short-sightedness. The time has come for you both to pay for your greed."**

"I do not lie. Yes, there have been many clashes between our peoples. I doubt there is a corner of the world that have not heard of the struggles of Becknor and Everfrost. But the entirety of the recent war was only ten days, and that was a season ago. Furthermore, ours had never been a struggle for gold. Everfrost only seeks food enough to feed their people, sadly their leaders think only of providing through military might. While the people of Becknor seek only to defend themselves from an act of genocide. Perhaps that is why the Valley has never fallen under the vengeance of dragon-kind. Perhaps the wars waged by Becknor are looked upon as just."

**"Only the self-righteous, children of men could claim any war was just,"** Talio bellowed. **"If there was such a thing as a just war, the dragon would not exist."**

"Please understand great Talio," Lydia began. "Though I do not deny that our histories have not been sordid, we all began as nomadic people seeking peace. Two thousand years ago, the first settlers came here because of the isolated nature of these mountains. Wishing to put the bloody wars behind them, they looked upon the lush fields of this valley and saw an opportunity to build a life where the only struggle was one of tilling the fields. A life with their hands caked in the rich soil of this land, not dripping with the blood of their brothers. Freedom to learn the art of irrigation, cultivation, and harvest, to never again study war."

"For the most part, the Goblin Kingdom in the mountain is no more deserving of dragon retribution than our people. Just four centuries after my people settled here, a peaceful tribe of goblins settled within Everfrost, hoping to mine it for its minerals and perhaps earn the coin necessary to purchase back their own lands. Lands that had been stolen from them in the last war. But the winters upon Everfrost are harsh and unforgiving. Our ancestors, who were even more isolationist than the people of today, did have compassion for the starving goblins and offered a share of their harvest.

"It was the last of their Great Overseers, who became the first of the Dread Overlords, Geebal Parsh, who persuaded his people to take their iron and their bronze and fashion weapons and march off the mountain, and take our lands for themselves. At first many resisted this notion. All they wished was to go home. But Lord Parsh dealt with them quickly. He murdered them openly for all to see. They marched on my people out of fear. The goblins of Everfrost have never attacked out of greed, but out of fear of the lash. To this day, even after nearly dying by their hand, I believe there are still those who wish peace. It is my hope, that given time, those within Everfrost who wish peace will again find their voice. One day, they will push their fears aside and demand change of their Overlord. There will be a lasting peace in these mountains again, if you give us time."

Lydia felt handicapped. Negotiations normally took place face to face so that you could look your partner in the eye. Most kept a steely expression but it was the eyes that told the story. Within you could see if your words were truly reaching their heart, as they were staring back to see if your words held any sincerity. So as silence fell and held after her plea, she could only hope her words had penetrated deep into Talio's heart.

**"You are a masterful speaker, Lady Regent,"** Talio said calmly. **"You speak knowledgeably, especially of your own past. I must say that there is very little doubt that your words come from your heart. And even such as I am moved that you would not only speak on behalf of your own kingdom, but also for your enemies who would see you dead. Your hope for peace is a noble sentiment. A sentiment, that was no doubt, once shared by the dwarf."**

Lydia's heart sank. Her words had bounced away just as an arrow would have bounced harmlessly off his scales.

**"Not just the dwarf but also every race now long dead. All exterminated for their land, power, and riches. It is because of the greed of the surviving races: man and goblin included; that the Divine created dragon-kind. We are Divine retribution. Only with an eternal threat of death, has there ever been a lasting peace."**

Lydia took a steadying breath, she could not afford any emotion in her voice in what she was about to say. If it came too forcibly it could anger him into action, if her voice cracked it would embolden him all the same.

"But great Talio, is it still the will of the Divine to burn indiscriminately? After three thousand years of dragon retribution, was not the world in ruin? The forests were nearly gone, there were no cities, barely any villages and was not the surviving races on the brink of dying out. Had not dragon-kind been too willing and too efficient? Is this not why the Divine sent the Ten?"

The Ten were first magicians and wizards to use the Pure Magic. A

Divine power to bring healing and reconciliation to the world. And if Talio had been alive then, or knew his history, he would know that it was a time that even Vindicta the Terrible first began to show mercy.

**"Yes, yet was it not a few centuries later that one of the human descendants of the Ten betrayed some of his brothers by murdering them? He took their power and pervert it into the darker arts. And so began the War of the Wizards, to which dragon-kind was called upon again. We are moving in circles Lady Regent,"** he said as his growls turned more menacing. **"Surely, I have not awakened for no purpose at all. My kind is very sensitive to the turning of the world. If war has returned to your little valley, then no doubt the rest of the world must be at war."**

"To that, you would be wrong," Lydia lied. "And if I may be so bold myself, great Talio, you are ready to point out the treachery of but a few of my people, and yet you have failed to remember your own history. Not all dragons were loyal to their Divine Purpose. Were there not the traitors who betrayed your First, Vindicta?"

**"And history shows that they paid dearly for their treachery. Retribution was swift. So this is how you seek to dissuade me? By insinuating that I have no more moral right to fulfill my purpose because of the treacherous actions of a few?"**

"Why not? Considering you are trying to use ancient history as a reason to punish a peaceful people," Lydia said quickly. "But I would only seek to remind you of the revelation of your forbearers. For the first time, they knew that one side can be justified in defending themselves in a war of aggression. Did this not lead Vindicta to agree to the Concordance of Understanding?"

**"Temporary treaties, and agreements that most of dragon-kind reluctantly agreed to only because of Vindicta's grief. Grief from**

losing far too many of our kind. **But true dragons still hold to the**
**Divine Purpose. All who study war must be purified in flame. And**
**Talio is one such dragon.**"

It was over then. Lydia was puzzled. It was said the dragons loyal
to Vindicta were the more reasonable. She could have, perhaps, understood
the dragon's stance if a war was ongoing. Nowhere in history had a dragon
attacked months after a skirmish such as the Ten-Day War.

"My Lady," Hector whispered into her ear. She eyed him coolly
despite the danger they were now in.

"You will never speak reason to this one," he continued. "He has
knowledge but lacks wisdom. He is too young and has far too much fire in
his blood. Look beside the children and you too will see."

Again Lydia chanced a look around the corner of her hiding place.
Talio was moving his head from side to side sniffing the air as she looked.
Ignoring him she looked to the far side of the pond. Again she noticed the
two piles of rock but this time, she recognized them. One looked to be
sulfur and the other coal. She joined Hector in understanding.

"He is trying to recreate Rial's fire," Hector whispered to her.

Lydia smiled. Talio had yet to mature into adulthood. It was
doubtful he could breathe fire. For the first two centuries of its life, a young
dragon's fire glands were not fully developed. Although they could not
produce fire did not mean they were totally defenseless. Aside from their
still impressive size and teeth, the fire glands could produce a very acidic
mixture that could melt steel in an instant. But without the ability to breathe
fire, he could not fulfill his "Divine Purpose." Nor would he be able to melt
gold and transform it into dragon-stone to build a nest. He would be forced
to go back into hibernation until the fire glands fully developed.

"The pond; the water must be rich in minerals. By drinking the
water, then eating the coal and sulfur, he's hoping to recreate the formula to

help speed up the maturation process. He lacks one key ingredient. He needs just a small amount of oil produced from any variety of," her voice trailed off as she looked to Hector. A strange look had come over him.

"We need to draw him away."

"What are you thinking," Lydia asked worriedly.

"A balanced knight knows the value of a strategic withdraw," he said more to himself. With those words, Lydia could see that her Hector had returned. And it was at the precise moment she did not need him.

"Hector, whatever foolishness you are planning...."

Interrupting her in midsentence, he said, "If this should go spectacularly ill for me, will you please give my end a more epic spin."

"Hector, please, do not...."

"Gather the children and follow my trail back to the exit."

**"I call these paltry negotiations concluded,"** Talio bellowed. **"Take heart, for today I will remove the very thing that causes war in your valley. Before I take your gold, I shall burn the land itself until not one single green leaf grows ever again. Now come forward, Lady Regent. So that I may end you in a way fitting your kind."**

Lydia could only watch as Hector snatched up his torch, held it high over his head, and began to scream like a wild man as he ran away, arms flailing.

**"Watch how swiftly your champion flees. Oh yes, a great and mighty man of valor this Hector is. No matter, I shall end the coward swiftly and come back for you and the children."**

Lydia felt the gust of air as the dragon leapt over her hiding place. She could see his massive form moving through the shadows, and hear the crunch of rock under his massive weight, as he set out after Hector. She waited for his thundering footsteps to move farther down the corridor before replacing the helmet upon her head and moving for the children.

# CHAPTER THIRTY-FOUR

Galen was running, granted, at nearly eighty years, the running looked more to be a brisk walk. The acolyte at his side continued to beg him to sit and let him go to Aristide. Heart beating out of his chest as it was, the moment the acolyte had delivered his news, he knew he needed to see to this himself.

Galen was at full stride as he passed through the gate. Before him were ranks and ranks of the Knights of the Valley, their armor glistening in the late afternoon sun. Battle tested as they were, the look of concern upon their faces was understandable.

Galen looked up to see Aristide approaching on horseback. He was still wearing the black armor of the Inner Circle but had shed himself of his rank's red cape.

"High One," he began. "I have mustered up a good two thousand. Another thousand shall depart by the time we arrive."

"You, and whatever knights are upon horseback, must ride with all haste ahead of the rest," Galen said. "Cassius has commandeered a wagon and loaded it down with blasting powder. He means to destroy the cavern."

"I do not understand, does he not know…."

"He knows Captain. He means to use this opportunity as an assassination attempt upon the Regent."

Aristide asked no more but took the reins of his horse and urged it on, issuing orders and calling to the other knights on horseback as he went.

Galen sat upon the ground to regain his strength. He had been a fool. He should have set fire to the words of his father's the same day their remembrance stones were set down. If he had, Cassius' fell words would have found no soil to grow within him. Now he could only sit and pray that his inactions had not brought harm to Lydia and all with her.

＊ ＊ ＊ ＊ ＊

Cassius urged as much speed as he dared from the horses. Blasting powder only needed a single spark to erupt. It would have been for naught if he had blown himself up.

The group of farmers milling about the opening were his next problem. They would need to be dealt with.

"Good and brave people of Green Plains," he addressed them as he dismounted the wagon. His two conscripted knights flanked him as he approached the crowd. "This is no place for you. A legion of knights is at my back as we speak. The concern for your children is understandable and admirable, but I fear you will only get in the way. This is work for blades and spears."

Turning to the knights he ordered them to escort them away. Turning back towards the wagon, a nearby woman's voice addressing him brought him to a halt. He looked to see that she had laid her hand upon his unfeeling shoulder to get his attention.

"Forgive my interruption master," a raven-haired woman addressed him. "Many of us are desperate for any news. Could we not wait within view of the cave? And if the Lady Lydia is successful, would it not be better for the children to see their parents first upon emerging."

"I understand your concern," he lied. "Yet, this field is a small one and we will need every last space to prepare. But worry not, I do not doubt that after this day your children will be beyond further harm," he said offering a smile.

She eyed him a moment longer. *A smart one this girl,* he thought to himself. He could tell she did not trust him. Reluctantly, she turned and joined the others.

Cassius waited until the last farmer was out of view and began to work. He had never intended to unload the wagon himself. Hands that felt no sensation at all were a liability. Luckily, the barrels were small enough for him to wrap his arms around and squeeze them to his numb chest.

For the second time, fate had decreed that he act completely alone. The last time it had left him scarred and forever injured. If Cassius' life ended today with Lydia's, he would count it as a fair payment.

\* \* \* \* \*

The children crowded in around Lydia as she led them through the labyrinthine caverns. Following Hector's marks were easy enough. Until the next mark pointed towards a fork in the path that neither Hector, nor herself, had realized was there. Coming to a halt in front of them, Lydia was at a loss.

"I know the way," a small voice at her elbow spoke up.

"Leave the knight be," one child snapped while another said, "Stop lying Myron."

"How do you know," Lydia asked looking down upon a small boy with dark brown hair. His eyes locked confidently with hers.

"My uncle told me about this game that he and my mother used to play. She would bring him down here and try and make him lost. He taught me how to rememberize my way back if I ever was down here. Even though I have never ever been here," he added quickly with a hand upon his stomach, that she was sure was meant for over his heart, and then turning his gaze nervously away.

"Surely not," she said wryly. Motioning him to take the lead she said, "Show us the way then." Without having to stop and look for Hector's carvings the procession moved much quicker. Lydia knew that very few would have tied their fate to a small child's sense of direction, but then she trusted Hector to teach his nephew well. Lydia smiled, Hector to the rescue. Even when he was absent he was always nearby. Hopefully, her Hector was now here to stay. If he survived Talio.

* * * * *

It was the strangest thing. Hector was almost giddy in his attempt to lead the dragon away. Perhaps it was due to the fact for the first time in months he was not riddled with self-doubt. There was action and reaction.

The realization came upon him then about the promise he had made. His family had misinterpreted his promise long ago. They wanted, needed, to hear him say that he would know throw his life away foolishly. It was their way of attempting to make him rethink his choice. Give up knighthood as soon as possible. But his promise had been to live. And that was precisely what he was doing now. Though, taking chances such as these would never qualify as living to them, but then he could never have chosen knighthood and lived in the shadows. A life secluded away within the Barracks or perpetual guard duty was impossible for Hector. Knowing the events that informed his decision, they should have known better. There was only one way he could ever have lived his life. Fully dedicated and willing to go to the end. Only once in his life had he failed that standard and death came as a result. He would not fail again.

So as he turned another random corner, and Talio thundering behind him, Hector once again was at peace. If today was going to be his end, he would do so without regret or remorse. He would have bought time for Lydia and his nephew to get to safety and his promise would be intact. And as for the promise within the promise.

*Do you love her?*

If he lived, then he would reflect upon it.

**"I had truly hoped for a confrontation with a great warrior that was worthy of song,"** Talio growled closing in behind, snapping Hector back into the moment. **"Now this has become nothing more than a cat chasing a rat. If only the children that had sung your praises could see your cowardice now."**

Hector came to a forking tunnel and took refuge in a deep gouge to the side. Talio rushed past him moments later and stopped a moment to consider the two paths before taking the one to the left.

Quickly, Hector ran for the right branch before calling out, "I may be the rat, but the cat is fat and lazy."

Hector was making great effort to stay as far away from the marked passageways by making as many quick turns that were available. He had no time to leave new markings on the walls as he went. His old childhood navigation skill was being stretched to its limit. If there were many more turns, these caverns would be his final residence.

**"I know every nook and corner. Your attempt to flee is futile. You only run to your doom."**

Hector could sense a difference in Talio's voice. It was closer than it should have been. As for what happened next, Hector would never really know for sure what it was that had tipped him off; the direction of the voice, a subtle change in the air, or perhaps there had been a rumble in the cave floor? Knowing something was coming, Hector made his next move before his eyes had even seen the great dragon launching himself out of the shadows.

Still moving forward, Hector kicked his own feet out from under him and began to slide. Almost in the same instant, Talio's open mouth appeared above him. The great jaws of the dragon snapped shut in a thunderous clap just above his head. Sliding onto his back, he watched as

JACK O CRABTREE

Talio's long body flew over him. At the last instant, the tail of the dragon whipped around in an in vain attempt to crush him. The thrashing tail kicked up large chunks of rock just to Hector's left ear. Looking that way, Hector spied his next avenue of escape. A small, floor-level opening into a neighboring side cavern.

Rolling quickly to his knees, Hector tossed his torch through the opening before dropping down again and rolling through. Behind him he could hear the sound of liquid hitting the ground where he had been laying, Hector glanced back to see the rocks melting.

"Some harbinger of woe," Hector mocked the dragon as he was back on his feet. "Not old enough to breathe fire, and you threaten death and destruction. The blind, stupid cat chases his own tail; while the rat escapes with the cheese."

A growling roar of outrage echoed down the corridors as the entire rock wall before Hector cracked. Talio had begun to throw himself against the other side. Hector smiled. He could now make his escape as Lydia and the children should have reached safety by now.

As he retrieved his torch Hector turned to continue his sprint, the smile faded from his face. His luck had run out.

Hector's clever escape had become a not-so-clever mistake. A high-ceilinged, dead end chamber with a handful of stalactites lay before him. The rock wall behind him shook again as an angry Talio was intent on breaking in. Hector noticed more fractures had formed. It would not take long for the dragon to join him.

* * * * *

Cassius' overly sensitive ears heard the hoof beats of the approaching horses long before anyone else would have. He cursed himself for not having the acolyte dealt with. He had not even unloaded a third of the barrels. There was little chance that the barrels stacked in the opening

404

would collapse the entire cavern. Galen and Aristide had been too quick for him.

No, he was not beaten yet. Moving to the front Cassius unhitched the horses and drove them away. As quick as his clumsily numb fingers would work, he set a fuse to one of the barrels in the back.

"Stop him," the voice of Aristide called out somewhere behind. Ignoring the sound of their approach, Cassius lit the fuse and began to push the carriage forward. At first, the stubborn wheels refused to move, but once they began to turn there was no stopping them. Quickly the weight of the wagon and barrels took over and Cassius watched as it began to roll quickly for the cavern opening.

Cassius turned to see a group of knights riding hard towards him. He smiled at their futility just before losing consciousness from the blast.

* * * * *

Lydia had seen the wagon and the barrels nearly too late. As the realization of the barrel's contents dawned upon her, she quickly turned to the children and commanded them to stop and hit the ground. For a heartbeat, they looked up at her questioningly before obeying. As she watched the last child get down, the barrels went off. The shock lifted her and threw her over the children. She landed with a tumble that sent her helmet flying.

She laid there for a moment, ears ringing. She felt movement around her and looked up to see the concerned look of the children.

"I am uninjured," she told them, as she got back up upon her wobbly feet. Looking down she saw that her armor was merely dinged and scratched. The Kingdom's smithies were going to find their pay increased shortly. Retrieving her torch, she Looked upon to the children and said, "Come, let us see the state of our exit."

The blasting powder had done its job extraordinarily well. Behind them, there was the sound of rock slides echoing towards them. The blast had weekend the nearby walls. A worrisome memory of Hector telling her the weakness of the caverns in Green Plains, flashed into her memory. Looking forward, Lydia could see a number of large boulders blocking the way. It would take days to clear the debris. Days they did not have if Talio made his way back.

Thankfully it was not a complete blockage, as a beam of light made its way through a small opening at the top. While they all gathered looking upon the devastation, movement towards the top caught her eye. It was a Knight of the Valley looking through.

Seeing her he called out, "My Lady, are you injured?"

"What the blazes were you thinking," she demanded at once. "Have the Knights of the Valley and Galen lost their senses?"

"It was not us M'lady. This was the work of Master Cassius."

Cassius? Nicodemus has warned of thorns among the people. Had she already attracted too much attention? Shaking her head, there was time enough later for conspiracies, again she focused on the knight as he called out again.

"It will take some time, but we will get you out," the knight promised.

"Work as fast as you can. There is a very angry dragon down here, and I have faith your brave captain has made it even more so," she said, as she turned towards the children. She was about to offer them a word of encouragement when she took note of their size. Calling back towards the opening, "Brave knight, would you say that opening is large enough for a child to pass through?"

Inspecting the opening he said, "Easily M'lady."

"I shall send the children up one at a time. Get them back to the arms of their parents."

One by one the children climbed the rock deftly and with haste. As they made it to the top a pair of strong hands pulled them through. Towards the end, the boy that had assisted her, Hector's nephew, was standing by her side.

"That was brave of you. To have the courage to speak up and lead us out as you did," Lydia said, going down on one knee to look him in the eye. "There are adults that lack even half of that kind of courage."

"Thank you," he said graciously. "But I have a family reprentation to uphold."

Lydia grinned and said, "Of course you do." For the first time, Lydia noticed the girl who had never left his side during the ordeal. Not the girl actually, but the flower in her hair.

"Forgive me child, but your flower," she said.

"It is called Divine's Prominence," Hector's nephew answered.

"Divine's Providence," she corrected with a smile. "And that is precisely what it is. It looks very lovely in your hair, but I am afraid I have need of it," she said plucking it from her. "I hope you do not mind."

Cheering, both children began to hug each other. "Hurray! We are not married anymore!" Lydia just looked upon them puzzled as they joined the last of the children to freedom.

"Is that the last," the knight above called out. "My Lady, where are you going?"

"To return a favor to your captain," she said making her way back into the cavern. With one hand she plucked all of the petals free and discarded the stem. Retrieving her helmet she placed them inside. Retrieving her torch, Lydia worked her way back to the pond. There was still work to be done.

\* \* \* \* \*

Upon Galen's arrival, he took note of three things. The knights gathered around the collapsed opening, the children being ushered to their waiting parents just over the next hill, and the mangled and dying form of Cassius. Aristide stood over him as if he could take flight any moment. Galen joined them and was shocked to see that his traitorous second had awakened.

"How fortunate you are to have lost all sensation," Galen said grimly. "You would surely be wailing in agony." Bones were shattered, his flesh was ripped open, and he looked to be completely paralyzed.

"But fear not Master Cassius," Aristide spoke up. "For soon you will feel again. The fires of the abyss shall welcome you with their loving embrace."

Cassius laughed. An agonizing wheezing and rattling, demonic sound. Galen's skin crawled at the sound.

"Oh hypocrisy, thy name is Becknor. How many have you murdered, noble Aristide, in the name of keeping the peace," Cassius wheezed.

"Only those who would take peace from the innocent."

"Time is short traitor," Galen interrupted. "I would know why your hatred is so strong for Achelon that you would do," Galen looked up and said, "All of this."

"Actually, I am rather apathetic when it comes to Achelon. I only used the hate you were taught to control you while you were still malleable to act against the true threat."

"Lydia."

"You have no idea the destruction she would have led our Valley to. A storm was coming. Today, I have acted for the good of all. Just as I did thirteen years ago. The fire was never my intention, but it proved fairly effective."

With one last choked laugh, Cassius's body shuddered violently and then he was gone.

Galen and Aristide exchanged worried looks. A murderer had been in their midst all this time and they were nearly too blind to see. What other threats was there lying in wait, camouflaged by respectability?

\* \* \* \* \*

With one last ram, the rock wall cracked and crumbled to the floor. Great boulders rolled across the floor and to all corners of the chamber. Lastly, Talio made his entrance swiftly. With a great growl, he announced his presence. The growl turned to a roaring chuckle as the dragon discovered Hector's predicament.

**"Oh, how sad,"** he mockingly moaned. **"The witless rat has run himself into a trap."**

Hector had taken notice of a small crevice to the side where he hoped to hide and then double back once Talio was far enough into the chamber. He had dropped his torch in the center of the room to attract Talio's attention. Being the only obvious heat source at first, the dragon went for it instantly. Talio lowered his head down so that he might sniff the ground near it. His wings were tucked in close to his back and his tail swished back and forth behind, blocking Hector's exit.

Closing his eyes for a moment, Hector shook his head. Could he not have one easy path today?

**"The strong do not shy from a fight. They turn and embrace their fate."**

"Aldred Zen-Joffa would disagree with you," Hector called out loudly, his voice booming throughout the chamber.

Talio raised up to listen, and replied with what Hector guessed was a laugh, **"Aldred Zen-Joffa is a myth."**

Despite certain death, Hector could only shake his head. It was not every day you met an infamous immortal, and when you did, the rest of the world either called you a liar or thought you mad.

**"I have seen the destruction of the Great Wasteland and the Glass Desert first hand. Even as I flew over, I doubted the story of the Great Weapon of Desolation. Your kind is incapable of such destruction."**

Hector only had moments now before Talio ferreted out his hiding spot. There was nothing at ground level he could use, was there anything high up?

**"I will admit that your kind is an ingenious lot. Before coming here I traveled the wild lands of the Great Northern Expanse. I saw the machines that they have built there. Machines powered by fire and steam."**

Just the stalactites, nothing that could do any real damage to Talio. But perhaps they did not need to.

**"Destruction of the magnitude of the Glass Desert could only be carried out by a fleet of dragons. Only dragon fire is that pure and hot."**

There! On the opposite side. One of the stalactites looked perilously close to falling. Hector drew his dagger. He hoped his aim was sharp enough and double hoped the rock was as loose as it appeared.

**"Nothing in this world can match the holy destructive power of the dragon."**

Hector's dagger flew through the air unnoticed. It made contact slightly off the mark and did nothing. Moments later, the stalactite wobbled and fell to the cavern floor. Upon hearing the crash, Talio turned his head and spewed a stream of acidic fluid. The rocks began to steam and melt.

The dragon had moved, but not enough. To Hector's frustration, Talio's tail still blocked his exit. Sighing, he knew he had only one option. Hector drew his sword and rushed Talio. With his head turned, he did not see Hector coming.

With a running leap, Hector found himself landing upon the dragon's tail. Instead of trying to squeeze back into the main chamber, Hector began to run up Talio's back. Feeling Hector upon him, he began to try and buck him off like a wild horse. In response, Hector leapt forward and landed on the dragon's neck and stabbed his sword down.

Beckish steel was not the greatest work of ironmongery in the world. But it was strong enough and had a fine cutting edge.

Hector's sword worked its way into a groove between two scales and found purchase there. Not enough to do mortal harm but enough for Hector to hold on, and cause Talio great pain.

**"Off vermin,"** he growled as he tried to shake Hector loose by swinging his head violently from side to side. Hector began to try and pry away one of the dragon's scales. Howling in pain, Talio jumped towards the ceiling in an attempt to crush his tormentor. Seeing this, Hector let go of his sword and rolled to the side. He tried to control his fall but his feet flew from beneath him and he could only manage to land on his knees. From there his momentum caused Hector to spill over face first onto the stone floor.

Shaking the cobwebs, Hector looked up to see Talio still thrashing himself into the ceiling, trying to loosen the sword in the back of his neck. Stalactites and boulders crashed to the floor with each impact. Hector had to roll to avoid them. Looking up again, Hector saw that Talio had only succeeded in forcing the blade deeper, hopelessly embedding it. The dragon began to howl in pain as he clawed at the back of his neck.

Not waiting to see what happened next, Hector scrambled to his feet, reclaimed his torch, and made way through the now open exit.

\* \* \* \* \*

Lydia took a rock and began to crush the petals up inside the helmet. Carefully, she ran her finger across the bottom of the overturned helmet. Feeling the fine oily substance she nodded with satisfaction and moved to the next step. Lydia measured out a portion of the sulfur. The measurement needed to be as precise as possible, otherwise the mixture would either be inert or boil away in a steamy stench. Walking to the coal pile, she again took a stone and carefully crushed a few lumps of coal until it was a fine powder.

From deep inside the cavern, she heard Talio scream out in surprised rage. She was both concerned and proud of Hector. For the dragon to make such a noise, he must have delivered a memorable blow.

Finally, Lydia mixed in the coal and made her way to the poolside. The water was the problem. Having run across the rocks it was potentially rich in the minerals needed to complete the formula, but there was also the equal chance of minerals that would have made it unstable. Unstable was good, but she did not want to burn her own face off.

Carefully Lydia cupped water in her hand and added it to her mixture. Taking her borrowed sword she stirred gently. If any of it managed to splash out onto her it would prove to be excruciatingly painful. Pulling the sword away she saw faint scorching on the blade. Her little alchemical stew was as mixed as it was going to be.

Talio had been mistaken if he believed Rial's fire could be so easily replicated. It required the oil from one of several varieties of sunflowers. Divine's Providence worked well enough. When properly mixed it became liquid fire.

Four thousand years earlier, an alchemist by the name of Rial Prentice had come across an injured and dying dragon. Long before the Concordance of Understanding, there was much more animosity between dragons and all the people of the world, if that was possible. Prentice did something highly controversial in her day, she nursed it back to health. Her second unthinkable act was to help the dragon regain the ability to breathe fire. Rial's Fire was the result. Rial's first intention was to turn her formula into a paste and attempted to open a small incision in one of the dragon's fire glands and pack in the paste. She nearly killed them both. The acid mixture within the gland caused a giant fireball. Later she would find consumption by the dragon was enough to restore its fire.

For her efforts, Rial had the gratitude of dragon-kind and the ire of an angry king. The latter would later have her beheaded for her trouble and make her formula an instrument of war. The king and his kingdom were now long forgotten to the sands of time, as he was destroyed by the vengeful dragon.

Tossing the sword aside she removed her belt and fastened it around the helmet like a makeshift sling. Keeping it firmly in her right hand, and taking up the torch in her left, she made her way towards the direction of the sounds of Talio's rage.

The journey was not long. In the distance, she could see Hector running towards her. As he approached her tried to pull her by the arm but she shrugged him away.

"We must make haste," he told her panting.

"Not yet," she said firmly.

"Lydia, we have to go."

She allowed a brief smile at the mention of her name and not the title, but said, "When it is done."

The words were barely out of her mouth as an angry Talio rounded the corner, and sniffed the air.

"Talio," she called out. When he turned to regard her, "Come, let me give you my response befitting your kind."

Growling he started running towards her. Lydia thrust the torch in Hector's hand and began to walk toward the dragon spinning the makeshift sling over her head. She could hear the mixture sloshing inside the helmet but the force of the spin was keeping it in place.

"Lydia, no," Hector called out behind, but she ignored him. She was counting the distance. She needed Talio close or he might not provide the last ingredient needed. The cavern shook at Talio's approach. His eyes gleamed, as if anticipating ending her, but she smiled back as to say not on your best day. He was just yards away when she let loose her helmet, and turned quickly away as it soared towards the dragon.

Sensing something flying towards him, Talio launched a quick acidic attack towards it. Which was all Lydia had hoped, and a mistake that the dragon would not forget for centuries.

As helmet and acid met in midair a bright fireball lit up the corridor brighter than the noonday sun, effectively blinding Talio. His face, now scorched, his eyes blinded, the dragon cried out in immense pain and began to thrash about wailing. As he crashed into the walls about him, the ceiling began to collapse. That was the last Lydia saw of Talio as he was buried in stone.

Hector was at her side instantly, pulling at her arm and shouting, "We must flee!" Lydia looked up to see that between Cassius' explosion, the combustion of Rial's fire, and the thrashing of Talio, the entire cavern system was beginning to collapse.

"The way out is blocked," she shouted back. "Cassius has buried us."

Hector opened his mouth, stopped and then said, "No matter, just start running."

They ran blindly, turning down side passageways when the way before them began to collapse. Far behind, they could still hear the muffled cries of Talio, but they became fainter the further they ran.

The days of confined to her chambers, and the heavy armor, were now beginning to take their toll. Her breath was ragged, heart beating out of her chest, and her legs began to cramp. Again Hector grabbed her by the arm, just as she was about to give in, and pointed. It was daylight pouring in from around the corner. It could be an exit or it could be an opening impossibly high to escape. Regardless, they both ran for the light of day. Chancing a glance over her shoulder, Lydia saw the last of the caverns were collapsing and were beginning to overtake them. As they rounded the last corner they were greeted by the sight of trees and tall grass.

"Jump," Hector called.

Debris was falling around them as they both came tumbling through the opening and onto a grassy hill. In unison, they turned to see the entrance disappear in a cloud of dust. Just above it, flocks of birds were taking to the air as the trees they had been resting in moments earlier, began to sink. Then, as quickly as it had begun, the ordeal was over. The rumble from below lessened. Shortly, silence fell upon the scene.

For a moment they both laid there in the grass, breathing heavily. Neither willing to speak. Lydia half waited for a blinded, and scorched Talio to come bursting through any moment. She supposed Hector was doing the same. Once she felt safe to do so, Lydia turned over onto her back and looked away from the sealed cave. For a moment she looked up into the sky, taking deep breaths. She then turned her gaze to Hector just as he was turning to her. For a moment their eyes locked and then they both burst out into laughter.

After recovering he asked breathlessly, "Still wish to ride across the countryside?"

With the biggest grin she could muster she answered "More than ever. There are several more frivolous whims that need chasing down. But, I think I will wait till the end of my regency before embarking on another adventure."

"Good," he said with a contented sounding sigh and rolling onto his back. "Another seven-day sleep would be good about right now."

# CHAPTER THIRTY-FIVE

Hours later, Lydia, in fresh clothes and letting her hair flow freely again, sat in her chambers at the table by her window. As much as she hated being confined in these miserable rooms this morning, she relished the chance to be home within them this evening. She watched as the sun set on a very eventful day. A plate of food was before her, untouched. For one, she was simply too tired to eat. And secondly, at long last, there was a breeze. A gentle breeze, but a breeze nonetheless. It blew in through her window making her even drowsier. She leaned her head against the cool stone of the window seal and continued to look out until a soft tapping came at her door.

"Enter," she said softly. She smiled when she saw that it was Hector. At long last, her Hector, here to stay. "I thought you would want your armor back," she said pointing towards a corner on the floor, near the door. "What is left of it that is."

He waved his hand and said, "It can easily be refurbished and the smithies can replace what is missing."

"Come sit with me for a moment, if you have the time," she said lazily. Her eyes were becoming quite heavy.

"I can spare a moment," he said sitting opposite her. "I understand Galen has finally relented. Your journey today has proven your health is excellent. I hear you will be attending a session of the Royal Court tomorrow, the full Court."

"And now all I want to do is lay her and sleep away the next week. Why can they not leave me alone," she said feigning tears but smiling. "I suppose this is Galen's way of punishing me for breaking my word."

"Yes, a day of politics. I cannot think of a worse punishment. Moneychangers scheming ways to loot the treasuries, farmers asking for more share in the profits, land disputes, the Captain of the Valley asking for more resources."

"Oh, what have I done? Quick, fetch me a spade so I can spend more time with the dragon," she said with a little laugh. "Any word on Talio?"

Hector shook his head and said, "I have knights scouring all of Green Plains. The collapse of the caverns is extensive. If he is still in the Valley, he is probably buried under much rock."

"That would not be too difficult for a dragon to dig out," Lydia said stifling a yawn. "But he is injured. The heat of Rial's fire is brutal. He will be blinded for some time. He will need to go back into hibernation and heal."

"Which gives us perhaps a handful of years. But I have had a thought," Hector said apprehensively. "It was something Talio said. That dragons are sensitive to the winds of war. If war had returned here then it must be raging elsewhere in the world. From all reports from Isaac's Hold, the Alliance has sent no small number marching east. Which begs the question…."

"Where are the dragons," Lydia finished for him. "I find that a troubling puzzle as well. Twenty-four known dragons throughout the world, most of which are loyal to the Concordance of Understanding, and would at least wake to investigate the war. And in all of this, only one has awakened?"

"Something darker afoot," Hector asked.

"If there was, we truly would be the last to know. We are the 'strange valley-dwelling kingdom of no consequence' after all. Good for wheat and little else." Smiling she added, "We can keep a wary eye on the horizon, but let us leave the wolf howling at the gate to the kingdoms and realms of consequence. After all, the greater world is their domain, ours is this little valley."

"Agreed," he said pleasantly but she could see he was building up his courage. "I suppose you want to finish our conversation on the road."

"Actually, no," she answered after a moment of thought. "Truly, I would like to know, yet I saw the pain on your face as you tried to relate the third trial to me. Whatever you faced must have been dreadfully personal and painful. I will not enquire again. Besides, I heard all that I needed to hear."

"Which was?"

"The vision of my future he shared with you. It clears up a lingering question I have had for years."

"If I may ask," Hector said cautiously, "What question would this be?"

Lydia let out a little laugh and said, "I am afraid if I told you it would hurt your opinion of me. You might even think me a silly girl."

Hector smiled and said, "I witnessed you go face to snout with a vicious dragon and gain the upper hand. I am incapable of thinking you silly of anything."

"Thank you," she said fighting another yawn. "Thirteen years ago, after my parents died I suffered terrible bouts of loneliness. I felt as if I had no family at all. Even though Gaius took me in, I was lost. I feared I would never feel whole again. Then he came."

"Who," asked Hector.

"The Dream Man," she said, as this time the yawn won. Her eyes were now almost too heavy to keep open as she added, "At least that is what I have come to call him. I began to dream of the man I would spend the rest of my life with. At first, I was much older in the dreams. Much closer to my age now. It is a dream that has stayed with me my entire life. Whenever life is the hardest, he would come to me and sit with me. Even now. At times it was not even a romantic notion that I would one day marry, but a comfort to a lonely little girl that she would one day have a family again. Though, I was beginning to think my mind was slightly cracked for believing such things. Until today. Now I find that you have seen him too. So now I know it to be true."

She closed her eyes for just a moment. It was indescribable how good it felt to close them.

Laughing again she added, "It is so funny."

"What is?"

"You know the field where we first met," she said now only able to keep her eyes open for a heartbeat at a time. "I had asked the carriage driver to stop when I laid eyes upon it. You see in one of the dreams he came to me in that very field. In that field of windblown flowers, I would meet the man of my future for the first time. There the story would begin. And you know the strangest part," her eyes refused to open now.

"What?"

"In the dream, he was dressed just as you described. Yet, in the dream, just like all the others, I never have seen his face."

Sleep took her then, otherwise, she might have asked Hector why he looked so pained. When she woke, she was still sitting there by the window. Outside, night had fallen. Hector was gone and so was the plate of food. The maiden must have carried it away, but had let her sleep where she was.

With what was left of her strength Lydia got to her feet and made way for her bed. There she fell into the deepest sleep she had known in months. No nightmares came, no dreams at all for that matter. Just the best rest she had had in all her life.

# EPILOGUE

**Five Years Ago....**

The wind blowing through her hair helped calm her nerves. It was one thing to be home after a five-year absence. It was another to come home and find, on your sixteenth birthday, that you will now be seeing to the welfare of your entire Kingdom. When word had come on the road that the king had passed and had appointed her as regent with his final words, her stomach had been in knots. She had eaten nothing of substance in the last day and a half. This was a great responsibility.

Yet, the moment Lydia had laid eyes upon the field, it all changed. Against the wishes of the carriage driver, she had commanded him to stop. He kept going on about rendezvous and such business, but she knew she had to do this.

Removing her shoes just outside the field, she strolled barefoot into a sea of white. She closed her eyes and skimmed the top of the flowers with her hands. The sensations were exquisite.

*Home,* she thought to herself, contentedly. The Great City-State of Isaac's Hold was a wonder to behold, but it was not the Valley. There was no place to walk barefoot and feel the earth beneath your feet. There was wind, but it brought with it the smell of a city of a million but not the bouquet of flowers. There was no such thing as quiet in Isaac's Hold. So many living inside, there was not a single hour that did not have some

423

commotion. Not here in glorious Becknor. Not here where it was so quiet you could hear the ruffling footsteps of an approaching man.

Lydia heard him approach. Was this the moment? Was this where the story began?

She turned, but did not exactly see what she expected. It was a Knight of the Valley, the insignia upon his chest plate said he was a high lieutenant. He was passed his years of required service but he was not much older. Three to six years older than her, she estimated. His brown hair was cut short and to the code. He was taller than her, grey eyes, and a strong jaw and chin. She suppressed a laugh when she first looked upon him. The bizarre, quizzical look upon his face was priceless.

"May I be of service to you," Lydia asked him.

"I have been sent to escort the Lady Lydia, our new Regent to the Palace," he answered.

"Then I am afraid I am the harbinger of ill news," she said. His face began to twist into worry. Again she had to suppress a laugh.

"What is this ill news?"

This time, she did laugh and say, "The strange girl before you is Lydia. I am afraid your new regent takes to flights of fancy on occasion."

"Well then, that is not ill news at all," he said. "We are Becknor, historically many of our leaders take to flights of fancy on a regular basis."

She smiled and nodded in agreement. Then her eye caught the sight of her carriage leaving without her.

"Should I not be inside there Lieutenant, um?"

"Hector, son of Felix. I am afraid this was Galen's idea. The carriage is to take the long way through the Valley, as a kind of decoy. He felt riding in quietly on horseback would be less conspicuous. Especially in the case of Everfrost wishing to sow confusion."

*Or distract any political rival who wishes to assassinate the last of Achelon,* she thought bitterly. Out loud she said, "At least he sent me some company."

"That he did My Lady. May I escort you to your horse?" She nodded her consent and moved to walk beside him.

"It is none of my business, My Lady," Hector began.

"Please, Lydia."

"Of course, My Lady. But may I ask whatever possessed you to go for a walk?"

She could feel her cheeks warm slightly as she answered, "You would not believe me if I told you. Let us just say, that it was a whim." He nodded thoughtfully at her words. She could see that something she had said had affected him. "Did I miss speak," she asked worriedly.

He looked towards her for a moment, speechless, but then said, "Not at all. I was reminded of something I was once told. A whim lies somewhere between natural instinct and the prophetic. It can be the whisper of the Divine urging us towards our destiny or a self-set trap that leads down the path of catastrophe."

She thought the words over carefully and nodded. "Then Hector, let us see where this whim of mine takes us."

# AFTERWARD

Self-publication can sometimes be a misleading term. Yes, you can do it all alone, but this is rarely the case. For many, there is a small army of friends that help or give support along the way. These generous people, are an invaluable resource. If any reading have any thought of self-publishing and are on a budget, your friends can be of help in the editing process. They can at least point out structural problems or massive plot holes in your story. However, be sure not to abuse their generosity. Unless they are willing, do not send the fortieth draft of your story for them to read when all you did was change four pages.

So, in a moment I would like to list some people that have been important to the process. Though this is not a definitive list, I have tried to make sure everyone that has helped over the years is named. Whether they read through and offered constructive critiques, some have helped edit, some even inspired something story related without knowing, while others were present before the first foundations were laid with words of encouragement.

Finally, for some of the names listed below, I have lost touch with over the years, but then life is a journey and such is its way. I hope this book finds its way into your hands one day, if nothing else, someone has shown you this page. If you are reading this I hope that you are well.

In no particular order:

Derek Gillespie (mapmaker extraordinaire), Aaron Whittaker, Cortney Gibson, Chereign Kelsor, Ryan Pruitt, Matthew Mikles (no, I'm still not writing that scene), Hubert L. Mullins (great author; read his books), Rita Hughes, Heidi Hairston, Sheldon Norton, Stuart Tullis, Joshua Stolte, Michael Falkner, Eric Gellar (thanks for the *Outrageous* fresh restart), Dr. Pedro Jorba, Flavien Huynh, Bill Simpson, Amanda Bulat, Carrie Bland, Paul DePaola, and Lindsey Andrews

Thank you all!

**Hector and Lydia will return.**

# ABOUT THE AUTHOR

Jack O. Crabtree calls southern West Virginia home. From this base of operation he continually plots world domination, in fictional setting only of course. Defenders of Becknor is his debut novel and is currently working on the follow up.

Made in the USA
Columbia, SC
17 November 2024

46304825R00262